Also available and

All the Best Nights

END OF THE DAY

———

HANNA EARNEST

carina
press

carina press®

Recycling programs for this product may not exist in your area.

ISBN-13: 978-1-335-47511-4

End of the Day

Carina Press
22 Adelaide St. West, 41st Floor
Toronto, Ontario M5H 4E3, Canada
www.CarinaPress.com

Printed in U.S.A.

For romance reasons

END OF
THE DAY

It had started with one of his smiles, quick and airy like popcorn. Crave-worthy, until you've had too much. Copious, but lacking substance.

Easy for her to ignore, which she did, squeezing lotion onto her wrist and dabbing at it with a practiced finger. "Relax your face for me."

He cocked his head and offered another diverting smile. She disregarded that one too. She had a job to do and a point to prove.

When his mouth opened, she cut him off, sure she knew the score. Dirty-blond hair escaped from behind her ears as she shook her head and launched into half of a conversation she'd been forced to recite again and again since arriving in LA with a fresh face.

"Yes, I am new in town but no, I'm not interested in dinner. Or a tour of Rodeo or Mulholland or any big-named boulevard." She held up a hand to keep him from interrupting. "I'm not hiking with you to a secret spot with an 'unbelievable' view of the Hollywood sign or watching any movies in a cemetery, whether or not they are classics—frankly, those both sound like really solid ways to get murdered and I'm not into it." She tutted over a potential protest. "I'm sure you do know the best taco truck around, but I'm looking forward to discovering all the 'bad' ones on my own. And, no, it's not because I have 'a thing against actors.' It's that—"

His face lifted, skin glazed by the bulb-ringed mirror at her back, and she met his gaze for the first time. Twin white crescents formed under his deep brown irises as he looked up at her from the makeup chair. Puppy-dog eyes, she'd thought. Sweet and decidedly affable. The ensuing sly smile—slower than the others, one she could have made a meal out of—should have dispelled any notions of decency.

"It's that…" She blinked and finished with a lie. "You're not my type."

"You're mine."

With his first two words he had her forgetting all semblance of professionalism; he had Benjamina Wasik faking a gag. Mouth open, tongue out, complete with a chortling sound from the back of her throat.

That should have been the end of it. But Milo Fox's real smile only widened. "Fair enough."

Chapter One

The waiting area outside Max Field's office (two un-comfortable black-and-chrome Wassily chairs and a table so low it barely held her upcycled cognac-colored bucket bag off the ground) had one redeeming quality: the glass double doors that allowed Benj to watch the action inside like a movie. Well, more like a silent film she had to decode through pantomime. A based-on-real-events drama that would have had her at the edge of her seat, if the Wassily didn't tip back at a forty-five-degree angle like it was readying to launch her into space.

Normally, she loved a scene, happily sitting in the role of spectator. Today, she wanted to leap up, burst through the doors, and join in. But she didn't. Maybe it was the angle of the chair, the ab-day effort it would take to rise out of it, or maybe it was the years spent internalizing her mother's three cardinal rules: *Don't interrupt. Mind your business. Tell yourself true things, Benjamina.*

A shameless gossip, Benj had always had the most trouble with the middle one. Two out of three wasn't bad. But her mother wasn't the sort of woman who rounded up.

Besides, she was still trying to interpret meaning

from the advice she'd gotten that morning from her brutal-yet-accurate astrology app: *Don't lose your head—you'll need it tomorrow.*

What was she supposed to do with that, Daily Star–t?

So Benj sat all the way back, legs crisscrossed in the slanted seat to avoid the jungle-gym feeling of hanging by her knees. She already felt like she was waiting outside the principal's office, no need to increase the grade-school vibes. Someone had tattled. Someone had snitched. And the only thing they all agreed on was that the culprit hadn't been called into Max Field's office.

Yet.

A spasm tightened the muscles behind Benj's knees. Her exposed toes gave an impatient wiggle. Each intake of air flickered in her chest, shallow and unsatisfying. The atmosphere in her limbo grew thinner as she wondered what would happen next.

On a good day, she could sense the thrum of LA's anxiety—the fine line between what was actually happening and what was made up—and separate herself from it. Today wasn't a good day. Today the city's troubled relationship with reality pulsed in each too-fast beat of her heart. Today it wasn't fun to be part of Hollywood's crew.

Because maybe by tomorrow she'd have lost her seat.

Benj closed her eyes, tried harder to draw air deeply through her nose and release it slowly out her mouth. Tried harder to ground herself before speculation sent her into orbit, with or without help from the damn chair. Not that sitting outside Max Field's office, watching the trio of Fates inside was any less surreal than a trip to the moon. It was that she was accustomed to holding the scissors. And for once she was following all three rules. She *was* minding her business. This episode could result in her losing her best friend *and* her best client. Benj coughed on an inhale. That wasn't a circumstance she could just breathe away.

Another sky-high spike of anxiety had Benj's eyes popping open, her elbows jolting wide. She pressed her fingertips under her temples. Her knees bounced, fluttering the pages of a forgotten notebook open between them. A pencil slid down the book's gutter and Benj caught it just before it tumbled into her lap.

The page showed an earlier attempt to ease her nerves, to focus calmly on what was right in front of her. A sketch of the moment—not the past or the future. Translating the scene into soft-penciled lines, she'd drawn Nelle center frame. The pop star was known worldwide for her catchy, heartfelt music, but Benj knew her as the kindest, hardest-working, most-deserving Somebody in a town that considered itself Everybody. She'd drafted Nelle shoulders back, chin raised, refusing to play the victim. Hopefully refusing to be convinced of Benj's supposed treachery.

In much more severe lines, she'd drawn Mina Hassan, who'd taken over as Nelle's main manager. She'd unfairly exaggerated Mina's mouth—or had she? When that mouth was almost certainly in use intoning disapproval of Benj's continued employment. Benj had been on Mina's watch-list ever since Super Saturday, almost a year ago, when she'd gone rogue and lobbed Nelle's trademark hair. The incident had proved—to Mina, at least—that Benj's role as best friend made her an unreliable employee. She'd crossed the line, endan-

gered the Business of Nelle, the source of all of their
incomes, just to make her friend feel better.

Benj would do it again in an instant.

On the opposite page, she'd outlined Max Field himself, the man who used to be Nelle's senior manager.
It didn't bode well that he'd trained Mina, taught her
how to be the cutthroat go-getter that had gotten Nelle
to where she was now. If they teamed back up against
Benj…would there be anything she could do to defend herself?

Max sat behind his desk, AirPods visible, rubbing
his stomach and looking unsettled. Or possibly hungry.
Benj darkened the shadows under his eyes without caring which. Neither he nor Mina mattered, apart from
their sway. Benj only cared about what Nelle thought.
She cared if Nelle was okay. If she could only see
Nelle's face, she was sure she'd know what her friend
was thinking. There were clues to be read there: a pink
flush high on the cheekbones could be good or bad
(humiliation or indignant disbelief). The tell would
be in her honey-toned eyes.

Inside the office, Nelle nodded. The brittle tip of the
pencil's graphite shattered against the page. It could
be good, Benj comforted herself. Maybe they'd figured out a way to stop the approaching media storm.

Or maybe Nelle had bought the accusation her man-
agement team was selling.

The moment slipped away from Benj as she replayed
the events from the night before. It had all started as a
normal girls' weekend. She and Nelle had done mani-
cures and moon water, Pinot and palm reading. Things
that, admittedly, didn't sound particularly normal but
were, by Hollywood standards, quite tame. Learning

from a very convincing internet psychic that the letters
found in the wrinkles of their thumb knuckles represented initials of people they should look out for was
way less bizarre than overplayed goat yoga or buccal
massage. Less pricy too.

"Basic witch shit," Benj had joked, admiring her
filed-to-a-point matte-black nails and expecting Nelle
to laugh.

Nelle hadn't. Nelle had said, "That's what we should
call it."

"Call what?"

"Our beauty line."

She'd said it casually but Benj knew better than anyone how her friend worked. And *that* was Nelle speaking their future into existence.

Then Security Steve had called to let them know
about the "actor at the gate."

In the office, Mina pointed at Max, and Benj's
thumb twitched. Last night, she'd found two unmistakable *M*s.

A bag landed in the empty Wassily beside her, and
Benj startled at the pop of impact. A subsequent rustling sounded as the brown paper found no traction on
the chair's leather and slid to the back of the seat. The
smell of freshly fried tortilla chips invaded the room
and Benj leaned forward to confirm via a stamped-on
logo that takeout from the overpriced, overhyped (and
under-delicious) Taco Chance On Me was resting at
an alarming angle next to her.

"You might wanna—" She cut herself off, eyes flar-
ing at the food's negligent owner leaning one shoulder
into the wall.

In Timbs, black joggers, and an army-green field

jacket, he sported the uniform of Hollywood's fashion
militia—complete with grey beanie. But the boots were
scuffed and dirty, dried paint splattered the thigh of his
pants, and his jacket was torn along the left sleeve vent,
like he'd been caught on something and ripped himself free. Well-used work clothes he wore like James
Bond's tuxedo, jacket pushed back, one hand infor-
mally tucked into a jogger pocket. His gaze trained on
the inner office spectacle, he was profoundly unboth-
ered by her presence and the precarious incline of the
bag, which had probably sent ingredients sideways,
mingling incorrectly over the partitions of a biode-
gradable container.

Adrenaline exploded through Benj's body as she
held back her warning. She wasn't about to give Milo
Fox a heads-up that his lunch was in peril. Because
it *was* Milo Fox on the periphery of her space. Even
under that beard-and-beanie combo, chin-length hair
curling out the sides, she could tell. Even though it had
been three years since she'd seen him—not counting
sitting across from his identical twin at Nelle's dinner table last night. That's who had joined her in the
World's Least Comfortable Waiting Room: Milo Snake
Emoji Fox. His treachery earned him worse karma
than soggy tacos.

Despite the dark-framed glasses bridging his nose
and a full beard covering the other half of his face, his
features underneath were easy for her to call up. Benj
had spent an embarrassing number of wasted hours
thinking about Milo Fox's face. At first she'd done so
from a professional standpoint—doing his makeup on
Twin Pistols 2 had been her big break and she'd wanted
to establish a reputation of competency. So, yeah, she'd

pored over his headshot, memorized his leading-man hair—dark, dark brown, not quite black. Cropped close to his head then, not long enough to curl, though she could tell it wanted to, that it would, given the chance. The cut accentuated his oval face, that perfect dip of his inoffensive concave nose. In the headshot she'd studied, his wide mouth had been slightly parted, his forehead ridged with two straight lines. He'd looked thoughtful, considerate. Bright-eyed and selfless. So much boy-next-door charm oozing from the page, the gloss had gone tacky. But he was an actor. It was his job to sell a fantasy. At the end of the day, it wasn't her professionalism that had burned him to memory, but her hothearted rage. As a warning against future hurt.

Now Benj's heart timed the seconds in palpable bursts as she waited for their reunion to become mutual. But the minutes passed and Milo didn't recognize her. Didn't even notice her. Benj swallowed a laugh, suffocating it in her throat. Why would he? He'd made it abundantly clear how little he cared about her the last time they'd been face-to-face.

She hurtled over the memory of how close their faces had been before she tripped on it.

Never trust a Fox, she'd learned three years ago. Too bad Nelle hadn't listened to her last night and turned Milo's scheming brother away at the door.

"Why wouldn't I let him in? He's not the villain, that was the other one," Nelle had said, spoiling the big twist of *Twin Pistols 2*. Given her firsthand experience, Benj hadn't minded. Or disagreed. "I met him at that tequila party last year, and I can say definitively he's very charming and not at all a creep."

Nelle must be fuming now. Something she and Benj had in common: they hated to be wrong.

Benj's knees butterflied up and down again, unsettling the sketchbook pages with a noisy ruffle.

"They wrapping up?" Milo polished his glasses on the hem of his shirt. "Look, I know you've been waiting longer but I just need one thing. You won't mind if I go in first."

The notebook stilled. Her voice wavered from the force of her heartbeat. "I won't?"

"Great—" He started his smile and his reply almost before she'd answered. His line ready, her acquiescence scripted. But he stopped short, his mouth flattening as his head lifted toward the sound of her voice.

His attention brought her pulse closer to the surface. "'I won't?' was a question. I'm questioning your assumption." Her blood positively thrummed with opposition. "I do mind, I mind a lot."

Milo fit the frames back over his eyes and Benj hated the flaming heat, the telling color that seeped through her skin at his review—eyes roaming over her from across the room, lingering on her hands with a heavy look she could almost feel. She shut the notebook with a snap. Reciprocal recognition finally charged the air between them, like flipping a switch. His gaze shifted to her platinum hair. "You lightened it." He drew lines over his eyes to indicate her winged eyeliner. "And the—"

"Can we not?"

"I was just trying to explain—"

"Why start now."

The left side of his face winced, his head rolling to the side with it. He smoothed the motion into a nod, mouth quirking with a flash of inflated amusement. "Fair enough." That man-of-mystery hand slipped back into his pocket.

And that was it.

That was all he had to say.

Benj had, if she was being honest, pictured this moment. On off nights, when she needed a pick-me-up. It had seemed inevitable, that they'd run into each other. Until his disappearing act. Despite her penchant for gossip, she'd done her best to avoid the details, to avoid anything related to Milo Fox. But of course she'd heard about an accident on set. Both brothers liked to do as many of their own stunts as they could—a habit no doubt inherited from their acting-legend grandfather, Grant Fox. She'd seen Milo dive headfirst into fight scenes and high-speed motorcycle chases. One of them must have gone wrong because the third and final installment of *Twin Pistols* had been delayed, production shut down while he recovered.

What Benj knew was that Milo had left town to recoup. That had been a year ago—he'd probably lost track of company time, drinking and gambling in Monaco or some other high-profile glitterati hotspot. The only difference his funemployment had made in her life was that the scenarios in her head had grown more inventive than a run-in on Sunset. More victorious. She'd imagine herself somewhere fantastic, like Tokyo—no, *Paris*—getting out of a car with Nelle, the hotel staff rushing for their bags. She wouldn't even notice Milo sitting at the café across the street. But he'd see her.

He'd see her just fine. He'd see her doing well. See her full of success, of purpose, unaffected by his meaningless cameo in her life. By his malicious attempt to derail her career for the benefit of his own.

That wasn't how it was going.

You lightened it.

After all this time, after what he did, he'd started with those three words. Offering one for each year. None of them adding up to an apology. Not one of them *sorry.*

Maybe, Benjamina, there'd have been more if you hadn't interrupted.

Like this was her fault? Not a chance.

Benj struggled to control herself, to keep from hauling in the great gasps of air she wanted. Air she needed. To light into him, tell him off. She had a whole lot more to say than three fucking words. But what would be the point? Milo Fox would never care what she thought about him. She had to keep it to herself. His kind thrived on attention and he wasn't going to get it from her.

Still, her head shook with the effort of staying silent. Soft, lavishly pale hair feathered over her cheeks, fresh off a purple shampoo. Even though she knew the power was in her silence, the execution pained her— she inverted her lips and bit down.

It was Max Field who saved Benj from the effort, distracted her from the cause. With a dull thwomp of glass, he propped open one of the doors and Nelle marched through. Ushering Mina from his office next, Max let out a sympathetic sigh. "If there were something we could do, ladies, I'd be all for it."

Benj unfolded from the Wassily, abs straining against the slant as she searched out her fringed faux-suede flats on the floor and toed them back on. She shoved the notebook into her bag and stood, trying to lock eyes with Nelle, eyebrows raised in question.

Nelle didn't meet her gaze, her head down, thumbs in motion on what was either a very long text or the draft of an email to her lawyers, asking to cancel Benj's existing contract for the upcoming tour. Maybe even to draw up a restraining order. Benj's stomach twisted at the thought—she didn't care about the tour really, unless it meant losing Nelle's friendship—but she was depending on that income. LA rent didn't come cheap and neither did the proper upkeep on platinum hair, even for a salon insider. She wasn't about to ask her parents for help again. It had been humiliating enough the first time—the long pause before her mother agreed louder than any *I told you so.*

There were too many maybes. Too many unknowns. Making it impossible for her to predict what would happen next. But she knew she smelled a rat.

Mina stalled in the doorway, refusing to fully exit. "They are both clients of the firm, Max. Nelle's image is at stake. We're on the verge of her album launch—I'm talking losses in ticket sales, merch, streaming. She's an asset we should be protecting. I can't understand why you don't want to help."

Nelle let the phone hang at her side, her gold-coated index finger tapping against the case. She had to hate the situation being reduced to profit loss. Nelle's concern would be personal: Bran Kelly's reaction. How was her husband going to take a tabloid shot of another man caught leaving their house at dawn while he was wrapping up a tour, off playing a show in Brazil?

Benj's heart wrenched on her friend's behalf. No-good, conniving Foxes.

Max held the door wider. "I want to help! But there's nothing I can do. He's out of town—"

"Since this morning?" Mina pushed.

Patient, formulated words left Max's mouth. "It was a scheduled retreat to prepare for a part. This whole thing was an accident. An unfortunate part of the business. Regrettable. But unavoidable."

Benj bit her lip again to keep from interrupting. As if Jackson Fox skipping town wasn't at all damning. Even Mina had to raise a red flag at that.

"An accident?" Mina reeled to Benj's relief. "A coincidence? Or a setup."

"We've been over this. If it were a setup, who gained what?" Max held up a dewy palm. "Not your client. Not mine. Not press from stories like this."

Tension pulled Mina's mouth down, her head turned just barely in Benj's direction. Benj's stomach plummeted with the implication. Who profited from a setup like this? Whoever sold out. Only three people had been at Nelle's last night. Only one of them lacked the zeroes in her bank account for plausible deniability.

And Nelle still hadn't met her eye.

"I'm sure if Jackson were available, he'd also do anything in his power to help mitigate the impact. Is that my lunch?" Max spared a glance at Milo and the takeout bag.

Milo didn't respond. He'd gone rigid, ruining his laid-back display against the wall.

Max gestured again for Mina to step through the door, gripping the polished bar tighter when she didn't budge. "Jackson has no reason to start something in the press."

Mina pursed her mouth momentarily. "Maybe let

him know, just in case, that I'd finish it. He may be signed with you, but she's signed with me."

Was it wrong to glean some joy from the irony that Mina had learned how to defend a client from Max?

The placating smile dropped from Max's face. "We don't need to make this an issue of him versus her. Of you versus me. It's all in the family, Mina. There shouldn't be any infighting. Not when there are other, more plausible threats." Max nodded not-so-subtly at Benj, and the second insinuation of her guilt, the confirmation that she had been named as lead suspect, the most motivated to take Nelle down, brought Benj's stomach back up, the acidic burn of anger licking a flame up her throat.

"If it isn't a fight, why'd Jackson send in his second?" Blank faces met Benj's question. She gestured obviously at Milo, and the others turned in almost comical synchronicity to look at him.

"*Is* that my food?" Max asked again.

Milo shoved off the wall and grabbed the bag. The containers inside lurched loudly as he swung it forward and now, knowing it was Max's and with his opinion of her confirmed, Benj was glad for the sloppy treatment and hoped the avocado had browned and the tortillas were disintegrating from sauce displacement.

"Two chicken tinga, extra mango salsa?" Milo offered the bag to Max. "Took it off the delivery guy downstairs for you. Same old Max. No new tricks."

"Milo?" Max squinted. "Don't tell me you've been in town, kid, because—"

"No— Flew in this morning." Milo scratched at the paint on his pants and Benj noted the deep tan of sunbaked skin on the back of his hand—the Mediter-

ranean hadn't been a bad guess. He sure didn't look
unwell. But he did look edgy. He looked like someone with a secret.

Her interest piqued at the hint of a story—what *had*
he been up to? Curiosity was a bad habit, potato chips
she couldn't stop eating once the first one dissolved on
her tongue. She forced her attention to her nails when
Milo asked, "Where's Jack?"

Max rubbed his stomach again. "Let's talk inside.
The ladies were just leaving."

Pervasive tension ricocheted around the room. A
standoff with too many sides. Benj willed Milo to step
into the office. To be gone again. So she could go back
to forgetting he existed. Mind her own business. He
was a bad omen—a symbol of broken trust. The human
representation of failed friendship and cutoff careers.

Max shifted his weight against the door and Mina
finally gave up the threshold. Movement eased the
tension and Milo started forward—only for Nelle to
block his path.

"You're Jackson's brother?"

Milo huffed out a dry, humorless laugh. "That's
me."

"If he's responsible for this…" She paused to consider her words. "He can't hide from it. He can't outrun it. He can't outrun me."

"You're talking to the wrong guy."

"Yeah, I guess I am." Nelle let Milo go, coming to
Benj's side.

Milo crossed into Max's office and with a soft
whoosh of air, Max pulled the door shut.

"*If* he's responsible?" Benj twisted her ankle, suddenly afraid to look into Nelle's eyes and see their verdict. "You know I had nothing to do with this, right?"

Nelle squeezed Benj's arm, and relief tingled from the spot. "Of course I know that."

Benj looked up and saw eyes fierce with loyalty—and compassion.

"It might be blameless happenstance, like Max said." Her friend offered the wrongdoer an out.

Not on Benj's watch. "Nelle, I love you, but there's no fucking way this was an accident."

"I agree." Mina positioned herself at Nelle's other side, squaring off against Benj. Nelle might not think Benj had tipped off the paps, but her manager clearly wasn't convinced. "We'll get to the bottom of how it happened later. Right now we need to deal with it. I thought Max could call in a bigger favor but we've only been able to buy a delay. It'll be news soon enough."

Nelle nodded. "I'll ride it out. We knew this kind of thing would happen."

"Ride it out?" Mina's lip curled. "With album promo about to start, we can't have your brand taking a hit like this. You're supposed to be happily married—"

"I *am* happily married—"

"Not according to tomorrow's top story."

Nelle closed her eyes. "Solutions, please."

Helplessness hollowed Benj out. What could she do? How could she make it better? What did she have to offer? This wasn't a fashion emergency, something a fresh look could fix. In this moment, her skill set was proving as useless as her parents had claimed before she'd moved to California.

Inside the office, the picture through the glass had changed, resetting for the next act. Milo sat in one of the chairs facing Max's desk. But his head was turned in her direction. Their eyes locked and warmth bloomed anew under her skin.

He was watching her now. Just like she'd wanted. Except she wasn't midscene, flaunting her success. She was in the midst of losing it. Trust Milo Fox to reappear with a front-row ticket to her downfall—the encore of a show he'd produced three years ago. And what had she done then? Benj rocked back, curling her toes in her shoes for balance. She'd found her footing, established herself. Not even her parents could deny it now. Nelle had given her that chance. There wasn't anything Benj wouldn't do to repay her.

Mina's next suggestion reaffirmed Benj's fear that her professional future was in jeopardy. "We clean house so it doesn't happen again."

Holding Milo's gaze, Benj responded instinctively. "Say it was me."

"You didn't do this, Benjamina," Nelle said with enough force to break Benj's stare-down with Milo.

"No, say it was *me* Jackson was there to see. It's like any other blemish. We'll use cover-up."

"Work the narrative." Mina tongued her front teeth. "But we'd need Jackson to corroborate and he's out of pocket."

"Luckily we have a stand-in." They followed her gaze back to Milo. "Make the story me and 'Jackson.' What'll it take to spin it? A competing photo-op, some phony canoodling?"

Mina digested the idea with a skeptical scowl. "You want that attention? You want your name in print?"

Another allegation that couldn't have been more wrong. Attention was the last thing Benj wanted. She'd grown up with the weight of watchful eyes, with her shortcomings itemized. Mina's assumption that she'd organized this whole thing for fifteen minutes of exposure hardened her resolve to prove otherwise. "I want to help Nelle."

She didn't know if Mina believed her, but the other woman went for her phone, thumbing open her screen.

"You don't have to do this, Benj—"

Mina shushed Nelle, her phone pressed to her ear. "Joe? You're gonna want to hold it a little longer. Give me a few more hours, it'll be worth it. I'm not stalling. I'm trying to save you from running slander."

Nelle lowered her voice. "Am I missing something? Is this a different Milo Fox than the asshole who broke up with you?"

A succinct enough summary. Benj hadn't had time to get into the whole story last night. And even if she'd had the time…there were reasons she'd never mentioned Milo to Nelle before. Whatever Mina thought, Benj really didn't want the spotlight. She hadn't come to LA to star in the drama. Sure she liked a good story—just not about herself. Especially not about her being wrong. So last night she'd been vague, downplaying what really happened while trying to keep the memories from flooding back and overwhelming her. To keep the past where it belonged, the details of Milo Fox behind her. Beneath her. Sunk.

She couldn't risk remembering the way Milo kissed—that one perfect moment he'd leaned into her, his hands tangling into her hair, fingertips waking up her scalp. That one perfect moment before she'd realized what he'd done.

She couldn't admit, out loud, how mistaken she'd

been. How much she'd assumed, filled in on her own, while knowing so little about someone. But she could deflect until no one asked any more questions, until the focus was off her.

"We were just friends, we never dated. It didn't get that far before he got me fired."

Nelle's chin lowered next, intensifying the concern in her gaze. "But he broke your heart?"

Benj wanted to lie. To convince Nelle it was all fine and done and nothing. But the truth worked its way out of her in splinters. "He broke his own heart. What happened to mine was collateral."

"Okay, yeah, no, we'll figure something else out."

"Too late," Mina interrupted. "Unless we deliver, Joe's gonna run something even worse."

Nelle clicked her screen on again, her brow creasing at the empty notifications. "Worse than that I'm cuckolding a husband who doesn't know how to answer his goddamn phone?"

"They can always say worse."

Vibrations buzzed from Nelle's palm and she swore gratefully at the ceiling before answering. "You know for a man with a watch fetish you have the shittiest timing, Kelly—"

She disappeared around the corner, phone glued to her cheek, and Mina leveled another demoralizing look at Benj. "It's not going to be flattering. The angle they run—probably 'actor dates below his pay grade,' I'd guess. Is that worth the boost in Instagram follows?"

Shrugging off the dig, Benj tipped her chin up. "I can take a news cycle."

"For Nelle?" Mina pushed.

Benj held. "Right."

"You might want to help Nelle, but what about him?" The manager bobbed her head toward the interior office. "Somehow he doesn't strike me as the giving type." Mina's accusing, dubious eyes bore into hers, forcing Benj to look elsewhere. To look at Milo.

"He's not. He's singularly selfish." Behind the glass, Milo had stopped staring at her, refocused on himself. She'd missed her moment to triumph. But maybe she still had a chance to satisfy her hunger for payback. "I just have to make it about him."

Easier said than done. His affection was fickle. His attention exploitive. The thing he'd wanted from her he'd gotten.

So what did he want now?

Milo adjusted the beanie at his ears and forehead, covering the only part of his face not hidden behind beard or frames. He'd said he'd just gotten in. And he'd come straight to his manager's office. But Max had been as surprised to see him as she was. Which meant Milo was flying low for some reason. Keeping his movements to himself. She didn't have to know why. Even if her curiosity coated the question like grease.

She wiped her fingertips on her thigh and smiled. If Milo Fox had been watching, he'd have seen success. He'd have seen purpose. He'd have seen the moment Benjamina Wasik decided how to finally get him back.

Chapter Two

Milo lowered himself into the chair facing Max's desk slowly. Reluctantly. Resentfully aware of the geriatric twinge in his lower spine, his back aching enough to take his mind off the itch that came and went under the scar on his knee. Between the early-morning drive to BWI, the cross-country flight, and waiting for three hours outside of his own goddamn house for Jackson to show and let him in, he'd spent too long sitting in the last twelve hours. Too long thinking about the traitorous way his body had changed so easily, while his emotional evolution had taken so much effort.

Full midday sun streamed into the top-dog corner office, reflections winking off every gleaming angle of the metal-rimmed bookshelf behind Max. Crystal awards—recognition he'd earned by never letting go of a bone—sparkled above his head like a crown of diamonds. Bright sparks of light Milo could almost feel, like static electricity.

A melee of designer perfume clashed in the air from the meeting that had just ended, and combined with the glittery light, the sensation suspended him in a memory of walking behind his mother through a department store's polished labyrinth. The jewelry cases had risen above his head, and he'd held tight to Sophie's hand, Jackson ahead of him, holding on to Mom's, Dad and Pop backing them up. A family procession on the way to meet Santa, twin boys in matching sweater vests and bow ties, matching wish lists in their pockets. He'd blushed at the coos coming from the makeup counters, daunted by the bronze-cheeked women that manned them. If only that impulse had stuck.

"What was that all about?" Milo nodded to the women congregating on the other side of the wall. He wanted to ask a more specific question. He wanted to ask about Benjamina Wasik. What was she doing here? What did it have to do with his brother? Self-preservation—no, he wrestled his inability to name it for what it was. Guilt. Guilt stopped him from asking.

Their history was…a tragedy in one unforgivable act. And he was still reeling from the shock of seeing her, the shock that she'd seen *him*, considering he'd made it all the way to LA without anyone shouting "You almost had nothing!" at him.

Then, predictably, his brother had pulled focus. Milo concentrated on that instead of the rising tide of feeling that flooded him being near Benj again. "Jackson in some kind of trouble?"

Max unpacked his lunch and the container released a tantalizing waft of spice. Milo's stomach growled. He hadn't had breakfast, or lunch, let alone any decent Mexican food in a literal year. That was at least one good thing about his trip back. And something he could fix.

"Don't worry about that. Your brother got papped coming out of Nelle's house. No big deal for him. For her…not such a flattering look. The ladies are taking it too hard because they're the kind of women who think they can fix anything."

"You make that sound like a bad thing."

"It is if she tries to pin it on our guy—good thing Jackson's got us." Max frowned as he picked up a taco only for the chicken to fall through a torn tortilla. "Hassan's got nothing. She's been outplayed. That's why she's so frustrated. I get it. But I've been a resource to her. A mentor. You gotta respect the people who got you where you are. And I told her that the call came from inside the house. She's about to learn a hard lesson about trust."

Milo hazarded a look at Benj, what was meant to be a glance. She certainly looked like she was in the hot seat with Hassan, agitation tensing her angled jaw. Maybe it wasn't just her look that had changed, maybe she was the kind of person who sold secrets now.

She turned, her face finding the light, her gaze meeting his, and Milo sat stunned, staring into those pale brown irises, emphasized by a ring of expertly drawn liner. An image of her putting it on filled the space behind his eyes. Her long, artistic fingers curling around the pencil. Her steady hand hovering above a cheek, capable of strokes as delicate and detailed as architectural plans. The lightest scent drifting from her wrist. Crisp like apples and soft like bluebells.

Her hair was lighter, which explained why he hadn't placed her right away. But when she'd spoken, when her dark brows had arched in challenge, awareness had knocked the breath from his lungs. Milo felt it happening again now, his chest all but hollowing out, until she broke the spell, looking away and releasing him. Not a little disoriented, he turned back to Max and the comedy of errors that was his lunch. If Milo was light-headed it was because he hadn't had breakfast. And cravings only heightened the emptiness of hunger.

"What can I do for you, Milo? You all fixed up? Finally ready to get back to business?" Max opened a disposable utensil bag with a pop. "I gotta tell you, it took you long enough. Coulda given me a heads-up to get the ball rolling—but that'll give you time to get back into shape."

Fucking ouch. Milo dropped a defensive hand to his stomach. Even through a layer of fabric Max could tell ripples were missing from what he surely considered Milo's glory days, playing opposite his brother's action hero. When neither of their ripped and battered shirts ever made it to the end credits.

"I think we've got some leverage from your accident. Studio's probably a bit nervous, bet I can get them to offer you up something they would have saved for someone bigger. We'll land you something that will put you everywhere. I've got an idea that could really be something and we might be able to make 'em go for it—but don't tell your brother I said that. I'll talk to Gigi. She and I always do right by you, yeah?"

Max winked and waited for Milo to respond with the requisite excitement. Everything his manager was saying was exactly what Milo would have wanted to hear a few years ago. Gigi certainly had done right by him in the past. He'd been a nobody on the first *Twin Pistols*, but for the sequels she'd negotiated a significant pay increase from low six figures to mid seven. He had that *Twin Pistols 2* cash in the bank, but it'd go quick if he invested in the wrong thing. The third installment's paycheck hung in the balance, money he'd need a real compelling reason to walk away from.

Milo managed to raise his brows in feigned interest, which only made Max sigh. "Kid, you gotta start thinking about what's next."

"I have. I've been talking to Gigi." His agent was the one who'd broken down the options in his contract. "Let's deal with Jackson first. Where is he, Max?"

"He call you?"

Milo nodded.

"We had a check-in dinner last night. A few drinks. He was real jazzed up. Talking my ear off about big-picture stuff, mentioned some ideas and people who'd approached him. But I was ready for bed. Told him to find another audience, maybe a nightcap—not my finest moment." Max wiped at his mouth with the back of his hand. "I picked him up this morning and got him out of town, told him to unplug for a week. Get focused. He probably went to that off-grid spot of his— the monastery that's God-knows-where in the desert."

"You didn't tell him about the pictures."

Max's face approximated remorse. "He didn't need to know. It'd just distract him. We landed a part in Petra Modrić's next film. That's our priority."

Milo gripped the armrests like he had when turbulence hit midflight. "Petra Modrić?"

Modrić was a big-time filmmaker with a bigger-time reputation for being unapologetically eccentric in her demands of actors. The payoff was a guaranteed trophy season, full of award-show accolades. Modrić meant media attention, in-depth features, photoshoots, the works.

She was a huge deal. She'd worked with legends. She'd worked with Grant Fox.

It was Jackson's dream come true: to follow so directly in their grandfather's footsteps.

And he hadn't mentioned it. Not to Milo, at least. Sophie must have known, probably why she'd been badgering him to reach out to their brother. For once, Milo hadn't. Milo had stalled, having trouble pulling the trigger on what he needed to say. He'd had too much time to think this year, and his old strategy of heedlessly forging ahead had paid the price.

"He didn't tell you?" Max licked a bit of sauce from his messy fingers, missing nothing. "Must've wanted to save it for in person."

"Yeah." A phone vibrated on the desk, drawing Milo's eye. The screen lit up for a few seconds before it went black, an open abyss on the crystal desktop. He was physically closer than he'd been to his brother in a year, and yet they'd never been more out of touch.

Last night's voice mail had been their first contact in six months, when Jackson had heard Milo's idea and called it selfish, among other things. "Let me know what you decide," he'd said. Even though they both knew for Milo to bring it up, he'd already decided.

Listening to the voice mail in the dark that morning, Milo had found Jackson uncharacteristically hard to understand, rattling off a double-speed, disordered monologue, a demo reel of emotion. Jackson had slurred from accusation to enthusiasm to need. Ending with Milo on an impromptu cross-country flight.

He'd finally stepped out to face the music, and Jackson wasn't here to listen.

Max leaned forward on his elbows with a sympathetic look, misinterpreting Milo's silence. "He had to fill his schedule somehow, kid."

"Of course, I know."

"You see, his franchise flick hit a major delay, with some major unknowns. His costar went missing, wasn't fit to film. A year is a long time to keep a studio waiting, Milo. Lucky for you, I know one of the producers and he wants to get this film in theaters as soon as possible and get his best set of actors working again. While Jackson is off prepping, we can meet with—"

"No—let's wait for Jack. I want to discuss it with him first."

"What's there to discuss? Script was approved, production was a go. You'd be wrapped by now and we'd be talking junket dates if you hadn't smashed your—"

"Not yet." He put too much power into the words and Max sat back. Milo pulled his hat lower on his head self-consciously and gave it another take with less. "Not yet. But I do need your help. Can't get into the house. My phone isn't working, neither is my key fob. The app gives me an error on the code."

"He changed it. He didn't tell you he was feeling anxious—"

"Oh, yeah." Milo nodded like he was remembering something. He didn't want to admit how in the dark he actually was these days. "Do you know the new code?"

"I do." Max eyed him carefully. Too carefully. Milo could feel him trying to put the parts together, looking for gaps where the pieces were missing. Like he was some broken machine Max had to keep operational. Too late, but Milo had to tell Jackson first.

"It's his birthday."

"Shoulda known." Milo forced a quick smile, feeling it flicker on and off his face like a bulb on an over-powered circuit. "Thanks, Max."

When Milo stood, he hoped the audible creaking that accompanied the move was coming from the chair, not his aging joints, his reconstructed knee. Sitting in Max's office brought back a rush of that old imposter syndrome, and he fished in his jacket for his phone and clicked the screen on out of habit. The face ID stuttered and rerouted him to a pass code prompt. He suppressed the thrill it gave him every time the phone didn't recognize him. His beard deserved a lot of credit, but Milo knew it was something else. Something deeper.

He'd made a change. He was different. It wasn't just his knee that had been reconstructed—he'd taken a shot at fixing his life as well. The proof was making it through LAX undiscovered, a feat that should have been impossible with a face as famous as his. Theirs. He'd come back and it felt like the city had moved on. Forgotten him. It had been too fucking good to be true—thinking he could find Jackson and leave town again before anybody noticed.

Milo risked a surreptitious look at the door. The women had exited, Benj was gone. A coward's rush of relief flowed through him, his guilt ebbing momentarily, before trickling back.

The phone on Max's desk buzzed again and didn't stop. Max swore and jammed the heel of his palm into one ear to answer the call.

With a one-hand salute, Milo took his cue to go. He paused in the waiting area, the room haunted by the ghost of his past.

Can we not?

Benj hadn't been fooled by a little facial hair. She

hadn't registered any deep, soul-level changes. She'd known just who he was—now and then. She hadn't wanted anything to do with him either time. And, whether or not he wanted to, there wasn't anything he could say or do to change it. She'd never give him the chance anyway. That ship had already sailed— and sunk.

Milo made it to the underground parking lot before Benjamina Wasik proved him wrong.

The elevator doors opened on her like curtains parting, the framing damn near as cinematic as the timing. His mouth split to match, surprised by the second-chance sighting of a woman he never expected. One arm behind her, she clasped the opposite elbow, forcing her shoulders back. Her loose blue-and-white-striped button-down was open at the collar, drawing his attention to the pale smooth skin of her throat. Her chest rose with an exaggerated breath and he followed it up to her face, where she watched him with a look hard enough to hurt.

"You need to do something for me."

The doors started to shut and Milo battered through the narrowing opening. *Apologize.* He knew. It was three years late—but she'd been waiting. He faltered. "You know I didn't— When I—I don't know what to say."

That was one thing he had liked about acting: having a script. Someone else crafting the perfect wording that allowed him to say the right thing at the right moment. All he'd had to do was repeat it convincingly.

Benj released her elbow and hooked her thumb under the strap of a bulging bag that hung from her shoulder. "You don't have to say anything. You just need to come to the beach with me."

"To the—why?"

"So the paps can catch us together." A slight hitch of her voice ruined her attempted detachment from the statement.

Max had been right: she was angling for some fame of her own. Milo shrugged away the offer, and the sinking realization that they'd both changed. Half a shame to be sure: Benj had always been perfect.

"Yeah, I'm gonna pass."

When she started toward him, her finger in the air as a warning, he zeroed in on it, sure that if it had wavered like her voice, moved side to side by any margin, he'd be hypnotized into doing whatever she wanted. Those fine, pale fingers had always mesmerized him. He loved their classic sculptural quality, the inherent confidence of marble. Confidence that meant her hand was steady as always and he was spared one humiliation at least.

"You need to come stage photos with me. This afternoon. For the paps—"

He bent his knees to meet her eye. "I don't think so."

A wicked light flickered back at him as she finished. "—as your brother."

Milo's knees locked, the left glitching painfully, and he shot back up. "As my what?"

"I need Jackson."

The words cut under his skin, sharp as daggers slicing along old scars. Peeling him open. His voice felt rough when he spoke. "You and Jackson? You two are an item? And he hooked up with your boss?"

She drew her finger back into her fist and exhaled

a frustrated breath. "Let's try again: Your brother is messing with people's lives in the press. You and I are going to fix it by creating a diversion. You'll pretend to be him and I'll pretend not to be disgusted by the both of you. Thus saving my *friend's* reputation and album launch."

"You want me to pretend to be someone I'm not to protect someone else's income stream?"

"Her marriage, actually, but close enough."

"No."

"No?"

"No." Milo repeated his new magic word, testing its strength. He'd known he'd have to use it coming back to LA. Known he'd need to arm himself with a secret weapon, something he hadn't had before—the courage of his own convictions. He had to be clear. He had to protect his own interests. He never expected Benj to be the first one he'd use it on.

Under her glare, Milo faltered, grasping at excuses, cursing the liability that was his mouth. "I'm not here to—we don't—we don't even look remotely alike anymore. Jackson's still the clean-cut Hollywood hunk, right? And I'm— No. That's insane. That would never work." Besides, he had his champagne problem to deal with (technically, a sparkling-wine problem, what with it being California-made): he didn't want to be a famous Fox anymore.

Cold-hard insanity was what erupted in Benj's eyes before she advanced again, forcing Milo directly under the dusty beam of a lit ceiling panel.

"Let's see what we're working with: You're too tan, but I could fix that with foundation. The beard can go."

He rubbed his jaw, leaving himself open to her

next attack. She snatched the hat from his head and he grabbed her wrist on reflex.

Benj continued examining his hair. "Too thick. Needs more than a trim. Are these highlights natural?"

She reached her free hand up to run those alabaster fingers through his dark curls—an agonizing fantasy of contrast while comparing him to his brother. Milo caught that wrist too to halt her. His heart hammered at her nerve. And then stopped altogether, skipping beats he was sure he needed, when she lifted up on her tiptoes, her soft, lush breasts brushing his chest, her nose at his ear, inhaling.

Her scent invaded his space with her: apples, bluebells. Something new that woke him up.

An eternity expanded around him, contracting with a whoosh when she lowered herself to the ground again. His pulse stuttered back into rhythm.

Benj's voice started thick but evened as she pushed forward. "Ocean. That's…good. That's—overtreatment won't be a problem when I correct it."

"*When?*" He repeated the presumptive word, the evidence of her glaring certainty, and dropped her hands. "I never agreed." Talking to Benj was like working with yesterday's dailies. They weren't on the same page at all. Getting purposely papped absolutely did not play into his plan to get out of LA unseen. "He could be seeing someone."

"Is he?"

Milo should know. Milo should know what was going on in Jackson's life.

Benj answered herself. "I haven't read anything about him dating anyone. Unless you know something

I don't, that's just another excuse. So what is it really? You don't think you can do it?"

Milo pushed his coat back and gripped his hips. He should have added an amused grin, but he couldn't seem to make himself. A practiced show of indifference would have to do. If she wanted a full-on scene, she'd have to pick a different partner. He was done acting.

"You don't have the chops to be Jackson Fox?" Her bottom lip protruded in a falsely sympathetic but wildly effective pout. Heat rushed up his neck. "All you have to do is stand there. I'll make you look the part."

Milo huffed out from under the lamp, his vision going green in the dim light as he made for the glass-paneled door of the vestibule. She'd been close to the truth, but the imposter syndrome had nothing to do with his acting ability and everything to do with his fabricated designs on the Hollywood lifestyle. He'd never wanted to be an actor like Jackson, he'd only wanted to want it the way Jackson did. Want anything the way Jackson did. And now he was walking away from it.

"You need to do this for me," Benj called after him.

It was the anguish, the snapped band of her voice that stopped him. Emotion he knew she wouldn't have wanted him to catch. The same note he'd heard at the end of Jackson's voice mail. The one that finally got him on a plane. The unbearable tone in both their voices that he couldn't bring himself to label heartbreak. Not when his past indecision had done it to them both.

"Why's that?" Milo waited, his palm hot against the glass, knowing what she could say to clinch the deal. Knowing she'd have him, if she'd just take her shot. All she had to do was name him for the Rumpelstiltskin that he was and demand a deal to her liking. Anticipation tightened his throat. He was almost looking forward to it—being called out. Maybe then he'd have the chance to settle up, to earn more lasting relief from his guilt.

"You'll do it," she threatened, her voice back under control, "or I'll tip off every media outlet I know, personally handing them the scoop that Milo Fox is back in town."

Chapter Three

For a moment, Milo didn't react and Benj wasn't sure he'd heard her. Wasn't sure he cared. Then he spoke. "That's not…" His voice trailed off and his head shook. He rounded on her. "That's not a scoop." He snatched his hat back so quickly the rush of fabric from her grasp burned her fingertips.

"You sure?" She fumbled her phone from the bag at her hip, glad she'd had practice holding it up in a menacing way. "Looks to me like you're trying to keep a low profile. Why? You got a morning show booked? Want your prodigal homecoming to make a real big splash? Pity to ruin the effect with news breaking early."

Two creased lines on his forehead paralleled her doubt. Was she wrong about his motives? It had happened before. The strap of her bag dug into her shoulder, growing heavier and more uncomfortable with every second. She wasn't sure what to do if this didn't work.

An SUV rattled over the grate near the bottom of the ramp and Milo yanked the hat over his head, angling himself out of view until it was gone.

Benj bit back a relieved grin. "If you want to stay

under the radar until you're ready to break the news yourself, be your brother for an afternoon." There were only three cars left in the garage. The Tesla Roadster charging in an extra-wide spot had to be Max Field's. Which left her Subaru and a black pickup truck she assigned to Milo. A layer of dust covered the truck, obscuring the natural shine of the paint. "You just flew in, right? Do you have a Dopp kit in your luggage?"

If Benj hadn't been watching him so closely, she'd have missed his nod. Like he was so unwilling to agree, he couldn't force his chin to drop more than a millimeter. Once she'd secured that little bit of assent, she disarmed, putting the phone in her bag and heading to the elevator. "Great. Meet me upstairs in the washroom." Her thumb found the smooth curve of the call button as she watched for his reaction in the dull reflection. "If you're not there in five minutes, I start making calls."

"To rat me out?"

"Round of applause, everybody, he's got it now."

"You're bluffing. You're not serious."

"People always think that." No one could *possibly* take a woman seriously when she liked talking and makeup and had a favorite internet psychic.

He hadn't moved from the door, and Benj's worry surged back. She'd been so sure he was hiding something. That this would work. But maybe she'd declared premature victory—the skepticism in his voice implied it.

"Who would you call?"

The Up light shut off. Doors motored open. Benj had no choice but to forge on. To hope she'd played it right. If Milo took off—she couldn't afford to lose him, but she'd sure make him pay. She stepped inside and faced him, selling it with all she had. "Oh, *everybody*. If only I had a dollar for every reporter who tried to pick me up because of who my best friend is..." She trailed off and tapped her bare wrist, his eyes darkening at the motion. "See you in five."

As soon as the doors closed, Benj shook out a body full of nerves. She twisted her knuckles together and brought her hands over her head, stretching her elbows apart until her fingers were hot and red and couldn't take the strain.

"Fuck!"

That's how it felt to be near Milo Fox again. A battle raging inside of her, where winning was giving him nothing but losing and letting him have it would feel so good. And this plan—this plan *was* insane. Even if she managed to turn Milo into Jackson, who would believe the story they were trying to tell?

Her arms dropped to her sides. No. That was much too defeatist.

Benj drew her hands back up, cupping the air and swirling her palms around each other. In addition to psychics, the internet was full of tips for how to deal with negativity. One recommended practice she'd adopted to combat it: fluffing her aura when life's density was getting her down. While it looked ridiculous, the real funny thing was that that shit actually worked most of the time.

Aura sufficiently fluffed, Benj dropped her hands to her sides, feeling better until the elevator door opened, letting in the signal her phone needed to ring.

"Mina?"

"Did you get him? Will he do it?"

"I think so." Benj shouldered her way into the bathroom, the sleepy eco-efficient lights flickering awake sluggishly, contrasting with Mina's sharp reply.

"You think?"

"Yes." Her decisive response echoed in the tiled room, spiking her nerves the same way Milo's firm *no* had in the parking garage.

"Better." Mina broke down the details, confirming that she'd lined up photographers and giving Benj the address. "And I'm sending Nelle back to Washington, so as far as anyone's concerned: she's been there since yesterday rehearsing."

"But last night—"

"Your apartment was being fumigated. She said you could stay at her place. And you invited a plus-one."

"That seems kind of shitty of me."

"I'm sure you won't be the only one to say so." Mina paused. "You need to know: I don't care what Nelle thinks, if you're playing us, you won't work with her again. Or anyone in my orbit. I'll make sure you're only booked by ex- and wannabe-*WoCA*s or for tween socialites' birthday bashes. And that's because I'm generous."

Benj took a false step and wobbled to the side. Her fluffy aura had lost volume faster than oily hair. She wasn't worried about the specifics of Mina's threat—those *WoCA*s, *Women of a Certain Age*, made up Benj's reality TV of choice, so working with a cast member would be more of a thrill than a hardship. It was the promise behind the threat that knocked her off balance. Mina would do it: she'd shut down Benj's professional relationship with Nelle. She'd end it all. The shows, the red carpets, the barely there dream of Basic Witch

Beauty. And maybe Nelle would push back, maybe Nelle would even fire Mina—but that wasn't what Benj wanted for her friend. Mina understood Nelle's goals, her purpose. Mina plowed through the obstacles Nelle couldn't. Mina was a great manager who protected her client, and did it well. Nelle deserved to have the best team possible. Whether officially on the team or not, Benj wouldn't get in the way of Nelle's success.

Mina's warning concluded with a slow, serious challenge. "You'd better make this look good."

Benj steadied herself and held her own eye in the mirror, hoping the truth would take the edge off her fear. "That's what I do."

After Mina hung up, Benj continued staring down her reflection. It didn't matter that she and Milo had a past. That being near him made her soul rage like it was trying to vibrate out of its bodysuit. That even his refusal had drawn her in. There was something different about him. A coolness he hadn't had three years ago. She'd just have to ignore it. She had no choice now but to follow through.

"I can do this," she told herself. As long as he showed.

He would show, right?

He had to. He was protecting his anonymity too closely to brush off her threat. Whatever reason he had for backing out of the limelight, it mattered to him. And after what he'd done to her, she refused to have qualms exploiting that weakness.

Benj slid her bag onto the quartz counter and smoothed back her hair, tucking the blunt ends behind her ears, ready to unpack and get to work. Out of the satchel came a jumble of receipts, a glass water bottle, and the notebook with her sketches. She took a minute to scan the receipts for business purchases she could write off and flattened those under the cover of the sketchbook, setting it on the stainless-steel ledge beneath the mirror. Then she got to sorting the products that had jostled to the bottom of the bag, trying not to think about how much time had passed.

He would come.

She could do this.

From the kit in her trunk, Benj had grabbed three shades of MAC Studio Fix Fluid Foundation, and she lined all three bottles on the shelf despite being sure of her first selection. She had to bring Milo's rich tan down to a medium, taking into account his warm undertones, and without making him look yellow. NW35 should do the trick. Next, from a clear plastic pouch came tweezers, moisturizer, liquid contour, and a highlighter. Each item a touchstone to her professional self. This part, at least, was simple. Where she lacked confidence in her blackmailing skills, she had no doubts in her ability to manipulate the eye.

Five minutes had to have passed. She didn't dare check her phone to confirm. Willful ignorance kept her from panicking as she dug around in the bag for a mini brush canister.

The heavy door opened with a laden whoosh. When she looked up, forgetting to hide her eagerness, Milo Fox filled the mirror over her shoulder, a scowl on his face that not even that thick beard could hide. His hands were in fists at his sides, one clenched around the handle of a leather toiletry bag.

She wasn't sure what to do with this Milo, the one who didn't deploy rapid-fire bursts of socially deflective grins. In the vestibule, she'd seen a change in his eyes—a disruption where pleasantness used to reign. It looked to her like indignance. At having his plans interrupted, having to do something for someone else.

Benj worked to control her features and gestured to the shelf where the other tools of her trade were lined up and waiting.

Milo tossed the bag onto the counter, the zipper tag hitting the smooth surface with an aggressive scrape. He didn't move any closer to her. He had come, but he didn't want to be there. This was the real Milo—self-centered, inconsiderate. At least he'd dropped the amiable act. At least he knew by now she wouldn't believe it.

She unzipped the bag and found what she needed. With a click the electric razor was on.

He still didn't budge—extremely committed to his role of unwilling accomplice—so she met him in the middle of the room. She brought the buzzing device to his face and paused, feeling like she should say something. Give him a chance to back out. Treat him like the friend he'd been once. Her shoulders crept toward her studded earlobes and she pushed them flat. He hadn't been her friend since his first act of war. She had a job to do—a job to protect. And three years ago, he hadn't offered her an option.

The razor cut through his beard with a staticky snap. The sound occupied the room as she followed the line of his jaw down. With short, vertical strokes she worked her way across Milo's face to the grim set of his lips. While her grip on his chin was firm, the pressure came only from her fingertips, the barest hold she could manage while maintaining control. She diligently avoided flicking her gaze to his eyes, keeping intense focus on each section of beard until only a fine stubble covered first his left cheek and then his right.

Leaving Benj to deal with his mouth.

She'd done this before. Shaved Milo Fox. Back then she'd maneuvered purposefully closer to him. It was part of the job—makeup artists had to breach the boundaries of personal space—but with Milo she'd relished the right of invasion. The innocent flirtation. One time, as she'd brushed stray hairs off his upper lip, he'd cupped the back of her thigh, just above the knee. Where no one could see. They'd shared a look fueled by impatience, powered by need. A shiver had rocked her, head to toe, and then he'd let go, and she'd believed his intentions were genuine.

Now Benj tilted his chin down with a rough jerk and set to work on the mustache she'd created across his lip, refusing to acknowledge its full, smooth bow— reminiscing instead about the betrayal that had come out of it.

Milo remained silent, except for one little grunt when she pushed his forehead back with the heel of her palm to shave under his jaw. Satisfied by the job (and the nervous bob of his Adam's apple as she'd buzzed over his exposed neck), she knocked the razor against the sink and clipped a half-inch guard over the blades. Milo scrubbed at his face, looking side to side in the mirror, checking himself out before finding her eyes in the glass.

"I was gonna go along with this for you, but I don't see it happening, Ben."

Her shoulders prickled at the nickname. That one

letter he liked to drop, his own way of getting closer
to her, carving away the space between them.

"On your knees."

He balked, finally, at her command. "Is this an execution?"

"I can't reach." She motioned to his hair. Her chin
barely met his shoulder. She couldn't access the top
of his head.

With his beard gone, she could see the moment stub-
bornness set his jaw. "You'll manage."

This was the real, unaccommodating Milo she was
dealing with. He wasn't going to bend. And she shouldn't
have liked the challenge of it.

Benj closed her eyes, shaped her mouth into a ring
and exhaled. A one-second meditative attempt to keep
herself on task. It helped in that, the moment her eyes
opened, she noticed anew the little storage closet next
to the door. Inside she found supplies and emerged
armed with a dustpan and a bucket.

The bucket clanged against the floor when she
dropped it upside-down behind Milo, the sound clatter-
ing through the room. A hollow drum beat once, twice,
as she climbed onto it, one foot at a time. Her hands
found their way into his hair automatically, finally giving it the practiced ruffle she'd tried for in the garage.
She familiarized herself with the grain, sinking her fingers to his scalp. It was thick and soft and curling into
her grasp. Shame to have to cut it so short, really.

His reflection blinked up at her and he swallowed
twice before saying, "Seems like a lot of work to prove
your innocence."

"Your point?"

"Maybe Max is right, maybe you're responsible for

the whole setup." His tone was dry, accentuating the cracks in his character. The desiccated delivery chafed at her nerves. It wasn't that he didn't care about anything, she'd found out the hard way, it was that he only cared about himself.

She gripped his hair tightly, ignored the pained groan that vibrated from his throat, and forced his head into a better position. "Use someone who trusts me to get what I want? Sounds familiar, but it's not *my* MO."

He shook her off. "You're really going to make me do this?"

She extended her palm over his shoulder. "Razor."

After a long moment, he handed it back, took off his glasses, and the buzzing resumed.

Benj worked methodically from the back of his neck, shearing off the loose mess of wavy surfer hair he'd shown up with. She wouldn't need to worry about those natural highlights, because she cut them away. She cut it all away, and, in the process, reset him back to how she'd met him on the set of *Twin Pistols 2*, when she'd thought the bad cop he'd played to his brother's good was scripted.

A crease deepened between his eyes as he watched her progress. Dark hair littered the floor around them. She clicked the razor off, reached to brush a feathery lock off his shoulder, and missed when he surged closer to the mirror. He put down his glasses and ran his hands over her work again, not content with seeing the change but needing to feel it.

"I still don't look like him." Pride laced his determined dissent.

"I'm not done." She stepped off the bucket. "Sweep that up and wash your face while I get organized."

Benj rinsed her hands while Milo cleaned up. He shook off his jacket, revealing a baseball shirt with orange shoulders and an Orioles bird emblem on his left pec. He tossed the jacket on the counter and bent to splash water over his shaved cheeks, letting it drip onto his shirt when he stood.

She frowned. "I said wash your face."

"I did?"

"You don't have a cleanser you use?"

"Is that your angle? You're going to upsell me on some overpriced pyramid-scheme skin-care essentials?"

Excavating through her bag, Benj uncovered a pack of facial wipes and tossed it at him. "Shut up and use one of these."

Milo did as directed, eyeing her warily as she pumped white cream out of a bottle. "What's that?"

"Moisturizer, your skin is dry. You could use a mask, or at the very least some eye patches for the puffiness—"

"Right, yeah, send me your affiliate links."

She clicked her tongue, weighing the price of defending herself. "You can use plain yogurt as a mask. I'm not trying to sell—"

"Can we get this moving?"

Benj snapped the lotion cap closed. "You asked! Shut your mouth if you don't want to talk."

A short fuse had been burning in his eyes and now it detonated, the whites exploding wide. "So it's my fault if I'm a little wary of you putting shit on my face? I was very orange for a very long ten days last time."

"Well, you shouldn't have gotten me fired." There it was. The past forced its way out of her, to the forefront. A debut of backdated hurt.

He huffed. "You got yourself fired."

And her attempt at composure disintegrated. "I told you to shut your fucking mouth, Milo Fox."

Chapter Four

Shut his mouth. He *should* shut his mouth. Once again, left to his own devices, just being himself, Milo had done the wrong thing. Said the wrong thing. To be fair, he'd thought his final act in Hollywood would be privately telling Jackson he quit—he hadn't had a lot of time to process being coerced into playing his twin for some cameras. So, yeah. He'd snapped back. He was frustrated. Couldn't seem to cover it up with an easy smile.

Not that Benj would have been fooled by one. She'd seen his worst. It was almost a relief not to have to hide it.

Maybe he should tell her the truth. Maybe she'd let him off if she understood that he didn't want to be part of this anymore. Any of this. The cameras and the plots and the stories. Maybe he would have, if he didn't need to tell Jackson first. If Benj hadn't been *so* clear that she didn't want to hear anything he had to say. She wanted him to be a human cutout. The only reason she'd enlisted him instead of a cardboard standee of his brother was the inconvenient third dimension, making his sole appeal a surface-level solidity that completed the effect of "living man."

Milo found himself in the mirror. Only it wasn't him exactly—not who he'd woken up as, anyway. It was a version of himself he hadn't seen in a year. Since before he'd gone home to the family farm on the Chesapeake Bay. His father's side had planted tobacco there for generations until his grandfather had turned three acres into a sunflower field dedicated to his late wife. The tobacco was long gone by the time Milo came along, but the smell never left the tobacco barn—neither had Pop's spirit, with the field kept up by Milo's older sister. In another month or two the seeds would go in, and then, late in the summer, they'd have neat rows of yellow-gold faces—and for the first time in a decade, he'd be there start to finish. He wouldn't miss it.

Milo turned to face Benj, an apology twisting his tongue, tying it up. She didn't deserve one now, not in the midst of her blackmail routine, but he was going to force the words out anyway—until her eyes squeezed shut and he noticed the rapid rise and fall of her chest. The effort she exerted to keep herself together. Breath by breath, the pace slowed, and when she blinked her eyes open with a deep exhale, he decided what would be best for everybody was if he did what she asked. Keep his fucking mouth shut.

"Can you just—" She motioned to a lower, accessible section of counter.

Lips firmly together, Milo perched on the edge, sinking just below her eyeline. He tried not to flinch when Benj applied the lotion onto his face.

"It's just moisturizer," she said again. "To prep your skin. Like I said: it's a little dry. Could be the salt water. You were beach bumming?" Not how he'd describe diving into the frigid Bay each morning. "Planes can be very dehydrating. Sun too. You should probably stay out of it."

Not a chance.

"For career longevity and all." She stalled with a thoughtful pause. "I guess it doesn't matter as much for you."

His heart galloped, jolting away from him before the rest of her thought eased his suspicions, the unfounded shock that she knew what he was up to.

"Male actors aren't thrown over the second they begin to show a little wear."

Milo exhaled, bringing his racing pulse back into normal bounds. Without his glasses, the room blurred around Benj, making her stand out. The soft cotton of her shirt gaped invitingly, revealing the strap of a plain light blue bra—and probably more, Milo knew from experience. How many tantalizing hours had he spent sitting in the makeup chair, peeking down her blouses? *Not enough.*

He forced his attention away, sure she'd be able to feel the red heat that splotched his cheekbones. Her thumbs smoothed over his forehead, chin, and nose, spreading warmth underneath his skin wherever she went. He had the urge to lean into her touch, to let himself forget that she was bribing him to sit there. But he had too close a view of her face, the strained professionalism she adopted. So he held himself back, checked the memories like baggage, refusing to remember how good this could feel. He kept it stowed away.

Or, he tried to. In three years, he hadn't been able to rid himself of the memory of Benjamina Wasik's expert hands. Or the way she talked, like it was natural to think out loud, to be so open. And after the accident, yearning for her steady brand of comfort, the ease of just being, had sent him all the way back to his childhood home.

With a rough stroke, Benj brought the lotion up to his hairline, pausing at the little scar that trickled into his forehead. Milo jerked away. To hide his discomfort and buy himself some space, he grabbed the water bottle she'd left on the counter. Fresh and extra cold, he gulped it down, washing back the apology she didn't want, cooling his heated cheeks.

"Hey!" she protested.

"Planes can be dehydrating." He tilted more water into his mouth.

She grabbed the bottle from him, splashing his crotch.

"Hey!" he echoed, but Benj drowned him out, "You're wasting it!"

He wiped his mouth. "Is the drought that bad? I took two sips."

She capped the bottle, speaking softly to herself, like she didn't care if he heard. "I was going to use it to clean my brushes. It had intention." She glared at him. "You just can't help yourself, can you. Always taking."

Milo bristled, rising from the edge of the sink. "You can get more. There's a faucet."

The bottle disappeared into her bag, another part of her tucked safely away from him. "No, I can't actually. Not until next month. It didn't come from a faucet. It's moon water and now it's half gone."

"Moon water?"

"Don't say it like that, like *moon water.*" She tucked her chin and pitched her voice lower, practically ogre-

esque on the last two words, an exaggerated imitation
of his skepticism.

He braced a hand on his stomach. "Tell me it's po-
table."

"It's not hose water, it's moon water." As though he
was actually supposed to know what that meant. "Calm
down. I had some this morning." Her palm on his
shoulder forced him back onto the sink. She scanned
his expression, one eyebrow quirking up. "Wow, the
color just drained *right* out of your face. Makes you
look so much more like him."

Milo clamped his mouth shut again, interest in her
lunar aquatics dissolving like the protein powder Max
wanted him to be living on. That is to say: not entirely.
But he'd had plenty of practice choking down the grit
at the end.

That strained professionalism returned, but Benj
continued narrating what she was doing. "Cleaning
up the eyebrows next."

He refused to wince as she plucked the stray hairs
along his brow, thinking—rightly—that she'd enjoy
it too much. And when she spread another potion on
his face, he closed his eyes. He didn't need to see her
loathing so clearly. Not when he could feel it in every
harsh stroke of her accomplished thumbs.

"I'm lightening your tan to match Jackson's complexion better. And this is a little highlighter." She
dabbed under his eyes. "Too dark. Here as well."
Something soft feathered under his jaw. "His chin has
more definition, so I need to contour yours."

"You can stop," Milo grumbled. He couldn't take
much more comparison, much more judgment. "Talking, I mean. If it will make you go faster." He opened

his eyes in time to catch the placid focus leave her face, replaced by aggravation.

"You're right. There's really nothing we need to say to each other."

She finished his face in silence. But when she nudged his shoulder to see the completed product, he couldn't contain his surprise. "Holy shit. You really did it."

Benj rinsed an egg-shaped sponge in the sink, shrugging off his compliment. Refusing any niceness from him. "You're literally twins, it wasn't that hard."

Twins. Like he could forget. He'd spent a lifetime sharing a face with someone else, being confused with someone else. All through high school he'd been congratulated on school plays he hadn't starred in. Never mind that Milo'd never even set a foot on the stage. Never mind that they were two people. They were living one life.

And Milo had finally admitted to himself it was Jackson's.

The first time Milo was stopped on the street, he'd been called a liar by a man who refused to believe he wasn't "that blind kid"—Jackson had just finished a five-episode arc on a medical drama. After that Milo'd been accused of being the prisoner from *Redcoats*— "You are. I know you are!" But the angriest stranger had been the one who'd followed him to his car shouting, "Find something new and stop ruining everything!" when Jackson was rumored to be up for Inigo Montoya in an ill-fated *Princess Bride* reboot.

And then *Hey Batter!* had happened. The movie had absolutely bombed, Jackson's industry appeal imploding with it. Milo had thought that might be it. Jackson had given it a solid go, they'd had fun, for the most part—at the beginning. But as the endless summer stretched in front of him, Milo was closing in on his limit. He hadn't found what he was looking for in California, he hadn't had the chance.

But instead of that being the end of Jackson's career, Max had brought over the screenplay for *Twin Pistols*, marking the beginning of Milo's run.

He still remembered the sound of the script hitting the kitchen's calacatta countertop—a sharp, stirring clap.

"I know you were hoping for a period piece, but this is the part I can get you." Max pointed at Jackson. "And I think it'll do what you want it to do—prove that you're hero material. The real deal. The thing is, to get it, you gotta bring 'em something they didn't know you had." Max had looked over at Milo. "It might not be such a bad thing—I can sell twins for double."

"What do you think?" Jackson had asked.

Milo didn't think—he'd been tired of being mistaken for someone else. He'd wanted to exist on his own merit. Still did.

Benj started packing up and Milo stepped closer to his reflection, fascinated by the miniscule nuances she'd found that made him see his twin in the mirror.

"Don't!" she ordered, startling him. "Don't touch your forehead. I had to use extra cover-up on your hairline. Where there's that scar."

She palmed a bottle of foundation but didn't put it away. She held his eye, looking like she might actually want him to speak. Waiting for him to fill in some blanks.

Milo only shoved his arms back through his jacket sleeves.

When he picked his glasses off the counter, she continued the instructions. "And don't wear those when we get to the boardwalk."

As if he hadn't already gone into this blind. He slipped the frames back on, the bamboo wallpaper behind her coming into focus, widening his view so it wasn't all about Benj. "We done here?"

"Almost." She secured the bag's strap over her shoulder and hooked her thumb under it. "Now we just need to 'get caught.'"

Back in the parking garage they separated, Milo agreeing with a grunt to caravan behind Benj's car. A few hours in California and he was right back to following someone's lead. He climbed into the truck and slammed the door. Gripping the wheel and shaking his head, he waited for Benj to pull out. Her lights clicked on, but she sat in the front seat, frowning at her dash. Then, with a sigh he could virtually hear from across the lot, she thumbed open the phone attached to her dash and began talking.

The lights flashed on the Tesla opposite the elevator doors and he spared a glance at a confused-looking Max. Milo extended four fingers in a motionless wave, palm flat against the wheel. Maybe the lack of Jackson's signature enthusiasm helped Max place the imposter because he waved back, even as his brow remained furrowed. Milo would have rolled down his window to explain, but Benj's backlights blared red as she backed out of her spot. He'd have to call Max later. Now, gritting his teeth, it was time to get this show on the road.

Out of the garage, cheery late-afternoon sunlight greeted Milo. He wanted to let it warm his face, but without his beard and hat, he felt suddenly overexposed. At the first stoplight Milo pitched sideways, diving for the prescription sunglasses in his glove box. The switch in lenses did little to alleviate the feeling of being on display and he sat at the light, heart pumping, willing it to turn green so he could drive out of Beverly Hills and not stop.

Someone honked and Milo felt it like a knife in the back of his skull.

"Hey!" The man in the convertible next to him waved for Milo's attention.

Milo lowered his window, unmuting the city sounds and making him wince. He'd worn noise-canceling headphones on the plane and wished he could put them back on.

The man set his voice deeper, rolled the words around in his mouth like marbles and then spit them out. *"You missed your train for nothing, sweetheart!"* His head fell back with a laugh. "Pretty good Grant Fox, huh?"

For the first time in a year, someone was shouting his grandfather's lines at him. This was exactly why he was done with this city. Milo repressed the desire to flip off the stranger, and instead did what used to be instinct, what Jackson would do: smiled and winked.

Milo gunned it when the light changed and swore when Benj pulled onto the 405 South, a road—a parking lot—he had learned to avoid at all costs. But somehow, for Benj, the cars parted. Whichever lane she was in *moved*. He kept on her tail, and what should have been gridlock for three hours took them a miraculous forty-five minutes before Benj led them smoothly off the exit at Rosecrans Ave. Two blocks later she slowed, pulling into the tiny lot of a whitewashed mechanic's garage. Blue and red plastic letters spelled out Eddie's Auto Repair, the word *brakes* beneath shortened to *bra*, dirty outlines remaining where the other letters were missing.

Milo idled next to a single scraggly palm tree. Was he supposed to follow her in? This wasn't the beach. He grew more suspicious of the detour the longer he waited. He told himself just to leave, but was still waiting when Benj reappeared around a cinderblock wall. She yanked open the side door of his truck and started loading in her shit: a big boxy case she put on the bench next to him, a hefty weekend bag shoved in the wheel well, and, once she'd climbed in herself, that overfilled purse swinging from her hip to her lap.

She motioned impatiently at the road. "Can we get this moving?"

He held his arms straight, pushing back into the seat. "Where's your car?"

Her hand spun a vague circle, her wrist pivoting gracefully even as she brushed him off. "The check engine light keeps turning on. And then turning off before I get it here. Eddie can't fix anything until he pulls the code or whatever. It turned on in the garage, so I brought it in. It was on the way. Now we can arrive together, since I don't know if they'll be waiting or not. And then you can drop me at home."

"The garage is open on a Sunday?"

"Some of us are walking the line between having a life and making a living."

He stared at her over the trunk between them.

"So. Let's get moving." She gestured to the street again.

Fine. Fine by him. The sooner they did this, the

sooner he'd be able to get home and figure out what to do about contacting Jackson.

Milo's elbow knocked the trunk and he cursed as he pulled back into traffic. She hadn't told him where to go but he had enough information to guess at their destination. "I'm assuming you want me to head to the pier?"

She raised a single thumb without looking his way. His grip tightened on the wheel.

The Manhattan Beach Pier was scenic. Romantic. A place plenty of people would flock to on a springy Sunday afternoon.

"We're never gonna find a parking spot."

"We will," Benj said airily. "We're on a mission for Nelle. You'll see. Things always work out in her favor."

Whether it was Nelle's guiding spirit or dumb luck, Milo spotted someone walking to their car just after they'd passed Manhattan Ave. He double-parked to wait. The street slanting down and the pier rising up gave the impression of sitting at the top of a roller coaster. A familiar buzz of adrenaline sped up his pulse, a throb of energy unwilling to be contained. He shifted with nowhere to go, Benj's black box pinning him in from the side.

The sun had begun its descent and blazed through the front windshield. The air inside the truck grew hot. With his elbows tucked in to prevent further injury, Milo began to sweat under his jacket. A toxic concoction of perfumed products emanated from inside the damn case, filling the cramped space, making it stuffy and unbearable. But the silence from Benj was the heaviest layer, the most oppressive, the weight that made him want to buck.

The other car finally vacated the spot and Milo claimed it with a sharp swerve, pulling up and reversing so hastily that the makeup case knocked into Benj. While she protested, he jumped from the too-warm cab, freed himself from his coat, and hauled in an excessive gasp of fresh air. The glittery artificial side of LA's coin he could do without, but the California sun? The wild edge of the coast? That almost felt like coming home. Eyes closed, he held his face up to the sky, half expecting to feel the ocean breeze in his hair before remembering that Benj had cropped it too close to his head for that particular pleasure.

He found her waiting on the curb, hand outstretched, her pale almond eyes daring him to reject it. Despite the fact that he'd gone along this far, she still expected him to leave her high and dry. He could guess why. Her smooth, strong fingers curled around his, pulling him forward.

Hand in hand they walked toward the hexagonal building at the end of the pier, lapping the closed aquarium's wraparound boardwalk in a truly lackluster performance. Whatever show she'd wanted the photographers to witness was falling as flat as his participation in her charade. Milo couldn't see the paps she'd promised, but he knew they were there from the trepidation that prickled his neck. He'd almost forgotten the feeling of being watched, like seasickness, nausea from motion out of control. Big thanks to Benj for making sure he had one last taste of it. The feeling brought him right up to the end of his limit, ready to call it a day.

When he started back down the pier, Benj stopped, their arms stretching awkwardly wide between them. Smiling a big fake smile, she dropped his hand and leaned her elbows on the wooden rail. "I'm not ready yet." She had to know they hadn't pulled off the stunt, there'd been no money shot, and as much as she seemed to hate this too, she wasn't going to give up.

Again, Milo thought about leaving. He'd done his part. He'd let her extort him, shave him, force him back into the spotlight he was intent on putting behind him. He'd let her use him—just like he'd used her. That was their common ground. She hadn't done anything he hadn't done first. Which was why, as tired as he was of standing there, he dug deep to do it a little longer.

Milo kicked a rock over the side of the pier and watched it fall into the ocean. The light scattered off the waves, a natural sparkle so different from the metallic shine of Max's office. Normally he'd be in no hurry to leave the beach. When they'd first moved here, while Jackson had been building his career, Milo had spent his days braving the surf. Impressing himself with his ability to face old fears. Convincing himself his grandfather would be proud. He'd gotten a job renting wave runners to tourists, just for an excuse to stay barefoot in the hot sand. He had fish tacos for lunch and Coronas whenever he got thirsty. There had been definite perks. He'd been nineteen, wanting for nothing, his world tasting like lime and smelling like coconut.

The wind blew sideways, ruffling through Benj's hair before it reached him, mingling with her signature scent. Energizing him. Tormenting him. Making him want more.

He rested against the rail beside her, his back to the ocean. "You wanna give 'em a real shot and be done?"

Chapter Five

"Oh my god yes."

At that moment, Benj wanted to be done with Milo and his brother and this ridiculous scam more than anything. Milo might look like Jackson, but neither of them were selling *budding romance*. Somewhere nearby photographers were taking passionless photos that would be used to dissect the validity of Nelle's defense, used to dispute the fact that Benj and Jackson were an item.

Soon she'd be discussed by strangers who didn't know anything about her except what they could see. And Benj knew her looks would be the first casualty. The easiest target. Her hair would be too light, her body too heavy, sparking speculation that she was a trashy blonde, or, perhaps, if the stranger was feeling generous, that she had the potential "to be hot," with long legs and a rectangular build—if only she weren't so "filled out."

She could already sense the skepticism from their audience, knew just how onlookers would wonder, to themselves and out loud: *We're supposed to believe he was with* her *over Nelle?* The headache pounding behind Benj's temples made it hard to break down the bullshit in that thought, made it harder to force more facial expressions that would undoubtedly be picked apart.

Benj *so* wanted to be done. She wanted to help Nelle and then she wanted to be in her bed, under her covers, preparing for the fallout. With the help of a few *Women of a Certain Age* marathons and a Costco-sized bag of chocolate-covered pretzels, she could probably hole up inside for a few days, maybe until this was completely over. She might even be able to make herself forget the whole thing, emerge in a week like none of it had happened.

But there could be no forgetting what Milo did next.

Twining their fingers, he pulled her close, overlapping her hip with his, lining her up against him. The heat from his body seeped through their shirts while Benj stood stiff as a board, fighting the urge to pull away.

He smoothed his free hand around her back, hooking his thumb through her belt loop, anchoring her to him like he could tell she might bolt. "Relax, the camera picks up tension."

"Right, I should be super comfortable this close to you. After what happened last time." Her face lifted to his, his mouth just above hers.

"That's not going to happen again. I'm not going to—I won't kiss you." He turned his head and breathed in her hair, raising it from her scalp. Excruciating minutes passed before he spoke while she held herself still. Then his voice came from far away, a murmur she'd have missed if the wind had decided to take it. "Just pretend. Pretend it happened different. That we happened different. That we had a real chance."

They'd had a real chance. He'd ruined it. The muscles in her calves tensed. "I can't."

Milo squeezed their entwined fingers, his palm kissing hers. "Try."

He nudged her closer still until Benj curled her arm behind him, resting her hand on his shoulder. She kept her gaze on the water where the waves crashed against each other, some trying to reach the shore, others pushing back, the turmoil echoing the clatter of her pulse.

He spoke into her ear, coaxing her to remember why they were here. His voice sticky slow and painfully sweet. "You want them to believe it, you need to believe it too, if only for a moment."

For a moment. She had to set aside her anger. She had to set aside her past to ensure her future. She had to tell herself untrue things.

So Benj let herself pretend.

The waves swirled, their story churning in her mind.

When Benj moved to Hollywood three years ago, her first job was on the set of *Twin Pistols 2*. She was twenty-three and on her fifth career (sixth, if she counted frying cheese curds at the local Cranberry Festival—which she did not). Capricious, her parents said. Looking for the right fit, Benj countered.

The *Twin Pistols* gig only lasted a month before Milo Fox got her fired. She'd told him from the start she wasn't interested. But, okay, sure, she'd walked that talk back, flirting with him in the makeup trailer as he spun side to side in the chair, making it impossible for her to do her job. She'd stilled him with her hands, running her knuckles under his jaw to tilt his gaze up, wiping a smudge at his lip with her thumb.

A Wisconsin-bred Girl Scout, she knew how to start a fire. She'd thought he understood: just a touch now, leave the rest for *when they weren't coworkers*.

The bottom of her striped shirt was tied up and his abdomen pressed the hard knot into her soft stomach. She'd been wrong about Milo. If she hadn't known it the moment he kissed her in front of the entire *Twin Pistols* crew, she knew it after, when he texted production, kicking her off the set. It took her a few months, and that very humbling request for a loan from her parents, but she'd found her way, scored big with Nelle, and tried to never look back.

In her head, Benj didn't change anything about those first weeks. Not the flirty looks, the teasing touches, not the conversations that had started light and grown heavy, saturated like the air before a storm, seeping into her as she read into the details. She liked almond croissants and he liked ham and cheese—was there a trendier duo than sweet and salty? Conversations that seemed to bring her closer and closer to the truth of him, to the big, sweet heart she thought existed under all those flaky layers. Ha.

She remembered the start as it had been, the mornings she'd gone in to work, excited to check the call sheet and see the number two next to Milo's name. The letters that spelled out something special, the promise of something grand coming her way. The pieces of her life falling into place.

Benj lowered her chin to her hand, her fingers a barrier between her and Milo. She breathed him in automatically, his scent clear as cut grass, warmth wafting off his tan skin like freshly baked bread. Impossible to ignore. Closing her eyes, she did what he asked, she did what she hadn't let herself do in three years, and re-imagined their chance. She rewrote it so they were both patient. Not a line was crossed. In her make-believe version, Milo never disappointed her, never hurt her.

Leaning against him on the pier, Benj imagined it was real. That production had wrapped and they'd made it through together. The story had continued on, blossomed and grown into something better. Something genuine.

The fantasy came easily to her—too easily. Her disloyal mind readily accepting alterations to the truth. The potential had been alive between them, irresistible. She'd been so sure once that she could love him. Sure enough to try.

Her breath evened. Her body went soft. Settling, comfortable and quiet, while all around her was motion. Holding still, taking it in, she gazed out over Milo's shoulder, her focus drifting. Kites waved gaily from the beach. A skateboard rattled over the wooden planks behind her. The waves played beneath them, the wind above. A seagull landed on the railing, tucking its grey wings close to its body and surveying the scene alongside her.

She relaxed into him, the knot at the front of her shirt shifting up, out of the way, unnoticeable. She let him gather her closer, suspended in time.

The photographers Mina called had surely gotten the goods, the idyllic moment between two would-be lovebirds. Benj could go, knowing they had done what she'd set out to do. Yet she stayed put. She lingered in the moment, resting in a fantasy so *tangible*—Milo's warmth through her clothes, his easy hold. Loose and confident. Like he knew he had her. He could have *had* her.

It was easy to believe, easy to pretend, because she'd wanted so badly for it to be true. God, she *still* fucking wanted it to be true.

Benj's delicate tether to the present snapped.

The wind whipped toward her, stinging her eyes and she untangled their bodies, her sudden motion startling the gull back into flight.

"Ben—"

"That should do it."

She stared Milo down until his mouth shut. He held his hand out to her and she weighed what it would look like if she didn't take it. Were the paps still watching now that they'd gotten their show? Was it worth the risk?

Down the pier stood a pretzel vendor and with another unhinged, exaggerated smile, Benj made a diagonal dash for it. She bought two, shoving one into Milo's hand, giving him that to hold instead. She double-fisted her own all the way to the car, taking overpoweringly salty bites that turned immediately flavorless as she chewed, and hiding her hot face behind the flapping blue-and-white checked paper. Embarrassment erupted inside of her, taking up so much space she could barely swallow. Every time she saw these damn photos, she'd be mortified by her willingness to let go of the truth. For what? For a moment of pretending he'd actually wanted her back?

No, the truth was that she'd done it for her friend. Benj gripped it tight, squishing the doughy pretzel in the process. She'd done it for Nelle. With any luck, the evidence *would* be inescapable for a few days, saving Nelle from Jackson's scheme to use her name to raise his profile. That should have made Benj feel better. It would later, she assured herself, when she had some space from Milo. Space she wasn't going to get crammed into his truck, she realized as he opened the door for her.

She balled the last bit of bruised pretzel and paper in her fist, no longer needing the prop. His hand hovered at her back, but he didn't make contact. She'd have flinched for sure if he had. Soon she'd be home and she could hate him again in peace. Hugging her bag to her lap, Benj didn't fully exhale until the ocean was behind them, the sun chasing them from the horizon. Her mouth was so dry she drank the rest of her moon water, not caring what else she could have used it for.

"Where do you want me to—"

"On the next block," Benj decided on the fly. Asking him for favors had backfired. The side mirror reflected her glassy eyes back at her. She shouldn't have let him get to her. But now that she had, she might not make it home before she came undone. "I'll get a car."

He adjusted his grip on the wheel. "You wanna wait on the corner with all this stuff?"

It didn't sound ideal, but did she want out of this car more? Hell clap emoji, yes clap emoji.

"Ben," he started again, his voice warm and tantalizing, like it had been on the pier. "I can drop you at home. Just tell me where."

The icy energy keeping her tight melted, leaving her overwrought nerves soupy. Her eyes burned and now she couldn't blame the wind. Did she want to wait on the corner with all this stuff while *sobbing*?

The same paps might drive by and catch her looking a mess. Mina wouldn't like that.

"Carson," she choked out. She'd take the ride. Compose herself. A two-step process starting now.

Benj blinked the emotion back—refused to let Milo Fox do this to her again—and skimmed her notifications to distract herself. She hovered over a check-in from Nelle, then closed the text app without responding. Benj wasn't in the headspace yet to break down everything that had happened since they'd parted ways. It had only been a few hours, but it was so much to type. Eddie had left a voice message letting her know that her car wouldn't be ready for another week. Considering her plans to go underground the next few days to avoid Milo's fake face, she didn't think that would be a problem—until she completed her communication triumvirate, checking her email, and found herself lingering over a frantic plea from a soon-to-be bride. The wedding was in one week, the invitations sent, the A-list RSVPs tallied, and her beauty team had fallen through. *Creative differences, not contractual*, the bride made sure to say. *The compensation is on par with what you'd expect from a wedding like this*—here she dropped her Big-Named parents' big names.

And they were big names. *Huge*.

It had been almost a year since Benj had taken on an extra client. Working exclusively with Nelle kept her busy, kept the bills paid. She'd even moved into a new apartment—well, a studio—and finally didn't have to worry about coming home to a naked roommate using her homemade quilt as a yoga mat.

But with Nelle out of town and Mina's threats in the back of her mind, Benj couldn't bring herself to type her usual polite-but-firm refusal. Even if the bride wanted to have a consult…tomorrow.

Benj blew out a slow breath and replied, finding it refreshingly easy to fake her enthusiasm through the phone.

I'd love to! she typed, setting up the meeting for the next morning.

Whatever clout Mina thought it lacked, working events for the kids of industry giants was profitable.

Milo took the 405 again before Benj could warn him not to and they suffered through a silent gridlocked hour and a half before her exit in Carson, giving the busy bride enough time to write back asking Benj to come to her mom's house in Beverly Park. Benj chewed her lip, already pained by the surge price of the car she'd have to hire to get there and back.

By the time they pulled up across the street from her apartment complex, night had stained the fabric of the sky. Milo kept the engine running. Benj paused with her hand on the door latch, giving him one last chance to say something and hating herself for wanting to hear it. Nothing good ever came from Milo Fox's mouth.

Of course, he said nothing, his gaze fixed out the front windshield, an impatient crease forming between his brows. The live engine hummed in her ears like a swarm of bees, the sting coming from the seed of hope he'd planted under her skin.

She held in her thanks. He didn't deserve it. This afternoon had been owed to her, a farce for a farce. She'd consider the ride home interest. A fine on over-due compensation.

On the curb, she slung her purse and weekender

over opposite shoulders and wrenched her kit across the bench.

"Wait—" Milo's eyes narrowed. "Benj, hold up."

Benj did not hold up. She was over holding in and holding up and holding out hope that Milo Fox was a decent guy. The only thing left to hold were her bags on the way out of here. She marched behind the truck—and he met her at the back bumper.

"I know that guy."

Incapable of ignoring the juicy undercurrent of his tone, she looked around immediately. "Which guy?"

Milo tilted his head back and to the right where a thick-necked man occupied the front seat of a jeep. "He's a pap."

"Why's he here?"

"This is what you wanted."

"I didn't—I didn't think they'd come to my house," she admitted. Suddenly the other side of the street felt very far away, the safety of her door even farther.

A car passed and Milo shot a palm out in front of her. She glared at it, and the insinuation that she was a toddler who hadn't learned how to cross the street.

His fingers flexed. "They shouldn't have gotten here so quick."

Benj pushed his arm down. "Well, he'll get the scoop on me coming home and—"

Milo caught the handle of her kit. "Is one of those your balcony?"

Balcony was a generous word for the little cement porch off her room. But she nodded.

Milo tugged unexpectedly, loosing the kit from her grasp. She grabbed back for it, missed, and he tossed it into the open bed behind her. "Get back in the truck."

"Oh okay—the *fuck*, Milo?"

"I'm not leaving you here with him outside all night."

"All night?" She strained on tiptoes to reach her bag. "He'll get—" she caught the handle "—his shot—" heaved "—and go." The bag rose a few inches and dropped back into the truck's bed. She didn't have the leverage necessary to lift it over the side.

"Not this guy." Milo opened the driver's door. He extended his arm, blocking her from crossing the street again and corralling her back inside of the cab.

The straps of her other two bags crisscrossed her chest like ammo bands, and she stood deciding whether to unload. How dare Milo make any demand on her?

She was almost home. That was her window, right there, so close she could almost see the comforting square of her bed.

Except. If she could see it from here, what was the neckless man's view like? The idea of him parked outside her house all night had her suppressing a heebie-jeebie-induced shiver.

And there was the jut of Milo's jaw. He might sound bossy and outrageous but he meant business. He wore that same look he'd had on earlier when he refused to budge a step closer to her in the bathroom. He wasn't going to bend. He wasn't leaving here without her, and if she made a break for it, what kind of scene would he cause? One the pap would catch? One that had the potential to ruin the love story they'd tried to set up that afternoon? Making everything she'd been through *pointless*.

Her options straight-up sucked.

Milo had her pinned in, repeating his order. "Get back in the truck."

Fire burned in her chest.

And Benj did as she was told.

Chapter Six

Benj scooted across the bench seat, as far as she could get away from him, until the bag on her hip hit the passenger door. Milo had the car in drive before she could think twice—before he could either. His fingers felt wrong curled around the steering wheel when they wanted to be wrenching the camera from the creep in the jeep and smashing it on the pavement.

That guy. That fucking guy.

It had taken Milo a few minutes to place him and then the only thing he wanted more than confronting that slimebag was keeping him away from Benj. Did she even understand what she was getting into, inviting these vultures into her life?

"You can calm down," Benj said after a moment. Forced to sit nearer to him than before, maybe she could feel the new heat coming off him. The heat that nearly choked him. Black, like warning smoke. "You can at least drive slower. And it wouldn't kill either of us if you'd use a blinker once in a while."

Milo forced his foot off the pedal.

"He caught you in a bad light, huh?"

"Not me."

"Jackson then?"

Milo grunted. Her gaze was hot, boiling the story out of him. "A few years ago. After *Hey Batter!* Jackson wasn't in a great place."

"So he what? Blew some cash? Some drugs? Some hookers?"

"All of the above. Max took care of the photos." He should tell Max the photog had resurfaced. Maybe he'd be able to help, like he had the last time.

"You don't know what he would have—"

"He shouldn't have been there." Milo ripped the sunglasses off his face and lunged for the glove box, hoping a switch in lenses would help with the darkness clouding his vision. He needed to get ahold of himself. He normally didn't get angry like this. But it had been a long day. He'd been traveling. Planning to talk to Jackson had him geared up.

"And you shouldn't have talked to me like that."

The latch wouldn't catch as he tried again and again to shut the box. "None of this is the way it should be."

Benj must have at least agreed with that, because she didn't argue with him further. She did push his hand out of the way, black talons flashing, so she could manage the contents of the glove box and click it closed.

"You really need to fluff your aura."

"What are you even talking about?"

"Forget it."

As Milo wove north, silence clung to the air between them. So thick Milo spun the radio dial for relief. He should have guessed Nelle's voice would come pour-

ing from the speakers along with the beat of her new
single, "La-La-La, Bye-Bye."

> *Hush up,*
> *You poor little baby.*
> *Hush up,*
> *Don't say that you played me.*
> *Tried to make me go down,*
> *But you're the one who blew it,*
> *So hush.*

Milo grunted again, a sound that might have been
a laugh, if he'd been in the mood to joke.

"What?"

He shouldn't answer. He recognized the protective
note in Benj's voice. The ring of bias. The sound of
someone readying for a fight. If only he hadn't used all
his self-control driving away from one already. "That's
your friend?" He nodded at the radio. "She's why you
made me do this?"

"You know that's my friend. What's your problem
with it?"

Milo paused, trying to put his thoughts into words.
"You said we were saving her marriage? But—" He
extended his hand toward the dash, where Nelle was
proving his point without him having to say anything.
Benj's glare forced the explanation out of him anyway.
"She's decimating the man on the radio. And sneaking around with my brother. Why's she letting you go
through the trouble—since you're such good friends
and all."

Benj didn't need to take a beat, she was always ready
for another round and this one had been brewing. "She

is my friend. My *best* friend. And she isn't sneaking around with Jackson. Nelle and Bran are as real as it gets—they're perfect for each other. Your brother showed up last night. *He* wanted to 'pick her brain'—"

"About what?"

"I don't know—he couldn't remember the name of some guy they met at a party. Don't ask me why he couldn't just call."

"Jackson prefers to do things in person."

"How nice for him. He's still the one who had 'too much wine' to drive home and crashed on the couch. And incredibly, conveniently, '*accidentally*' someone was there to snap him leaving first thing in the morning."

"Max said he didn't even know about the photo—"

"And you believe him? Ha. No. He set *her* up—and then he ran away and left us to deal with it. So you can—you can just—"

"Shut my mouth?" Milo turned, forgetting how much closer she'd be when he did.

The red light glistened in the sheen on her brow. "Yeah. Actually."

Milo rolled down the window, letting in the smell of hot asphalt and cheap weed. She'd worked herself up and he didn't want to argue anymore. The soft, warm air did little to cool her ignited temper and she started in again when the light turned green and exhaust joined the mix.

"And whoever Nelle wants to 'decimate on the radio' is her business. More power to her. Her husband isn't bothered so why are you? He worships her. He'd decimate himself on the radio to please her. Have you *heard* 'All For You'?"

"No," Milo lied.

"Yeah, right." She huffed out a laugh that told him she hadn't actually found anything funny. "You know, as a man, it takes a lot for what a woman says about you to affect your career. But for a woman, one word from a lead on a film and there goes her first industry job."

His teeth ground together. He never should have started this. He wasn't going to win. He eased his molars apart to change the subject, to put an end to it. "You have a place I can drop you? A hotel or—"

"A hotel? Full of tourists who read the tabloids with breakfast? I don't think so." Benj turned the radio down, so low it might as well be off. She rubbed at her temples before looking sideways at him. "How far north are you going?"

"The Bird Streets."

With a slow nod, she said, "That'll do."

"So We-Ho or a friend's…?"

"The Bird Streets."

"I'm not following—"

"Just take me with you."

"To my house?"

"I've got somewhere to be up that way in the morning. And it's been a fucking day. So if I'm gonna be ambushed by another photographer, it might as well be to my benefit. Let them think I'm spending tonight with Jackson too."

The light ahead of them turned from yellow to red while Milo was still deciding whether to punch it. He ended up slamming the brakes. The truck lurched, the seat belt catching at his neck, trapping him in. Benj glared harder at him. She pushed down the arm he'd stretched out in front of her and he let the red lights across the street burn dots into his eyes until he had to close them.

"Green light."

He blinked his lids open. Benj motioned for him to drive, conveying all of her aversion for him in the acerbic flick of her wrist.

Milo drove the rest of the way home with all the patience he could muster, concentrating on the road, doing his best to ignore the quiet intensity of the cab, the way Benj seemed to grow tenser with every block. Was she waiting for him to say something? Or dreading it?

Either way, Milo kept his mouth shut. Whatever reason she thought he had for participating in this pretense didn't matter. As far as he was concerned, today was the day they squared up. Whether she still hated him tomorrow wasn't on him.

Even if he wished she didn't.

Even if he would change it if he could.

That anger she was holding, he certainly deserved some of it—but he couldn't account for why she was still so mad, so untouchably furious. He'd felt it when she'd made up his face, he'd felt it through the tension of her fingers when they'd held hands. It had only gone away on the pier, when he'd convinced her to pretend he wasn't the guy she'd known.

Back then he'd been different. Still faking it, even to himself. And he'd fucked up. He knew it. But then she'd moved on to something better. Why was she still harboring so much resentment? When he looked back on that time, after he'd pushed through the guilty sludge of it all, he remembered her…well. He revisited the knowing glint of her eyes, her smart mouth, the way laughter burst out of her like a solar flare, sudden and bright. Details he'd searched for in every woman he'd been with since—bits of Benj, denied the whole.

Tomorrow she'd be gone and he'd have to remember how to forget the way the sight of him deadened the glow behind her eyes.

"You did get me fired," Benj said suddenly, like she couldn't hold it back anymore.

Milo rolled his neck, everything inside crackling like tires on a long gravel drive. "I didn't—"

"No." She interrupted, turning in her seat to face him, using his new word against him. "No more make-believe. Let's go over it together and get the facts straight. What happened was I turned you down. I told you why. It was my big break and I wasn't going to get involved with the movie's star."

He grimaced at that. He hadn't been a star. He'd been the star's brother, on-screen and off. He'd been cast not because of merit, but because he looked the part. "I remember. I wasn't your type."

What is your type? he'd asked.

Tall, dark, and not a coworker, she'd said.

He'd clicked his tongue. *Two out of three.*

Her eyes had sparked. *Not good enough.*

"And you *agreed*. And then you kissed me. You kissed me in front of everybody. And production fired me—"

Milo started shaking his head before she'd finished. "No, *no*. You turned me down, you told me why, I agreed. And I kissed you." His heart flailed at the memory, train wheels spinning off the track. He exhaled. "And then you spiked my sunscreen with self-tanner out of spite."

"False. Fully false. I only—" she held up a point-making finger "—*allegedly* tampered with your complexion *after* I was fired."

"That's not how I remember it."

"So admit you remember it wrong."

He couldn't. It didn't make sense. "Why would they fire you because I kissed you?"

"Oh, wow, Milo. Okay, so there's this thing called professionalism. And because of you they didn't think I had any. You forced them to fire me."

Milo tongued his teeth and tried out her version of events. She'd turned him down, but there was something there they couldn't discount. She'd told him why, and he'd agreed because he understood. The problem was temporary, he was going to wait it out. He'd agreed and then he'd kissed her because he'd been so convinced of his own self-importance, so hard up to make a good movie, one worthy of Grant Fox's legacy, he'd convinced himself the trade-off was worth it.

It hadn't been. And the old guilt coupled with the new knowledge of why she was rightly so very pissed at him stung like a bee sting on a bruise.

"That's it? No response?" Benj vibrated with so much pent-up energy it was a wonder the windshield hadn't shattered.

Milo didn't know what to say. Nothing would make it better. After a pause so long she probably thought he was ignoring her, he managed to tell her, "I didn't think that would happen."

"Really? What did you fucking think would happen?" She shot back another response, always quicker than him, always pressing her advantage.

He didn't know what she wanted—for fuck's sake, he'd only *just* figured out what *he* wanted.

I don't know.

He didn't say it. It wasn't enough. Couldn't compete with whatever she'd say next.

And they'd finally arrived. For the second time that day Milo pulled up past an overgrown privacy hedge to the house he and Jackson had been left. A parting gift to a pair of fourteen-year-olds from an otherwise broke grandfather, a man they'd hardly known. The only thing he'd ever given them, the scarcity imbuing it with undue meaning.

Unlike at Benj's apartment, there was no photographer waiting outside Grant Fox's reimagined midcentury modern at the top of the hill. Milo punched the updated six-digit code into his phone and whispered his relief as one of four garage doors opened. The scent of lilacs followed them in, sweetening air that smelled like new rubber. Back in Maryland, the garage smelled like paint thinner and dried tobacco. Desperation laced the way he missed it.

Milo climbed free of the cab. The garage door lowered and everything went dark. He froze. Enveloped in black, he couldn't tell if his eyes were open or closed. The hollow sound of collision reached him. Benj cursed.

"Hold on." He made blindly for the light switch, flicking it up with no result. *Really, Jackson?* If his brother couldn't be bothered to change the lightbulbs, the least he could do was pay someone else to do it.

Benj swore again from somewhere near the bumper and Milo moved toward her.

"Here." His outstretched hand found her elbow just before her front collided with his.

The scent of her washed over him, edging out the wrongness of the garage. He followed her arm up, bringing her closer with a hand on the nape of her neck. He felt the catch in her throat through his fingertips. His ears rang with the sound of it. The taste of need lingered at the back of his tongue.

A reminder of how much he'd wanted her and how little he'd done about it. Desire he wasn't brave enough to name locked him in place. Was there something he could say to make it right between them?

A palm at his chest forced him back. "There's no one here to see, Milo." Her words were icy, her palm hot, and he turned away from them both, the jagged car key in his fist cutting into his index finger.

He'd had his shot. He'd blown it. And he was leaving town as soon as he talked to Jackson. It was over with Benj.

Milo found the door to the hall and flipped on the light, sending a beam across the smooth cement for Benj to follow on her own. A newly installed alarm system beeped at him and he stared at the panel in the wall. Max had said Jackson had been anxious—probably because he was living alone for the first time in his life. He wanted his brother to feel safe, but something about the upgraded security fortified the unsettled feeling Milo had uncovered this year. Jackson wanted this life badly enough to live somewhere that required defense measures. To Milo it felt like being locked into a life that wasn't for him. A reminder that being born codependent didn't mean he had to die that way.

Benj dropped the largest bag off her shoulder. "Tell me you know the code."

He thumbed in the numbers as the beeping intensi-
fied. "I know the code."

The beeping stopped.

Milo stooped to pick up her bag, surprised she hadn't
asked, specifically, what the code was. But she wasn't
watching him, waiting for him to explain. The view
had pulled her attention. It did for most people. This
was a house meant for entertaining, breezy and cool.
Grant Fox had loved to host—just not his family. Milo
hadn't been here until his grandfather had been dead
half a decade. Jackson thought the bequeathed view
was supposed to make up for that.

Milo waited patiently behind Benj as she took in the
open layout. They'd done some much-needed upkeep
and remodeling a few years back, when the money
started rolling in. The two bedroom suites were entirely new, but they'd kept the living space the way it
was—expansive and inclusive of the kitchen and din-
ing, all open to a terrace edged by an L-shaped infin-
ity pool. Night was settling over the landscape beyond
and the pool glowed indigo. Lights speckled across the
hills, dustier the deeper they went into the valley, obscuring the rise on the other side.

He'd stood side by side here with Jackson, taking
it in that first evening. Dust powdering the surfaces,
white as cocaine—some of it was probably cocaine.
Jackson had grinned, ear to ear, the Thalia to Milo's
Melpo, a tableau of an old running joke as he said,
"Look at that. The valley can be your night-light."

Benj drew forward across the slate-tiled floor. "Is
that an O'Keeffe?" The blue-and-salmon-colored
desert scene stood out against the fireplace's whitewashed brick, and Milo glanced that way, frowning

at the bare mantel beneath, where a gold-plated Oscar used to sit.

"Sure is." Milo wished he knew what she was thinking. She'd studied art in college and, as she stared at the O'Keeffe, he knew she was seeing so much more than she was willing to say. "We've got one of her barns too. And a Thiebaud. I prefer both of those but Jackson has a thing for the desert."

Ever since he went there to dry out.

Benj ripped her gaze from the painting to look at him, disbelief weighing down her mouth.

"We found all three in the garage," he offered as explanation. "Really, really lucky." If Grant Fox had remembered they were there, he'd have sold them for sure. The man had needed cash near the end and the only thing he'd had any attachment to was this house.

"Lucky? Finding priceless art in your garage?" She clasped her hands under her chin as if in prayer. "Tell me you aren't still storing the other two in there."

"Benj. Seriously. They're on loan to a museum."

"Must have been nice, showing up in Hollywood, this place just waiting for you." She shook her head, running her hand along the back of a plush mustard sofa. "Your lifestyle, your achievement, your Thiebaud, guaranteed from the start. It's true, huh? That Grant Fox left this place to you and Jackson because he wanted the two of you to have the same success he did."

"That's what they say."

Her gaze left the slanted ceiling and found his face. "You don't think it helped? You think you'd be where you are right now without your position literally grandfathered in?"

"No." Her eyes flashed and Milo rushed the rest out

before she could misinterpret him again. "He didn't have any fortune left, so he did his best to leave us the fame. We wouldn't be here without him. But he wouldn't be relevant the way he still is without us."

Milo started down the hall before she could ask him to explain that last part. In his room, the same view met him from floor-to-ceiling windows. He took off his glasses and rubbed his face on his sleeve.

"I'm in here?" Even as a blurry outline in his periphery, Benj crossing the threshold into his room made his throat thick. And he couldn't bring himself to send her down the hall to Jackson's bed.

With a nod, he folded his glasses instead of putting them back on and tossed down her bag. He paused at the door frame.

"Yeah?" Benj put a hand on the knob. Waiting, again, for him to say, *something*.

"I—No hard feelings."

She closed the door in his face. That hadn't been it.

Milo put his glasses back on, ignoring the smudges from his fingers. He retrieved the other bags from the truck. Leaving her makeup case under the narrow table by the front door, he took his luggage to Jackson's room on the other side of the house. Jackson had his own corner of glass, his own hillside view, his own end of the pool that bent around the terrace. Everything the appearance of equal, even when they both knew it wasn't.

On Jackson's dresser he found the missing Oscar. They'd watched a clip of Grant Fox accepting it on YouTube. Watched him thank his agent, without a word about their young mother, who remembered watching it from home. Grant Fox had wanted to be remembered

and instead had watched his star fall. He'd tossed aside
his chance to have a family, chasing that high and never
achieving it again. And Jackson had moved the damn
thing into his bedroom.

After a hot shower, Milo dropped a pillow at the
foot of the bed. His not-as-young-as-it-once-was body
flagged, facing away from the windows, the large mirror Jackson had mounted over his dresser. In Milo's
room, the same spot was taken by an oversized print
of a field of sunflowers. Home.

For a moment Milo pretended he was somewhere
else. Maybe Alaska or Sweden—somewhere the sun
didn't always set. Where tomorrow wouldn't come and
he'd never have to explain this to Jackson. Never have
to let Jackson down.

With the weight of the phone on the center of his
chest, Milo played the voice mail again.

"Hey, uh, it's me." The uneven emotion in Jackson's
opening line had Milo closing his eyes. "Are we ever
gonna have this talk? Or are you too chickenshit?"

Milo sucked in a breath and the phone pitched forward, catching him in the throat. He thumbed hastily
through the menu, like he should have done last night,
calling Jackson back immediately instead of trying to
think of what to say first. He'd overthought and now he
had even more to explain and no one there to hear it.

*"Your call has been forwarded to an automatic
voice message system: three one zero—"*

Milo cut the recording off, frustrated both that Jackson hadn't answered and that there was a part of him
relieved to be off the hook—at least momentarily.

He was going to tell Jackson. He'd fucking flown
here at the drop of a hat to do it. He just didn't want

to hurt another person he loved. He didn't want to let Jackson down, not when Jack had been counting on *Twin Pistols 3* to keep his star rising. But Jackson was already working again—he'd landed a Modrić. He'd be perfectly fine without Milo.

A yawn accompanied the sudden blur of his vision. Milo was tired was all. Too tired to get up and turn off the lights. When he closed his eyes, the rest of the voice mail ran unbidden through his head, amplifying the need that had cracked his brother's voice when he'd said, "I don't think I can do this without you."

Milo woke from a dead sleep to late morning sun and the intercom's merciless buzzing. He stumbled blearily down the hall. Benj's case was gone. He'd missed her—but maybe she had come back? Leaning his face on the wall, he groped at the buttons.

"You forget something?"

"Are you trying to screw me over, Milo? Or just your brother?" Max sounded like a wild dog foaming at the mouth—knowing him, it was probably cappuccino.

"What?" Milo blinked at the sun slanting off the polished floor.

"That little publicity stunt with the blonde yesterday— you might have just cost Jackson his next job."

Daily Star–t
Monday, April 18

You want to go dark right now. It's not the worst idea you've ever had.

Chapter Seven

"Okay, see. *This* is what I wanted. I knew you were the right choice."

Benj waved off a cloud of lavender-scented setting spray as her client, Skylar Davies, jumped eagerly from the director chair to evaluate her face up-close in a giant framed mirror leaning against the wall.

"When I saw Nelle's *Vogue* cover, I knew. I told Ivo, I was like: I need to upgrade my glam. And he was like: Babe, we're getting married in one week, and I go: But I want Benj."

Benj had never heard her name used like that before. Like it had its own gravity, its own clout. It almost made her forget the imposter-syndrome-inducing headline she'd woken up to that morning.

Fox and the How?

Mina had been helpful enough to send her a screen-grab. And a text that was either ominous or comforting but probably not meant to be comforting, because, well, consider the source.

Could've been worse.

Thanks?

"I told you my original squad wanted me to go natural? Like, they were full-on pushing *elegant* and *classic*. They did not understand the assignment."

Benj nodded. Three things made Skylar a dream client: she was on time, she knew what she wanted, and her nonstop wedding talk kept an ever-curious Benj distracted from her own life, immersed in a world all about Skylar.

Benj readily absorbed the vision: the theme was art deco floral, the colors emerald and gold and cream, the dress was Versace ("Met Gala Versace, not Cannes Versace"). Five hundred of Skylar's most-famous friends, family, and acquaintances were gathering on a downtown rooftop to watch Skylar take her vows under a custom stained-glass awning and leaving with a favor bag filled with Baccarat candlesticks and Tiffany picture frames. And the crowning glory: none of it had anything to do with Milo Fox.

"Pippa!" Skylar shouted into the foyer, the call getting lost in the chandeliered rotunda. The eldest daughter of Lee Davies, who'd made his own headlines for "retiring" from the Premiership in favor of a multimillion-dollar contract to play soccer in America, Skylar most certainly had a beauty room or a luxurious en suite (or both). Yet she'd had Benj set up in the living room. Presumably for the foot traffic. Everyone from house staff to Skylar's parents had passed through, and Skylar had done her best to get them each to stay, deflating most thoroughly when her parents made their excuses to go— her mom was preparing for a meeting and her father was off to the airport to "collect Evie."

"Evie's his favorite," Skylar had confided, her eyes

faithfully closed, her face lifted for Benj to work. "Obviously, or he'd send a car to pick her up. Don't get me wrong, I want both my sisters at the wedding. That's something Ivo and I have in common—family's everything to us. But she's—she can't help the way he is about her. You know it's like: this Sunday is the one day I want him to be that way about me."

Her honesty pulled Benj all the way in—and, if it hadn't, the vanilla oat milk latte Skylar acquired for her from a passing housekeeper would have done the trick. She wanted to deliver on everything Skylar wanted, to create a look that garnered attention, that fit the bill—and fashion-spread drama? Benj had that in the bag.

Skylar's medium-deep skin was already smooth and flawless thanks to a full La Mer care regime. (This was not a client to whom Benj would waste energy pitching more affordable alternatives.) Benj had lightly covered and contoured, then highlighted Skylar's cheekbones with a peachy blush. The pop came from overlined, crisp-edged plum lips and a vivid cat-eye that swept back over a neutral glitter on the lid.

"Pip-pa!" Skylar called again, as if there were any chance her voice could carry through the entire Beverly Park palace. "I really want her to see. Can I get her?"

Benj hesitated. All she had to do was take a photo of the finalized look for reference on the real day. Then she could go home. The *Women of a Certain Age* marathon and the chocolate pretzels were waiting. But Skylar wanted to find her sister—wanted to share her excitement—and wasn't that Benj's favorite part of her job? Making people feel good?

"Yeah, of course."

Skylar's Givenchy mules slapped the marble steps out of the foyer and Benj rested on the back of the couch. Except, without Skylar there to fill the silence, she had no distractions. No way to stop herself from hearing his voice in her head.

No hard feelings.

Three more words. All wrong. She had feelings. She had concrete emotion that only crumbled when she went soft against him. Milo had been so warm, so solid, so exactly like she'd remembered. So completely satisfying.

Benj pressed hands to her heated cheeks. "Nope. We're not doing that."

It was done. Over. No more Milo Fox.

So why did she still hear him—not in her head, but in the *fucking foyer.*

"I know she's expecting me, but it doesn't seem right just to walk in." Milo Fox, phone flat to his ear, came into view, taking two hesitant steps across the marble tile.

Benj groaned her disbelief. "This can't be happening."

The audacity of this man, to narrow his eyes at the sight of her.

"Max, I'll call you back." Milo pocketed the phone and pushed back the sides of his ripped-sleeve, army-green coat without dropping her gaze. "You really have it out for him."

"Out for who now?"

"Jackson. I'm—"

"Leaving. Why would you even come here?"

Voices sounded from somewhere upstairs and Milo

lowered his to a harsh whisper. "I'm trying to fix my brother's life since you started messing with it."

"I'm not taking that on. You two need to stop messing with *my* life. Did you follow me?" How had he gotten past the intercom at the fence?

Milo surged toward her. "No, I didn't follow you."

She moved to meet him. "We don't have time for this: Skylar's going to be back any second."

"Who's Skylar?"

"Skylar Davies. She booked me for her wedding."

"I'm here to see Petra Modrić. She booked Jackson for her movie."

Benj blinked up at him, unsure if it was the measly granola bar she'd had for breakfast, the surprise of him, or his physical proximity that slowed her ability to understand what he was saying. She swallowed. "Wait. What?" He opened his mouth but adrenaline finally kicked her mental wheels into motion. He was here to see Skylar's mom about a role. "You're pretending to be Jackson? Looking like that?"

His under-eyes weren't as dark as yesterday. Last night's rest seemed to have taken the edge off, and he looked healthy and balanced. Like a side of green beans and mashed potatoes. Homegrown and farmfed. But his jaw was still too full, the stubble he'd grown since yesterday unable to cover the difference in shape from Jackson's angular jut. She plucked the damn beanie off his head—again—and shoved it into his chest while maneuvering him into the director chair—Petra Modrić's chair, god, what were the odds she and Jackson would be working together? Benj forced Milo's chin up and, as quickly as she could, dotted his face with contour, highlighter, and base, leaving a smattering of tricolor smudges.

Milo glared at himself in the mirror when she stepped away to grab a brush. "Great thanks, this looks much better."

"Shut up," she said, wedging herself between his legs and getting back in his face. "It'll look right when I blend it." The brush fanned over his skin in concentric circles, bringing the smudges together.

"This isn't like yesterday with the cameras—anyone who gets close to me will wonder why I'm wearing makeup."

"Maybe not. It's Hollywood, everyone's made up. If you're worried about it, keep your distance." He'd at least had the foresight to wear contacts, but without the glasses between them, his eyes bore directly into hers. "I'm fucking helping you right now, FYI. You shouldn't still be trying to be him."

"I didn't really have much of a choice. She knows he's in town thanks to the pictures of us. And she wanted to see him."

"What if I hadn't been here? You couldn't have upped your wardrobe? I've *never* seen Jackson in anything that looks remotely worn." She glared down at the green-and-yellow John Deere logo on his shirt. "Or merchandised."

Milo's eyes winced closed as her brush neared his lower lashes. "Yesterday wasn't the first time I've played my brother, Ben. No one's ever caught on but our sister. It's not only in the look."

"Oh yeah, what's your trick then?"

He faltered. "I can be less me."

"But—" Unconvinced, Benj brought the brush

under his chin. "Your scar and this damn jawline are dead giveaways."

A startled gasp escaped her when he caught her wrist. He forced off the hand she'd braced on his forehead.

"Yeah, got it. I'm jowlier than my chiseled counterpart."

Could he feel her pulse thrumming in his grasp when his chin lowered, eyes looking up into hers? Big and round and deeply brown, with lashes so thick and dark that if she didn't know better, she'd think he'd already tightlined and root stamped. It was a shame he'd only done cop movies so far, he'd have made the prettiest pirate.

"Can I finish?" she asked, becoming aware of the heat of his thighs on either side of her hips. She was close enough to feel the raised outline of his phone through his pocket. He tipped his head back, giving her permission and access to the underside of his jaw. She brushed at it brusquely, wishing she could brush off whatever ingrained instinct it was that made her want to make him feel better, like he was Nelle or Skylar or someone deserving her help. But that badge was sewn into her makeup. "I didn't say you were jowly."

He scoffed in response.

"It's just that Jackson—"

"Jackson eats perfectly portioned, perfectly measured fuel. To look the way he's supposed to. And I don't—I don't do that anymore."

"Yeah. I saw it in your fridge. Funny he had a full week of food, what with his *planned* trip out of town."

It was uncharacteristic of Milo not to immediately

take up for Jackson, but his defensive silence didn't crack.

She twisted her wrist free and rested the heel of her hand on his collarbone for balance. No, she didn't need to make him feel better. But she wasn't the kind of person who made people feel bad either.

"Before Bran Kelly's Gordon McKane shoot, he did a full body makeover. Arms, abs, *thighs*, the works." The bristles of her brush slowed, smoothing over his features with a lighter touch. She concentrated on his skin's finish, to avoid meeting his eyes while she spoke. "And I get that he wanted to look good. But, even at the time I thought, like what a powerful statement it would have been to just go in as he was. To be real about it. Let people see a human body without expectation."

Milo's quiet stare brought a frustratingly familiar heat to her cheeks.

"They probably would have drawn a six-pack on him in post anyway, though, so…wouldn't have mattered." She lifted her hand from his chest and tried to take a step back but Milo caught her around the waist. He guided her palm back to the warm spot on his shirt. His forearm slipped up slightly, under the loose edge of her crop top, coarse hair tickling the smooth skin of her back.

"Mi—"

He cut her off by standing, pulling her closer, bringing his lips almost to hers. The kiss landed at the corner of her mouth. Off target. He breathed a path up her cheek to her hair, whispering in her ear, his voice rough and low. "We have an audience."

Hazy waves of heat crested through Benj, distracting her, slowing her reactions. He was everything a deep breath was meant to be, grounding her body, separating it from thought, from ego. From concern and consequence. Giving in to him was instinctual, immediate. Soothing her reflex to counter. It felt so good to let him take control.

Head heavy, she allowed it to fall back. Milo's eyes held hers for a moment, two. And then he glanced behind her. With a blink, his eyes changed. Their steamy intensity evaporated. He planted a second, easy kiss on her cheek and released her.

"Hey! Skylar, right?" He whistled. *Whistled.* Whut. "Stunning."

Benj reached to steady herself on the chair. She landed awkwardly in the canvas seat, the lightweight frame skidding back a few inches.

Skylar left her sister in the entryway while Milo sidestepped around the couch, making a show of admiring the abstract artwork on the opposite wall. His steps bounced, his eyes sparkled with liveliness. Even his words sounded more animated. "This is *fascinating.*"

He'd shed the resolute reluctance he'd been wearing like a second skin and suddenly he looked and sounded exactly like his brother.

"You and Jackson Fox?" Skylar raised her brows at Benj. "I had no idea!"

"I did. It's been all over my socials." Pippa's cheeks flushed pink and she looked down.

"My algorithm is completely skewed from wedding planning." Skylar was momentarily distracted by her own reflection. "I look like I'm wearing a filter." When she glanced back and saw Milo again, she got right to business. "Mom's in the theater, Jackson. Do you remember where it is from last time?"

"Last time…" Milo trailed off, some of the luster leaving his eyes.

Nausea swept over Benj—Jackson had been here before? Did Skylar know him? What had Milo said in greeting—Her blood pounded in her ears and she couldn't remember.

But Skylar smiled. "It's not a problem. This place is a maze, honestly. Ivo still gets lost trying to find the tennis court. Show him will you, Pip?"

Milo gestured for Pippa to lead the way. Benj was glad she seemed too shy to look directly at him. On his way out he pointed both index fingers at Benj. "Let's time this better next take." And then he winked.

Benj's mouth gaped wordlessly. She was skull-emoji deceased.

Skylar echoed the finger guns, approaching Benj with a laugh. "Okay, girl, spill. Is this serious? When did it start?"

"Recently," Benj said carefully. "Really recently."

Skylar eyed Benj's overnight bag next to the doorway. "You were there last night, weren't you?"

Benj grabbed her phone, trying to shift the spotlight back on Skylar. "We should get a shot of the approved look. If you're happy with it and want to—"

"Obviously yes, consider yourself booked. Jackson should come to the reception! Ivo won't mind."

"That's really nice, but I'll be—" *done pretending to date him by then*.

Right?

This was supposed to be over already. She hadn't planned for any reshoots and or touch-ups. It certainly would be over—in more ways than one—if Milo fucked up his meeting with Skylar's mom.

To cast Jackson, Petra Modrić had to have auditioned him, talked to him. Maybe they'd even had lunch. The chances of Milo fooling her were so low they were subterranean. As soon as she realized, the whole cover-up operation would explode, scattering shrapnel and making a worse mess for Nelle. Mina would have her way, and Milo Fox would sustain his legacy: getting Benj fired from yet another dream job, with rent coming due.

Benj snapped Skylar's picture and clipped on a smile, revisiting the lessons she learned from Milo: how to work the angles and make sure she landed on her feet. She needed a backup plan. She needed to take care of herself first. Right now, that included some hustle.

"You know I do hair too?"

Chapter Eight

Shit. Shit. Shit.

Mistakes had been made. Milo had jumped in too quickly, without thinking things through. Old habits and all that.

Now he realized how right he'd been when he'd told Benj this wasn't going to be like yesterday. Yesterday Milo only had to keep his mouth shut and let Benj do her thing. Today he had to talk. He had to say the right things. He had to sound like Jackson.

Shit. Shit.

Shit. Jackson wouldn't swear. Not here, not meeting with Petra Modrić. Jackson's goal would be closing this deal. Confirming his commitment. Saying anything he needed to make this movie happen. His focus on the task at hand would be absolute, not tugging him back upstairs. Jackson wouldn't be thinking about how close he'd been to kissing Benj again. How he'd tasted coffee at the corner of her mouth, how the smell of it lingered on her impossibly smooth skin. Details Milo couldn't shake. He'd held her close. And then he'd had to let her go.

In good news: anything Petra Modrić wanted from Jackson would be easier than that.

The air cooled as they descended into the lower level of the house. Pippa left Milo in front of a set of paneled swing doors. Hesitation crept up his back but he shouldered through before it reached his brain. And then, for the first time in his life, Milo entered a darkened theater with a sense of relief.

Milo had been a scared kid. Anxious moments in a movie would send him running in a loop through the house until the scary music was over, he didn't believe anyone who tried to explain how planes stayed in the air, and why would he swim in the Bay knowing there were sharks? But the dark—Milo never felt right in the dark. He'd worried it could consume him. That the shadows would swallow him whole, leaving no trace of him behind. Today the dark was a welcome cover. Today he hoped they would.

Petra Modrić sat at one end of a row of three oversized velvet recliners. Milo dropped into the other end, leaving a seat open between them. He probably hadn't needed Benj's mini-makeover. If she'd known the meeting was in the black of Modrić's home theater, she might not have bothered. Then he wouldn't still feel the imprint of her palm on his chest.

Milo had woken up with a clean slate. His debt paid. So he couldn't account for the fact that the feeling of her—guilt, he'd called it—remained. Still there, and significantly worse. An ache growing in his throat as he thought about her upstairs, packing up, leaving before he had the chance to—to what?

Rolling his neck, Milo forced his attention to the screen. It took a long minute—more proof he needed to focus—for him to recognize the movie playing. The dialogue dawdled at the back of his mind, but his muscles still remembered that blocking. His chin still smarted from the blow of Jackson's stage punch landing for real. They'd kept going, neither of them able to stop. The cameras had rolled through it all.

"This is my favorite part."

Milo glanced at the director next to him. She was known for character dramas, films that were quiet and real and excruciatingly honest. Like the four-part ensemble piece Jackson had signed on for—Max had coached Milo on the details that morning, "It's a boring fucking play about two marriages but your brother's gonna squeeze a trophy out of it."

Modrić's hair was swept back, creating a crown of silver above her brow that flashed light-to-dark in the action-sequence's strobe effect and matched a glittering excitement in her eyes. When her lips moved, his own voice dubbed over them.

Almost had you.

She mouthed along with Jackson's line next: *You almost had nothing.*

"Shit. This is your favorite part."

Modrić laughed, deep and full. "You didn't believe me?"

"I guess I just…" Milo faltered. He sounded too uncertain, too much like himself.

Luckily, Modrić's attention was still half on the movie. "What was it you said last month? 'There's nothing like the impact of a line worth repeating.'"

"That sounds like me," he lied. It most definitely sounded like something Jackson had stolen from Mom. She'd had a complicated relationship with her father. As Grant Fox's only child, people assumed she'd grown up in Hollywood, never wanting for anything, when in fact she'd never shared a roof with the man and often wanted a lot more from him than she'd gotten. His interest in her childhood had been inconsistent at best. His interest in her children and the simple life she'd chosen in small-county Maryland, nonexistent. But she'd found a way to separate all that from his films, introducing them to the man who fathered her through a DVD box-set of the Complete Grant Fox Collection. She loved his movies, and through her eyes they'd learned to see their grandfather as a soldier, a cowboy, a hero before they'd ever met him.

A close-up of his own face loomed above Milo. There was an artificial laceration at his hairline, put there by Benj, just before he'd kissed her. The placement matched his real scar and he'd been confused after the accident, trying to wipe it off, make it go away as easily as before.

"Your brother's pain here is so real. The betrayal so acute."

Milo scratched at his armrest having dropped his eyes from the screen. He nodded like he could see it. He didn't need to—he'd felt it. Made sure he felt it. He'd manufactured that pain on purpose.

God he'd been a fucking stupid punk. Like any of this mattered. Who cared if Flash's betrayal of Thunder looked real? (And how had he not realized what a punk he'd been playing a character named Flash?)

Modrić paused to watch the movie's climax, the soundtrack swelling around them. Milo's voice filled the room with it.

You're gonna have to shoot me.

Milo lifted his eyes in time to see the camera cut back to Jackson as Thunder.

I know, his brother said, his voice raw. A tear slipped down his cheek, clearing a trail through the fake dirt and blood.

If it were me, I'd enjoy it. His own delivery surprised Milo—Flash sounded like he meant it.

I'm not you, Jackson said back.

Not yet.

Petra turned the sound down after the shot rang out. "How's your brother doing? Is he still recovering well?"

Milo's hand smoothed over his knee. The injury that Jackson hadn't gotten. He locked his fingers in his lap. "Milo—he's fine." Modrić waited and Milo's fingers squeezed together. Jackson wasn't succinct. Jackson loved to share. Apparently he already had. "You know, his knee healed pretty quickly, in a few months. It was the head stuff…that wasn't as easy to deal with."

"Concussion was it?"

"Yeah. Traumatic brain injury." Detaching from the story made it easier to get out. "Milo had some short-term memory loss. Lasted longer than we thought. Made the early days harder. Got easier for him after he went home."

"Some things you can't rush."

Milo thought of the mash of grain and seed he'd left to ferment back home, the list of potential partners he was working his way through, diligently ensuring he put his foundling company into the right hands.

"Exactly." Their eyes met, Modrić's warm with compassion.

"But he's better now?"

Milo nodded. "He is."

"He didn't die."

His gaze shot up, following hers to the screen.

"Flash. Despite being shot, I'm sure there are action-movie reasons for how he survived. And when he's back, you'll finish the trilogy?"

"That's—Up in the air a bit. It's the plan but…"

"Things change?"

Milo's head bobbed faster as he repeated her. "Things change."

"Well, even if you don't finish, I kind of like this ending. Resolution isn't always tied up in a bow. But I wonder, though, how will it be working together again. Do you still feel guilty?"

His mouth opened. For a moment only air came out. "What?"

"You said you felt guilty. Because it was your stunt he was doing, when he was hurt."

Fuck. Milo wanted to look down again, to hide his confusion. If he could read the genuine emotion in her eyes, he was sure she could read his. Jackson hadn't just met Modrić a few times for auditions and callbacks, he'd confided in her. And the way she was looking at him was with enough force to see through him. See who he wasn't.

Panic swelled inside Milo, rushing loudly in his ears. Modrić was expecting guilt in Jackson's eyes, so Milo showed her his own. He let his mind wander back, not just upstairs, but all the way to the day he'd kissed Benj. It had been three years but he hadn't forgotten a thing: not the way she'd melted into him, not the little whine of pleasure that escaped her throat, not the way her eyes had blinked open, hurt already clouding her irises. He said slowly, "I really wish it had gone differently."

Modrić hummed. "Then that's not guilt. That's regret. You're lucky, you won't have to worry that another opportunity to make it up to him will come your way—when someone's intertwined in your life that tightly, you know it will. Jackson—"

Milo's shoulders pricked. "Yeah?"

"This performance—" she motioned to the credits rolling on *Twin Pistols* "—is really something. It has a natural depth. That's what I want for *-endships*. And I want you to help me get it."

"I'm all ears," Milo said. Max's advice had been simple: *Say yes. Say yes to anything she wants.* Milo hadn't needed the direction. He knew this character: Jackson would agree to anything Modrić wanted.

"Our movie is about people who know each other—who've *known* each other. I want that to come across. I want the audience to sense there's more they haven't seen. To wonder what underlying moments exist between Lear and Dahlia and Sam and Zuri." She pointed the remote at the screen. "I want *this*. I want real brothers. Real friends."

She wanted Milo? How could he be Milo when he was already being Jackson? "I'm not sure I—"

"I want you all to know each other. Personally. Off screen. I want the messy real stuff that doesn't get written, there in subtext because it can't go away. A layer underneath the script."

"You want the cast to have drama? Before they—we film?"

She quieted him with a wave to show he'd gotten it wrong. "The opposite of drama, I want history."

Whether he understood or not, all Milo had to do was get on board. "Sounds really fascinating. I'm in."

"Excellent. I'll send you the details for tomorrow night."

His abdomen tightened with surprise. "Tomorrow night?"

"Are you available?"

Jackson would say yes. Jackson was three hundred miles away in the desert somewhere, at a silent retreat, and didn't know this was happening—and Milo could *hear* Jackson saying yes.

Modrić rested a hand under her chin. "The whole cast is having dinner together. You'll go, yes?"

Milo made a noncommittal noise.

"And I'd like everyone to bring a date."

"A—Why?"

"I don't want you performing for each other, or holding back. Having someone from each of your lives there will keep you each accountable." Modrić pressed a button on the remote and sconces lit along the wall.

Milo jumped up. Benj had done her best, but this woman wouldn't be fooled by a bit of makeup.

"Jackson?" Her eyes narrowed looking him over. "You didn't ask much about him today. Your grandfather. Do you still want to know what my experience was like working with him?"

"Some other time."

"And, Jackson?"

Milo pressed his lips together and raised his brows. His chest hammered while he held his breath.

"I thought we discussed you'd grow a beard for the part."

His head snapped down. "Yeah. Yeah, this is just the start. We don't film for a few weeks yet, right?" He backed down the aisle, desperate to escape. "You'll see—it'll all fill in. Looking forward to tomorrow night!".

The theater door was still swinging when Milo hit the first step. He had his phone out by the landing, and was pounding out an SOS to Max as he exited the building. This was a disaster. He'd barely made it through that meeting, but a whole dinner? He didn't even know where or when it was. Modrić might text Jackson's phone the info. How would he—

"Did you do it?"

Benj appeared from the shade of the carport's wall. She closed in, speaking more urgently, a tremor in her voice unable to hide her concern they'd been found out. "Did she believe you were him?"

Guilt rose from his gut at the sight of her, sticking in his throat.

Her hands came to her hips, palms out, shortening her cropped shirt and revealing a swath of skin from the top of her high-rise leggings to the bottom of her ribs, along with the tantalizing curved underside of her breasts in a neon bra. Her skin looked soft and fair and ripe for exploring with hands or lips or both, given that he'd be on his knees begging for the chance.

That ache was back, in his throat and lower. Modrić's words filtered from his mind through his veins: *That is not guilt. That's regret.*

"Did she?" Benj repeated. Her hands flew up in the air to punctuate her question. Her shirt dropped lower, its wide edge flirting with the tight top of her pants and accentuating the little dip of her waist. From there the black smoothed over the slight flare of her hips and back in, the fabric blending into a triangular seam between her thighs—

Her hands dropped to her sides, balled into fists. "Can you please fucking answer me."

What was the question? Milo puffed out his mouth. Oh right: Had he successfully bamboozled one of the most powerful women in Hollywood? "I think so. Yeah."

"Okay. Good." Her fathomless eyes softened with relief. "Now can you leave please? Before your luck runs out?"

His phone buzzed with a response from Max, and though he hated to look away from her, he did. He needed to see that Max would get him out of this.

Already on it—finding out where dinner is.
—MF

"Goddamn, Max. Fuck."

"*Milo.*"

His knees went weak. Both of them, not just the one that had an excuse. It was the sound of his name from Benj's lips, infused with her needy frustration. But she shouldn't be saying it, and he certainly didn't deserve to hear it like that.

Milo tossed a look over his shoulder to confirm they were alone and break his gaze away from her. He had to think. He couldn't think when he was looking at her. He hadn't thought any of this through since he'd seen her and now—now look at the mess he was in.

Eyes on the sky, he reviewed the situation.

Max wasn't going to get him out of dinner. Which meant his choices were: Abandoning his foolhardy attempt to talk to Jackson in person. Or accepting that until Jackson was back in town, Milo was playing the part of the peppy celebrity twin.

It wasn't much of a choice given that he hadn't been able to make the call. He had to tell Jackson, once and for all, that he was done, and he was relying on a face-to-face meeting to ensure that he'd actually do it.

His eyes lowered, finding Benj again. She'd had a part in this too—the inciting incident that led him here was her doing. She was going to have to help him see it through and he was going to have to convince her to do it.

Just not here.

"How are you getting home?" Milo's was the only car parked in the drive. "Can I give you a ride?"

"No."

"But Eddie still has your car."

"Which is why I'm waiting on a Lyft."

He shook his head, surprised by the smile muscles tensing the side of his mouth. From the moment they'd met, she'd laid down how it would be—she'd been in charge, telling him off. It only ever turned him on. And now it was his turn to tell her what needed to happen. Milo toed some gravel back into the grid between the cement pavers. "I don't know, Ben, I think me leaving you here would be a dead giveaway."

She adjusted the straps on her shoulders and wet her lips. "Fine, great. Thanks, *Jack*, I'd love that." She started for the Maserati he'd taken from the garage and said in a more natural tone, "At least you had the sense not to drive your truck here."

She was ready with another plan by the time he'd stowed her kit in the trunk and taken the wheel.

"Drop me off and then I think you should go. Like

out of the city, better yet the state, because we can't have another close call like this."

"No."

"No?"

The engine roared as he accelerated and he had to speak louder. "No. I agreed to go to dinner. Well, Jackson agreed to go to dinner."

"You did what?" Benj topped his volume, though the car's excess rumbling had subsided.

He inhaled. The air was rich with her scent—crisp and soft and revitalizing. No matter which sense he used to take her in, the effect was overwhelming. Maybe keeping her involved was a bad idea. Too late now. "Modrić set it up. For the cast. Tomorrow night— and I need you to come. As my date."

"Why the fuck would you say yes to that, Milo? Why the fuck would I!"

"I didn't have a choice. I'm not going to get Jackson fired over this. He's *my* best friend." Milo nodded. That was still true. That would always be true. "We could do this unless—" Milo blew out some air. He wanted to extort her as mercilessly as she'd extorted him, but he knew he'd regret it. And he couldn't take any more regret where it came to Benj. "Unless it would be too hard for you. After what I did."

"What did you do?" She tilted her head, her tone innocent, forcing his guilt into the open. No. Not guilt. He named it again: regret. Because he didn't feel bad about kissing her, he couldn't apologize for it—he only wanted to take it back so he could do it again.

The contacts he'd worn irritated his eyes and he scrubbed at one with a knuckle. He was tired of making her mad. There'd been a time he made her smile, made her laugh. He stretched his jaw. "What I did—I thought it would make the movie better, okay? Jackson was in my head, saying people thought we weren't living up to the Grant Fox hype. It got to me because—" He hadn't realized yet that he didn't give a fuck about Grant Fox. "Because at the time, I wanted what Jackson had. And I knew, I knew if I really felt like I'd done it—crossed a boundary—I could use that. I could take it and use it for the scene. I could steal the scene from him."

He waited for her to react. Expected another decibel of volume not yet on record.

Her quiet, knowing comeback caught him off guard. "I know."

"You know?"

"You told me. You said acting is the easy part. Feeling your real feelings is what's hard."

Of course she'd figured it out. Milo might have moved without thinking, but Benj was a step ahead. Crop tops and skintight shiny black pants aside, what really did him in were those sharp eyes. That smart mouth.

"And I think it was really fucking selfish, Milo."

Selfish. That label again. Maybe that's what he was. Or maybe he wasn't selfish enough. If he'd really been selfish, ignored what Jackson wanted, what some man he'd never even known had thought, he might still have her.

He wanted her. Milo felt it in every nerve ending in his body. He'd felt it three years ago and been too afraid to admit that it was real. That would have meant confronting that he'd built his life around something that hadn't actually mattered to him. Well, he'd already done that. There was nothing stopping him and Benj from claiming that second chance Modrić had predicted.

Milo adjusted his grip on the wheel. "I shouldn't have kissed you like that. I wish I had done it right. I still think about doing it right." She'd called him lucky, so Milo rolled the dice, took the risk, hoping they could start over. "You still melt, every time I touch you. And I don't want to be someone who hurts you again."

He hadn't stopped to think that the thing stopping them from claiming that second chance was Benj.

"Milo, let's be clear up-front: I don't care about you touching me as long as this works. Go on and make me melt. It's just a superficial reaction, nothing deeper. Nothing I can't handle. I know better now than to let you under my skin." She leaned an elbow on the door, resting her head on the heel of her palm. "As far as I'm concerned, you missed your train for nothing, sweetheart."

Chapter Nine

Okay so maybe it had been a little dramatic to use his beloved grandfather's most iconic burn on the man. But that line had entered the catchphrase lexicon for a reason. To mess someone up. And who was more deserving of mess than Milo Fox? Milo Fox, who'd managed to make a barely there apology something that curled her toes. Made her head swim with longing. Whose voice and words flooded parts of her he had absolutely no right to access.

How even dare he.

Milo's mouth was still hanging open, and a thrill ran through her at how well the jab had landed. He blinked at the road. He cleared his throat but said nothing. His knuckles grew white gripping the steering wheel, like they had last night leaving her house. Only now it was her provoking him, not some sleazy pap.

The thrill swept out of her as abruptly as a changing wind, a cold front blowing in off a lake. The heat of it cooled and condensed in her chest, replaced by a heavy need to make him feel better. Benj breathed the need out, little by little, only speaking again when she was sure it had passed.

"But you're not sorry about getting me fired?"

"I didn't—"

Her elbow slid off the door. "Don't do that."

"Ben—"

"I saw the text, Milo!"

"What text?"

"The one you sent production, telling them to replace me."

"I didn't do that. I didn't send any text."

Really? He was unbelievable. Sticking to that script. Vibrations shook Benj's body, unrelated to Milo accelerating through a yellow, zipping the Maserati past Wilshire.

"Slow down," she snapped. "God, do you always drive like such a maniac? Do you want to have another accident?"

The car braked suddenly. Benj lurched in her seat. Her heart raced, pounding in her neck. She swallowed, watching his jaw set hard enough to crack.

"I shouldn't have said that." Little tremors pulsed in her fingers and she stretched them wide. "I'm over-caffeinated and underfed. Neither the boiled chicken with quinoa nor the steamed salmon with brown rice in your fridge appealed to me."

Milo kept his eyes straight ahead, his suggestion annoyingly reasonable. "Then you should eat."

"Thanks so much for the input. As soon as I'm home, I'll get right on trying that." Except her grocery situation after three days away would be pretty dire. She'd have to order something. And wait for it. Her stomach groaned at the thought. "Actually, no, take a right on Santa Monica."

"I said I would take you home, Ben." Milo's voice sharpened, his own frustration cutting through.

"You can still do that. After I eat."

"So, what, I'll wait in the car for you?"

Would he? Could she make him? His forearms were taut, a winding coastline of veins pushing up under his skin. All of him, as deep as he went, straining to hear what she'd say. Listening for her command. Yeah, she definitely could. But was she going to?

Milo looked over at her, a shadow under one eye from where he'd rubbed off the concealer. Looking unfinished, incomplete.

Benj sucked in one cheek. "You don't have to wait in the car. You could eat too. You sound a little hangry yourself. And if someone sees us—great, right?"

He eased the car onto Santa Monica. "Just tell me where."

Before she could answer he'd spotted the right place and pulled into an open spot on the curb.

The stand was hard to miss on the corner of the next block. Light-up letters along the low, flat roof spelled out LOS TACOS, and a pale purple picket fence surrounded a patio of teal picnic benches and electric palm trees.

They left the car and joined the line without speaking, though Benj held back a few choice words when she felt Milo's arm hovering behind her, helping her across the street. While he stared reverently up at the letter-board menu, Benj studied his profile with equal intensity. She'd made a bigger deal out of his jaw than necessary. He might have lost the notorious Fox edge line, but Milo couldn't look anything but good. He wasn't molded to precise specs in a gym, but he projected masculine strength in the way he held himself. Upright and solid. At least on the surface.

Underneath, he was less reliable. She trusted him like a glass bridge, an ice shelf, liable to crack and drop out from under her at any second. She couldn't figure him out. When he wasn't obtuse, he was intuitive. When he wasn't clumsy, he was careful. When he got it right, it was *so right*. He'd used to listen to her with such overwhelming intensity, she'd get dizzy on her own power. He'd used to smile that smile that was just for her. He'd convinced her so easily that he cared. That's what she could never seem to reconcile when he'd gotten her fired. He'd only ever been in a blockbuster, he wasn't supposed to be that good of an actor.

"It's up to you," Milo said as they approached the window. "I'll take whatever you want."

Benj stepped up to order for them both. "Two carnitas tacos, two fish—and do you want a kale salad?"

"Yes carnitas." The conviction in his tone drew her eye. "Never kale. I have standards."

"Oh. You're one of those." She waved a hand to stop him interrupting. "No—no need to explain your meat-eater machismo, I get it. Make that three carnitas." She winked at the clerk. "And a guac."

The clerk rang them up and Benj looked expectantly at Milo. He'd pulled out his wallet but was standing there, staring at it. She leaned over his shoulder as his fingertip rubbed over the name at the bottom of his Black Card.

Milo Fox.

His eyes met hers, asking the question.

She dropped her chin, answering it. *No. You can't use that. Obviously.* Benj sighed. Tipped. Paid.

Milo followed her to one of the sun-soaked tables. "Thanks."

She slapped the chrome stand onto the wood with a dull thud and almost dislodged the card with their order number. "How many millions did Max get you for reprising Flash in *Twin Pistols 3*?"

"I'm paying it back."

Benj let out a breath and told herself something true, out loud so Milo could hear it and hopefully stop scowling—it was extremely un-Jackson-like. "I'd've spent more on a ride—and I'd much rather have the tacos." The set of his jaw eased and clamped back down as she added, "And I should probably buy lunch for all my nemeses. Enemies closer and all."

"I'll bring cash tomorrow night."

A waiter set a plastic basket of tortilla chips in front of them, along with a bowl of guacamole, ringed with pink radish slices, splayed out like the petals of a flower. Hungry as she was, Benj hated to ruin the effect. She plucked one out anyway and crunched into it, the contradictory cool spice inundating her mouth. "I don't remember agreeing to tomorrow."

Milo leaned back to stretch out his leg and pull a buzzing phone from his pocket. He silenced the call and dropped the phone on the table next to the chips.

Sophie Miller the screen said. Avocado, cilantro— those were the reasons Benj tasted green on her tongue. "You don't need to get that?" That hint of acidity? Had to be the lime.

"Not now. Apparently, I'm hangry. We'd only get into it." Milo loaded a chip with dip and ate it, chewing as an approving hum vibrated from his chest. His head bobbed and weaved through the second and third chips like he was jamming to a private beat. When the waiter returned with two more baskets, Benj was surprised he didn't pump a fist in the air. Inside the baskets, the tacos she'd ordered were nestled side by side. Milo scooped up one tortilla, golden fried crust peeking out from under an adobo crema and a pile of purple slaw.

He took a bite and her knees bounced expectantly under the table. "What do you think?"

His brows bunched together and he examined the taco's filling. "This isn't fish."

"It sure isn't. It's cauliflower, in the style of fish."

"So...what's in those?" His eyes narrowed at the carnitas and she bit into one with a shrug.

"Hibiscus flowers."

"And the cream?"

"Cashews."

She waited for him to protest, egging him on when he didn't. "Go on. Tell me it's rabbit food. Trash kale some more."

Instead, Milo took another bite. And another, finishing the "fish" taco and moving on to the others. "Kale trashes itself. It's not rabbit food. It's not food at all. It's natural pesticide. My Pop planted it to keep bugs off his tobacco. They wouldn't even eat it." Halfway through the first carnitas-style taco, his shoulders had begun to rock—the music back. "You're vegan now?"

She didn't like the way he said it. Like he was collecting information about her. Getting to know her again. She'd have preferred derision—*vegan?* with an inflexible sneer.

"Is it a moral thing?" he probed, loading another chip with guac.

"Environmental reasons." She managed to cut herself off. With anyone else she'd have launched into some stats, a convincing lecture mostly stolen from her most climate-conscious friend, Arlo, but she didn't want to give Milo any more insight into who she was now. What she cared about. How individual impact mattered to her.

"You care enough about the planet to give up almond croissants?"

No, she wasn't going to fall for that. The ability to remember one little detail did not a good guy make. Looking around, Benj caught sight of the woman at the next table pretending not to fix her phone in their direction.

"Camera." Benj covered her mouth with a napkin. "You'd better flip your Jackson switch."

But Milo had already done it, his elbows dropped casually to the table, a quick smile cracking his face but not his eyes. Easy and insalubrious. *Popcorn*, she thought, struck by the familiarity of the memory.

Milo's impression of Jackson was alarmingly reminiscent of the version of Milo who'd dropped into her makeup chair three years ago. Before that first real smile made her think there was more to him. He hadn't been lying about one thing at least: he'd had plenty of practice pretending to be Jackson. It's what he'd been doing when they first met.

Her head tilted to take him in from a different angle, that buttery smile activating her curiosity. *Did he know?* Did he know he'd been playing Jackson then too?

She couldn't be sure. She could never be sure with Milo.

"What?" he asked, the smile fading from his face. "What are you thinking?"

"Say something as him."

A hint of confusion tightened Milo's face and released. "Like what?"

"I don't know. How would he pick up a girl? What's his move?"

Milo's lips pressed together and she wondered if he wouldn't do it. His finger ran along one of the gaps in the table. He flicked up his brows. A conspiratorial wink paired with a quick grin. "Let me get your number, hon—I'd love to take you out some time."

"Now do you." Her voice came out flat. "How would you pick me up?"

Milo stared at her from across the table. "You or some girl?"

"Me."

She refused to look away, even as her face warmed. Her breath deepened as the seconds passed, as their eyes held. She was sure now he wouldn't do it, and yet anticipation drew her to the edge of the bench, made her resentful of the five planks of wood that separated them.

Then the solid earth of his eyes shifted, warming with an inner glow, rich and inviting.

"Hi."

The single word flipped her stomach, had her head spinning like she'd stepped off a tilt-a-whirl. She was drunk on a syllable. Reeling back in search of balance. They had skipped the pleasantries three years ago. If he'd've said "hi" to her like that on day one it would've been over for her.

"How…" she trailed off. *How could he be both?* Both the guy she started falling for, the one whose unfiltered attention was as relaxing and intoxicating as a sauna—and the one who'd been vindictive and cruel and iced her out, putting an end not just to what they'd started but the career she'd moved across the country to build. "How could you ask them to fire me?"

He muttered a swear and clasped his hands above the table, thumbs shrugging. "Right. It's my word against the alleged text."

"Not alleged. Verified. I saw it. You signed it."

"Really." Those disbelieving thumbs popped up again. "Who signs a text, Ben?" His lips parted, his eyes closed. He swore, louder now, and picked up his phone. After a few swipes he held it out to her. "Was it like this? Was it initials?"

Already on it—finding out where dinner is.
—MF

"MF—that's not me. That's Max. Max Field. Do you believe me now? I didn't—I wouldn't do that."

She stared at the screen. At the evidence—the proof that Milo wasn't as duplicitous as she'd believed. The phone went black, reflecting her dismay back at her.

For three years she'd had such a good, loud reason to despise him. He'd messed with her career. He'd come for her livelihood. And now…she had to let that go. And what she was left with were quieter feelings. Hurt and disappointment. Soft feelings that were harder to deal with because she'd been the one who allowed herself to get carried away. After only knowing him a month, she signed him up for forever. She'd been wrong, but he'd still misled her. He wasn't the villain— but he wasn't a hero either.

Benj pushed the phone out of her face, their hands stacking on the table, the phone sandwiched between them. She blotted the shine above her top lip with her napkin before crumpling it in her lap.

"I don't want to be your enemy." He went to push his short hair back and ended up scratching hard at his scalp, like he was frustrated not to find more there now that she'd taken it away. She'd made him into something he wasn't. "But I get it. It's my fault you thought I'd do that. I should've been someone you could trust. If I had been, you'd never have believed it." Milo touched the knuckles of his free hand to the inside of her wrist. "Ben?"

Her eyes closed. Heat radiated up her arm. Distracting and enticing, but not nearly as enticing as his mouth. That was the real problem—where *his* power was. That mouth. And what it did to her when he used it right.

"Okay."

"Okay?" He brushed his knuckles gently over her pulse and she opened her eyes in time to see it. That dangerous mouth curving into a slow, genuine smile.

Her toes curled with it. With that look that made her wonder if the best way to shut him up was to confess her uncontrollable feelings for him and sit on his face.

How very dare he.

Benj yanked her arm back and flexed her feet. He might not have gotten her fired, but she'd been burned by Milo Fox once, badge earned. It wasn't going to happen a second time.

Chapter Ten

Milo single-palmed the wheel, rolling the car up to the curb outside Benj's apartment and scanning the street for paparazzi, satisfied to see that the asshole who'd been there last night was gone. He'd asked Max to do something about it. Looked like the manager had made a call. Pulled some strings. That was what Max did. That was how Max had gotten Benj fired. Milo jammed the gearshift into park. He had some questions about that. Questions Max was going to need to answer for.

As the car idled, Milo breathed out some of his anger. He couldn't blame Max entirely. He'd betrayed Benj's trust first. He'd proved his willingness to hurt her before Max had gotten involved. He was the reason wanting her now was an ache he couldn't soothe.

Benj thrust her door open, jolting him in his seat. Milo clambered out after her. The tan leather had been hot against his back and he pulled his shirt away from his body, feeling momentary relief before the material clung to his skin again. He'd felt something similar at the taco stand, convinced he'd finally cleared things up with Benj, convinced he'd said what she needed to hear to give him another shot. Her "okay" had been the last word she'd spoken to him, which made a pretty strong case for things not being okay at all.

Benj beat him to the trunk, hauling out her kit before he could offer to help. Milo rested one hand on the Maserati's low roof and rubbed his neck with the other. His shoulders popped when the trunk slammed shut. She moved to the sidewalk and he turned to keep with her, knowing he had no right to push, but needing her answer.

"So tomorrow—"

"I'll do it," she confirmed, though he didn't miss the resignation in her voice. The resentful way she dropped her case on the cement. "I mean, you can't go with anyone else. And with me calling you Jackson, maybe they won't question it."

He started to nod.

"But I have a condition."

Fair enough. Milo leaned back against the car. "I'm listening." He was always listening when she talked.

Benj moved to the edge of the curb, the sun's blaze backing her up. "You don't talk to me."

He squinted up at her. "Not sure what it's going to look like to everybody else if Jackson ignores his date all night."

"Oh, *Jackson* can talk to me. Jackson can touch me and kiss me and do whatever he needs to do to make sure this story stays solid." A foreboding glint lit her eyes. One black-on-white fingertip pointed at him, inches away from stabbing his chest. "*You* can't."

Milo crossed his arms, his pulse throbbing in the bend of his elbows. Half of her words distracted him— *touch* and *kiss* and *do whatever*—but the other half held a riddle he couldn't puzzle out.

Benj kept going, either unaware or unconcerned that

she'd left him behind. "Just text me what time we're supposed to be there and then we'll work out when you'll come by here. Early enough so that I can fix up your face again—but shave first, will you?"

Milo found some traction in the last part of her proposal. "Can't. Modrić told Jackson to grow a beard."

"Oh. Okay."

That word again. He trusted it about as much as she trusted him.

"Good, we won't have as much to do with your ja—" She bit her lip. "That is, I can do a lighter contour with a bit of brow filler. Then, with a little concealer, we're done." Her eyes lifted to his hairline. "We'll be good to go. If you can keep your mouth shut until we get there."

Milo flattened a hand between them. "Let me just make sure I've got this. You want me to chauffeur you, play doll, and flirt with you in public, but not say a word when we're alone?"

"Looks like I was pretty clear."

"And if I do it your way—"

"You get what you want."

Her.

She hadn't meant it like that, but Milo heard it anyway. In agreeing with stipulations, she had inadvertently sweetened the deal. She'd given him a way to prove he could be trusted with a second chance.

Benj took a step back to gather her bag and Milo pitched forward, propping one foot on the curb.

"Ben." He heard her breath hitch. Saw the flush she could never hide when he moved in close to her. The hope fluttering inside the cage of his chest stretched its wings wider. "I need your number."

As always, she fought him for control, drawing

her phone from her bag and swiping it open. "What's yours?"

"Four-one-oh," Milo began.

"Hold on." She made a point of responding to something else before looking up at him. "Four-oh-one?"

"Four-*one*-oh."

"Where even is that?" Her voice was razor-sharp with irritation.

Milo's own frustration was a close second. She'd told him she didn't want to hear anything he had to say but was still spitting questions at him. "Just let me do it."

Benj held the phone out to him, waving it impatiently—or maybe trying to disguise the quiver in her hand. "Fine. Text yourself."

Her eyes wouldn't meet his, and even if they had, he knew those pale irises. How impermeable they were. Light and hard as unstained oak. They would only block him out.

Milo lifted the phone out of her grasp and bent over the screen, cupping his left hand against the light. She'd opened to her texts, but not a new blank message like he expected. Instead, the thread glaring up at him was decidedly *not* blank.

I miss you. Dinner before the show on Friday?

Benj had responded moments ago:

I miss you more!
My week is still up in the air—can I let you know?

A bearded memoji grinned back, holding two thumbs up.

Jealousy cranked Milo's blood to a full-blown boil. He whipped his head up. Questions crammed the space between his brain and tongue.

Who was this fucking guy? And had Milo been closer to her type before she'd shaved off his beard?

But Benj's gaze was still bouncing around him, scattering in every direction but his. She wasn't waiting for a reaction. When she noticed him watching, her ankle twisted. "Where is that for real? Four-one-oh?"

"Maryland," he ground out. Was she playing with him?

"And you never changed it? When you moved here?"

Milo's jaw clenched tighter. He could only shake his head.

She motioned for him to move it along and he fixed his attention reluctantly back on the screen.

Whether it was an intentional move to rile him up, or an accident between the two of them handling the phone, Milo had gotten an eyeful of something he didn't want to see. Something that shouldn't be his concern. His wanting her wasn't a condition she was bound to respect.

But if it was part of some game… Well, she'd already told him the rules. He could touch. He could kiss. He could do whatever he needed. As long as someone was watching.

She only knew the old Milo, the one that settled. Those rules wouldn't keep him from getting what he wanted. They'd ensure he got it.

Milo thumbed a new message open and typed in

his number, sending a message to himself. His phone buzzed a receipt in his pocket.

Back in the car heading north, he tried Jackson again. The call went straight to full mailbox. If he'd been more like Jackson and kept his own mailbox full, his brother never would have been able to leave that voice mail. He wouldn't have had to hear Jackson voicing his own inner fears, his brother questioning the growing distance between them, anger and sadness punching up the words, "Is this how it's going to be now?"

Milo swallowed hard and tried Max next. This time the call went through, ringing and ringing, but the result was the same. No answer. And when Milo's own phone rang a few minutes later, it wasn't Max calling back, but Sophie. Without Benj there, he had no excuse for putting off Soph's call any longer.

"Hey," he answered.

"What the fuck is going on, Milo?"

Milo immediately wished he'd taken an extra second to come up with that excuse. Now he did it on the fly. "I'm driving and the damn Bluetooth won't connect— can I call you later?"

"No. Fuck no. Why am I looking at a picture of you, with a headline about Jackson?"

"Don't worry about it, Soph—"

"No. No, no, no. You don't get to tell me what to worry about. You get to tell me the truth. Or I'm telling Mom."

The threat was serious enough that Milo sucked in a breath. His maladies had been the source of enough of Mom's worry for the year. She and Dad knew to ignore press about their sons, and even if they saw this particular story, he was sure they wouldn't find anything amiss. Unless his sister told them there was cause for concern. Sophie Miller was the only person who'd never, ever mixed him up with his brother. It earned her the truth. Or, as much of it as he was willing to part with.

"Jackson was in a jam. But he's not here to get himself out of it."

"You're protecting his interests?"

"Right."

"I thought you weren't doing that anymore."

"Things changed."

"Seems like things are exactly the same, Melpo." She used Jackson's nickname for him to drive her point home. It worked. When Milo didn't answer, Sophie continued. "Have you talked to Max?"

"Yeah, but I didn't tell him." How she was able to infuse silence with so much disapproval, Milo would never know. "I want to tell Jackson first."

"You already told him."

"I want to do it right."

"That's not an excuse not to do it because you're scared?"

"No."

He exhaled when Sophie changed the subject. "And the ficus?"

"The what?"

"The woman in the photos. *Benjamina.* Weeping fig. Are she and Jackson serious?"

Milo issued an indignant dismissal. "No. Of course not—she's my—She's not involved with him for real."

He knew immediately he'd worded it wrong if his intention was to make Sophie drop the subject. Even through the phone's flat silence he could hear his sister's interest pique.

"She's your what?"

"We used to know each other."

"When?"

"A few years ago. We worked together."

"That's it?"

A spasm pulled at his knee and he adjusted the angle of his leg as much as he could in the small space. This was the second day in a row he'd spent on his ass and it wasn't just his knee that was feeling it.

"Yeah. That's it. She didn't want to get involved with a coworker." Milo rushed ahead before Soph could ask any follow-up questions about those particulars. "Look, if you hear from Jack, can you tell him to call me. Immediately. Before anyone else. So I can explain?"

He heard the slap of a hinged door closing and imagined Sophie entering the screened-in porch off the kitchen. She'd toe off her boots just below the single step and then head inside to put on water for tea, setting one mug on the counter instead of two. He ached to be there, blowing off steam together as they watched the sun go down over the field that was now hers. She'd also inherited their mom's knack for boiling memories into stories that stuck. One evening, early on in his recovery, she'd raised her mug to the straight rows of growing seed and told him, "I was standing just over there with Pop once. It was midspring. You and Jack were out there harrowing the field."

"Probably fighting over who got the wheel." They were always getting in trouble for messing around, plowing off course.

"Out of nowhere he goes, 'Hon, do you know why I farm?'" She'd paused at the same moment the wind died down, a dramatic silence undercutting the memory and leaving Milo suspended, waiting for the drop, hot tea scalding his tongue. It had been peppermint, he couldn't forget. Soph grew that too. Grew it, dried it, and brewed it—all right there—infusing their history in every sip.

"He said, 'I farm for the curve of the trees against the sky.'"

Milo swallowed, gulping down the beauty of the words, the purpose his Pop had felt on their land.

"Then he shouted at you two miscreants to—"

A grin broke Milo's face as he joined in.

"'Get that motherfucking tractor back in line!'"

The sudden wave of homesickness was so appealing, he wanted to paddle hard for it and let it carry him to a shore on the other side of the country. Instead he pressed a button and the sunroof droned open, washing him with light. The sun wasn't setting yet in California, and that's where he'd ended up. For now.

"I'll tell Jackson to call you—but you should work on that explanation." Water clattered inside a metal pot in the background and Sophie raised her voice to be sure he heard. "Because, Milo, it's a bucket full of holes and it's spilling everywhere, making a fucking mess."

"Yeah, yeah. I got it," he said, deflecting her big-sister advice. "Love you, Soph. Enjoy your sunset."

He shoved the phone back into his pants, his own warning sitting unread in his pocket.

Don't start something you can't finish.

Daily Star–t
Tuesday, April 19

Something's off. Is it you? The best way to find out is to turn yourself on.

Chapter Eleven

The intention behind Benj's gag rule had been to make things easier. Knowing she had him muzzled should have made it a breeze to see Milo Fox at her door, a cinch to get on with their prep for the evening, absolutely not an issue for them to be alone together. With Milo's mouth out of play, it should have been all business between them.

But Benj had underestimated the effect the rest of Milo had on her. The head rush she got when she moved in close enough to smell the toasty warmth of his skin. His dark liquid irises bubbling like root beer ignited a flush on her cheeks every time their eyes met. And the worst of it, a very personal problem: the unexpected wetness between her thighs brought on by his submission.

He'd listened when she'd said to up his wardrobe game, arriving in black jeans, a dark blue Oxford shirt, and a buttery brown leather jacket. Once she'd ripped the beanie off his head and tossed it aside, the look was styled to her discerning standards. He conformed when she told him to sit at the edge of her bed. (Where else was she going to put him? She had one chair and it was loaded with magazines.) He followed each of her commands with a steady, reliable frown.

It should have been easier. But it wasn't.

The jacket, for one, sidetracked her. The leather was tough and soft at the same time—that ideal masculine composition. And Milo wore it with obscene confidence—an absolute disaster for her revving sex drive.

"Take that off if you're hot," she said.

If.

Milo was smoking. Even without the friction of conversation, he was burning up all the air in the room. He shrugged off the coat, which did little to alleviate his rakish appeal. An unfortunate development for Benj, who'd been thinking his new clothes were the problem.

Maybe if he weren't wearing any?

No. *Immediately* no.

That was exactly the kind of unreliable thinking that had gotten her involved with Milo in the first place. She'd had a rule. She should have stuck to it. Things would have been easier if she had.

With the sky already dark out her window, Benj transformed Milo quickly. His thick stubble gave her less to do and she was more efficient from experience— she was also desperate to regain some distance, to douse the slick, loose, *good* feeling that pulled her attention lower every time she told him to tilt left, to tilt right, to hold still. Every time he did exactly what she wanted him to do.

"Head back." Her fingers pulled at the thick cotton of his collar. "Jackson had his top button done up last time I saw him."

Milo's chin rose allowing her to close the shirt at

his neck. Her hands smoothed the fabric molding over his shoulders. Her thumbs slipped into the grooves of his collarbone. When he lowered his head and found her eyes, Benj snatched her hands back as if burned.

"Wait in the hall while I get changed."

He left, simmering now with luscious frustration but never saying a word.

A girl could get used to that.

Just not her.

Benj made the effort to get ahold of herself. They were about to be in public, about to perform their trick tableside for an audience of six—and whoever else was out people watching on a Tuesday night in LA. A plant in the crowd of Milo's magic act, her job was to convince everyone else she was into him, but before they left, she had to convince herself that she wasn't.

Benj had done her hair and makeup before Milo'd arrived. But she checked both again, standing at her bathroom mirror, a cascade of heart-shaped plastic philodendron leaves her backdrop. With her schedule, she'd only kill the real thing, but she liked having the pop of color in behind her, the scene of all her best pep talks. Girl, did she need one tonight.

It was time for some truth: Yes, she was still attracted to Milo. Yes, the details of their past had been rearranged. But no, it didn't change the outcome.

So she relined her lips and perfected the glazed finish on her cheeks. She pulled half her hair into a bun, took it down, and put it back up. She sorted all the products she wasn't bringing with her back into their respective clear storage drawers—an advocate of see-through containers, Benj hated not being able to find what she was looking for.

All of that was part of her finely honed process, and not because she was avoiding Milo in the hall.

Benj had already picked an outfit—a grey three-piece sweater set that took no time to put on—so it couldn't have been that long before she emerged from her door. From the icy once-over Milo gave her to the ensuing hunch of his shoulders, she knew it must have felt longer. She knew he was over waiting on her.

The night air helped cool Benj's head—but it didn't last. Once in the car, Milo's irritation swelled to a dull, deafening hum. The silence ached, compressing her in her seat while Milo drove with furious patience, never speeding, never braking too quickly, as if to prove to her she'd got it wrong. Her comfort was in his control all along.

By the time the car stopped, Milo's silent fuming had turned noxious, becoming so overpowering Benj couldn't focus on anything but her own shallow breaths. At this rate, she'd be sapped before they were seated at dinner.

A valet approached her door too slowly and she flung it open herself, bailing out of the car, lunging for fresh air, for escape. She didn't get far. Long strides gave Milo an advantage and he cut her off, slipping an arm around her back and using her own momentum to haul her closer.

"My turn." His rough whisper scraped her neck. "Stop, hold still, look at me." He pulled away, giving her space to obey. She met his eyes, leaning back as far as she could and feeling his hands lock behind her. "Can you do this, Ben?"

"Let me go, Mi—"

He squeezed her closer and shook his head.

"Jackson."

His eyes flashed and went dark, houselights flickering before the show. The weight dropped out of his voice, and with feathery lightness and the intention to be overheard, he said, "You're right—they're probably waiting for us. We'll save this for later."

Milo eased back and offered her a hand. Benj took it and let him lead her forward, watching each of his springy steps in immaculate bone-colored sneakers.

This was not Milo. This was Jackson. This was the show.

She needed to make sure she knew the difference.

As they spun through the revolving door, she refocused on their task…and finally realized where they were. Milo stopped at the hostess stand while Benj scanned the room in disbelief.

Not *those* red booths. Not *those* brass fixtures. Not *that* smooth walnut bar and the familiar face of the bartender behind it. His was one of many phone calls she'd "missed" in the last day and a half. The near-constant alerts on that thing—Daily Star–t coming for her, friends and family "just checking in," and strangers flooding her socials—it was too much. Too uncomfortable, making her want to squirm and hide.

There were a thousand other restaurants in this damn city. It was just her luck to end up here.

"Fuck," Milo said, echoing her thoughts. "I didn't know."

How did he—

"I didn't realize Cormac's was a steakhouse."

Her brows knotted. What was he talking about?

"You're vegan."

Milo's real, misguided concern startled a laugh out

of her. A sharp, out-of-place cackle that turned heads. Milo stared and she clapped a hand over her mouth. Her nerves: officially shot.

The steakhouse shared its name with the owner, who happened to be one of Nelle's husband's former bandmates. Cormac turned up at the Kellys' almost as often as Benj did. Along with Arlo, the third member of Bran's trio, they'd celebrated holidays, they'd celebrated each other—they'd formed a circle of trust. And tonight she might break it. She might have to lie to Cormac's face.

Cormac tapped the bar, calling Benj over, and she raised a finger to buy a second, a minute more of time she needed to right herself. She pulled her sweater around her body and dealt with Milo first. "The menu options are pretty low on the list of things wrong with this evening, don't you think?"

"It's high on my list to keep you satisfied." Milo/Jackson grinned—she didn't know which. "I've seen you hungry."

It was supposed to be easier, that he could only talk to her in public. But now Benj didn't know what was part of the act.

A black-vested server led them to a rectangular table in the center of the room, four high-backed upholstered Parsons on each side. Milo'd been wrong by the car: no one was waiting. They were the first to arrive. He shifted one of the center chairs out for her but Benj didn't sit.

"I'm gonna get a drink. While we wait."

"This looks like the kind of place where a waiter would be willing to do that for you."

"I want to take care of it myself." She glanced at

the bar where Cormac stood, unmistakably watching her, his wide, muscled shoulders lit from above by a cluster of sparkling globe pendants.

Milo followed her gaze. "I see."

"I'll be right back."

"Why rush?" He shook off his coat and positioned himself at one end of the table, gesturing to the empty seats around him. "It's just me."

As she made her way across the restaurant, Benj felt the weight of both their gazes, front and back.

Cormac started talking as soon as she was close enough to hear. "I thought I was going to have to come looking for you."

"Oh yeah?" Propping one foot on the brass rail underneath the bar, Benj folded her arms over the counter, hoisting herself up and offering a cheek to Cormac.

He bent forward to kiss it. "One Mrs. Kelly has been all *up* in my grill trying to get me to track you down. Can you call her?"

"I will." Benj rested her chin on a raised fist, hoping he'd been filled in. "How much do you know?"

"Enough to want that asshole out of my restaurant."

She was going to need him to be more specific. Benj had to know what she could say and what she couldn't. "Because he…?"

Cormac matched her questioning tone. "…fucked with my friend?"

Still not specific enough. Benj frowned and Cormac put two hands on the bar, his big shoulders bunching at his neck.

"What? I'm not allowed to be mad that Jackhole over there tried to jam Bran up? You know he does it to himself enough—he didn't need any help."

Benj exhaled. Mina must have told Nelle to keep the swap under wraps. Cormac didn't know the whole story—that Milo was Jackson and Jackson was gone. That wasn't so bad. Benj could dip her toe into the lie, before taking the plunge back at the table. "Well, that Jackhole is helping me smooth things over now, so let us have dinner and then I'll get him out of your grill too, okay?"

"What about you?"

She traced a circle around a knot on the bar top. "What about me?"

"Oh it's like that?" He slid a black cocktail napkin edged with gold foil into the cave of her palm. "Tell me what I can get you at least."

What did she need? Some sort of sedative, something strong enough to curb all the feelings competing for her attention. Something that could stop her mind's spinning and her body's panic, make her slow down and breathe, ensure she owned what she was trying to sell. What she needed was Milo's syrupy, barely there border-state drawl when he whispered in her ear on the pier, telling her to pretend.

"Bourbon."

Cormac drummed on the bar—*bah-duh-bah*. "Coming right up."

While he picked a bottle off one of the crowded, towering shelves behind the counter, Benj turned to her table, where Milo was now on his feet, shaking hands with Lewis Abreo, the internet's most-recent boyfriend. Lewis's thick hair was combed back, and he was clearly on a curl regimen that worked for him. If there was a lull in conversation tonight, Benj was going to find out what he was using to get that kind of definition and shine. And then Milo was kissing Jem Horner's cheek and she was sifting a hand through her long auburn locks and introducing raven-haired Vanessa Vu—who, coming off back-to-back Best Supporting Actress wins, didn't actually need an introduction.

It was a lot.

Even for Benj, who wasn't new to *Stars, They're Just Like Us: Out to Dinner Edition*. She was industry, but she wasn't talent, and she never knew which people she met would make a point of proving that distinction.

Although, as they settled into their seats, Benj noted the three other diners, the ones who didn't have famous names and faces. She also noted the empty seat next to Milo, where she was supposed to be.

Cormac placed an etched tumbler half-full of amber courage on the napkin. Benj stood back, swinging her ever-present bucket bag to the front of her body in search of her wallet.

"Get out of here with that."

She smiled at him, picked up the drink, and started for the table.

"Call Nelle!"

She waved over her shoulder to show she'd heard him. She did need to call Nelle. Nelle was the one person she wouldn't have to lie to. It was just…the longer she waited, the more truth she had to tell, the harder it got.

This was starting to feel like some kind of cosmic punishment—all those years she'd eaten up other people's stories—now she had to put her own up for consumption. All she wanted was to keep her head down, do her job, and live her life. Unobserved. Unjudged. Uncontested.

That wasn't in the cards tonight.

Milo got to his feet as she approached. Benj set her drink down and slung her bag over the back of the chair, making it even heavier for Milo as he nudged it toward the table beneath her. She was smiling her hellos around the table when Milo reached across her and carried her drink to his mouth.

"What'd you get?"

"Bourbon, Jim Beam maybe."

Milo's eyes closed, his head rolled loose on his neck. He set the glass carefully back down in front of her and rubbed his bottom lip.

"No."

"No?"

"That's not Jim Beam." He charged up his grin, but she saw the effort. "Must be a good friend behind the bar—he reached right up to the top shelf for you."

Lewis, who was sitting across from her, offered some speculation. "What is it? Wild Turkey?"

"Pappy Van Winkle," Milo answered, flicking his brows up with intrigue.

Lewis whistled.

Benj raised the glass, tilting it to catch an orange glow. "Is that good?"

"It's exceptional." Lewis twisted in his chair to look for the waiter. "Worth every penny."

"It's expensive?" Benj lowered her voice, asking Milo directly.

"He must be a very good friend."

"He is." Benj smelled the bourbon, and Milo's dark eyes glittered in the restaurant's moody lighting.

"Taste it. You'll see."

"I won't know what I'm looking for," she worried out loud. "I might not appreciate it."

"Does it smell good to you?"

She nodded.

"Then take a sip. Hold it in your mouth." He drew closer with each directive. She watched him watch her, doing everything he said. The evening taking another reversal. "Breathe. Swallow." His eyes dipped to the deep rise and fall of her chest. "Feel it? That slow burn?" He dragged his gaze up to hers. "That's all you have to appreciate. That, and the sweetness."

"What makes it so sweet?" Lewis interrupted.

Milo's mouth set and for a long, rude moment he didn't answer. Then he scratched at his growing beard and smiled at Lewis. "Payoff from the wheat."

Benj freed herself from the heatstroke that was as much the fault of her sweater as Milo's smoldering gaze. That slow burn? She fucking felt it.

It would have been so much easier if she didn't.

Chapter Twelve

"You want one?" Lewis asked while the server waited at his elbow.

It took Milo a minute to respond. "I would."

He was finding the conversation hard to focus on. For one thing, he was annoyingly sensitive to the buzz of noise in the restaurant. A throb had started inside his head, which made him appreciate the low lighting at least. For another, he'd been trying to understand Benj's outfit since she'd met him in her hallway and that task was still taking up brain power. It was at least one sweater, which made sense. She'd always been cold on set. Scoffed at him when he'd lamented California's seasonal deficiency and pined for harsher weather. "You only say that because you've never spent January in the Midwest, you don't know what winter is."

But she had removed that original sweater, a loose oversized cardigan, revealing a second series of sweaters underneath. Sweater material, at least, the same soft grey wool taking the form of a pair of shorts that angled up on her hips, wide cuffs banding the tops of her thighs, and a matching cable-knit bra that cupped and presented her breasts like an offering of first fruits.

Breasts he'd felt warm up against him, but which had never met his eye quite like this.

He called it what it was: distracting.

But not distracting enough to keep him from considering the disquieting presence of that outrageous glass of bourbon in front of her. What kind of "friend" produced that kind of pour? The bartender who, with a look, had Benj bending over the bar, her actual sweater rising to reveal the lush curves of her bottom in those strange, enticing shorts? Was it part of Benj's game, another way of reminding Milo that being with him was just for show?

No. She couldn't have planned this run-in. She hadn't known where they were going. Unless she had a friendly bartender in every restaurant in the city. Milo didn't see why not—look at her. She had a radiance, a draw, that winning smile. She'd have this table eating out of her hand before the meal was over, feeding them exactly the story she wanted.

That thought drew him right up against the rules Benj had laid out. The rules that could be a trap but felt like his only recourse. Here, in this restaurant, he was Jackson, and Jackson had the green light to make this convincing, however he saw fit.

Might as well get on with the show.

Milo brushed the pale hair back from Benj's collarbone, fighting the nerves in his gut. Would she flinch? Wriggle out from under his hand?

Not Benj. Her commitment was absolute, and she leaned into his touch, allowing his hand to slide over the base of her neck and settle there. He watched the side of her face, the playful iridescence under her eyes, the pink blush that curled up her cheeks to her temples.

Each accented feature of her seemed to come alive, glowing brighter from underneath her makeup.

Christ, she was good.

Testing her resolve, Milo dipped forward to press a kiss to the bare curve of her shoulder. A soft smile pulled at her matte, petal-toned lips. He could almost believe she was enjoying it. Vanessa Vu had better watch her back.

He wanted to know: How far would Benj go to prove a point?

Touch. Kiss. Do whatever he needed?

He increased pressure in his fingertips, a firm squeeze that brought her gaze to his. The restaurant's noise faded away, the pain in his head retreating. Her heart-shaped mouth parted and his throat constricted, straining against that final button she'd done up at his collar. He hadn't thought through what he'd do next. He'd only wanted her full attention, like she had his.

That mouth of hers. Soft and full and waiting. He could kiss it now and she'd let him for sure. But he didn't want it like that.

Milo could feel eyes on them from around the table. He tried to think like Jackson and said the first thing that came to mind. "You're gorgeous."

"We can talk about that later," she replied, knowing full well that later he wouldn't be allowed to talk at all.

"Sure thing, hon." Milo released her, flashing a smile.

Jem leaned forward to ask Lewis, "Did you see it?" At his nod, she leaned back and met Milo's questioning eye. "You looked just like him."

Milo swallowed. "Just like who?"

Red hair shook over Jem's shoulder as she laughed.

"Grant Fox. It's your smile. I know everyone remembers him in *Hearts of Gold Rush*—"

Milo braced himself for someone to say the line, to perform the obligatory sacrament that followed every reference to the film. It was Lewis who deepened his voice to rumble through it, backing up a bit in the script for the full effect. *"You let it blind you. Out here where you needed your wits, you fooled yourself into thinking you'd be mine. You're gonna make me say it, aren't you? You missed your train for nothing, sweetheart."* He looked to Milo for approval on what was admittedly a spot-on impression.

A long second passed and Benj kicked him under the table. Milo raised two thumbs as Jem continued.

"Right that, and all those old war movies—but I thought he was unbelievable as Walt Whitman. Sure, it wasn't critically well received, but what a departure from his previous roles. Did you ever get to talk to him about that choice?"

"No." Milo knew exactly why Grant Fox had made that choice. He'd wanted another trophy. He'd wanted to be back on top. The man had given up everything to get there—everything except the cocaine that eventually stopped his heart a good twenty years too soon.

"But he'd always played fighters, and soldiers—and then to play a poet—"

Milo cut Jem off. "They aren't mutually exclusive. You can be both."

"Of course! Any great actor has that range."

Milo frowned, feeling misunderstood and wishing he'd better articulated what he meant. He hadn't been talking about playing parts. He'd been talking about real life, about his paternal grandfather who had served in Vietnam and penned his grandmother deeply romantic letters. Al Miller had been both a soldier and a poet, without any fanfare. Milo could have tried to explain, but he wasn't sure he was up for changing the Grant Fox conversation tonight. Milo turned back to his menu and Benj. "I did some recon while you were at the bar. You could order the niçoise, without the anchovies or egg."

A heavy sigh met his suggestion. "What about the cheeseburger without the cheese or burger?"

"You're welcome to my bun," Jem offered.

Benj sent a tight smile back. "You're sweet."

"Food allergies?" Vanessa asked from the other side of Benj.

"No, I'm vegan. We didn't realize—"

"Oh shoot, I'm so sorry—"

"Don't be, it's fine. Jackson didn't tell me where we were going."

"But I should have asked if anyone had dietary restrictions."

"It's fine, really," Benj assured Vanessa, whose regret appeared genuine. "I'll pretend I'm in Paris."

Milo caught her eye. "Rules don't apply there?"

She explained with a twirl of her wrist. "I make exceptions for the exceptional."

"Paris is overrated these days. I've had much better meals in London." Jem added in Milo's direction, "Does anyone want to split the crab cakes?"

He shook his head. "I'm a filler-fearing Maryland man, I don't eat crab cakes outside state lines. There has to be something you can eat—"

Milo's knee jumped, surprised by the warmth of Benj's hand. He could make out each of her fingertips through his jeans, five sensational seeds of heat. And fuck if he didn't wish they'd go up on pointe, those sharp nails digging into his skin. He started to lean toward her again only to be forced back by a waiter coming between them, setting a large dish on the center of the table.

"Fried Brussels sprouts with sriracha, honey, and lime—on the house."

Jem's head angled with surprise and Milo suspected she was trying not to wrinkle her forehead. "That's not on the menu."

"It sure isn't." Benj turned in her seat to mouth a *thank you* at the bartender. He held his hand to his ear miming a phone call. Who the fuck was *this* guy?

"You're friends with Cormac?" Vanessa asked.

Milo, who had been sipping carefully at the bourbon the waiter had delivered, almost spit it out—which would have been a shame if Cormac, the restaurant's owner and Benj's *good friend*, had poured him the luxuriously smooth bourbon he'd ordered. Instead, Milo choked down a sip of truly subpar alcohol, fire racing down his throat. That was certainly a ballsy move. He half faced the bar, eyes watering, and raised the caramel-colored swill in salute.

Cormac, busy polishing a glass, only nodded.

"We're basically in-laws," Benj confirmed. "His best friend is married to my best friend."

Jem let her brow wrinkle now, demonstrating perfect control of her features. "Who is your best friend?"

"Nelle Kelly."

"That's right, I think I heard something about that. Or was it that you work for her?"

"It's both. I've worked with lots of people. I'm a makeup artist."

"Well, that makes me feel better, because all this—" Vanessa waved a hand at Benj's face "—is downright intimidating for a Tuesday night."

"And do you like that, working for Nelle?" The question out of Jem's mouth raised Milo's shoulders, but Benj answered her with composure, sincerity. With nothing to hide.

"I love it. I love being able to make people feel good in their own skin."

"So you and Cormac? The Kellys haven't tried to double and set you up?" Vanessa's husband asked, from somewhere Milo couldn't see, dissipating some of the charge between the two women at the center of the table. Milo felt bad he'd already forgotten the man's name. They'd been introduced while Benj was at the bar, and Milo's attention had been split—he couldn't seem to pull his focus off her.

Benj laughed, and Milo breathed in the sound. "Oh no, he's a full-on Aries and with my Cancer moon— fire and water, not gonna happen."

Vanessa spooned some sprouts onto a plate and handed it to Benj. "You believe in all that?"

Benj lifted one shoulder, adjusting her plate. "I believe in deeper meanings, in inherent connotations."

"Astrology is too determinist for me." Jem leaned her elbows on the table, making sure to catch Milo's eye. "Big fan of choosing whatever I want over here."

She was seated diagonally across from Benj and the line between the two women tensed with current once more.

"It's always been accurate in my experience." Despite Benj's pleasant tone, Milo could tell some power balance was being worked out. And Benj's hand on his back confirmed it. "Although—" Benj traced her fingers across Milo's shoulder blade and up into his scalp. "Gemini isn't a great fit either and we're making that work."

"Jackson?" Jem played with a strand of her red hair, twisting it one way and then the other. She'd been cast as Jackson's wife in the movie, and she'd introduced the man to her left as her "gay husband," both red flags waving in the breathy way she said his brother's name.

"Yep?"

"I want a turn. What makes my drink sweet?"

"What are you having?"

"Vodka soda."

Milo grunted a laugh. Benj's nails grazed his scalp, and god help him if he didn't respond to it, needing a few rapid blinks to keep focused on the world outside of his pants. "Not much sweet about that."

Benj let her arm slip slowly off his back, one nail dragging at the fabric and drawing a shiver out of him. "Next time choose a Shirley Temple," she suggested.

Across from them and sitting back so Jem couldn't see, Lewis pulled his mouth straight, teeth clenched. Then he attempted to bring the conversation back in line. "Is it just bourbon, Jackson, or do you know your whiskey too?"

"I—" Milo stopped himself. He tilted his glass, pooling the thin liquid inside. He had to get this right. Couldn't bond with Lewis over something Jackson knew nothing about. "It's not actually my interest—it's my brother's. Something he picked up from our grandfather."

"Of course Grant Fox would be a whiskey man." Jem

leaned in again. "Do you really live in his house? Is it true he bought it off an Italian mobster and there's a bullet hole in the front window from a shootout in the '50s?"

"I heard Jane Fonda walked through wet cement at a party and her footprints are still there," Vanessa added. "You have to have us over."

"Not that grandfather, actually." Milo put down his drink and took a sip of bubbly water, swallowing the harsh snapping that fizzled over his tongue. "My father's father. He made moonshine when we were growing up."

"What's moonshine exactly?" Lewis's sister, Ani, spoke up from between Jem and her brother. Milo assumed she'd come as Lewis's date because bringing anyone unrelated to him would make too much of a statement. Like Jackson bringing Benj.

"Unaged spirit. Pure. Raw. Burns like you wouldn't believe. But it can be sweet, when made right."

"What's right?" Benj asked next. "How'd he make it?"

Again, it took Milo longer to answer than it would have Jackson. He knew what to say, knew every part of the process. Had done it by hand, by heart. It's what had kept him going for the last year, when it was hard to remember what had happened the day before. He'd check his calendar, read his notes—how long had the seeds been malting, when had the mash started fermenting? He'd count the days, waiting for the next step. The next. The process had been a map, it had set him on the path that led back to his own life.

He couldn't bring himself to describe it as anything less than a lifeline, the thing that made him feel like himself again. And he didn't like the way they were all watching him—he could even feel that bartender's gaze. The attention made him hot. He didn't want to share. But Jackson would.

Milo shot back the rest of the cheap bourbon and tried to keep his voice even, offhand, like his crack about crab cakes. "He malted the sunflower seeds from the field he kept for our grandmother. Called it sunshine."

He knew he'd failed when he felt Benj's hand warm against his spine. He sat back, forcing her off, hoping no one noticed. He had to try harder not to let any more of himself show through.

When Lewis followed up, saying he'd love to try sunshine some time, Milo lied, telling himself he was only saying what Jackson knew. "No one makes it anymore."

For the rest of the meal, he shut himself down and played his part. It wasn't that hard if he didn't think about home or how badly he wanted more of Benj than he could have. He was here, he was Jackson, for the time being. This was the game. LA had never been a place for the truth—it had always been a place for hiding it.

It wasn't anything new. Old habits and all.

Chapter Thirteen

Benj had switched to water by the time the waiter brought the check. After two sensational glasses of bourbon and an equally intoxicating fill of Milo's hands on her body, her head was beginning to spin and she feared what would happen when she stood up and attempted to walk straight.

"This was fun!" Vanessa announced.

"So fun!" Benj agreed. In Vanessa, at least, she'd found a fast friend. Someone authentic and easy to interpret. Someone who said what she meant and meant what she said. A revelation, here or anywhere. Even if they'd mostly talked about their favorite *WoCAs*.

"Let's do it again ASAP." Vanessa handed a credit card across the table to Lewis. "Petra said she wanted us to get together as much as we can before filming."

"The cast," Jem interjected, passing her own card down the table. "Petra said the cast should find ways to bond."

"Well, let's keep the plus-ones welcome," Vanessa replied decisively. "This turned out so well."

Even as Benj squirmed in her seat at the thought of having to do this again, she admired the casual way Vanessa used her power, leaving no room for argument. Next to Benj, true to his word, Milo pulled a wad of cash from an inner pocket of his coat.

"Okay, high roller," Lewis joked, watching Milo count out bills.

"Lost my wallet." Milo tossed off another breezy smile, but Benj saw the turbine spinning behind it. "Can't find my phone, either—so if you make plans, text Benj."

Vanessa waved her clutch. "Already got her number. And I know the perfect place—Hubs and I were thinking of going tomorrow. Any objections to day drinking?"

So their next performance would be a matinee. Benj wasn't ready to think about that. Not when this evening hadn't yet wrapped, when the cut was still looming a few lines away. Soon she and Milo would rewind, go back to being themselves. That was where the danger lurked: speeding away in the getaway car, faced with how good it had felt to be bad. The moment they stopped pretending was racing toward them, head-on. She needed to pump the brakes, slow down enough to minimize the impact.

Benj stood, self-consciously adjusting the hem of her shorts. "Hey, babe?" she said, like it was the most natural thing in the world.

Milo's focus stuttered slowly up from his level view of her hips. "Yeah, hon?"

"I'm gonna go thank Cormac while you settle up."

"Gimme a sec and we'll go together."

When their gazes met, Milo was no longer lurking in the shadows of those dark eyes but taking center stage. He'd retreated after telling Lewis about his grandfather—the one no one had heard of. He'd brushed her off and played Jackson so well through the main course and dessert, stealing bites of her squash and sorbet with more of those fleeting grins, that Benj had wondered: What was he hiding? Where was the lie?

That wasn't something she could pursue and still keep her distance.

She reached for her sweater and Milo caught her hand, bringing the back of it against his lips. Her head swam with the temptation to give in to the warm glow of his mouth.

Benj freed her hand from his, their palms sliding slowly apart. "You can meet me at the bar."

Rounding the table, she said her goodbyes and walked to the bar, the air growing clearer the further she got from Milo. She hoisted herself onto a stool in front of Cormac's station. "If I order an Arnold Palmer, will you let me pay for it?"

"The fuck you think."

"Then I'll take an Arnold Palmer." Benj nodded, agreeing with herself. This was a good idea. A mild hit of caffeine, just enough to wake her up and get her home. "And can you put it in this?" She shuffled her bag and removed her water bottle.

"A roadie? Really?"

"I'm ready to get out of here." Benj shook the bottle at him. "Come on, Cormac, be a pal."

"Is that all he is?"

Benj rolled her gaze up to Milo, hoping he'd slipped his easygoing Jackson mask back into place. No such luck. With that glower, that tone, she expected a possessive hand to clamp over her neck, but he offered it out to Cormac instead.

Cormac glanced at Milo's extended arm and took the bottle from Benj.

"Benj and I wanted to thank you." Milo's hand curled into a fist and rested on the bar. "That bourbon was really something."

Benj sat back with a sigh and searched her bag for a compact. She was in dire need of a touch-up and fairly certain the impending man-off wouldn't require her input.

Cormac mixed her drink behind the bar and focused on Milo. "You're good to get her home?"

There it is, she thought, brushing an eyebrow up with a fingertip. She'd have loved to be wrong this once, but she'd already been sidelined by their need to one-up each other's manliness.

"I'm fine. She's fine."

"I'm just asking. Maybe you should chill out," Cormac escalated, and Benj put her lipstick away without uncapping it.

The run time on this showdown would be short, what with Milo proposing a second option. "Maybe you should lose her number."

"Fuck off. You don't want to do that here, man."

"I think I do."

"Is he for serious, Benj?"

Benj snapped her compact closed and found both men staring at her.

"Well, Cormac," she said, taking advantage of the opening—how nice of them to include her. "I think what Jackson means is that, if you wouldn't mind, he'd like you both to take out your dicks and lay them on the bar. That way, you can discuss between yourselves which one I'd prefer. It is a strange request because Jackson is normally so friendly."

"How 'bout Jack and I talk out back?"

"I'm up for that too."

Benj climbed off the stool, swatting away Milo's steadying arm. "You're both exhausting. Cormac, stay where you are, Mi—date and I are calling it a night. You'll be there on Friday?"

Cormac nodded and Milo dug in his heels. "So this is what's up in the air for Friday?"

"Up in the—Did you go through my phone?" Anger flared hot and red across Benj's cheeks. Embarrassment extended the flush. She didn't wait for him to answer, already understanding what had happened. "I didn't close it, did I? When I was getting your number."

"What's on your phone?" Cormac paused, a lemon in one hand and a knife in the other.

Milo tilted his head at Cormac, keeping his eyes on Benj. "Beards don't do it for you?"

Benj glared at Milo. "It's none of your business—" And then Cormac. "Or yours." And then Milo again for good measure. "I don't have to tell either of you anything about anyone I'm texting with."

Cormac put down the lemon, keeping hold of the knife. "Someone bothering you?"

She should just tell Cormac it was nothing. Milo had misunderstood a text from Arlo. But Milo would overhear and she wasn't ready to let him off the hook. She'd rather twist the hook and watch him squirm. "Nobody's bothering me."

Milo lifted his fist and rubbed his growing stubble with a knuckle. "So who is he, Ben?"

If it hadn't already kicked on, the nickname would

have activated her fight mode. "What does it matter?
What are you going to do about it?"

Cormac's arms bulged as he tightened the lid on her
bottle. "I'm curious to know a name myself."

"Okay. Here's a name: Arnold."

Milo leaned in, but Cormac was already shaking
his head.

"Palmer."

Cormac slid her bottle back to her, the glass scraping heavily across the wood. "You're real cute, you
know that—"

"Good night, Cormac." Benj plucked up the bottle
and wove her way through the restaurant, spinning
out the revolving doors without a glance back at Milo.

He caught up to her at the valet stand and traded in
his ticket to the runner. They stood side by side, alone
on the sidewalk. It was almost over. But Milo wasn't
done yet. "Would you have told him? If I wasn't there?"

"What does it matter?" She shouldn't have asked.
Shouldn't have turned to face him. She should have
kept her mouth shut until she could hustle him into the
car, where Milo couldn't talk any more.

The Maserati pulled up to the curb, but Milo's only
move was to mirror her body, put them face-to-face.
Stalling, knowing his advantage was almost played out.

"Are either of them your type?"

"Yeah, actually. I like 'em without something to
prove."

"That explains the different rules for Cormac. You
let him take care of you. With the drinks and the food."

"I didn't *let* him, he just did it."

A muscle ticked in his jaw. "Fair enough."

"What do you care? He's not the one who sent the

text. And even if he was, it's none of your business, like I said. Unless you're not hearing me—"

"Oh, I'm hearing you." Milo closed the inches between them, grabbing her ass and hauling her against him with a rough squeeze. "If I want to take care of you, I should just do it. And I was listening, when you said earlier that you loved your job. Loved making people feel good. But who makes you feel good, Ben?"

She didn't answer. Couldn't. It wasn't anger burning under her skin, it was something else. The heat he drew out of her. The fire he ignited. The one that made her melt.

He breathed against her ear. "Or is that something else you want to talk about later?"

Agitation underlined his purpose. He was angry. Jealous. And it was working for her. She always fell for it when he stopped pretending.

She dug up enough air from the bottom of her lungs to answer him. "Get in the car, Jackson."

His hands braced her hips when he stepped away, helping her regain her balance. Where did it go when she was pressed up against him? A camera clicked and light flashed in her periphery, signaling that some paparazzi who haunted the restaurant's entrance had returned from a smoke break.

Benj suffered Milo's hand at her back as he guided her to the open passenger door. She crammed her bag into the wheel well, kicked off her pumps, and tucked her feet underneath her. Another photo was fine. Was whatever. What got under her skin was the way her body was so keen to trust that he'd take her weight. Her memory wasn't short but it apparently didn't reach to her extremities.

She remembered it all. The flirting and the lead-up and the need. Their entire history hinged on anguish. The misery of wanting. Anticipation left unsatisfied. Her pulse throbbed low between her legs, making her question why she wanted to keep it that way. Why didn't she demand the fulfillment she was due?

She chugged from the ice-cold lemonade-and-tea combo Cormac had sent her off with. It did nothing to cool her rising temp. If anything, the sugar and caffeine worsened the energy coursing inside her. A coil of need that tightened every time she braced for another turn, intensifying with every block that brought her closer to home. With or without a spoken apology, part of her was ready to accept what Milo could offer.

Benj had her line prepared well in advance of Milo parking outside her apartment. She practiced it once in her head as she bent to put on her shoes. And then she said it.

"I'd like you to walk me up."

Direct and to the point. Not a command, but an assessment—designed to see if he was really listening, if what she wanted really meant something to him. As drunk on his absolute submission as she was earlier, loopy with control, she didn't want to do that now.

Well, not yet.

First, she wanted to see what he would do with what she'd given him.

Milo turned the engine off.

Benj led the way up her walk. She held open the vestibule doors for him, keeping ahead until they turned down the short hall that ended at her door. Then she slowed, her nerve going slack. He came up alongside her, passing with a sideways glance. When he leaned one shoulder into her door frame, his mouth was set tight.

But his eyes were open, taking everything in, brighter and more alert than she'd seen them yet tonight. When he was like this, she stood no chance against him.

The beige walls glowed yellow in the warm light of two sconces. His shadow fell over the door, and she struggled to fit the key in its hole. He took over, sinking the key into place with a metallic rasp. The noise grated at her ears, loud as any clatter, jarring her senses.

She grabbed at his wrist when he went for the knob, then looked up, finding her own small reflection in his big, soulful eyes.

That wouldn't do at all.

Benj eased herself back into the door's nook, keeping hold of his wrist and angling her hips out. "You want to take care of me? Show me. Do it. Be the one who makes me feel good."

She lowered his hand to the seam of her shorts and waited.

Milo braced his free hand on the frame above her head and leaned over her, searching her face for signs of weakness. She tipped her chin up and worked her fingers under the cuff of his jacket sleeve. Her other hand stroked over his chest. He swallowed, drawing her attention to the tight collar at his neck. She popped the top button free.

His knuckles brushed down, over the linking pattern of her shorts. Her mouth opened, her fingers inching up his forearm. She thumbed the raised, erratic path of his vein, her nails digging into his tan skin when he shifted his hand to cup her between the legs. His limbs were steady though his breath was rough.

Their eyes locked as he rubbed through her shorts, pushing the fabric up and into her, so she could feel the shape of his hand molded against her. Pressure danced from one finger to the next as he felt her out, found the places he could do the most damage.

His face drew close to hers but she knew he wouldn't kiss her. Not when he hadn't all night—it was a line he wouldn't cross. Not again.

She had no intention of crossing it either, even as the memory of what his kiss had done to her that first time flared in her mind, sending liquid heat down to where his hand was working her over. But she forced the thought back, divorcing her past from what was happening to her here, now.

It felt good to separate her mind from her body. To fly above and watch herself indulge. The heavy rise of her own chest in her lower periphery made her pant harder. Her swelling breasts threatened to burst from the confines of the bralette, dropping her and Milo's mouths in perfect symmetry. She loved to see it.

But when Milo brought his hand to her overflowing chest, fitting his palm to the curve of her tit, his low groan distracted her from herself.

I still think about doing it right.

He might be an absolute smoke-show, but this wasn't about him.

Taking hold of that wrist too, she dragged his hand to where *she* wanted it—clasped around her throat. That little denial, that refusal to let him choose set her off. And under those dual points of pressure—his right hand caressing her, the friction of fabric on her clit, and his left pinning her in the corner by her neck— she finally let herself come undone in front of him.

Every part of her squeezed unbearably tighter. She shut her eyes as the unreasonable relief of orgasm rippled through her. She gripped both of Milo's wrists, feeling skin and leather, needing an anchor in the dark of her own mind. The slow stroke of his thumb on her throat coaxed her back to her body.

Benj opened her eyes to find Milo watching her. Her head spun again, worse than when she'd risen from the table, tense and teased and tipsy. For a long moment she considered letting him help her through the door, imagined tumbling into her bed, taking him with her.

Losing her balance.

She could tell herself it was nothing—nothing new, nothing special, nothing she hadn't done before. But the truth whispered in her veins: Milo was different. Milo was special. Milo would wreck her. So Benj let go of Milo long enough to wobble through her door and slide to the floor on the other side alone.

Daily Star–t
Wednesday, April 20

You're still messy if you make your bed and lie about it.

Chapter Fourteen

The table on the winery's terra-cotta patio was cluttered with wineglasses, each sparkling in the afternoon sun. A hillside field lined with grapevines stretched out behind Lewis and the two Vus, pastoral perfection under a wild blue dome of sky. To Milo's left, Benj laughed, tipping her head back, allowing a yellow ray of sun to sneak under the stiff brim of her hat and light up her face. Absolutely flawless.

"Jackson." Jem touched Milo's arm and his mouth sprang into a friendly smile.

"Yeah, hon?"

"Do you think we should order some food for the table?"

He nodded immediately, the answer easy. The six of them had been "tasting" wine for almost an hour and no one was making use of the spit bucket. "Let's get a spread."

Milo inclined the other way, settling his arm along the back of Benj's chair. Her hair was pulled into a low bun at the nape of her neck. When she turned her face up and leaned into him, enveloping him in the shade of her hat, a loose strand of blond feathered over his arm. Perfection.

"Hungry?" he asked.

"Famished."

"Consider me on it."

"Thank you."

Her palm ruffled the short hairs of his stubbly beard, and the restlessness he'd been trying to deny rippled under his skin. If this were real, he'd have kissed her. His mouth would already be covering hers, licking into her, tasting the wine without dirtying another glass.

But perfection was never real, was it? It was always artificial.

As much as Milo wanted to be living this untouched moment, soaking in the sun and the grapes and Benj's natural charm—none of it was actually happening to him. The picture-perfect day in the winery was a set, the friends around the table a literal cast, and Benj— Benj was a double threat: she wasn't only starring in their production, she was directing it. Leaving Milo to figure out: What did she want out of him?

After last night he had no fucking clue. Challenging him to get her off in her doorway couldn't have been about her friend's PR nightmare—for one, he'd been the only one watching, the only one to see how her eyes had melted just before she'd come. And for another, thinking that she'd asked him to do it as Jackson was unendurable.

Milo had short-circuited outside that door after Benj had closed him out. Unable to… Unable to… Simply: Unable. Without the ability to. To think. To be. To leave.

His veins had buzzed, his cock had throbbed. He'd sure shown her, huh? That thought was laughable. He'd rubbed his neck where she'd opened his collar, holding his own throat the way he'd held hers, a firm cuff her grip had demanded. All of it her call. Benj made the rules, she owned the game. And for ten minutes, gasping and clawing at his wrists, she'd owned him.

No. She'd owned him long before that. She owned him every time she glanced his way.

At the table, Milo fingered Benj's skin through a cut-out in her green khaki jumpsuit, just under the decorative knot at her bust. He let his thumb explore higher, stroking the underside of her breast through the thin lace of her bra.

Her breath hitched and she shifted closer to the edge of her seat, one noodle-thin strap slipping down her arm. Her lips parted, then pursed, reminding him how badly he'd wanted that door to open. How badly he'd wanted her to let him in. No rules. No games. No wondering if she wanted to get off, or wanted him. Milo pulled his hand out of her top to hook his fingers under the strap to guide it back into place, his knuckles against her warm skin.

"What's happening behind that hat?" Vanessa teased.

"Nothing unseemly." Benj turned back to the table and Milo folded his hands in his lap.

Nothing unseemly. Not like last night, when she'd broken on his fingertips. Or when he'd gotten home and repeated the torment alone in his shower—desperate for a different ending. Desperate to know whether she was just that good at pretending, or if there was still something between them.

It wasn't like he could ask her. She was sticking to the game plan this morning. Even in text, she'd used the bare minimum number of words to communicate the details of their unit move to Maison Vineyard and

Winery. When he'd written back, suggesting a time he could pick her up, she'd responded with a single thumbs-up. And then, in what was clearly a move to keep the two of them from passing the scene of last night's crime, she'd met him and his Range Rover at the curb.

That was the only clue he had that she might regret hooking up with him more than she enjoyed it. Unfortunately, given their history, his fear that she wanted to take it back held too much water to be discounted. Milo rubbed a pain from his knee. But she had enjoyed it. He'd made sure of that. And it wasn't like she was shying away from his touch today.

Benj looped one arm over the chair's top rail, the other cradling a wine goblet to her chest. Her foot rubbed the back of his leg under the table, where only he knew. "Which wine's been your favorite, babe?"

Her dialogue was simple, effective—it was unnerving how competent she was, but she'd always been so easily herself. Milo's attempt to banter back felt clunky in comparison. "Which one has been your favorite?"

"I asked you first. Even though I already know."

"Let's have it."

"You liked the green wine. The one we tried inside during the tour."

She had him. He'd been most taken with the young, unripened wine that hadn't yet been aged. Milo dipped his chin in a nod, seen.

"The one that wasn't ready?" Vanessa didn't look convinced. "How do you figure that?"

"It reminded him of home." Benj's mouth curved open slowly, her tongue pressing pink between the even rows of her teeth.

Milo's pulse jumped. He'd been called out and the urge to shut her up with a kiss nearly overwhelmed him. "Your turn."

"It's between the sauv blanc and the cab," Jem answered, looking over from her conversation with the server.

Benj lifted a shoulder. "I liked the rosé."

"First astrology and now rosé?" Jem huffed a breathy laugh. "B is for basic."

Benj's response was cold—sharp and pointed as an icicle. "Among other things."

Milo caught the server's eye. "Separate from the food, I'd like half a case of the rosé we tried. A bottle for everyone as a souvenir."

"Now that's very considerate. Who knew you were so thoughtful?" Vanessa leveled a look at him and he smirked it off.

"I'm just trying to make you like me."

Lewis raised his glass. "So we shouldn't expect this generosity to carry over to any scenes we share?"

"Definitely not—" Milo felt the conversation coming easier now. "Benj'll be the first one to tell you I'm selfish as all get-out. I never want to share." He reached down to caress her bare ankle. "I just can't help myself."

Benj agitated her wine, the shallow tasting pour lashing the inside of the glass like a tiny, contained hurricane. "Wasn't I talking about your brother?"

Milo blinked at her, trying to understand what he'd done wrong. She was the one blurring the lines first, talking to him like he was himself—flaying him open, like she wanted them all to see who he was. But this response felt like a warning, a redirection, reminding him to stay in his lane. To be who she wanted when she wanted it. Her eyes were shaded by the wide brim of her hat, but he was sure they'd gone icy and hard.

Clarity pulled Milo's mouth flat. No matter what he did, under his growing beard, the concealer, and Benj's evenly applied tinted SPF, he was the wrong guy. The one who didn't belong here, sitting next to her at magic hour, sipping wine and sharing laughs.

"I've never heard that about Milo." Jem leaned over him to address Benj. "Do you know him well?"

"I—No. I don't know him well at all." She crossed her legs the opposite way, pulling her ankle out of Milo's grasp. "I was teasing Jackson the other day. Joking about how I would tell them apart." Benj spoke with airy lightness that Milo couldn't match.

He flicked a fly away from one of the three glasses in front of him. "It's his selfishness you'd recognize?"

"Babe, I didn't mean to upset you." Benj gave his knee a meaningful squeeze. "I know how close you are to your brother. Let's forget it."

In other words: Cut it out. The show must go on.

Fuck that.

Impatience hurried his breaths. He didn't want to be here. Listening to Benj, once again, throw his alleged selfishness in his face. She was so sure of his core flaw despite—as she had just said—not knowing him well at all.

Truth be told: Milo was damn proud of being selfish. It was a skill he'd had to hone. To work on. Born with a partner he loved and admired and would do anything for, learning to be selfish, to put himself first, had taken dedication. It had taken forever to get where he was, but now he was committed to doing whatever Milo Fox Miller wanted most.

A *big* thanks to Benj for the reminder.

"What can you tell us about the next *Twin Pistols*? How are they bringing Flash back—it's not like they can make another one without you."

Milo's attention snapped to Lewis. "Milo was Flash."

"My bad." Lewis formed his favorite mouth-pulling grimace. "Hard to keep straight."

"They're two different people, Lewis." Jem's touch on Milo's arm was light but significant. "I remember you saying your brother fell in to acting. He wasn't like you, wanting to take after your grandfather."

Milo moved to wipe his forehead, dislodging her hand. "He did in a different way. I wanted to be a movie star, Milo just wanted to be brave."

Benj rested her head on her hand, looking sideways at him, and Milo felt the truth piling up inside him, forcing its way into the open for her viewing pleasure. "When we were eighteen, he was fucking around on the Army website and saw this promotion where you put in your address and they'd send you a free hat. So he signs his name without thinking." Like with Modrić, Milo found the story easier to tell from Jackson's point of view. "The hat arrives on our steps. And about a week later so do the recruitment officers. Milo was too chickenshit to even answer the door. Our Pop did it for him, sent them on their way."

He'd found Milo in the closet. "What was that all about, son?"

"I wanted a free hat."

Pop had frowned. "Try wanting something more. Especially if you're putting your life on the line for it."

"Then I asked Milo to come to California again and he finally agreed."

"What was your pitch?" Benj asked.

"I said think how proud he'd be."

"I don't remember Milo in much before *Pistols*." Lewis probably hadn't meant to strike a nerve.

"He wasn't in anything." Milo pivoted, revealing one of Jackson's lesser moments, instead of another of his own. "My manager said it would be bad for me while I was trying to establish a real career to have Milo out there in toothpaste commercials. Said everyone would think it was me. So Milo took a back seat."

That was the full picture: Jackson had sold him on a joint dream, only to put him on standby when they arrived. And Milo had stayed, because he had something to prove and the view didn't remind him of home. He'd stayed because it was easy for him to pretend he was where he wanted to be.

Milo had forgotten about that damn hat for ten years. He'd braved flights and oceans and falls to soothe the blister of cowardice that had stayed with him, but the cap itself—a thick-knit grey beanie—he hadn't remembered it until he'd found it in a drawer last spring, when he'd gone home to recuperate. It had almost been too late for him, he'd already put his life on the line, when he remembered Pop's advice. *Try wanting something more.*

"He's good though. He has that quality." Vanessa pulled her hair over one shoulder. "You want to know what he's thinking. You want to watch emotion cross his face. He makes himself so vulnerable."

Lewis's mouth pursed sympathetically. "How's his recovery been?"

Milo nodded. "Fine. Good."

"Does he have anything lined up?"

"He doesn't, no. Much to our manager's chagrin."

"What is he looking for next—"

"You'd have to ask him," Milo interrupted, his tone unnecessarily sharp. He was done entertaining them with fragments dragged up from the deepest parts of him. The table's energy shifted, like a cloud passing over the sun. But the sky was open and empty and the shadow over the table was Milo's doing, some inner darkness he couldn't hold in.

Good. He'd been afraid Sophie was right, and he'd come back to LA only to fall into old patterns. Afraid he'd already forgotten the clarity of self he'd developed while healing in Maryland. He'd been afraid the moment would come when he was standing face-to-face with Jackson and he wouldn't remember what it was he wanted to say. Or he'd remember, and be too afraid to pull the trigger and say it.

But he still felt himself—it had to mean he was stronger, if playing Jackson wasn't coming as easily to him as it once had.

Without meeting anyone's eyes, Milo pushed his chair back and stood. "Excuse me. I think I need to fluff my aura." His attempted smile barely nudged one cheek.

Milo's long strides took him quickly to the edge of the grass between the start of two vines. His gaze followed the long row all the way back to where it met the curve of the sky. If he were more selfish, he wouldn't be here, staring at this field of bramble and twig. He wouldn't care how Jackson received and reacted to his decision. He'd be where he wanted, able to see open water on the horizon, the sun coming up—not going down.

But he did care. And not just about Jackson.

"You okay, babe?"

His shoulders rose as Benj wrapped her arms around his neck.

"Not now, Benj."

"Yes, now. They're all watching, so let's kiss and make up. You know you want to."

The wool hat scraped his cheek and he ducked back. "Not like this."

Her hands tightened at his neck, drawing him down to her. "What are you so angry about? You're a ticking time bomb, aren't you—just waiting to go off. Should I be concerned we're going to have another yesterday?"

"What happened yesterday?" He swiped the hat off her head, leaving her to squint up at him.

Strain crept into her voice. "Your out-of-character hostility toward Cormac."

"Nothing else? Nothing unseemly?" He palmed the opening at the back of her jumpsuit, his thumb finding a notch along her spine.

"Do you think something unseemly happened yesterday? Do you think I behaved inappropriately? I don't remember breaking any rules. And it's not like you didn't know what you were doing."

"It felt to you like I knew what I was doing?" He raised both brows and enjoyed a flush that burned up the sides of her face. "You didn't give me any notes."

"That's not the point of this conversation. Or any conversation." She was trying to shut him down, but those rules that had been black and white now included the soft grey wool of her cable-knit shorts.

He had an opening to find out what was going on in her head. And he still hadn't quit hoping she'd see that he could be trusted, that she wanted him as much as he wanted her. "Maybe it should be. Maybe we should be talking about how you felt last night."

"You wanna know how wet I was?"

Milo's mouth gaped. That wasn't what he'd meant.

But Benj kept talking, her hips swaying ever so slightly against his. "You wanna hear how easy it would have been for you to fuck your big hard dick into me?"

Milo swallowed. He was…no match for her. Outplayed, at every turn.

"What?" Her chin lifted. "You don't like to talk dirty? I bet you'd do it for me." She pressed closer to him, whispering in his ear, her voice dropping any hint of tease. "How's this for incentive: I'm here *for you* doing everything in my power not to fuck this up for either of us. So if you aren't going to kiss me and make it nice, at least screw your smile back on and do your job. You're a professional pretender. I know you know how to fake it. Whatever is bothering you, lock it up. If we're going to hide in broad daylight, we need your A game here." She freed her arms from around his neck and patted his chest. "'Kay, babe?"

Benj didn't pull her punches and Milo didn't need to read between the lines, but he picked apart the phrases anyway like marking a script.

Lock it up? He couldn't even keep the door shut.

A game? He didn't want to fucking play anymore.

I know you know how to fake it.

God*damn* that hurt.

"That's not what I was asking." Milo's protest sounded feeble even to his own ears, but he couldn't not push back, his ego smarting from her verbal lashing.

"Then what were you asking?" Her hands smoothed

imaginary wrinkles on his shirt. Her head shook. "I'm riveted. A captivated audience, waiting to hear what comes out of your mouth next. So if you've got something to say just—"

"I thought you'd want it sweet. Slow. When I picture it, that's how it is between us."

For once, Milo had to wait for Benj's response. She took her time, fiddling with his collar, making sure the top button was secure. When she eventually spoke, her voice was abnormally uncertain. "I didn't hear a question."

"Maybe I'm done asking. Maybe I'm done letting you call the shots."

Her body went lax for one tantalizing moment—and then she willfully stiffened. "Is this because you felt used? That unresolved twin shit that set you off at the table?"

He fixed his gaze on the top of her head, blinded by the white-blond of her hair in the sunlight and the white-hot emotion sparking in his veins. "You can go ahead and use me up, Ben, use me all until I'm gone. But don't go around thinking you know anything about me anymore. You only see what you want to see—and that's not me."

Chapter Fifteen

It was safe to say that Benj was a wine-addled disaster. Also safe to say that her twin comment had hit home. And absolutely perilous to admit she regretted it.

She could not feel for Milo Fox. Considering that man a whole human again, with hopes and struggles and dreams and all the trappings of personhood, would be absolutely devastating to her ability to maintain the iron curtain on their arrangement. The boundary that separated her—protected her—from that old possibility of Milo being More.

Benj exhaled, her breath shaky. It was too fucking late. She was already feeling Milo. Some damn muscle memory of finding him warm and attractive combined with new knowledge that he could make her come like shattering glass—effortless and thorough.

Infuriating as his accusation that she'd used him. Maddening as his refusal to kiss her.

Not like this.

Enraging as her *wanting* him to do it—to remind her—to prove he was exactly who she thought he was. So she could stop hoping he'd kiss her and be some-one else.

Before she could sort through all of her mixed-up

emotions, Milo was releasing her. He fit her hat onto her head, ran a finger along the rim, and pointed her back to the table. She blinked, and just like that it was curtains up.

"I'll be right behind you, hon."

Milo was pretending again, turning away from her and scraping at his scalp. The desire to shake him out of it knocked her sideways and Benj stumbled back. This was catastrophe.

She forced herself to head back to the table, flexing her thumbs as she walked, knowing an *M* wrinkled in the knuckle of each as she did so. Milo was someone she had to look out for, and while she was low-key thrilled that her faith in internet psychics was warranted, it was no less a warning than it had been in Max's office. She was still in trouble.

Their skeleton crew had thinned even more, leaving only Jem at the table, surrounded by food. A bowl of creamy spinach dip, a wooden charcuterie board of ungarnished meat and cheese, grilled romaine drenched in white dressing, and deviled eggs. Extremely sus. Benj felt Jem watching for her reaction and settled casually back into her chair. "Where is everyone?"

"Lew took a call, then Vu and her boo started whispering and ran off."

"Sounds eventful."

The forced pleasantry of the interaction confirmed to Benj that she and Milo weren't the only ones playing games.

The two women shared an unobstructed view of Milo down the lawn. He had his phone pressed to his ear—could've been a prop to buy himself time or a real call, Benj didn't know. She didn't know him, that was what he'd told her. Why did she want so badly to prove him wrong?

"Is Jackson alright?" The real concern in Jem's question caught Benj off guard.

"Fine. He's fine. Touchy subject, is all."

"The natural drama of twins." Jem rolled a thin slice of salami into a tube and bit one end. "All that attachment and competition. Up close it must be quite a show."

Benj shot her a quizzical look and Jem answered it, a flickering "gotcha" in her eyes.

"You worked on *Twin Pistols*. Damien mentioned it to me the other night, his boyfriend was a PA."

"It was a short stint. Like I said, I didn't really get to know either of them at the time." Benj crossed her legs and tried changing the subject. "Damien couldn't make it today?"

"Short notice. Not a lot of people are free in the middle of a Wednesday. Like you."

"And you."

Benj's foot swayed in the air, her leg rocking from the knee. Jem's blatant disregard was well past stale and Benj, who was in the business of building people up, was struggling not to engage. Not to stand her ground. But this wasn't an episode of *Women of a Certain Age*. She didn't need to engage in conflict for anyone else's entertainment.

"Do you not have a lot going on at the moment with Nelle out of town?"

"I'm booked this weekend, actually, for Skylar Davies's wedding."

"Oh, so we'll all see you there too. Petra's invited the cast."

"Of course she has."

Both of their voices had lost animation, neither of them pleased about that development. For Benj it meant another day with Milo, trying to keep the truth of her feelings for him at bay.

He started back toward the table, only to frown and change directions a few yards away. Benj was jolted out of wondering why by Jem's next question.

"He must still be reeling, from Milo's scare?" Jem straightened two of the wineglasses in front of her. "He mentioned how hard it's been to me."

"He did?" When had Milo done that? Unless Jem had talked to the real Jackson about it. "Wait, were you and Jackson—"

"We got drinks after our screen test. I have to admit I was surprised to see him with you. I thought—well, we had chemistry. And I wondered if it might go some-where. You know how these things happen on a set."

Boy did she. The long hours, the big emotions, the working together toward something substantial—intensity like a pressure cooker. Taking half the time to get twice as tender. She was sure she had known Milo then. But it had been three years and so much had changed for both of them.

"You should know," Jem added. "If something does develop with me and Jackson, I'm not going to stop it. It's nothing personal against you—I'm not coming for you—for me, it's about connection. When I make a real one, I act on it."

"Thanks for the heads-up, I guess." Benj had to give Jem props for her honesty—and her ability to keep that much volume in heavy, over-the-brow bangs. And she wouldn't take it personally—by the time they were filming, Jem would be dealing with the real Jackson.

Benj and Milo wouldn't be involved.

That thought should have brought a wave of relief. When it didn't, Benj wrapped both of her palms around her knee, pulling it toward her body, trying to hold in her question. She couldn't. "Jem, what did Jackson tell you about Milo's accident. What happened?"

"To Milo?" Jem angled her head. "A descender rig malfunctioned when he was doing a stunt fall. His head missed the mat."

Benj swallowed against a sudden surge of bile. The gruesome image of Milo falling, landing, slamming his skull into a cement warehouse floor made her sick. "I can't believe that could happen. With all the safety protocols in place?"

"Well, it did. And it's probably why the studio hasn't pushed him about the length of his recovery. They should be worried he's going to sue."

Realization pulled Benj taut, everything snapping into focus. An impending lawsuit explained exactly why Milo was protecting his low profile, why his manager was the only one he wanted to know he was in town. When that news broke, it'd be a media sandstorm, impossible to avoid, working its way into every little crack. If she'd thought about it for two seconds, she'd have realized that *of course* he was still feeling the impact of that accident. If she hadn't been trying so hard to ignore what he was going through.

Milo was right: She didn't know him anymore because she hadn't wanted to. She hadn't wanted him to be real.

"You think he'd really do that?"

"Who knows. I wouldn't. Not if I wanted to keep making movies." Jem finished her salami and sat forward to peel open the tight fold of a white linen napkin. "I'd be more hung up on the trauma of it. Of losing the trust you had in the process, the trust you put in people whose job it was to keep you safe. Getting over that would be really tough."

Benj released her knee and slumped in her chair, like she had against her door last night. She'd sat there, her legs sprawling across the wood-patterned vinyl into the kitchen, theorizing that it was her rules that made Milo so appealing. She'd labeled him off-limits from the moment she met him—it was no wonder she found him irresistible. That was basic psychology, a tried-and-true cliché: wanting what she couldn't have.

Only it wasn't the truth. If it were, she wouldn't be gathering all the bits of his story together. It would be enough not to know him, the impression of him would suffice.

"Jackson didn't tell you any of this?" Jem eyed her doubtfully.

"I—I didn't want to pry."

"Because you were involved with Milo before? And now you're with Jackson?" The other woman sat back, her gaze flicking momentarily over Benj's shoulder. "What's that like—do you have a preference or do you just go for whichever one is nearest?"

Benj retaliated with glib sarcasm, forgetting that Jem had shared her insights along with a warning, that she was acting on her own interests. "It's definitely more of an eeny-meeny-miny-moe type situation."

"Your mother told you to pick the very best one?"

"And here I am with Jackson."

A plate jostled onto the table in front of her—a dish of peanut sauce nestled between two spring rolls, the yellow, green, and orange of fresh vegetable muted under thin white rice paper. Benj looked up to thank the waiter—and met Milo's burning eyes, his sunglasses hanging from the square pocket at his chest.

Her lips parted. Her cheeks heated. How much of that had he heard? Judging by Jem's cat-got-the-cream smirk and Milo's dark stare: enough to leave a mark.

She'd hurt him. Clear as day.

"This for me?" Guilt that he'd gone out of his way to get her something to eat, only to overhear her positing his brother as the better twin, weighed down the attempted levity of her question.

Milo's jaw was locked too tight for a response. Benj dropped her foot to the ground.

She'd gone from disaster to catastrophe to crisis. The moment required a decision she was incapable of making. She wanted more and she wanted less. She wanted in and she wanted out. She couldn't trust Milo any more than she could trust herself.

None of it made sense. None of it was right.

When she reached for his hand, Milo lurched away. Feeling ignited under her skin and Benj reacted, grabbing his collar and pulling him back down. He'd already told her he was hers to use up, but that wasn't what she was thinking when she crushed her mouth to his.

She wasn't thinking at all. She was acting on a connection she couldn't explain away. She was giving and taking—opening her lips to the soft, slow sweep of his tongue.

When Benj was kissing Milo, there was nothing else

going on—no complications, no conflicts, no contra-
dictions. When Benj was kissing Milo, all the noise in
her head faded to black. When Benj was kissing Milo,
she was mad for the beat of her own heart.

Her hat tumbled off as her head fell back, laden
with want, the burden of giving in to him. He caught
her, his palms heating the sides of her neck, and delved
deeper, tipping her back and keeping her there. Less a
burden, then, as he held them both up.

Milo kissed like he was saying something, kissed
like he meant it. Benj whimpered into him, straining
up from her seat to get closer when he started to ease
back. She squeezed her eyes closed against the light,
trying to block it out and stay in the dark, unruly world
of his kiss. Leaving it had only ever changed her life
for the worse.

Their lips separated but she kept her hold of his collar, kept him bent over her.

"No notes," she breathed. Then details of the scene
came into focus—her motivation, their roles, the props
on the table—everything she needed to move on as
though the kiss had been part of the plot. "You're the
best. Thanks for thinking of me."

He nudged his nose against hers. "Any time, Ben."
And she let go.

Chapter Sixteen

The word for it was *déjà vu*. Milo had done this before. Kissed Benj, pulled away, and felt his world shift off-balance. This time, though, the sinking feeling, the heavy truth that dropped his heart into his gut was that in a seamless second-act reversal, he was the one who'd said no to this.

Hadn't he? He had—though that was before he'd said yes. Before he'd challenged her to use as much of him as she wanted. What a truly stupid fucking thing to say. As if he'd survive Benj hitting and quitting him. As if this situation had equal give-and-take.

Milo rebuttoned his top button and licked his bottom lip, carrying the airy sweetness of Benj's lipstick into his mouth. She tasted like every dessert denied to him during those years spent sculpting his body to perfection. The thickest, richest frosting of a tender, dewy cake. He wanted to go back for more until he was sick and dizzy. He wanted to ride the sugar-high rise of his blood as it woke up every nerve in his body. But he lowered himself into the seat opposite her and shoved a deviled egg into his mouth, hoping the vinegary bite of the fried caperberry garnish could cut his craving for sweetness. (It came close, but what was a deviled egg without Old Bay?)

Sophie had called it, though he hadn't realized it when he'd picked up earlier hoping she'd gotten in touch with their brother. Milo had tried him again that morning—Max too, to no avail and mounting frustration.

"How's Jackson's life?" Sophie had asked after breaking the news that she, also, hadn't been able to reach his twin.

"No change."

"You mean he's still got his job and his girlfriend?"

"She's not his—yeah, we're keeping a lid on things. Even if she still despises me," he'd confided accidentally.

"Oh, Milo." His sister's understanding had crackled in his ear. "You're still going to talk to Jackson, right? You're not not quitting to get her back?"

Milo bristled at the question, at the accusation that he wouldn't go through with his plan. "Quitting has nothing to do with losing Benj. It's about…"

"Finding yourself?" There was a hint of humor in Soph's voice because she just couldn't help herself when it came to teasing him, but it didn't take away from the truth. "Well. I'm sorry she still despises you. But that's to be expected. *Ficus benjamina* is the kind of plant that likes things just so. Not too hot, not too cold. If you want to move them to a new light, you need to be patient. You need to be slow, bit by bit. Give 'em time to adjust as you go. It's a long game."

Benj wasn't moving slow this time.

Milo chewed, swallowed, and chased the egg with someone's glass of water. He was mad. He was wild.

His lungs struggled to keep up with the chaos of his pulse. That kiss had hit him like a lightning bolt—striking fast and sudden and lighting him all the way up. He locked on to the rule of Benj's gaze, willing her to break it. She glanced aside, an unaltered smile parting her lips.

"And where were you two?"

Vanessa Vu and her husband slid into the chairs next to Milo, leaving an open spot for Lewis between Benj and Jem, whose features were forcefully blank. That little snippet of conversation he'd overheard had to be the tip of the iceberg because the vibe between the two women now was damn near arctic.

"We were checking in."

"You're staying here tonight?"

Vanessa nodded. "It's two hours back to the city."

Benj tucked back a strand of loose hair. "That might not be a bad idea. Maybe we should get a room?"

Oh, she'd like that, wouldn't she. Another damn pretense. The two of them "forced" to share a bed, her body next to his in the dark. No one to see, nothing to explain. Undercover seduction. Milo resisted the image—Benj pressing back against him, urging his hand down to where she wanted it—even as it aroused him. Another interlude she'd act like hadn't happened.

"I don't mind driving."

"Jackson—"

Hating the way she wielded his brother's name, Milo worked the outraged jump of his muscles into a surge toward the salad.

Benj's eyes flared. "I think we should get a room."

Benjamina Wasik liked things *just so*. It was her way or nothing. She was so confident he'd take whatever she was offering. He should just agree, but he was tired of trying to prove his whole self worthy when she was making it clear she was only interested in part of him.

"You know I was thinking the same thing." Lewis claimed the seat next to Benj, squinting into the setting sun. "What do you say we eat, have some more wine, and then all go to bed?"

"I did not have 'orgy invitation' on my Bingo card." Benj laughed and Milo steeled himself against the pleasure of the sound, focusing instead on how easily she could pretend for the others. That was the problem, wasn't it? They had kissed, but he still didn't know what was made up.

That kiss had sent him flying high. Feeling close enough to touch the sun that warmed his neck. In reality, it was always out of reach—and still more likely he'd make it there, to the sun—than back in Benj's good graces. Milo wasn't sure he could keep trying. Not when the idea of flying wasn't complete without the threat of a fall.

Lewis looked around. "Is that a no from the rest of you?"

Milo fit his sunglasses over his eyes. "One of many lessons I learned from Benj. Never a good idea to get involved with someone you're working with."

"We were just talking about that." Jem held her hands out for Milo to pass her the salad bowl.

He handed it over, glad he'd shielded his eyes before looking over at Benj again. "Were you?"

"She was telling me how you met—you and her and your brother."

"How did you guys meet?" Vanessa asked, sending the spinach dip around the table next.

Using a slice of bread, Milo scooped dip unceremoniously onto his plate, waiting to hear what she'd have to say about that. But Benj didn't have anything prepared. Instead she blinked slowly as if waking up. And like *that*, his *déjà vu* was back—this time without a reversal, this time it was a complete playback of how a smile could retreat from her face. First from her eyes, then her cheeks, and finally her mouth, as it formed the words without any joy whatsoever. "We met on the set of *Twin Pistols 2.*"

"Benj was my brother's makeup artist. Bastard didn't know how lucky he was." Milo forked salad into his mouth, chewing to keep himself from saying anything else.

"How'd you land that?" Vanessa prompted.

Benj lifted her head, her teeth in her bottom lip. "Trying to be someone I'm not." She cut one spring roll in half, and then the other. "My mother's always been very…critical. I'd been doing weddings and events back home, and she wanted to know where it was going. Which of course meant she had already decided it wasn't. She didn't care about anything I learned to do as a kid unless it earned me a merit badge. So I thought: Where do you get recognizable credit for hairstyling?"

"Welcome to California."

"Exactly. I busted my ass making calls and putting myself out there and finally someone offered to give me a shot on a set."

"That must have made your mom take your career seriously."

"For a bit. Until I couldn't get another job. And I had

to call her asking for money. The expectation I grew up with was that if you set a goal for yourself, you follow through on it. No excuses. No going back on your word."

Milo's heart throbbed as he filled in more parts of the story, the accusations Benj wasn't saying. He waited for her to glare at him, but she kept talking, her voice even. The story wasn't about him, even if he felt like he understood more than the others at the table as she continued telling it.

"I didn't need to come here. I was happy where I was," Benj said, putting voice to thoughts Milo had had himself. "I'm still happy doing weddings. If I'm with the right client, it doesn't feel like work."

"People don't know what a shitty trade it can be." Milo hastened to swallow an under-chewed bite and was still a step behind.

Benj's eyes flashed at him, her voice growing harsh. "It's not a shitty trade—"

Jem laughed. "Putting fake eyelashes on people is your calling?"

"Is wearing them yours?" Benj countered.

Milo cleared his throat, feeling the moment getting away from him. Worried if it did, he wouldn't get another to explain. "I meant: it's a shitty trade—between doing what you want, and what other people think you should want. Between making yourself happy and making other people happy. But it sounds like you found a way to do both."

"Oh."

He watched her take in air and let it out, like she needed a moment to herself before continuing.

Her breathless laugh surprised him, made him think

she'd pressed on before she was ready. "Except for my mother. There's no making her happy. But if I hadn't tried, I wouldn't have met... Nelle."

"So the job you did get was with Milo and Jackson." Vanessa leaned in. "Did sparks fly right away?"

"As soon as he smiled."

"And you were hooked."

"No—" Benj shook her head slightly and began again, as if she'd lost track of what she was saying, as if she'd remembered the point. "It was during a week of night shoots. I'm getting set up, and in comes Jackson to chat."

Milo's head tilted with interest. Beyond the intrigue of hearing about Benj's past, he'd always wondered if his brother and Benj had interacted on set. He'd convinced himself they hadn't—or why would she have kept flirting with him?

"And I'm yawning and yawning and he's standing there with his coffee. So I swipe it from him and he goes—"

"It won't be sweet enough for you," Milo finished for her, their stories clashing, the table turning on a disorienting swish pan.

He remembered that night and it had nothing to do with Jackson. That had been him. Milo and Benj, alone in the makeup trailer, just getting started.

"Oh, he'd been watching you!" Lewis jumped in. "Nothing sexier than when someone proves they've been paying attention."

Jem dropped the salad bowl back on the table. "That line between admirer and stalker is a fine one."

Benj kept her focus on Milo. "What did it for me was the next day. When he came back, sipping from another coffee, getting in the way, *again*. I stole another sip, bracing for the same bitterness. It was loaded with syrup. Just the way I like it."

"Too cheap to get her one of her own?" Jem supplied.

"Hey, he wasn't a high roller yet," Lewis said.

The side of Milo's mouth quirked up sheepishly. "I wanted us to share."

He'd wanted to have the thing she wanted. So he changed it. He was always changing himself back then, doing what he thought would make someone else happy. Making his decisions for other people. He'd spent the last year deciding he wasn't going to do that anymore. Deciding to do what he wanted.

And here he was fucking it up. Torturing himself for what? For who? For Jackson? For Benj.

Milo shoveled more food into his mouth, drank more water. He ordered a coffee black, the way he liked it. By the time the sun had set, his buzz was gone, replaced by the stone-cold sober sensation of being a fucking punk. He was trying to get away from the fast-paced uncertainty of Hollywood—and Benj was luring him back into bed with it.

"So that room?" she asked.

"No." He pulled the keys from his pocket. *Not like this*, he'd told her. It was time to mean it. Time to follow through. "I'm good to drive back."

The sidewalk outside of Benj's apartment was blessedly full—with people and a hazy film of weed—when Milo double-parked the SUV after a frosty, silent drive back to the city. His knee protested an attempt to hop out and meet her at the curb, so she was march-

ing up the walk when he called her name, called her
back to him.

"Ben."

She turned, her loose bun coming undone with the
force. "*What*."

Milo eased out of the car and stalked up to her, stopping close enough to force her head back if she wanted
to continue glaring up at him. Which she did.

"You asked why I'm angry? I'm tired of—" Words
failed him—the inability to describe inner frustrations
with the way he'd let his life play out—and his palms
shot wide. "All this shit."

"Well, *Jackson*." She looked sideways as one of her
neighbors passed on their way into the building. "If
you were so tired, we didn't have to drive all the fuck
back here tonight, did we?"

"We did. We did if we have any hope of being
straight with each other."

"Why would we want to do that?"

All the questions rattling around Milo's mind came
tumbling out. "Why would you tell that story about
how 'we' met? Who was that for? Why would you
want to stay at the winery? What would have happened tonight?"

Her chest rose and fell under his gaze. Her mouth
clamped shut.

"You don't know the answers or you don't want to
tell me?"

"Please say you're nearing your point."

Milo balled his fists, about to hit it. About to cross
the axis of action, redefine the space between them.
He'd been trying to play a clean game—why? It wasn't
serving him. The only sure way to get what he wanted

was to help himself. "Go upstairs and pack a bag. I'll wait here so you don't get any bright ideas in that dark hall of yours. Come with me and do it right. You want to share a bed tonight, it's gonna be mine."

Chapter Seventeen

Benj was not able to muster her wits quickly enough to realize the proper comeback to a demand like Milo's was to not come back. But she was well on her way, her bag packed and in the back seat of his Range Rover by the time that power move occurred to her. Her best counter would have been going upstairs and never coming down. She should have left him waiting. Shown him she couldn't be bossed or swayed from what she wanted.

The issue, of course, was that she wanted him. In the worst way—a base-level, penetrating need. There'd been promise in his demand—that he'd take care of her until she was satisfied.

The issue, of course, was that she knew he could do it.

The promise was nearer than ever now. Milo's garage doors were lowering, but the room didn't go black. He'd apparently found time to change the burnt-out bulb, and that little detail had Benj's mouth going dry. That little detail let her know there wouldn't be any more hiding in the dark.

Benj carried herself into the house, leaving him to follow with her bag. The view caught her again in her gut—a level of stunning that only real money could buy. She flipped every switch as she went, flooding the rooms with light, obscuring the windows with reflections, and bolstering her own bravado. The irregular black floor with its white grout led down the hall like a game of lava, and she stepped from slate tile to slate tile without touching any of the cracks, a way of quelling the urge to speed up her steps and run from the feeling of Milo stalking behind her.

She was sure he'd tackle her to the bed as soon as they reached it, sure he'd claim the victory the moment he'd won. But she passed through Milo's bedroom untrounced and stepped confused into the bathroom on the other side, stopping only when she had nowhere else to go.

Milo slowed in the doorway and she nodded to her bag, like this had been her plan all along. "You can leave that on the counter."

Milo moved with excruciating leisure, setting the bag softly to the side of the double sink. Benj waited for him to come to her but he stood his ground, a knowing glint in his eye. *Like he had her.*

Only because she wanted him to.

Benj pulled her hair over her shoulder, unlooped her arms from the straps of her top, and turned her back to him. "Help me with this."

He eased closer until she felt his breath on her bare shoulder, sensation rising up from her toes at the warmth of it. He undid the buttons of her jumpsuit one at a time, her strapless bra seeming to tighten around her lungs as the fabric gaped open. This was it. It had to be. He'd spin her around and strip her to her feet, taking her hard and fast against the sink.

But when he finished, his hands settled patiently on

her hips and his mouth pressed hot to her nape. Hotter still was the wet of his tongue licking her skin in smooth, deliberate strokes.

I thought you'd want it sweet. Slow.

His words from earlier pounded in her veins and Benj broke away from him. One hand holding up the garment, she braced her other palm on the cool marble counter. His silence—in the car, through the house, all the way up to this moment—unnerved her. Made it feel like they were still playing a game—one she felt like she was losing, even as her body hummed with triumph. What he'd said in the vineyard—how he'd known what she would have wanted—if they were being themselves—if this were real between them—

Those words were making it impossible for her to give herself over to him now and pretend none of it mattered more than the pleasure of letting go together. Made it impossible to pretend that this was the same as any time she fucked a guy who made her wet.

Milo didn't just make her wet. He had her trembling with desire. He had her aching for more and preparing to get it. Only *more* with Milo was a limited release. And she had to get her head around that before she got too greedy.

With anyone else she'd be in control. Any other time, she'd have been directing the action. With Milo running his own plays tonight, her head wasn't in the game.

Still clutching the top to her, Benj looked for him in the mirror—hoping to find a simple lust in his eyes, dark and uncomplicated. Only the doorway was open. Milo gone.

Benj's mouth unlocked as she spun in the empty

bath. Frustrated steps took her to the edge of the room where she watched as Milo stripped to nothing, tossing his shirt on a low chair in the corner, leaving his pants in a heap on the floor. The dimples of his bare ass clenched as he opened a glass panel and dove into the end of the pool just outside his door. The thick muscles of his tan shoulder blades glistened as he rose out of the water. His hair was blacker now than she'd ever seen it. One arm stretched out of the water, he gulped for air, and swam away from her.

An indignant laugh caught in her throat.

She shoved out of her clothes and took one step after him before a turned ankle brought her up short, forcing her to stop and take more careful steps. She watched him glide through the water. A moment ago, he'd been a shark circling closer. Now he was a white whale she longed to pursue. If he expected her to chase after him, that she was so hard-up for his cock that she'd go searching for it, he was capital-*M* Mistaken.

Switching directions, Benj headed for the shower, filled the bathroom with steam, forcing him to seek her out. But Milo was still doing laps when Benj emerged from the fog. She'd had time to think in the shower— though she wouldn't exactly call herself clearheaded. Not when her hands had skimmed her own body and she'd imagined them darker, rougher, driven by a purpose not at all her own. During her abbreviated, three-step skin-care routine, her lustful, frustrated thoughts had all come together in a new game plan. A bold one. One that would put her back in the lead, if she didn't lose her nerve.

She wasn't going to chase Milo, nor was she going

to wait for him to come to her. Not when she always
kept a small emergency vibrator in her toiletries.

The toy was tiny, a little buzzing bullet attached
to a wide elastic band that fit comfortably over the
three longest fingers of her right hand. Perfect for a
targeted attack.

Benj threw herself on the bed without toweling off,
her wet body leaving a dark imprint on Milo's light
grey duvet. She stared up at the wood-paneled ceiling
and turned the vibrator on with a rub of her thumb. It
hummed to life and she closed her eyes, listening, letting the sound overwhelm her senses. Simple as sci-
ence, her body readied—Pavlovian wetness coating
her center.

The first brush of the toy to her pussy jolted her hips
up and she pressed herself deeper into the blanket, the
pillowy down rising up around her like tall grass. The
recessed lighting blazed red through her eyelids and
she knew she was on display through the glass windows. Her hand circled faster at the thought.

Any moment Milo would walk in and find her, already in the throes, as it were. Halfway to heaven without any help. She didn't intend to count the head start
he'd given her just by being nearby. That would require an examination of *why* Milo Fox's proximity
sent her body into a frenzy. Why the toasty aroma of
his skin drew her in. Why she wanted to dive into the
dark pools of his eyes—even knowing whatever was
hidden in those depths could unman her.

She wasn't waiting on him—and she wanted him
to know it. He could keep his slow burn. He'd see her
helping herself to what she wanted, the way she wanted
it. She wanted him to watch, she wanted him to see.

Nerves tightened her stomach—anxiety chasing away her desire, pushing it out of reach—

Doubt opened her eyes a split second too late.

Milo stood at the end of the bed, the glass door behind him ajar, letting in the cool night air, heavy with the smell of lilac. Benj's flesh prickled, the moisture on her skin condensing even as his gaze stoked her cheeks to a fiery glow. He'd gone completely still, except for the nerve ticking in his jaw, the blaze roaring in his eyes, and the slow drip of water off his body, pooling at his feet.

Short-lived embarrassment dropped her eyes low—too low—down, past the coarse hairs of his chest, and the solid planes of his middle. Down. To the hard, smooth cock that strained up and out. Toward her. She blinked and thought, impossibly, that it grew thicker and more substantial—that it might actually reach her, given the chance.

She'd been speculating about his "big dick" earlier, trying—as now—to get a rise out of him. (Check and check.) That speculation caused her to exaggerate the ease with which he'd be able to slide inside of her. Now she wasn't so sure, but her body ached to give it a try.

Benj's fingers slipped up, the buzzing toy striking gold. And when she clenched, the hollow ache of her pussy was reason enough to demand her fill. Reaching out her left hand, she knocked her knuckles against the side table, where she knew he kept a box of condoms. She'd snooped the last time she'd stayed in this room. The place seemed to bring out the worst behavior in her.

Judging from the way he lazily stroked his cock as he crossed to her, Milo didn't mind. He stopped, stand-

ing over her, droplets falling from his hair and landing like rain on her soft stomach. His palms feathered
over her exposed breast with measured lightness. But
when he bent to cover one stiffening bud, his tongue
provided the roughness she craved.

Benj gasped, her knuckles knocking harder against
the drawer front. Milo released his dick to take both
her breasts in hand and squeeze, the heat of his mouth
trailing across her chest, his short beard scraping raw
sensation across her skin.

Her hand moved faster now. Faster and faster, a low
moan escaping her throat as a wave of—

Milo pinched her free nipple before snatching at
the wrist of her right hand and pulling it wide. The
vibrator buzzed louder, no longer muffled against her
swelling clit.

Benj whined her protest, the ghost of vibration making her even more aware of the void between her legs.
Milo, undeterred, brought her hand to his mouth, fitting it over her fingers to taste her and suck the toy
inside, completely disarming her.

When he let go of her wrist to open the drawer,
Benj lay paralyzed on the mattress, her elbows bent,
her palms up, as much a puddle as the pool water he'd
dripped on the floor. Days ago, in her one-room do-
main, she'd been in charge. She'd been drunk on her
hold over him, loopy with power. Here, now, she was
not in control. She was exactly where Milo wanted her.
Watching, breathless, first as he rolled on the condom,
and then took the vibrator from his mouth and fit the
band over the head of his cock, working it down to
the base.

As he knelt between her legs, she lifted up on her

elbows to watch—only for Milo to bring his head back down, lashing at her breast again, the hot tip of his buzzing cock searing her open pussy while leaving it unfulfilled.

He was intent on this slow pain. This torturous pace. His bed. His way. His win.

He had her. But she was going to have him too.

Benj slipped her hand between them, caught the scorching length, and thrust him home.

Chapter Eighteen

Milo sank and sank and sank into Benj. His hips drove into the warmth of hers even as he wanted to hold himself back. Even as he worried about going back on his word and hurting her. He couldn't. There was no resisting the primal need urging him on—urging him in.

She rose up to meet him, and he held himself over her so as not to crush those perfect tits he hadn't been done getting to know. Everywhere her body curled around him felt like warm satin. Her thighs on his, her arms soothing over his back—until the tips of her nails dug into his ass.

Milo groaned, his head dropping to her neck, his mouth finding more perfect, smooth skin. He inhaled expecting that kick of caffeine, the scent of her that would ensure he was awake and not dreaming. All he got was coconut. His eyes closed and he was nineteen again. The only kid in Hollywood without a dream of his own, except the simple desire to soak up as much sun as he could each day. Head heavy with longing, listening to the unspoken command of her hands, Milo pushed further into her and felt the moan work its way through her throat, the gentle vibration against his lips a counterpoint to the electric buzzing that had her writhing under him.

Benj had told him once that she loved the build-up. It had been in a different context—he'd been asking about how she got into styling. As always, she answered with depth he didn't see coming, open and honest, talking about the way it had started as a hobby, helping her friends get ready before a night out.

"My absolute favorite thing. Music and hairspray and anticipation clinging to the air. You know how all the best foods are appetizers? People like to be teased, it's why we get high on the feeling of a room building with buzz. It's those tasty little bites—the best bits that happen before any lights go out."

Milo's own experience echoed those themes—the best things progressed slowly. Seed to flower. Flavor growing from time. The best bits were happening beneath him, and he was damn ecstatic the lights were still on in his room, that he could see every glimmer of emotion that crossed her face. But true sweetness was a process he held dear, and Benj was rushing him.

Sunk completely into Benj, and reluctant to remove himself, Milo tried to slow things down by stopping the roll of his hips. She didn't appear to notice, continuing to work herself against his cock and the busy little spur at its base. To get her attention, Milo had to pull away. He braced himself and sat up, looking down at her, at the pink flush of her perfect skin. She clawed at his thighs, trying to pull him back to her and Milo watched his dick sliding in and out of her bare pussy.

Fuck it. He fell back onto her, thrusting with abandon. Benj knew what she wanted, who was he to disagree? He'd gotten what he wanted too: proof that Benj wasn't just using him for a performance. She couldn't pretend this had anything to do with their deal. She was here with him on her own accord.

And, really, faster was better—faster meant more moaning, less thinking. The indulgent flinch of her body under his as the vibrator reconnected with her clit. Their limbs twined together, and Milo felt the end coming, thought he knew where he was taking them, until Benj's voice, a harried, insistent whisper, provided the plot twist he didn't see coming.

"Talk to me."

"What?"

"Talk to me."

Their bodies were talking. Milo didn't know what else needed to be said.

"Not as Jackson—"

She might have been trying to clarify but Milo interrupted her with a growl and a hard thrust, driving into her, hating his brother's name on her lips.

"*Talk* to me."

Milo's forehead was already ridged with exertion and confusion pulled it tighter. What could she possibly want him to say right now? Her hair tangled in his face and Milo breathed it in, like he had in the vineyard, when he could taste the sun's heat reflecting off her.

What had she told him then? *You don't like to talk dirty? I bet you'd do it for me.*

"Look at me, Benj." Milo pushed up on his palms to look down at her, never stopping the roll of his hips. "If I'm not your type, why was that pussy so fucking wet for me?"

Her eyes widened with surprise and he worried he'd

gotten it wrong. But as he watched, her lips turned up and she dug one hand into her hair, the other massaging over her breasts. Her feet leveraged her hips into his, encouraging him to continue.

"Your pussy was just begging me to glide right in, hoping for as much dick as I could give it? Huh? That's what you want from me? You're getting it now."

She released another glorious moan, digging her heels into his back, spurs of her own. The words rolled off Milo's tongue, loose and easy. He'd never felt freer to say exactly what he was thinking.

"This should be a tight little cunt, but you've got it so slick for me, it took nothing to bury myself in it. I'm not gonna make it that easy for you—you're gonna have to work to get my come—wring this cock out over and over again."

"*Fuck.*" Her eyes squeezed tight and he had to look away.

Milo bit her arm inside the elbow and sucked as her pussy spasmed around his cock. His lower back pulled tight in response, every muscle in his body readying to come. He bit higher up her arm, sucked harder, until the feeling passed.

"Keep going," she panted.

"I'm not going to stop." He didn't know when he'd get to do this again, and he was damn set on making the most of it. "Not until you're begging me to."

"I won't." Her back arched. "I can take it. Fuck me. As long as you want."

So he did. He fucked her and fucked her and fucked her through another two back-scratching orgasms. Every time his cock threatened to spill, he locked on to the challenge in Benj's eyes as she held, refusing to yield, until he wasn't sure how much more either of them could take.

"You done?" he asked, sweat sliding between them, her legs loose at his waist.

The ends of her hair were drying in wavy chunks, not the sleek curtain he was used to. The vibrator on his cock had long-stopped buzzing.

Benj started to nod and Milo slammed harder into her. "Then beg."

Her poor cunt must have been aching, swollen and red from his raw treatment of it. She bit her lip and he pounded into her again, the tendons of his legs beginning to cramp. A whimper escaped her and he almost stopped. But he wanted it his way—being selfish had never felt so good. And he kept thrusting until she released her lip and tilted her chin back, exposing her throat.

"Milo—"

He started to come before she finished. His mouth crashed into hers, desperate and needy, open on a groan, hoping she'd give him the rest.

"*Please.*"

Daily Star–t
Thursday, April 21

Today you're a bagpipe—you can scream until you're out of air but not a lot of people want to hear it.

Chapter Nineteen

Gripping her phone in one hand and wrinkling a satin pillowcase in the other, Benj stood over the bed, seething at Milo's guiltless sleep. They'd both slept like the dead after last night, giving the day a head start without them, missing what had turned out to be an eventful morning.

"What the fuck did you do, Fox?"

The sheet slipped down his torso as his feet stirred the blankets at the end of the bed. He rubbed his eyes and squinted up at her. "You?"

Benj whipped the pillow at him with a satisfying thwack. "Why would you talk to the media?"

"I wouldn't?" Milo caught the pillow and pulled. If she'd let go, she would have kept her footing. Instead she'd grasped tight, and already looming over him, fell forward, her knee connecting with his ribs. His groan of protest urged her further forward and she climbed over him, pinning him to the mattress, and holding her phone over his face so he could wake up to Mina's voice mail too.

Nelle's manager spoke rhythmically through the speaker as she read. *"A source close to the couple can confirm the two are inseparable, 'practically liv-*

*ing together—she might even stay with him instead
of going on tour with Nelle.' The aspiring makeup
maven has been on the outs with the singer since she
was overheard badmouthing Kelly's husband's siz-
zling Gordon McKane campaign, going so far as to
say he was working against the body neutrality movement, continuing harmful body imagery messaging."*
A short, static silence followed, and then Mina's voice
punched through the air again. "My concern, as you
might be able to guess, is the phrase: *A source close
to the couple.* Let's think about that, shall we? Who
might be talking? And what else are they going to
say? If this gets messy, if there's so much as a Tum-
blr post debunking our story, I'm not going to be able
to recommend that Nelle develop the link between
your names—so this better be the end of it. You need
to land the fucking plane, Benj. And keep the optics
clean. No. More. Turbulence."

One of Milo's hands had found her thigh while they
listened, comfortably possessive over her dusty-rose
yoga set. And why wouldn't he be? He'd literally had
her begging for him last night. He'd had her salivating over those deliciously indecent things he'd been
saying. The key to dirty talk was conviction and Milo
fucking had it. When sex was the topic on the table,
Milo knew all the right things to say.

His other hand scratched at the scar on his hairline,
his ropy arm bent just as it had been all night, serving
as her pillow while she curled up next to him. Completely spent after he'd squeezed every drop of juice
out of her just to prove he could.

And now that she knew what he was capable of…
Benj swallowed. While technically she was dressed,

the way he was looking up at her made her feel naked and on display—another unfortunate, sidetracking echo to the night before. Before the begging and the salivating and the squeezing. A flashback to the last moment she'd lied to herself, thinking she had a handle on things between them.

Realizing she was in control of the pillow again, Benj brought it down on Milo's head once more, breaking off his all-too-knowledgeable gaze. "Were you even listening?"

"Ow. What? Yes—somebody sold a story. What else is new?"

"Not somebody. You. *You* talked to the press. *You* told them I'm on the outs with Nelle."

"Why would I do that?"

"I don't fucking know! But you were the only one there at Modrić's when I said that shit about Bran."

"Someone else must have overheard—a maid or—"

"That would be convenient, wouldn't it? Let's blame the people who are just doing their jobs." She hit him again and he snatched the pillow away from her, tossing it aside as he sat up.

"I didn't do that." Milo's eyes bore into hers, intensely brown and solid all the way through. "We're on the same team, Ben." His arm went around her middle, securing her to him, making her intensely aware of her spread legs straddling his lap. *Thank god* for the spandex barrier between them or he'd already know that she'd started to melt again, when she wanted so badly to ice him out. "Do you believe me?"

She hoisted off him, shoving at his chest. "It doesn't matter whether I do or not. This is getting completely out of control. You might be willing to gamble with your career, but I'm not. This is my *life*."

"Yeah, it's my life too."

"No it isn't, Milo! You can weather rumors and have Max pay off photographers and even have him sue production for you and you'll still be Grant Fox's grandson, prince of fucking film."

"I'm not suing anybody. Production paid my medical bills and they're updating their safety procedures and equipment—that's all I wanted. And fuck Grant Fox, that misogynistic coke addict." Milo rose from the bed, letting the sheet crumple to the ground at his feet, his body taut and bare. He took a beat, a powerful one. One that distracted her from the surface-level shock of seeing just how hung he was in the daylight—of realizing he wasn't the farm boy, he was the bull.

Fuck Grant Fox? What the fuck was that supposed to fucking mean?

Hours ago, she'd wanted him to talk. To tell her things. Real things. True things. To connect with her on a deeper, more meaningful level. He hadn't understood—and that was fine. That was better. Getting deeper would have only made it harder to climb out of this hole she was in.

Benj held back the questions surging through her mind. They didn't need answers. She fought the urge to prompt him, the urge to dig into him and get to the bottom of whatever had set his chest heaving across the room.

Every time Milo revealed something about himself, it was harder for her to remember that old version of him. The one she could easily villainize, the one that was categorically bad. Every time she learned something new about Milo, she liked him more. Just as he was.

She wasn't going to ask. She wasn't going to deliver him the upper hand. Not when he could so easily take it for himself.

And then, just like that, he did.

"Would you believe I only met him once?"

"Your grandfather, the actor slash misogynistic coke addict?"

Milo's smile lifted one cheek before dropping away. "Mom kept that to herself when we were kids. Waited to tell us the whole story—that he was famous for more lines than we knew—she let us fall for his act first. I guess she wanted us to love him, like she did. To know him the only way we could, through a screen, through the characters he played. It worked. He was everything we wanted to be. Brave and strong and heroic. We saw him the way the world saw him."

How could it be that Milo had known Grant Fox from the same distance she had? "And when you met him?"

"Mom got him to come to dinner because he was filming in Virginia for *Song of Myself.* We'd never warranted an extra flight." Milo moved closer, drifting slow on the memory. "I remember how lively he was—this larger-than-life persona telling Mom, 'This is the one. This is the part. This is how they're going to remember me.' But the power went out. I didn't—I didn't like the dark. Or the ocean. Still can't stand planes. So I was scared. I was a kid. And then—the one time, the only time—that I was face-to-face with *the* Grant Fox—this human representation of valor—he looks me dead in the eye and says, 'You're not scared, are you?' Then he hit me with that movie-star smile, quoted some line from fucking Whitman like I'd know what it meant, and told me, as the oldest, it was my job to set an example, to take care of Jackson."

Her stomach twisted as he hooked her with his gaze.

"You wanna know the punch line? I'm not the oldest. Jackson's got six minutes on me." Milo reached both hands to cradle her face, angling her gaze up to his. "That man didn't know me at all. But I let him tell me who he thought I should be. I let him shape my whole life. But when I stopped to think about it, I saw through the bullshit. How he left us this place. *Not* his daughter. *Not* our older sister. Us. Two idiot teenage boys—because we were the ones who could extend his legacy. That's all he cared about. As if we owed it to him. And I took it, like I deserved it. I'm done being a part of his bullshit. I'm quitting, Ben."

Benj was breathing hard, again Milo had sucked up all the oxygen in the room and left too little for her, painting himself as a reluctant prince, trapped in his hilltop tower. Her question sounded too light, almost flimsy. "Quitting what?"

"This." He held his arms wide. "All of this. Acting and LA and being someone for everyone else."

She could only take that one clause at a time. Milo was quitting acting? No way. It had been so important to him—he'd tossed her over to make his dumb movie better. Acting was who he was. "What about *Twin Pistols 3*?"

"They're gonna have to do it without me."

Benj pinched her waist, feeling inexplicable tears in her eyes. Emotion that she didn't understand, that wasn't completely her own. "Like Lindsay Lohan in *The Parent Trap*?"

"Like it isn't my problem what they do, or who is disappointed or who loses money—I don't care. There's an out in my contract about accidents and I'm taking it. I don't want this. I've never wanted it. I'm starting over doing something else—that's what I came here to tell Jackson. Once I do that, I'm gone." He held her face again, his eyes flickering to her mouth, waiting for a response. "Go on."

"Go on and what?"

"Call me selfish."

Internalized judgment had brought the word to the tip of her tongue. How could he not finish the trilogy he'd signed on for? People were supposed to follow through, no matter what.

Right?

Benj raised her chin. "I would. I'm just not sure, given that backstory, that I'd be right." She turned the volume down on her mother's voice, testing out her own opinion on Milo. "People should be allowed to change their minds."

"I didn't change my mind—I finally made it up."

Her head swam with his conviction. In that moment, she believed him, believed he knew what he wanted and that he wouldn't stop until he got it. But out of everything he'd said, there was one word that stuck in her mind—a word that, when she'd heard it, caused an unexpected, off-center thump in her chest. "What does 'gone' mean? Where are you going?"

"Home."

The way he said it, with such longing, such hope, answered any follow-ups she might have had. Home to Milo wasn't *here*. He'd never acclimated, hell, he'd never updated his phone number.

"That's where you've been?" she asked, already knowing the answer. Not beach bumming, not jet-setting. He'd gone home to get better. And home for Milo had never changed from that farm in Maryland where he'd grown up.

While Benj had her allegiance to Wisconsin—who wouldn't proudly rep a place that revered beer and cheese so openly?—she wasn't planning to move back, like ever. Her life was here. Not just because she felt free living out of view of her parents, but because she'd built it herself. Maybe he'd feel the same if he'd had to work harder to earn his own fame—fame he couldn't escape just by running away from it.

"But everyone will still know who you are—you're Milo Fox."

"No. I'm Milo Miller. Fox is my middle name. It's only a part. They don't know me. Took me the last year to put together that I didn't either. That I wasn't clear on what I wanted. I've fixed that now. I know what matters to me and what fucking doesn't."

Wetting her bottom lip, Benj tasted salt on her tongue. "And what do you want now?"

"For you to trust me. To believe me. I'm not going to hurt you again. I'd never be the source of an article that makes you look bad." They stared at each other, Benj warming under his touch, captivated by the simple truth in his eyes. A slow, triumphant smile began on his face. "You do. You do believe me."

"Okay. So what if I do? What are we going to do about the press?" Benj crossed her arms—and uncrossed them when Milo's gaze dropped directly to the peekaboo tit-slit of her razor-back yoga bra.

"Not much we can do but stay here today. Lay low. Maybe call a truce."

"A truce?"

"A ceasefire. No rules. No games. We can be ourselves."

"And what would we do? Here. All day. Together."

"What do you like to do? When you want to feel like yourself?"

"Draw."

"So, you can draw. I can swim."

"It's low impact? For your knee?"

He nodded. "And I like how it drowns out the world. Keeps me focused on my own thoughts. When you draw—"

"Yeah, same. I'm in it for the presence." She was in it to root herself in the moment. It was the best tool she'd found for grounding herself—until Milo.

"You draw. I swim. I've got some calls to make." The firm press of his knuckle under her jaw pulled her spine straighter, her body drawing up against his. "Or—"

"Or what?" Her interruption did little to derail him. She wasn't sure she wanted it to. But she had to get some things in perspective. For starters, at the end of the week this would be over. The gig was only booked until Sunday. Next week, Nelle's schedule kicked into gear with a press tour for the album's release, followed by a real tour that would take them all over the world. A hundred flights to Milo's one. They were both leaving. There was no future here, only a past and a present. A beginning and an end.

"Or. I could tell you I already miss you." The heavy

heat of his dick grew at her side and she told herself not every challenge required a response. "The way you feel wrapped around me. The sounds you make when your little pussy milks my cock. Helpless thing, can't stop herself."

"That's not fair. You said ceasefire. You're still playing to win."

"Who's playing? How wet are you now, Ben? I bet it'd take nothing to get into that tight, hot box between your legs. I could make myself at home without any effort. And you'd welcome me right on in." He traced down her spine, rounding a palm over her ass and giving it a rough squeeze. "If I were playing, I'd tell you I'm not going to touch you. I'd say it just to make you ache, thinking about what I *could* do to you."

"But you're not playing?" She was light-headed, swaying—maybe? Falling—for sure. The floof of his comforter caught her.

Milo bent over her, his hands pressing into the mattress on either side of her head. "No. I'm not."

In the face of that, without any other workable options, Benj did the least sexy thing a woman could do: tried to squirm out of her sports bra. A mess of elbows and elastic, she bought herself some space, a moment where Milo backed off, enough time and room for her to think about how to regain some desperately needed control.

"On your sink, next to my bag, there's a jar of coconut oil."

"Why?"

"Because, as previously discussed, I take moisturizing very seriously."

"Why do we need coconut oil?"

Benj kneaded her breasts and dropped back on the down, looking up at him as she tweaked her own nipples into hard points. "Because you've been thinking about fucking these titties for three years. And I'm about to let you."

Chapter Twenty

Maybe he had died after all, Milo thought, retrieving the requested jar of coconut oil from his bathroom. He grabbed his glasses too—this was something he needed to see in perfect focus.

Benj was waiting for him where he'd left her. In his bed. On her back. Tits-up topless. An aerial shot he committed to memory immediately. Her head rested on the pillow he'd wrestled away from her, her face was tilted up, and her eyes, tracking his movements, were full of daring.

He hadn't meant to tell her about quitting. He'd been so dead set on making sure Jackson heard it first. But it was like all those filthy truths he'd been lobbing her way somehow made the real talk easier. And Benj wanted to know. He could feel it like pressure in his eardrums, growing worse the longer he tried to keep it to himself. He didn't know why he'd even bothered—he wasn't sure there was anything he could deny her. Not when he wasn't running from uncomfortable feelings anymore, but naming them and facing them head-on.

Not when the result of giving in looked like this.

Each detail of the scene seemed to fragment into separate sensations. The spring sun bouncing off the windows, dancing over the floor, the bed, the walls. The metallic scrape of the jar's lid twisting away from the glass. The waxy give of solidified, opaque oil on his fingertips. The exotic waft of coconut as it melted on her hot skin. His hands slipping through the smooth valley of her breasts. The perfect mise-en-scène.

Milo straddled Benj's torso, the mattress giving way to his weight like shifting sand. His thighs trapped her ribs, and he felt very much on his knees despite his position over her. There was no doubt in his mind who was pulling his strings. His cock was tight, and so sensitive he worried he might come while lubing himself up.

But this wasn't a chance he was going to waste.

Running his hand down the length of his cock, he drew it up at the tip and let it drop down to Benj's chest with a rewarding slap he felt at the back of his throat. Her back arched at the impact and she squeezed those soft tits together, surrounding his cock with warmth, with the luxury of her perfect skin. Sitting up straight, he thrust his hips forward, his cock sliding through the glorious tunnel she'd made for him out of her generous cleavage.

He'd never made it to LA. Like he'd always feared, his plane must have dropped from the sky. Killing him instantly. That's how he'd ended up here. It was the only possibility that made any damn sense. When she opened her pearly-white gates so each of his thrusts ended in the lush cave of her mouth, Milo was certain: this was heaven.

He'd transcended. Beyond the push and pull of their hustle. Beyond any hardship he'd ever faced. Benj made everything so simple. Produced perfection so effortlessly. All he had to do was rock his hips and he glided over her, through her, into her. Even taking into account the twinging protest from his left knee, it was the most faultless, unbeatable movement of his life.

Milo never blinked, never lost sight of her, even as his groin constricted and his balls zinged with pleasure. Ecstasy wasn't the destination, because he'd already arrived—when he clamped his hands over hers, wild with possession and forcing her tighter around him, he felt the bigger payoff just over the horizon. Momentum brought him closer to it as his breath faltered, his pace roughened, and his knees crushed her middle. Benj whimpered then and Milo stopped thrusting, taking himself in hand and pumping his cock, teeth clenched.

"You know you want to," Benj urged, her voice hushed and throaty, her lips glistening in the sunlight that still ricocheted around the room. He couldn't tell if it was a challenge or an invitation—but her back arched again, like she couldn't wait for him to do it.

In three hard, fast strokes he did, shooting a blistering ribbon of come onto her bared breasts. His disbelieving hand reached for her, following the stream, painting in the pattern of light and shadow that splattered her skin.

Benj's eyes closed. "Get off me."

For the rest of his life, Milo would hate how slow he was to react—how it took him a moment to process her words. That she had to add a nudge of her hand to get him into motion. He sprang up then, knocking into the dresser behind him, mouth open, wordless with confusion, misunderstanding, zooming in on regret.

The apology Milo tried to voice died on his tongue

as Benj smiled, stumbling up after him. His heart thundered behind her as she pressed the hot silk of her back to his chest. She leaned into him, her hair tickling his neck. Relief and exertion weakened his legs and he relied on the dresser for support, Benj settling between his thighs, shifting her weight on to him. She drew one of his hands to her throat, and brought the other to her mouth, licking his thumb until it glowed in the bright beam of light that slanted across the room to find them.

Her hand on his wrist, Benj guided him down, under the waistband of her form-fitting pants. "Now get me off."

Milo applied himself to the task without hesitation, wedging two fingers into her and searching out her clit with his wet thumb. Benj made it easy for him to find—hiking one knee over his leg and opening herself up to him. A pleasing shudder rocked her body when he hit his mark, flicking the swollen, sensitive spot.

Her head turned toward him, a question passing her lips as natural as breath.

"Who do you have to call today?"

A smile pulled at Milo's cheek. Her desire for answers was incorrigible. Her dirty tactics—asking him now, when he wanted to satisfy her completely, the way she had done for him—were worse.

"I'm looking for a partner—for a business idea." When he'd tried to tell Jackson he was quitting acting the first time, Jackson had pushed back, asking him what he'd do instead. Milo had an answer now. He gave it to Benj willingly. "I've been making sunshine. The way my Pop used to—which is to say, illegally."

She squeezed his thigh with her knee. "You're a bootlegger?"

"Our secret, Ben." He drew his fingers out of her, slowly tracing the seam of her pink lips up to her clit and back down. "I can trust you right?" She nodded through a moan. And he sank his fingers back into her. "I'm done spending my time on what doesn't matter to me. On Grant Fox's legacy. Everyone wants to think they know where we came from. They don't know the whole story."

Pop was the grandfather he wanted to be associated with. The one who'd sat next to him in the high-school auditorium for every one of Jackson's shows. The one who'd had so many dinners with them it was impossible to remember them all. Grant Fox had given him one piece of advice. And Milo had based his world on it. It had felt precious, significant in its rarity. The best advice Al Miller had given him was buried under all the other good memories.

Try wanting something more.

Benj's hips rocked, driving his spinning fingers deeper.

"Sophie Miller is your sister?"

He nodded, his cheek against hers, feeling the flush of her skin through his stubble.

"What's Jackson's middle name?"

He curled his fingers, gripping her from the inside. Her whole body squirmed and he held her tighter to him, his hand cuffing her neck the way she liked. "Grant," he gritted out.

Milo eased back into rhythm when she left his brother out of her next question. "What's your Thiebaud?"

His grin was lost in her hair. "You'd love it. It's a dessert tray."

"Fuck." She started to shake. "Why do you hate flying?"

"Too high," he simplified. "Too far to fall and survive."

She was gasping, going tight and loose in his arms, coming undone, on the cusp of shattering.

"Did you...really...almost die?"

Milo fit his mouth to her neck, sucking at her skin, buying time to answer. She wasn't making it easy now, asking that he put into words what he'd felt a year ago, when he could barely string together a thought.

Her pussy spasmed around his fingers, an aperture closing out the light. Her lips parted but no sound came out. He could feel her holding something back—a shout or a yell—wished she'd let it burst from her, bright and uninhibited as her laughter. Instead she moaned, long and low and reserved. He stroked her through it, hugging her close to him as her body sagged, heavy as the realization in his gut that he'd give all of himself for a little more of her.

Her orgasm receding, he lifted his mouth, his answer an unscripted dénouement to her climax.

"Yes. I busted my knee—it still doesn't feel right. My head—couldn't focus on anything for a few months. I was living in a fog that just wouldn't clear. That's better now. But I still get headaches when things are too loud or bright. And I'll always remember thinking it was over." Milo had never told anyone how it felt to fall, unsure how they'd react to the clarity it brought him. Not sure if they'd understand or take offense at the way he now viewed his old life—a bad dream he'd gotten himself trapped in. But with Benj, Milo had found the freedom to speak, to share what had happened to him when the fog had lifted. With Benj, Milo wasn't afraid to say, "So I'll never forget how it felt to wake up."

Daily Star–t
Friday, April 22

There's nothing wrong with winning when you do it right.

Chapter Twenty-One

Something was buzzing. Something was *always* buzzing. While Benj groped around to try to find out what, her pillow heaved itself up and made for the hallway on its two feet. That only made sense if Benj accepted that she'd slept on Milo Fox. Again.

She sat up, squinting at the sun streaming into the room. They'd missed another morning, having stayed up late, doing all kinds of things that set her heart racing to remember. Like when they sat side by side at the edge of the pool, their feet in the water, the silence comfortable, the night theirs. Or before that, when she'd been boneless on the couch, listening in on Milo's phone calls, trying to capture the depth of his eyes in her sketchbook. He'd hung up and slipped the pencil out of her hand to violently scratch out the name on his list.

"What didn't you like about that one?"

"Pushy. Felt like they were already trying to take over." He slotted the pencil back into her curved palm. "Volume over process. My operation would be…boutique."

"How boutique."

"Sixty bottles a year."

"Milo—just make them yourself! You must know sixty people. I'd take one."

"You would?"

"Yes." She shifted in her seat, making a joke to deflect the intensity of Milo's attention. "Lewis'll probably take five. Be our little bootlegger." Her lower body clenched on the word like it remembered what she'd been doing the last time she'd used it.

"Tempting, if it weren't for the part about it being a felony. And, aside from the potential jail time, selling them under the table wouldn't get the other half of my story told." He stared at the list. "But everyone I talk to wants to make more money."

"You don't want to make more money?"

"If I only wanted to make more money I'd cash in on *Twin Pistols 3.* I want to make something that matters to me, I want it done the way I want to do it." He glanced at the open notebook in her lap and she closed it, embarrassed by the sketch she'd drawn of him.

"How convenient for you, that money doesn't matter."

"That's not—"

She'd cut him off with a kiss, sorry she'd started it. They'd called a truce, after all, and as her tongue tangled with his, she'd admitted to herself how much she enjoyed not being at odds with him. Her voice had come out low and husky when she'd broken away to tease him, "Tell me more about the way you want to do it."

The buzzing stopped. Benj crawled out of the bed and retrieved her sleep shorts from the floor. They'd landed there around dawn. She and Milo had made use of the earliest part of the morning before falling back asleep after exhausting themselves, fucking the way Milo had promised. Sweet and slow. Side by side.

No games, no dirty talk. Only one long kiss, one continuing embrace, Benj's leg over his, as they searched each other out and found a way to come together. And when she'd started to unravel, Milo had smiled into her mouth and pushed into her depths and broken the silence to whisper, "Just like that, Ben."

The memory had her stumbling into the wall as she pulled her shorts up. She caught herself halfway to the bathroom and glanced down the hall to see Milo leaning against a wall of his own. She froze, stopped dead in her tracks. Technically, it wasn't the sight of him that stopped her—though he looked damn fine in absolutely nothing, his knee bent, his ass bare—her own knockoff Michelangelo. What had stopped her short was the unmistakable voice crackling through the intercom telling Milo, "If she doesn't come out, I'm coming in."

Milo's head rolled on the wall so he could see her, his gaze muted under slanted lids. "Jig's up." He pushed a button on the pad and headed toward her, his big dick swinging with purpose. Michelangelo could never.

When he reached her, he palmed one of her cheeks, bringing her forehead to his mouth to plant a kiss on her hairline. Benj's entire being swayed into him, drawn to the warm swaths of his skin that she could feel through the thin satin of her sleep cami and shorts. Her fingers met in the dip at the base of his spine, and she fit perfectly under the curve of his arm. Her nose against his skin, she breathed him in, momentarily forgetting everything except the way it felt to be held close by Milo. Cared for. Secure. Like he wouldn't let go.

The front door shuddered under three heavy knocks.

Symmetry was an important aspect of Benj's work. Most looks were about balance—or disrupting it. Nelle banging on Milo's door like it was a hotel room in Chicago was a little bit of both. She should have seen this replay coming. Nelle had been blowing up her phone, threatening to come over. Benj would have responded, called her off, if she'd thought for a second Nelle would be huffing and puffing at the right fucking door.

Ducking out from under Milo's arm, her feet curling against the cool tiles, Benj made it to the door before Nelle opened up her lungs and started yelling. The latch snicked and her best friend stood on the threshold, using every inch of her limited height.

"How did you find me?"

"Oh, so you were hiding?" The accusation hung in the air. And then Nelle blew it away with a sigh. "I had the police ping your cell to the nearest tower—what do you think? I went to your place and you weren't there so I asked Mina for the Foxes' address. You weren't answering my calls. Or my texts. Or my restaurateurs."

"I know, I'm…" Benj faltered, not sure how to explain what was going on with her. Not sure she even knew. The last day with Milo had been like stepping out of time—a pause, a break from reality. With Nelle here, that day was swallowed up and gone, like the hour that no longer existed when daylight savings sprang them all forward. "You're supposed to be in Washington."

"No, I'm supposed to be meeting Bran at home before he heads to his show but I came here instead."

"It's Friday." Benj rested her face on the sharp ridge of the door frame. "Bran is playing the Greek. You haven't seen him in a month and you came looking for me?"

"Yeah, I'm like a really good friend, now let me in so I can see what you've been up to."

Benj hesitated a moment, feeling strange playing host at Milo's house. But he'd disappeared into the bedroom and the only one to see was Nelle, so she held the door wider.

Dropping a white-and-tan Fendi duffel on the slate floor, Nelle surveyed the living area, from the kitchen cluttered with takeout containers to the open doors leading out to the back patio. "Wow."

"You want to see Jane Fonda's footprint?"

Nelle ran a hand along the back of the couch, eyeing the throw pillows on the floor. "No—I mean, yes obviously—but after you tell me what you've been up to since Sunday. Or should I guess."

"You don't need to guess. I've been doing what we talked about. It got a little complicated but Milo and I figured it out. I didn't have time to call. We've been busy."

Nelle raised her eyebrows.

"Helping each other."

Her chin dropped.

"To keep the story straight."

"If I hadn't heard the same from Cormac, I'd say it looks like you two haven't left here all week."

"We needed a break. From pretending."

"If you're pretending out there—what's happening in here? The real thing? And this is what? A little sex intermission between acts? Wait, I can do better: an inter*sex*sion. I thought you fucking hated this guy?"

Benj lurched forward, shushing her friend. As if

Milo didn't know exactly what they'd been up to in this house the last twenty-four hours. As if he didn't know how she felt about him. "Can we not do this here?"

"Yes, I'd have very much liked this meeting to have been an email, Benjamina. But. The aforementioned skipping of calls and other communication methods." Hurt bruised Nelle's big amber eyes. "I thought you were mad at me for making you do this."

"Pretty sure I volunteered."

"Then why haven't you called me back?"

That was the million-dollar question. Benj flopped down to the couch. "If I called you. I'd have to talk about it."

Nelle lowered herself to perch on its arm. "And you're not talking about it?"

"I'm not." Not with Milo. Not with Nelle. Not even with herself. Benj didn't know how else to explain. She lifted her hands helplessly. "Yesterday I was a bagpipe."

Nelle slipped down to the cushion next to her and nodded knowingly. "I was a bagpipe last week."

Her easy acceptance of Benj's nonsense answer proved Benj had the best friend in the world. "I should have texted you back. Even just to say I wasn't ready to text you back."

"I would have appreciated that."

"You really haven't seen Bran yet? Even though he's in town?"

"I'm meeting him at the show. You wanna come with?"

Benj nodded. She needed to get back to her real life eventually. "I'd love to. You want me to make you look so hot your husband rethinks every moment he spent away from you?"

"Please. I was trying to figure out when it was appropriate to turn this into a business transaction."

Benj laughed and stood, hauling Nelle up after her. "Let's step into my office."

After grabbing a stool from the kitchen island and motioning for Nelle to bring along her bag, Benj started down the hall. Milo emerged from his door, fully dressed in dark jeans and a maroon hoody.

Since she was already playing hostess, Benj swung the chair at Milo and then Nelle, reintroducing them. "Milo, I think you know Nelle."

"In name—and what I've heard."

"Yeah, and, Nelle, you remember Milo."

"You're the guy now, huh?"

"Super." That was enough of that. Benj turned sideways, letting the metal legs go wide, forcing Milo down one side of the hall and Nelle the other. "Well. We've got some work to do, so—"

"I'm gonna make coffee." Milo hugged the wall, trying to avoid the chair. "You want some?"

"No, thanks. But—" Benj hiked up the stool "—save the grounds for me."

"Do you garden now?" He guessed again as she laughed and moved on. "Do you compost?"

"I shower." She added over her shoulder, "It's an excellent exfoliant."

Nelle was silently laying out her toiletries on the sink when Benj arrived in the bathroom. Too silently.

"What aren't you saying?" Benj set the stool in front of the mirror and readjusted it, pushing it toward the glass wall that looked out on the side of the hill for better light.

"You're not talking about it."

"No, I'm not." Benj balanced herself on the edge of the sink, going up on her tiptoes. She lowered herself back down. "So what's the look we're going for?"

Nelle hopped into the chair and folded her hands in her lap, the picture of poise, if you ignored the wicked look in her eyes. "I've got one of his concert tees—so, superhot superfan?"

Wetting her hands, Benj sifted them through Nelle's short hair, encouraging the curl by twisting damp strands into coils. She'd tease it up a bit later, zhuzh it into giving "already fucked."

As Benj prepped and primed Nelle's face, she relaxed. Steady hands applied Nelle's fake lashes and after a quick test on her wrist, she penciled around Nelle's eyes, using a Q-tip to purposefully smudge the black into a sooty line under the lower lash. She filled in the quiet less intentionally. It was natural to talk while she worked. The part she was unpracticed at was talking about herself. "And if I were talking about it?"

"I'd be all ears."

"I'm worried I'm doing it again."

"Doing what?" It was only when Nelle whispered back that Benj realized how quietly she'd spoken.

"Making this…more than it is. Getting ahead of myself. I mean. It's been like four days."

Nelle blinked up at the ceiling, her chin raised. "Sometimes that's enough."

"You knew Bran for a year."

"And you've known Milo for three."

"But it's different for us." She tapped excess powder off a brush and Nelle closed her eyes so Benj could create a smoky shadow on her lids. Illusion was what she was good at. Like pretending she'd moved on from what had happened three years ago. Maybe that was *delusion*—it certainly was when she told herself this time would be different. Benj shifted her feet. "I'm not going to make the same mistake twice, not now that I know better."

"People make mistakes. They do and they say the wrong things. It's only human."

Benj wished she could apply that logic to herself as easily as the shadow she swept over Nelle's eyelid. It was indisputably human to be imperfect, but she'd grown up with the expectation that she'd make all the right decisions anyway.

"I'm not falling for him again."

"Why not?"

"Because…" She'd already decided not to.

She slotted the brush into its place in the travel organizer open on the counter and closed up the eye shadow palette. Her fingers danced over the lipsticks and liners waiting in order next to it. To her core, she was intentional. Benj had learned to set her expectations and meet them.

She'd also learned to tell herself true things. And she knew deep down it was a problem that she discounted Nelle's comment about mistakes being human, that she resisted applying it to herself. She knew it wasn't right that she wasn't sure of her own voice when she'd told Milo people should be allowed to change their minds.

But changing her mind on this came with a risk. And not the broad fear of messing up, of having known better. Benj was afraid of feeling what she felt last time. Of going through that pain again. The goal she'd set was to protect herself—didn't that deserve her commitment?

"It can hurt," Benj said simply.

Nelle nodded, her eyes warm with understanding. "It can hurt."

"I wish there were a way to be sure it wouldn't. I want to know… I want to know if I can trust…" The way he made her feel. Special. Capable of magic.

She'd done that once and never fully recovered.

"What you want right now is certainty," Nelle said, sounding not unlike a Daily Star–t push notification. She sat back while Benj added two shades of lip liners to the growing palette on her wrist. "You're used to being the one with all the answers. The one who knows what to say. What would you tell me? If I'd sat here and laid this out for you?"

"I'd tell you…"

She'd tell Nelle she was a literal daydream who could do anything she wanted because she was full-stop unstoppable. She'd tell Nelle that because it was true. About Nelle. Nelle was rich and famous and talented and Benj was—well, not rich or famous, but she couldn't allow herself to downplay her talent. Wouldn't allow herself to perpetuate the narrative her parents created about her job not being good enough. That lob she'd given Nelle—that was iconic. And Skylar Davies had asked for Benj by name. She'd made a life for herself, one that left her happy and fulfilled, and she'd keep on making it, giving it her all, like she had every day since deciding to put herself first.

"I'd tell me…" Benj changed the start of her answer.

What did *she* need to hear? "That nothing is certain. And not to worry about forever. I'd tell me that if at the end of the day, I want another, I should take it."

"Choose a day, choose a week, whatever you want."

Benj shook her head. She couldn't tell Nelle Milo's secret, that he was talking about bucking the action star creed: he wouldn't be back. *If* that were true—it sounded unbelievable when she repeated it in her own head—it was stupid to even mention forever. Forever had never been on the table. If Milo proved he could back up his talk, they'd both be gone before next week was out.

And yet she knew Milo wanted her. She could feel it in the pure devotion of his touch. She had tasted the raw desire on his tongue. Maybe they did have a chance to try again. But if she gave it to him, what would he do with it? Could she trust him to prioritize what she needed from him, over his own wants? He'd made a start, chipping away at her doubt by following her rules, helping her protect Nelle's reputation.

Milo knocked at the door then. A steaming mug in one hand, he set a bowl of used coffee grounds on the counter.

Benj nodded her thanks and finished coating Nelle's mouth with a creamy pink lipstick. She could sense Milo watching her, still standing at the door, as she tried to keep her focus on Nelle, dotting highlighter in the corner of her eyes, the tip of her nose and chin. "You should change and then I'll do your hair and any touch-ups."

Sorting through her bag on the counter, Nelle held up two options, a denim skirt with two rows of buttons and a pair of patent-leather leggings.

"The skirt, no question."

Milo settled onto the counter to let Nelle pass.

Benj's phone buzzed. "It's Vanessa," she told Milo. "She's making plans for everyone to have another dinner tonight."

"Here we go again."

Benj stretched one arm across her body, holding it there with her wrist. "No—I'm not going. Nelle invited me to Bran's concert."

"One-man show then." He offered her the coffee, which was glossy and black the way he preferred. Jackson probably didn't stock oat milk or almond milk or coconut milk, but she couldn't help reading into that mug of unsweetened bitterness, filing it as counterproof that he'd pick her happiness over his own.

It was exhausting flashing hot and cold about Milo, her thoughts bouncing back and forth analyzing everything he said and did. The only reprieve she got was the balm of his touch, driving away her worries and planting her in the present.

"See you Sunday?" Her stomach flipped as she said it, at the realization that she wasn't ready to wrap things up.

Milo set the coffee aside and grabbed her hand. His agonizing, treacly eye contact had been sending her from the moment he'd walked in and started watching her with Nelle—and now he licked his thumb.

Fuck.

"Or—" Her breath growing heavy, Benj watched Milo try to clean up her wrist with his thumb. She didn't know how much more of him she could have, let alone how much more she could take. But she knew she wasn't done. "You could join us. At the show."

Only managing to smudge the lines of makeup, Milo brought her wrist to his mouth, sucking at her skin. Her pulse shot through the roof. Could he feel it throbbing in her veins, coaxed into a frenzy by the hot lashes of his tongue?

His hands found her face, cupping it and pulling her willing body into his. "What about Vanessa?"

She bartered for Saturday too. "Invite everyone over for dinner tomorrow. They all seemed interested in seeing the house."

On Saturday night she would have to go home, to prepare for work on Sunday. But she'd see him at the wedding, the final act where they could flirt and dance and close it out on a high note. Better than last time.

"I want you to come," she told him. "I'd like that."

Milo dug into her hair, raising a warning prickle across her scalp. "Just that, Ben?"

He was going to kiss her and she was inclined to let him. Nothing was more certain than that. Except that this would be over soon—and that she wanted to make believe a little longer. At least she wouldn't be caught out this time. At least she knew how to land on her feet. She could give in to him a little more, while keeping in mind the end was near. While keeping her heart at a safe distance. The answer left her lips before his mouth claimed hers, before she familiarized herself with his familiar sweetness, a counterpoint to the bitter coffee on his tongue.

"Just for now."

Chapter Twenty-Two

Milo had been looking forward to the weekend. No, he wasn't where he'd planned to be. He hadn't succeeded in announcing his retirement yet, or made his swift return to the family farm, or found the perfect partner to help him get Sunshine off the ground. But since their truce, Benj had been unquestionably more open with him—and not just when he was balls-deep in her pussy, willing to say anything she wanted to hear to stay there. Tonight, she'd even invited him into her real life, where he'd get to laugh and dance and slip one hand under her cropped tie-dye hoodie, the other into the pocket of her frayed jean shorts. Tomorrow, they'd have all day together before the cast of *-endships* arrived for dinner. And on Sunday, he'd be her date to a big showboat of a wedding that was sure to include drinks and food and laughs.

They had made new plans. Plans that kept them together. What wasn't exciting about that?

Then Milo climbed into Nelle's black SUV, and Benj turned to the driver and said, "This is Jackson."

He'd never heard three worse words. The final one set off a tiny missile that exploded in his chest. A real-life arret: the stop-motion magic of his anticipation disappearing from the moment.

The introduction stuck in the back of his throat, a hard lump he couldn't quite swallow. His contacts swam in his eyes as he held his breath. Right: he was Jackson. Of course. It wasn't that he'd forgotten, exactly, it was that he'd spent the last day and a half living his own best fucking life. Even when Benj had swiveled her hips between his knees, applying concealer to his scar, her touch had felt indulgent, lingering where she normally utilized efficiency, lenient where she used to be strict. It had felt like a return to their story—not Jackson's.

Milo let out a breath that burned like smoke, berating himself for getting hyped on an alternate reality. Nothing they had planned for this weekend was about *being* together—it was all to be *seen* together. Benj hadn't explicitly mentioned the PR angle when inviting him to the concert, but she must have thought about it. She must have figured that the perfect answer for that article alleging her rift with Nelle was a united front, a friendship parade at Bran's show.

Benj cared how things looked, cared that they got the job done right. Her primary goal since Sunday had been proving she and Jackson were a pair of indisputable, unproblematic lovebirds. He couldn't expect that to have changed after less than a week. After two nights in his bed.

Sitting in the row in front of him, Benj never looked back. She hadn't seemed to notice that Milo'd said nothing since reprising his role. While they crawled up the 101, she was fully engaged in conversation with Nelle, talking over more plans—ones that extended beyond his run. Milo didn't want to hear about the press stops next week, the six-month tour after that. He regretted ever leaving the house. He'd had Benj alone. All to himself. Why had he agreed to go anywhere?

Because she'd have left, with or without him. And being with her was all he'd considered when making his decision. If he'd have thought harder about it, he'd have remembered the catch, that to earn time with her, he had to continue playing his part.

The sun stretched long rays across the sky as Nelle's driver pulled into a parking lot to the side of the venue. A loading area surrounded by trees, it was mostly empty, barring three guys tossing around a baseball. Milo recognized the big-shouldered one right away: Benj's buddy Cormac. He barely had a moment to revisit the jealousy he'd felt the other night at the man's restaurant, when a second guy, the bearded one nearest to the car, handed the ladies out, earning a huge easy smile from Benj and Milo's eternal envy.

Milo wanted to bottle everything about that smile—except the bitter flavor of it being for someone else.

Benj brushed the man's shoulder. "I never got back to you about dinner, did I?"

"Don't worry about it."

She nodded and half turned to include Milo. "Arlo, this is—"

"Ben's date." Milo thrust his hand forward for a sharp, strong shake.

He ignored Cormac, who stretched an elbow over his head, muttering, "This fucking guy."

"He's not so bad," Nelle argued, hugging Cormac, completing the meet and greet. As she settled back on her feet, Milo sensed a tension mounting and followed the rest of their gazes to the third player, still standing across the lot. A quick squint brought the man's face into focus: Bran Kelly.

They all had eyes on Bran, but Bran was watching Nelle. He was watching Nelle like a sailor from a ship, finally sighting the shores of his homeland after months at sea. He'd taken off his hat, holding it over his heart as if he could hear an anthem in his mind, playing just for him at the sight of her.

When Bran started forward, the other two guys stepped back and Benj grabbed Milo's hand, pulling him closer—no, out of the way. Nelle waited, defenseless, eyes locked on the torpedo coming toward her.

At three feet away, Bran dropped his hat, at two he bent, and, as he took his final step, he wrapped his still-gloved hand behind her, never having removed the leather. He crashed through Nelle, his battering-ram momentum sending them into the broad side of the parked livery vehicle. Nelle absorbed the impact, teetering up on her tiptoes, her arms thrown around his neck, her mouth fusing to his.

If words were exchanged between them, Milo couldn't hear. He didn't need to. The intensity with which they came together said it all—a montage of brutal need. His throat went tight and he held fast to Benj's hand.

Cormac stretched his other elbow, his torso pivoting on his hips. "There's a crowd on the other side of this car that would love a preview of the show if you guys want to go for it."

"Greenroom?" Bran buried his hand in Nelle's dark hair, his mitt cupping her ass.

"Too far." She pulled at his bottom lip with her teeth, startling Milo.

Bran groped for the handle on the SUV's back seat door and popped it open. He leaned into the cab. "Albi, Cormac's going to take you over to craft services."

The driver climbed out from behind the wheel as Bran maneuvered Nelle back inside. Both doors slammed shut, and Cormac clapped his hands together. "So, refreshments?"

The three other men started toward the building, but Milo stood frozen to the spot, staring at the car, recalling Benj describing Bran and Nelle's relationship as perfect. He could see where she was coming from: Nelle and Bran weren't holding back. They gave zero damns about who was watching, and it certainly didn't seem like there were any rules between them. If that's what Benj wanted, he'd sign on the dotted line.

Benj tugged on Milo's hand. "Come on, Jackson."

That wasn't what she wanted.

When he resisted another tug, her eyebrows arched. "You're not trying to peep in there?"

"What? No." He let her pull him along to prove it.

"Good, you'd burn your eyes—it's nuclear at this point." Her tone was light, her steps fluid as she led him after the others. "Since he's been gone and she's been here. That's why I told her to wear the skirt."

He couldn't tell if she was putting on a good show or at ease among her friends. Wanting desperately to give her the benefit of the doubt, Milo cleared his throat. "Now she's going on tour? They don't mind that they never see each other?" Was that part of being perfect?

"Oh, don't get me wrong, they mind. But both their careers matter, so they do it when they have to. Now that they don't, Bran's coming with us."

His pace stalled. "But he just got home. He's going

to fly all around the world again?" Milo swallowed another lump lodging in his throat.

"He just got *back*. Home is where she is. I think it's like that when you know."

"Know what?"

Benj shook her head and dragged him forward, leaving Milo to mull over the longing in her voice as they made their way backstage. While everyone else ate and made small talk, he retreated into himself, fixated on Benj. She laughed easily and often. Her eyes glowed bright and sparkly, being with her friends a natural catchlight. Did she really want what Nelle had? A perfect husband, a perfect career, a perfect public profile?

"Jackson." Benj caught his eye from within the group and waved him over to her side. Her eyes widened with warning when he didn't budge. She excused herself and came to him. "You okay tonight?"

"No."

"Do you need some water or do you want—"

"I want you."

She laughed without hesitation. Like he'd been joking. "Then act like it. Santino wants to talk to you."

"About what?"

"I don't know, maybe he's a fan. It wouldn't kill you to try a little harder here." Benj worried her bottom lip, looking around the room. These were her real friends, this was her real life—Milo didn't want to ruin any part of it. Not again.

He pushed off the wall and she mouthed an exasperated *thank you*, towing him over to the tattooed singer who'd requested a word before motoring back to her group of friends.

Milo offered his hand. "Hey."

Santino pulled Milo in and thumped his back. "Long time, man."

Milo nodded like he knew what that meant. "Yeah. I haven't seen you since…" He trailed off, hoping Santino would fill in the rest.

"Must've been Lo's tequila launch. But I heard you guys talked on Sunday—did it go well?"

Milo risked a sideways glance at Benj, who was too far away to help. "Well—uh, yeah, really well."

"Glad it worked out. I might be interested in getting involved, if you need another investor—" Santino cut himself off with a grin, his gaze going over Milo's shoulder to Bran and Nelle's entrance—the "messy" look Benj had put together for Nelle one shade messier. "Would you look at these two cats."

Milo used the distraction to drop away into the background again. He pulled out his phone, hoping to get Max on the line—an outlet for his frustration as much as an exit strategy. Unsurprisingly, Max didn't pick up.

Milo wanted to tell himself he was hanging back to avoid the risk, but he forced himself to acknowledge that he couldn't get his act together. This setup was the worst one yet. The pier was supposed to have been a one-off, and he'd mostly been himself. Modrić's had been a surprise, and he'd jumped in without thinking. And while the cast dinners had been torturous in their own way, trying to puzzle out what Benj wanted from him, they'd gotten him close to her when she never would have allowed it otherwise.

Here he couldn't bring himself to wrap an arm around her or go in for a kiss. Now that he'd had her for himself, Milo wasn't interested in doing it for anyone else's benefit. How was he going to do it tomorrow? And Sunday?

The sun went down, the lights went up. The theater settled back into the hills, ready for the show. A side section of pit seats had been sectored off with metal gates and security. At their approach, the audience began to vibrate with excitement. Cameras flashed. More photos for Benj's campaign. People shouted for Nelle's attention. For Santino's. For his. It was like a zoo. Milo kept his head down, trying to follow Benj into the paddock.

A woman who looked like she wore business casual to bed stopped him at the opening. She didn't even glance at the lanyard hanging around his neck, examining his face instead. "You're pretty convincing."

Milo lifted his gaze from his feet. "Am I?"

"More so than your brother. As a cop at least. My mother was LAPD and her biggest pet peeve was watching actors reach across their chests to call something down." The woman brought her left hand up to an imaginary radio on her left shoulder. "You got it right. Jackson didn't commit to the details."

He shifted, his brother's name hurrying his pulse. "I am J—"

"I know who you are."

Benj backtracked to his side, lowering her voice conspiratorially. "Aya always knows everything. She's Bran's *entire* team, and her ear is plugged right into the ground."

The woman, Aya apparently, smirked. "Mina filled me in at lunch today."

Benj's mouth rounded with surprise. "She did?"

"It'll be news on Monday, so I'll let you in early." Aya's voice lowered, causing Benj to lean eagerly in.

"Mina's moving to my office. We figured it would be easier to deal with the Kellys and whatever they do next under the same roof."

"Does Max know?" Milo asked, thinking back to the tirade Max had let loose about mentoring Mina and the respect he felt owed to him because of it.

"Of course Max knows. Mina's a professional. She gave her notice and he's had plenty of time to work out his own plans."

"I can't imagine he's happy about it."

"Counter to what Max may believe, what does and doesn't make him happy has no impact on how the rest of us are making our decisions." Aya inclined her head toward Benj. "There are lots of things in the pipeline—including Basic Witch. This was a good move, but not if he doesn't play along." She looked at Milo again. "You're not convincing me tonight." With that, Aya stepped aside to let him through.

Released from scrutiny, Milo didn't move. Benj's shiny energy had gone matte. From what Aya had said, what he had done. No, what he *hadn't* done. He hadn't been enough Jackson for her today.

Benj recovered herself first and pushed him into the row behind Nelle. A whoop went up from somewhere when she looped her arms around his neck. He tried not to flinch.

"How's this for convincing?" she murmured at his ear.

Milo breathed her in, picking out the coffee that lingered on her skin and left it smoother than marble under the fingertips that he traced up her spine. He tried to soak in the comfort of feeling her up against him, and fight off the repulsion of her real motivation. "What's Basic Witch?"

Her body stiffened, then forcibly relaxed. Her head dropped back to look at him. "It's Nelle's idea for a beauty brand."

"Nelle's?"

"I'd help. It's my area." She blinked back some honesty. "But people would buy it because of Nelle."

His arms tightened around her. "And you only get to be a part of it if you take the Jackson story off her plate?"

Nelle called her name and Benj wriggled free, putting a finger to her nose before leaning over the seats.

Suddenly everything was too bright and too loud. The crowd's reactions battered harsh and unrelenting against his ears, a throb in his head he'd been trying to ignore pulsed painfully, and Milo ached desperately for the quiet of home. He fumbled into a seat, clutching his scalp. His heart pounded unpleasantly in his chest, but at least he was momentarily blocked from view.

A hand—Benj's hand, reassuring and warm—landed on his shoulder. He looked up, finding her eyes. The noise and the lights receded slightly, unable to compete with the cool balance of her gaze.

Milo swallowed. "We need to talk."

Benj nudged at his shoulder to get him standing again. "Show's about to start."

The problem for Milo was that it already had. They were on display. A side act. The B stage. He was afraid that's all they'd ever be. Afraid she really would use him all up, a means of getting what she wanted from someone else.

The lights dropped out. For a half a second, there

was silence. Darkness. Milo drank it in. Then the crowd was erupting. And Bran Kelly took center stage.

Benj's hips began to shake to the beat of the ear-busting opener. When she glanced back at Milo still in his seat, her head shook too. "I want you to dance with me!"

Not a question. Not a command. A statement Milo could do what he wanted with. An opportunity to score points or to lose them—which made no sense. Didn't she know she'd already won? That she could say jump and he'd ask nothing, because she'd already told him to keep quiet when he wasn't being Jackson.

She tugged on his bicep, trying to haul him up. Her touch changed, letting on her frustration. Her grip was rough and painful, her nails digging into his skin. He balled his own fists, like he had something to hold on to.

There was too much commotion for anyone to notice their struggle, but Benj looked around frantically anyway. That light in her eyes had stopped shining. He'd put it out.

Milo's hands flexed as he surged upwards, watching relief soften Benj's mouth. Some inner tightness eased in his chest when she took a breath, nodded her approval, and started swaying to the music again with Milo rocking his shoulders next to her.

If she thought he was playing Jackson, so be it. Milo was acting on something else. He'd spoken his truth when he'd told her, "I don't want to be someone who hurts you again." And Milo planned to deliver on that promise, no matter what it cost him.

Chapter Twenty-Three

He'd almost had her convinced he was someone else, but Benj had known all along that Milo Fox was selfish. She'd known it. She'd known it for three years. Milo Fox—Milo Miller—whoever Milo was claiming to be at any given moment—was unreliable. He said one thing, and then did whatever the fuck he wanted. Including her.

Ever since their truce, maybe before—ever since Benj had added sex into the equation, giving in to wanting him more than she wanted to protect herself from wanting him—the results had been blurry. Blurry, but serviceable. Except Aya had noticed tonight. Aya had found Milo's behavior concerning enough to flag it for Benj's review. And Benj's conclusion: too many goofs. Too many lines flubbed. Too many moments tonight where Milo had straight-up refused to play his part. All adding up to one giant mistake: hers. Thinking he could be trusted to do what he promised when her reputation was on the line.

Maybe the night hadn't been an actual disaster, but it was close enough—it could have been! The bottom line was she didn't trust that it wouldn't be a disaster tomorrow. He couldn't do this again, not in front of the

-endships cast. With Lewis watching, Vanessa watching, *Jem* watching, Milo needed to be all in. Or they'd both be found out.

Clenched between her teeth, Benj's inverted lips began to sting. She bit down harder, waiting to release them until Albi dropped them off at Grant Fox's hilltop getaway—not Milo's smuggler's hideout or prince's prison, but his villainaire lair.

After crossing the threshold, she marched straight into the middle of the living space, spun toward her adversary, and readied for combat. "We have to cancel tomorrow. Unless you can explain: What the fuck was that?"

Milo toed off his pristine sneakers by the door, one hand on the wall for support.

"Hello? You said you wanted to talk. So talk."

He straightened and scratched at his thick stubble. In another week, it'd be as full as it had been when she'd discovered him on Sunday. She wouldn't be there to see it.

Benj pitched a step forward. "Explain. Explain to me why you're suddenly so bad at this. Tonight should have been easy. It was supposed to be fun and instead you left me completely hanging."

"I danced with you when you—"

"That was not dancing, that was all shoulders."

"Now you have rules for what qualifies as—"

"Dancing's not enough! And it's not about the dancing!"

"Would you stop interrupting me?" He crossed the room easily with his long strides. "Better yet, tell me what you want me to say."

She held her elbow, her wrist swinging wide across

her body. Her fingers curled mildly into her palm. "I just want you to be honest."

Milo's shoulders popped. "When have I not been honest? I've told you things *no one* knows. Things I could go to jail for."

"Be honest about tonight. Explain—"

"I didn't feel like doing it."

Benj barked a laugh. "Oh okay, sure—why the fuck not, Milo?"

"I told you, I'm quitting acting."

"*If* that were happening, that's a professional context. This is personal."

"Yeah. It is fucking personal. For me. I'm done playing my brother. I can't wait until this is over. And we can stop pretending we're together."

His words pummeled her chest, unexpected blows she couldn't deflect fast enough. "Super, that's just what I wanted to know." His mouth opened and she steamrolled on, having heard enough. "Why didn't you tell me that *before* we went out to see my friends, and *before* we invited all of Jackson's colleagues over?"

"Because I didn't know!"

Benj's heart jumped in her throat. They were almost touching now, huffing in the same air. Too close if the intention was to stay apart.

Too close.

She'd let herself get far too close.

It was Milo who stepped back. He threaded his hands behind his head, his elbows wide. "We don't need to be doing this anymore. Not like this, for their benefit. It isn't our business. It has always been between Nelle and Jackson. Let them figure it out."

"It is my business. Nelle is my business."

"Is she? Or are you just as stuck as I was? Lying to yourself, living Nelle's life instead of your own?"

Benj felt as if she'd been slapped. The ringing silence seemed to confirm it. Milo stood staring at her, a crowd of one holding its breath, waiting to see what would happen next.

Don't interrupt. Mind your business. Tell yourself true things, Benjamina.

Milo didn't get to tell her the rules.

"Wow." She drew out the word. "Hot take."

"Ben, I—"

"No. My turn. You asked. I'm answering. I'm not living Nelle's life. And this is the part I want you to be clear on: you don't get to put your shit on me. I'm not taking that on. I make my own decisions. I do what works for me. I don't have a problem being true to myself."

"Like I do?"

"I didn't say it." She held his eye as he dropped his arms back to his sides.

"Okay, I deserved that. Can we start over?"

"Sure, let me just find the clapperboard and we'll go again."

His head rolled on his neck, frustration evident in his half-closed jaw. "I'm trying to apologize."

"Why start now."

"That's not fair. I've said I'm—"

"Milo." She raised one finger to stop him. "Your mouth has proved itself unbelievably capable—but you've never said you were sorry to me, which is the simplest fucking way to apologize."

He nodded for a beat. And then another. "How's this: I'm sorry if it takes me a minute to figure out what to say that will please you—when I know you'll only compare it to some giant gesture of an award-winning song. Or wonder if a pap got a good enough picture of me saying it. You know, the only actual problem you seem to have with my mouth is when I'm not playing along."

She didn't respond. She'd already told him as much. And agreeing to his assessment out loud didn't feel particularly flattering.

"And *forgive me* if I'm still wondering if it's me you want or my brother."

These were Milo's hard feelings, the ones he'd been carrying around, and Benj readied herself for him to unload until he got it all out. But he stopped himself, reaching suddenly across the distance between them to hold her hand. His fingers worked under hers until they were laced together. "What are we doing here, Ben?"

She didn't know. She thought she did. Now it looked like this bright idea of hers—to keep her distance and see the end coming—was as foolish as it sounded. But they still had two days to go.

"We're doing damage control." She squeezed his hand to hide the trembling of her fingers. "Tomorrow you *have* to be a better Jackson—and the wedding—"

"I know. I will." He stared expectantly at her.

Benj bent her ankle self-consciously. "So that's what we're doing."

"But after that…"

Possibility charged those three words.

Benj tried to untangle their hands, tried to settle the panic spiking in her veins. When Milo twisted his wrist to match hers, that panic gained momentum, running wild, her thoughts spurred into action.

There was no *after* with Milo.

She knew that. He'd just said as much. He'd said he was tired of being forced to be with her. Unless she'd misunderstood. What if he was saying—

No. He couldn't be. She wouldn't let him. She couldn't hear him say there was a way to make it work, make it last, because she didn't trust herself not to believe him. She wouldn't be outfoxed by a man who made promises she knew he was incapable of keeping.

"Let go of me."

He did, though he still held her in the grip of his inflexible gaze. A muffled buzzing filled the silence. Milo wrestled the phone from his pocket and swore at the call screen. Benj resisted the urge to throw up her hands when he picked up. As insulting as it was that he'd take a call right now, she needed the time-out to regroup, to push herself back. But when he switched the call to speaker, bad habits pulled her in.

"Max. I've been waiting for you to call me back since Monday."

"Kid, have I got some news for you—"

"Did you get Benj fired from *Twin Pistols 2*?" Milo dipped his chin at her wide eyes, encouraging her closer.

"Who? What?"

"Benjamina Wasik." Milo looked at her apologetically before adding, "'The blonde.'"

Benj bit the inside of her cheek, her head shaking. The worst of men lacked creativity.

"She did my makeup on set. There was a thing—I kissed her—"

"Is that that same girl—I really don't remember. Too

much going on now to be thinking about something that happened, what? Five? Years ago?"

"Humor me." Milo folded one arm over his chest, the other holding the phone between them.

For a moment, Benj thought the line had gone dead. Milo had tried, but he couldn't give her the closure she wanted on that time in her life. She started to curl her fingers over his arm to tell him not to bother.

Then Max spoke. "I had to get involved, Milo—you weren't focused. We were worried about your performance. Your heart wasn't in it. I'm always gonna help you put your career first. That's what managers do—"

"Let me stop you there. You're not my manager anymore." Milo shrugged one shoulder and nodded, like he approved of his own rash decision. "Wish I could say it's been real, Max." With a stretch of his thumb, he ended the call before meeting her gaze. "I don't want to waste time fighting, Ben. Not with Max. Not with you."

His phone arced through the air, landing with a bounce on the couch. Milo flashed his palms at her in surrender. His dark eyes glittered eagerly as he looked at her.

Had that just happened? What did it mean that he'd fired his manager over her?

Nothing, not if he was quitting acting anyway.

Maybe everything, if he didn't end up going through with it.

Closure was supposed to feel like an ending. This didn't. This felt like starting on a new path with Milo. She couldn't shake the feeling that if Milo was in control, she wasn't.

Milo's lips formed a circle and he breathed through

it, slowing everything down. "Let's do it your way. Skip to the good part. Let's kiss and make up." His fingertips found her hip, five light touches that had no business setting her head spinning like they did. He tilted his chin down, his brows rising into his forehead. Those brown eyes rounded with that exact Milo-made counterfeit innocence that had hooked her in the first place, despite her many misgivings.

That was exactly the kind of behavior that had to stop. The kind of behavior that almost convinced her Milo would do anything to make her happy. That look of pure, unadulterated Milo. Milo she couldn't cover up.

"There's no point." Benj sought refuge in her old excuses. "Nobody's watching."

"No point? What have we been doing here the last two days? What do you call all that?" Milo's arm swung toward his room and the couch.

"Method acting. Maybe I was trying to stay in character. You should try it."

Benj regretted the knock the moment it landed. It hit too low, cut too deep. Possibly fatal, considering Milo's eyes ignited with rage, a survival instinct to fight back. Fight for his life. His anger had been thinly veiled since Sunday, and now she'd pulled back the curtain.

"You were pretending to be with Jackson?" Milo scooped up her notebook from the coffee table, ripping through the pages until he found his face. "So this is Jackson?"

She bit her lip and he shook the pages, nodding theatrically, answering himself with a deranged mutter. "This must be Jackson."

Benj lunged for the sketchbook, grabbing it back. "That's not Jackson."

"Looks like Jackson."

"It's not." She snatched her pencil up next and slapped the book into the kitchen's island. On the spread opposite his face, she drew another, nearly identical, but with a chiseled jaw and a showy smile. No concerned lines on the forehead. No scar. No hidden warmth in his dark eyes. "That's Jackson. Do they look the same to you?"

Milo stood over her shoulder, heat wafting off him in waves that matched the fall of his chest. Fear lanced through her as his silence held. Had her short-fused mouth finally set Milo off? Pushed him over the edge? Had she done something unfixable, using his deepest vulnerability against him?

"Does it?" She hastily sketched a beanie on each page, covering the scar that would distinguish Milo without question. "How about now?"

"No," he ground out.

She released the breath stretching her lungs. She couldn't keep doing this. Every conversation they had made her think she knew him better, made her like him better. What did it matter if she liked him, if every time he opened up to her, she didn't know how to behave herself on the inside? "I think we need to reinstate some ground rules."

Milo's big hands bracketed her on either side of the counter, his front hard against her back. "But we have a truce."

"And I think we should end it. Go back to—go back to the original parameters."

He dipped his head to her neck, raising goose bumps

along her skin with his question. "Kiss and touch and whatever I need?"

Her eyes darted around the kitchen, searching for control and finding the stove's bright clock, glowing in the dark. "As long as you keep your mouth shut."

"Do you always have to have the last word?"

"Yes."

The loaded gun of his mouth moved over her ear. "But I've got more to say. More to tell you."

Fuck did she want to hear it. What if he said he wanted her for real? What if he didn't? What if he did and he didn't mean it?

Why put herself through that again?

She'd had a crash course in Milo Fox. She was wise to the pitfalls this time.

Benj squeezed her eyes closed, leaning in to the sensation of Milo while it lasted. She needed two more days from him, but only with her safeguards back in place. Only with her defenses up.

"We can start tomorrow," she offered on a whisper.

"Okay. Then Ben—"

"Milo," she interrupted once more, forcing her eyes open and her back straight. "It's 12:02. Time's up."

Daily Star–t
Saturday, April 23

Guess who's back, back again? It's your deep-seated fear of losing control.

Chapter Twenty-Four

If Milo didn't think too hard about it, Benj tossing him a condom was a good thing.

He'd been sitting on the patio couch under the pergola, the heat of a coffee cup soothing a twinge in his knee, when the foil packet landed on his bare chest.

Milo looked up to see Benj standing between two wood beams, her hair dry, though a towel was wrapped around her middle. As he watched she untucked one end from her bust and let it drop to the ground. It wasn't just her fingers that held the confidence of marble, her whole body was a study in alabaster grace. Every inch of her was pale and smooth, and his for the taking.

Objectively: a good thing.

Unquestionably, his dick thought so, tenting the thin material of his lightweight lounge pants. But when Milo opened his mouth to ask her what had changed since last night, the sharp shake of Benj's chin added a thicker layer to the proceedings. One he couldn't ignore.

Nothing had changed since last night. She was as at home getting him up as she was shutting him down, leaving Milo stuck between two desires—wanting to say to hell with her rules and talk out of turn, and wanting to prove he wouldn't push her boundaries again. He knew he'd fucked up at the concert, and after, that their fight was his fault. He was lucky she hadn't canceled tonight entirely, and he still had a chance to prove he could be trusted to care for her the way she asked. Of course, a third, naked-Benj-related desire was quickly shouldering its way to the front of the pack.

Last night, when she'd offered him a chance to tell her how he felt, only to snatch it back on a technicality, they'd gone to bed without speaking or touching. The condom represented progress on at least one front. If Milo didn't think too hard about the fact that they were headed toward a very distinct cliff, he could convince himself that progress with Benj was also a good thing.

"I want to shower before the caterers get here." Her open palm waved wide. Impatient. Demanding. "You know you want to." Undeniable.

Not without some reluctance, Milo pushed down his waistband and allowed his dick to stand tall in the afternoon breeze.

Benj drew closer, wetting her top lip. An encouraging sight that made him think she couldn't resist him either. She took the mug from his hand so he could maneuver the condom over himself. Then, still cradling the coffee to her chest, she straddled him, one knee on either side of his thighs. His hands skated up her legs to her softly curved waist. And then she was sinking down and he was rising up, and they met in the middle, the tip of him hitting home as it pushed into the slick opening of her pussy.

Benj's head fell back, coffee sloshed over the rim of the mug and onto her chest, making her gasp. The hot droplets seared Milo's abdomen as they fell and he thrust up into her, hissing between his teeth. Holding the cup to the side, and curling her fingers over his shoulder, Benj began to lift and rock above him. Her head rolled forward again and he caught the laughter in her eyes, the pleasure that penetrated deeper than the superficial flush of her cheeks. The mug had warmed the spot where it had pressed against her, leaving a pink stain on her chest, like her heart was showing through the pale veil of her skin.

Words he'd been on the cusp of saying last night rose in his throat. There was a truth he'd been dancing around, one he wanted desperately to name until she'd silenced him.

Milo bucked up, his stomach pressing against hers, his hands roaming her back in opposite directions, anchoring her to him with dual grips on her butt and neck. He licked between her breasts up to her throat, painting the worship she deserved into her skin.

Benj was a revelation. An eye-opening divulgence he'd never recover from knowing. A truth he admitted to himself, if not her. Coffee would never taste as satisfying, would never wake him up as thoroughly as it did when spilled on her body and sipped from her skin. No day would feel complete if it ended before he'd heard her laugh.

He was going to have her, if only she'd have him.

Benj gripped his shoulder, forcing him back into the cushions. Her hips picked up pace, the slap of her butt on his thighs ringing out as she urged herself on. He reached for her tit and she beat him to it, covering the mound with her own hand, fondling it right in front of his face. Playing dirty right until the end. Milo only had a moment to grasp for her hips before she leaned back, relying on him to ensure she wouldn't fall. Teeth gritted, he accepted the task and was rewarded by the feel—the sight—of his dick delving deeper inside of her.

Milo was helpless, holding her up, trying not to come too soon, watching coffee splash over one of her hands and the other drift down her stomach. His mouth dropped open while she teased her clit with those fingers he'd always found so captivating. She clamped down, her knees tightening, her box closing around him like she wanted to keep him to herself.

For several heart-stopping, bliss-filled seconds he let himself believe she might. How could he not? When she came on his cock like it meant something. And then he was coming, clutching her harder and spilling safely into her and not thinking about anything at all.

"Fuck," Benj gasped, falling forward into him. "Fuck, Milo, goddamn it."

He pressed his mouth to her neck to stop himself from responding. Her pulse fluttered against his lips, which was better than anything he could think to say. Except maybe, "Please. Please forgive me. Let me have you like this, all to myself, with nobody watching."

He tried to ask for it with the strokes of his hands up her back, successfully drawing a shiver from her body. She curved away again and he followed, sucking at the underside of her jaw. He asked her there, with the flick of his tongue, and again, mouthing silently into her ear and hoping she heard him anyway.

"I have to shower." Her knees squeezed him once more and she writhed on his dick like she wanted to do it all over again. Like she wanted more too.

She sifted her fingers through his shorn hair and

he wished he hadn't let her cut it, that there was more for her to hold on to, to tangle herself in. "People will be here soon."

Their guests would arrive and then he could talk, he could say what he needed to say—in character. As Jackson. He could be who she wanted him to be. His teeth scraped her collar and she whined.

"Okay." She lifted up on her knees. "Enough."

Like that was possible—maybe for her, not for him.

Milo pushed her blond hair back to find her eyes, needing to confirm that this hadn't been what she'd claimed last night. *Method acting*—part of the game. He'd seen that attack for the flash-bang it was the moment she'd pulled the pin and lobbed it at him, but the sound still echoed in his ears, the burst still blinded him with fury.

Benj caressed his cheek and stared back at him with those gorgeous eyes he couldn't read for shit. But the light was back in them. And that was worth the price of his silence. She pressed the half-empty mug into his chest for him to take. With a slight stumble, she scooped the towel off the ground. Her hips swayed on the way back to his room, her body loose and satisfied. Milo watched her go, his own priceless view, wishing there were a way to talk to her before everyone arrived—justifiably. Some loophole sanctioned by her rules. Better yet, he wished the rules away, the game over.

It would be soon, and what then? He'd pick the right moment and tell her that she'd woven herself into the fabric of his dreams—she'd probably laugh that off. Maybe he should start with something simpler, something she couldn't misconstrue.

Milo finished the coffee and took his own shower. By the time he emerged, his button-down buttoned all the way up, Benj was in the living room setting out candles in a long, flowy yellow skirt with a slit up the front and a short, clingy white T-shirt.

His arms were around her immediately, seeking out the sliver of bared skin above her waist. He drank in her surprised laugh as she spun in his grasp. Her palms landed on his chest and she looked up at him, her mouth forming in a stern line. The glass partition to the pool was open as always, and she squinted in the slanting sunlight that angled through the room. Milo turned, watching her face change, her eyes opening, her lips curving up like she couldn't help it. Like it was for him. For real.

Milo couldn't think too hard about that cliff, absolutely certain the fall would fucking end him. If he waited too long for the right moment, would he get another? He had to tell her he wanted her, just her. He wanted to take her out and take her home—take her wherever she deemed appropriate. Not for a photo op. Not for anything but himself.

He opened his mouth to say the only thing he knew she wanted to hear. An apology, a real one, one she was owed. An apology he hoped that would set them on the right path, even if it broke the rules for him to give it.

Her gaze moved from his, shifting over his shoulder. Shadows stilled the light dancing in her eyes. The smile fell from her face. Her skirt fluttered around them, the room's airflow changing directions with a sudden gust—the shift before a storm.

"Flash," boomed an alarmingly familiar voice behind Milo.

Benj met his gaze again, her eyes wider now with panic.

The world revolved around Milo when he turned with Benj in his hold. His brother stood in the door frame and Milo returned, "Thunder."

Chapter Twenty-Five

Jackson Fox was back in the picture.

He leaned into the door frame, scoring the bombshell drop of his arrival with a shrill whistle. He looked so much like Milo, with his own fledgling beard and pocketed hands, that Benj was suddenly thrown, unsure of which twin was which. Doubt had her looking harder at Jackson, and though his features were the same as Milo's, the man she was searching for wasn't present in his eyes.

Milo's chest moved steadily up and down under her hands, and a discomfiting sort of sheepishness heated her cheeks—like that time she'd been caught siphoning vodka from her parents' liquor cabinet and replacing it with water. Her first instinct was to pull away, only when she tried, Milo held her tighter.

Jackson watched with carefully employed humor. "Kind of awkward, but I guess I need to say it: hands off my girlfriend, bro."

"She isn't yours."

Benj pushed harder against Milo and his apparent jealousy, freeing herself as Jackson continued.

"No? I'm getting a lot of notifications that suggest

otherwise—but I might be mistaken. I have been out of town. Might have missed something important."

"Jack—" Milo started.

His brother pushed off the wall and made for a squared, clean-lined Scandinavian lounge chair opposite the couch. "Wait. This should be good and I want to be comfortable."

Milo waited for his brother to settle down before trying again to explain. "I called you. I couldn't get through."

Jackson hiked his ankle up to rest on the opposite knee. "Sophie said."

"You talked to Sophie?"

"I had a lot of messages—you, Max, Soph. I called the person I trusted to tell me what was going on."

"Which wasn't me?"

Benj heard it, the hard ask in Milo's voice. Jackson must have heard it too because he punched his shoulders up one at a time in an awkward motion she wouldn't have expected of his fluid style.

"Kicker is she didn't tell me anything. Told me to talk to you. So. Let's hear it, Melpo." Jackson gestured to each of them in turn. "Why are you pretending to be me, with her?"

Milo nodded, acknowledging the question but making no move to answer it.

Jackson's voice rippled with emotion. "Why are you back at all?"

Milo's head slowed to a stop and he stood still and speechless.

Benj bounced on her toes, knowing what he had to say, doubting he could do it. "He didn't have a choice. I blackmailed him and then Modrić—"

"Tell me you didn't talk to Petra Modrić." Jackson's foot dropped to the ground with a thud, his features no longer controlled. "Milo, if you fucked that up for me—"

"He didn't fuck anything up. He was trying to help you."

"Hey, hon, you wanna let me talk to my brother?"

Benj started forward, a flash of anger warming her blood. "No, I don't. I've been wanting to call you an asshole since Sunday and now I've got my chance."

"What the hell did I do to you on Sunday?"

"Like you don't know." She felt Milo's arm hovering near her stomach, as though to stop her from launching herself at his brother. She glared back at him.

Milo's eyes were shaded. "He doesn't know. Max didn't tell him about the photo."

"That's bullshit. Who else would it be? Who else would have a reason to set Nelle up?"

"Someone else must have—"

"It's always 'someone else' with you—there is no one else. Just me and Jackson and Nelle. And I know it wasn't me or Nelle."

The doorbell rang, cutting off any rebuttals.

"The fucking caterers." Milo rubbed at his jaw. "What do we do?"

"Caterers?" Jackson asked. "Are we having a party? What's the occasion? My homecoming? Yours?"

Benj's gaze flitted between them. "There can't be two of you."

"There have always been two of us."

"There's only one of me," Jackson countered with all the self-confidence she'd expect from a Hollywood A-hole.

Milo sucked a sharp breath in through his nose. But Jackson was right. She supposed she should be relieved. With Jackson playing himself, she wouldn't have to worry that the performance would lack luster. Milo had said himself he was over it. Now he had his out. The show could go on without him. She would have to go on without him.

The relief didn't come.

Benj put a hand on Milo's hip. She knew how to cut what wasn't working—she only had to trust her instincts and do it. "There can *only* be one."

"Highlander rules. I accept." Jackson stood, clapping Milo on the back as he headed for the door. "Looks like I'm up."

"You have to go," she told Milo.

His head was shaking before she'd finished. "No."

"Milo, you can't be here."

"Yes, I can. I just can't be him. I'll be me."

"You're making this too complicated—"

"I'm not leaving." He held up his palms as if to say *what are you gonna do about it*. She knew he wouldn't budge. What was she going to do about it?

"Come on in," Jackson greeted the caterers.

Benj shoved Milo toward his room and he stumbled back. "Well, go fucking shave at least so people can tell you two apart. And take out your contacts. And— just go!" Stubborn idiot. Doing whatever he wanted and making her deal with it. Now she'd have to fill his two-faced brother in as much as she could before everyone else arrived.

Jackson relocated to the couch and patted the cushion next to him.

Benj took the lounge chair. "We've had an eventful week."

He wore an amused smile, though his eyes held reproach. "Tell me about it."

Benj hesitated, glancing at the caterers busy in the kitchen. The fridge door barely made a sound when opened, and the cabinets all swooshed shut on soft-close hinges. With a sigh she got up and repositioned herself on the couch next to Jackson to ensure they wouldn't be overheard. She explained about Modrić and the cast in hushed tones, leaving out anything that didn't have to do with him directly. The best parts, she realized as she sorted through the story, those were the bits she kept to herself. The ones that were hers and Milo's alone.

"Milo was trying to make sure you *didn't* get fired."

"Clearly there was no other option." Jackson did little to conceal his sarcasm. "You two have it all worked out. Except the part where I haven't actually bonded with the cast and if Modrić finds out, I *will* get fired."

"She's not going to find out. If you follow my lead, I'll get you up to speed. Then after tomorrow we'll amicably 'break up' because of differing schedules and no one else will know what really happened."

His eyebrows pulled together, and she blinked until she didn't see Milo in his place.

"And then you and my brother are free to—"

"No, he's—"

But Milo hadn't told Jackson yet that he was quitting.

Jackson tried to fill in the excuse she left blank. "That would defeat the point? Of convincing everyone you were with me? What would people think to see you'd moved on to him?"

They wouldn't care—not if Milo quit. Not if Benj didn't hop actor brothers one week to the next. If they waited—

Waited for what? Milo hadn't quit. Maybe he wouldn't. She had to quit following her thoughts wherever they wanted to take her. Aya had said Basic Witch was back on the table, she couldn't gamble that on the possibility that Milo Fox had grown a backbone.

"So now what?" Jackson asked.

The doorbell rang again, signaling the start of the evening and the end of their impromptu production meeting.

Benj adjusted her skirt as she rose from the couch. "Now we try to land this fucking plane."

Chapter Twenty-Six

A clean-shaven, bespectacled Milo entered his living room to find it full of people he knew, all acting like they were meeting him for the first time. It was a heady concoction of false pretense and gaslighting that turned his stomach. He rushed through each reintroduction and kept his mouth mostly shut. Letting Vanessa and Lewis form the impression that he was rude was better than inadvertently giving himself away.

The only two outcomes Milo cared about were tied to the two people in the room keeping their distance. He'd missed his chance to talk to Benj before anyone arrived. And his plan to tell Jackson his decision as soon as they were face-to-face was shot. Milo had been going to rip the Band-Aid right off, just to prove he could do it. He'd planned to be brave and direct and entirely himself. None of that had worked out. He'd stood there staring at his brother, unable to force his mouth to form the words. The more Jackson prodded him to say it, the harder it got. He'd been stuck in a living nightmare, fighting urgently to run with legs that refused to cooperate.

Everyone had doubted whether he could go through with it—first Jackson, then Sophie, even Benj had thrown the word *if* at him. And he'd proved them all right.

Fuck that.

As the others gathered to sit for dinner, Milo tried to pull his brother aside. "Jack, can we—"

"Now you've got something to say?" Jackson replied in a low voice. He caught Jem watching and kindly made excuses for Milo in a louder tone. "Long day of travel." The others smiled, easily mistaking the shady mischief in his brother's eye for the excitement of reunion. "Milo didn't expect to find me hosting our dinner tonight."

"We told him he didn't have to stay," Benj added pointedly. "I bet he'll crash early because of the jet lag."

Milo's face heated, probably splotching his cheekbones. He hated the way they talked about him. The way they pushed him to the edges. "I'll be out of your hair soon enough," he said, exploiting his newfound freedom of speech and eliciting a hard look from Benj.

He let a smile spread across his face, slow and steady, until she looked away. Striking up a conversation with Vanessa about red carpet trends, she limited her frustration to the tapping of one foot, but he knew she wanted to do more to tell him off. She couldn't. There was nothing she could do to shut him up now. All her rules, all her leverage, had gone out the window the second she'd replaced him with Jackson. When Milo had gotten his wish.

He didn't have to pretend to be Jackson anymore. He'd been pushed out of frame. He was free to be himself. Free to watch Benj and Jackson play the happy couple across the table.

He was free to admit this was worse.

The speed and apparent ease with which Jackson and Benj had developed a rapport irked Milo. The cast change was seamless, even with no rehearsal and Jackson not quite off book. No one seemed wise to the fact that he'd occasionally look to Benj and raise his eyebrows as if to say, "Line?" while she filled in the necessary conversation. But it was the open way they exchanged smiles that made Milo unable to eat the vegan miso "cod" made with eggplant he'd paid top dollar for the caterers to prepare. It might as well have been crow.

While the company talked around him, Milo kept to himself, though his attention kept diverting to the winking gold pins in Benj's hair. She had one side smoothed back behind her ear and held in place with two clips, a *B* and a *W* for her initials. Every time she turned to his brother, the glossy gold of the letters caught the light from the kitchen and nearly blinded him.

Eventually he stopped trying to look away, telling himself it was so that his eyes would adjust to the sight of them together. Really, he didn't have the willpower to take his gaze off Benj. He most definitely should not have been staring at her so openly. He might as well have opened his mouth and announced to the table that he was completely infatuated with her.

That's what he wanted to do—expose her and Jackson, tell everyone he was the one who…well—who almost had her.

Almost.

But Benj had her friendships and her career staked on this familial farce. Milo only had his pride. He'd have nothing if he carelessly disrupted her life again. So he stared, holding himself back from doing anything thoughtless, and hoping that she'd glance his way with a look that confirmed they were feeling the same way: that this was torture.

She didn't.

And neither did Jackson.

Two of the most important people in his life were sitting across from him, pretending they were too smitten with each other to notice him. He'd been moved to background; he was an extra. He'd been written off. It was what he'd wanted—but not like this.

When Benj rose to get more wine, Milo nearly knocked over his chair leaping to his feet to help.

"I've got it," she hissed, ducking down in front of the wine fridge under the island. "Go back to the table and stop staring at me."

"How do you know I'm staring when you haven't looked my way once?"

"I can…feel you." She stood, putting two bottles on the counter, one of them Maison Rosé. "And I'm not *supposed* to be looking at you, I'm *supposed* to be looking at Jackson. That's the story: me and him. Do I really have to ask you to not fuck it up? I have a future riding on this."

So did he. Milo put the rosé back in the fridge. "I got that for you."

Benj took it back out. "No. Jackson did."

Ouch. He breathed into the blow. "What else did he do to you? Fuck you senseless? Did he make you beg to come on his cock?"

Benj's smile lanced through him with its false brightness. "Stop staring *and* don't talk to me anymore."

He beamed back. "Since when is it industry standard to oblige a showrunner who declines to renew your contract?"

Benj lowered her voice to a hiss again. "What did you want me to do, Milo? You were always a placeholder." She watched the hit land before glancing at the caterers cleaning up and forcing another smile onto her face. "Your brother and I can finish up with our guests. Do yourself a favor and call it a day."

The valley was mostly dark, but the sky still held a streak of color. "Day's not over yet."

"It is for you."

Milo caught her wrist where it hung at her side with the weight of the bottle, blessedly out of sight, though he hadn't had the forethought to make sure. He was so anxious to keep her for another moment, he wasn't thinking anything through. Nothing was working. He was losing her. "Ben—"

"What do you want, Milo? Really what is it you want to happen now? You're leaving as soon as you talk to him, right? There he is. Go and tell him how tired you are of all this shit."

"Why can't the only thing I want be you?"

Her lips parted wordlessly. She sounded winded when she finally spoke. "Because I'm with your brother."

"That's not real."

"It's real to everybody else."

"Prove it."

Benj jerked herself free. "Prove what?"

"That we're interchangeable to you."

"Can you hear yourself?"

"If you can prove it, I'll excuse myself and leave the two of you to wrap on your own."

"Don't tempt me. I'll fucking do it, Milo."

His shoulder jumped as a hysterical tremor rippled through him. "Then do it."

Benj exhaled through her nose and Milo followed her back to the table, feeling untethered. Feeling wilder than he'd ever been—raw and unfiltered.

She wouldn't do it. She wouldn't. He knew she didn't think he and Jackson were interchangeable. She had nothing to prove. And yet—Milo swallowed hard. He'd never seen Benj back down.

Benj presented the bottle to the table and a cheer went up from Lewis and Vanessa. Jem gave it a slanted appraisal and sighed.

"Not your favorite?" Jackson asked, his head tipping in her direction.

"My opinion hasn't changed—but the *L* in Benj's hair just took on new meaning."

Jackson looked to Benj for clarity. Her smile held an edge, whether for him or for Jem, Milo couldn't say. He chugged his water, attempting to clear the knot in his throat as Benj explained, "You remember Jem calling my taste in wine basic, don't you, babe?"

Jem wiggled her finger at them. "Wasn't it just before you two got in that tiff about Milo?"

"That sounds right." Benj's hand hovered over her glass before Lewis could refill it.

Leaning into Milo's space, Jem asked in a stage whisper, "Aren't you curious to know what she was saying about you?"

He recalled the moment well enough. Benj had called him selfish. "I'm sure it was nothing new." He could have let it go there, absolutely should have, in fact. But his mouth opened again. "Though I'm open to a recap. You wanna tell me how you really feel?"

With everyone watching, Benj finally turned her pale eyes on him. She held his gaze with a glare so intense, the tendons tightened in the back of his legs. Her shoulders rolled casually back and she lifted her hand, resting it possessively behind Jackson's neck.

A bold bluff. And one that worked.

Milo would respect the charade. He'd stand, signifying the end of his challenge. He'd throw down the white flag of his napkin and go. That would save both of them the heartache of seeing how it would all play out.

He had forced her hand onto his brother's collar, but her black nails scraped Jackson's scalp of their own accord. Milo didn't stand. He fisted the napkin in his lap. And stayed. He had to know how far she'd go to win. He couldn't call it off—he couldn't speak with his esophagus constricting the way it was, watching his brother lean toward Benj. Jackson nuzzled her ear, a physical "yes and?" that made Milo want to improvise a fistfight before the dessert course arrived.

Jem must have felt similarly nauseated, standing suddenly and excusing herself.

Vanessa laughed, breaking the awkward silence. "Raise your hand if you think Modrić's a genius." She planted her elbow on the table and flashed her palm. "When we get to the scene where Dahlia cusses Zuri out for sleeping with Lear, we'll all be primed with emotion."

Milo exhaled as Benj retreated into her own seat. She circled her finger along the rim of her empty wineglass. "Great, yeah, I hope Jem takes as much as she needs from this."

"She's not taking it from you." Vanessa brought her palm over Benj's hand, settling it on the tabletop. "Not really. Once we put it on the screen, we're giving it all away. That's why we all got into this, isn't it?"

For once, Milo had to bite his tongue to keep from responding. What was the point of showing vulnerability on-screen, when it had kept him from doing it in his real life?

Benj shook Vanessa off, rearranging the stem of her fork. "Always happy to do my part to ensure a good performance." Her eyes slanted his way, loaded as her reply to Vanessa, and training on him. A sniper ready to take him out if he compromised her mission.

Lewis passed the bottle to Milo. "Tell us what's new with you. We tried prying it out of Jackson but he was tight-lipped."

"That's unlike me." Jackson tasted the rosé, his mouth pulling down as he swallowed. "You must have caught me on an off day. Do you want to share now, Milo?"

Milo glanced at Benj before responding. "No."

"Go on. I heard it already—word is you're in final talks for the *Hearts of Gold Rush* remake." Lewis raised his glass in salute. "Hats off to you for knocking mine out of the ring."

Vanessa gasped. "I'd heard they might reboot—but that they didn't even have a script."

Milo looked away from Benj's shocked face to see Jackson's eyes broadcasting malice.

"You lying bastard," his brother said.

The merriment dropped from Lewis's voice. "I thought you knew? I was sure you two would have discussed it first."

"Where'd you hear that?" Milo turned to Lewis.

"Managers talk. Yours said—"

Fucking Max. "He's misinformed. It's not true."

"How is it not true?"

In every fucking way, Milo wanted to shout. "I'm not in any talks."

"You better not be," Jackson snapped.

Jackson knew Milo was over acting—why did no one believe him when he said it? Milo threw up his hands in exasperation. "And what if I were? What would you do?"

"Babe," Benj said quietly, drawing twin glances from them. "Let's calm down before somebody does something they can't take back." She glanced quickly at Milo and nodded toward his room, telling him once again to leave. He sat, rooted to the spot, watching her hands cup his brother's face. What would she do to make him?

Benj waited one more second, giving Milo a final chance to go. He didn't. And then he watched as she brought her face to Jackson's. Her lips pressed into Jackson's. Her tongue darted out slowly licking into Jackson's open mouth.

Milo couldn't look away. Couldn't move except to pinch his leg, bruising his skin down to the bone. He couldn't do anything but stare, his heart aching in his throat, taking in every detail of what he saw. Analyzing her proof. Comparing it to the moment she'd kissed him the same way in the bowl of that vineyard valley, the dome of sky curving overhead.

When Benj pulled back, Jackson looked lovingly into her eyes. "Thanks, hon. You're right." Jackson brushed the hair off Benj's shoulder, leaning back in, and Milo lurched to his feet. He'd watched Benj kiss his brother—but he'd torpedo the whole operation if his brother kissed Benj.

Which was exactly what Benj had asked him not to do.

She stared at him, eyes wide with warning. Eyes he couldn't bring himself to fully meet, his gaze snagging on the wet glaze of her mouth.

"Why don't I let you all enjoy your evening," Milo gritted out through his clenched jaw.

"I am enjoying myself," Jackson baited him.

It took everything in Milo not to bite. What he planned to do next wasn't up for public consumption. What he needed to say tonight would have to wait for privacy. He gripped his seat. Jammed it in to the table. And left.

Chapter Twenty-Seven

It was Milo's fault. He'd made her do it.

That was the half-truth Benj tried to sell herself after kissing his brother right in front of him. After pulling back, her lips wet, and seeing the color drained from Milo's face, the agony, the electric shock of her actions.

The whole truth was that Milo may have proposed the dare, but she'd chosen to take it. She'd decided to win. She hadn't expected Milo's retreat to feel like losing.

He'd asked for it. He'd deserved it. He had texted himself from her phone, Don't start something you can't finish. His words. Not hers. His advice. He should have heeded it.

Benj swished water in her mouth as discreetly as she could. She'd need something stronger to wash away the taste of Jackson that lingered on her tongue, strange and decidedly wrong. The bite of almond torte she forked into her mouth did the trick. Sweet and delicate and impossibly buttery, the dessert made Benj doubt Milo had remembered to ask the caterers to make the meal vegan.

But she couldn't forget the smug gleam in his eye, the confidence with which he'd voiced the caveat he'd uncovered outside Cormac's. *If I want to take care of you, I should just do it.*

Her doubt melted as quickly as the torte's powdered sugar topping hitting her tongue. She knew he'd just done it, even though she hadn't asked. Despite her running tally of his transgressions, she was developing faith in Milo.

Days ago, she'd reminded herself that the ability to remember one little detail did not a good guy make. If only it was one detail. She couldn't think of a cue Milo hadn't picked up on—whatever she wanted, he delivered. That didn't make him a good guy. It made him a better one.

Milo had grown. He'd aged. He'd experienced things that had changed him. She kept waiting for him to reveal his old self, his real self, for it to burst out of him, harsh and heartless. But each time she pushed him, he took it. When she had kissed his brother, he had walked away. He had followed through, when every taut, overworked muscle in his jaw had revealed how badly he'd wanted to renege, react, explode. How much more proof did she need that he had her back?

It should be enough. Enough to forgive him. So why couldn't she let go of all her hard feelings?

The others had finished their desserts. They had no reason to linger. Neither did she. She had Jackson for the wedding. She'd known the end was coming with Milo—that was supposed to make it easier. Eyes swimming with sudden emotion, Benj looked through the open doors to the patio. The other side of the dark valley was lit with bright, static spots, while the pool glowed violet, a shadow moving under the water.

Milo.

He'd gone to clear his head after she'd clouded it. She knew it was too risky to try talking to him again.

They'd gotten sloppy during dinner. She should let him be. Walk away like he had. But when it came to Milo, Benj had all the self-control of a five-year-old with a glitter palette.

She lowered her tucked-up feet to the ground, drawing Jackson's gaze when she stood. He eyed the fork still clutched in her hand and she placed it next to her unfinished plate. "I'm going to say goodbye."

An explanation and an excuse, two for one.

Jackson's eyes were so familiar and yet without the velvety edge she was accustomed to finding in that face. His voice was even more familiar when he asked, "How are you getting home? Do you want me to call you a car?"

Lewis put two hands on the table. "Are we breaking up?"

Benj nodded and Jackson glanced at the pool before addressing them all with a wry smile. "Sorry for any drama—clearly my brother and I need to talk when we're alone."

Talking alone. She and Milo never seemed to have that luxury. Between her rules and his roles, they'd had to get to know each other without the advantage of privacy. Their time together had been public, their admissions overheard, their confessions coded. Why should she expect their goodbye to be any different?

"We'll see you tomorrow," Benj heard Vanessa say as she abandoned her heeled clogs under the table and headed outside. Her skirt swirled around her ankles, the gauzy yellow layers catching in the night air as she walked along the natural stone pavers that lined the pool. They warmed under her feet when she stopped at the sharp corner where the two sides met.

Milo glided past, his arms carving out a path in the water. When he hit the wall, he flipped, going back the way he'd come. Maybe he hadn't seen her, maybe he didn't want to.

Benj didn't mind the delay. Gathering her skirt back, she sat, letting it bunch at her sides and dipping her bare legs into the water.

Milo swam past her again. And again. At the end of his third lap, he pulled up short. His head rose from the water, glasses gone, one hand slicking back his wet hair like he expected it to impair his vision, still unaccustomed to the short style she'd thought would make him look like his brother.

Staring at him now, Benj couldn't believe anyone— including her—had ever mistaken the two men. Milo was different than his brother—he was a rare find. Where Jackson's eyes were reflective and bright, Milo's were bottomless caves of desire into which she could fall forever.

But she'd come to say goodbye. Not to stare. Not to fall.

"We let this go on too long, don't you think?"

Milo treaded water, making no move to come closer, his mouth submerged. Light danced over the ripples colliding around him. Someone's parting line caused laughter from inside the house, the sound muffled and far away, coming from a different world.

His silence made her arms go tight, propping her shoulders up. "Milo? Do you get what I'm saying?"

His mouth rose from the water. "No more turbulence. Your new company's in the bag and you wanna run with it."

"Nelle's company," she corrected, smoothing back her hair.

"No."

Benj arched a brow. "No?"

"You think it's a coincidence that all of 'her' products are going to be branded with your initials?"

Her hands dropped away from the gold letters pinned in her hair. Milo was in dangerous form, paying attention and using it against her. Making her consider a better future than she'd thought possible.

She lifted her legs, holding them perpendicular over the water. They couldn't keep this up. Her feet dropped and she pedaled them, sending waves his way. "Don't do that."

He drifted closer, looping one elbow over the paver ledge. "I guess the only thing left is your apology."

Benj rubbed at her collarbone, looking away, knowing he was right. She had crossed the line with Jackson, she had deliberately done it to hurt him. "Milo, I'm—"

"Are you wet right now?" He looked up at her, skin glistening, irises dark and round and tempting. That look of imitated virtue that activated her Milo response system, flooding her body with heat.

Benj's feet stilled. "You wanna know if I got wet kissing your twin?"

"That's not what I asked." His fingers curled around her ankle and she kicked her foot under the water. His hand rose, squeezing her calf. "You don't need to answer. I already know you are."

Her mouth opened but she didn't argue, only hauled in air that tasted of chlorine and lilac when she felt his soft, clean-shaven cheek slide over her knee. His breath fanned her skin and she was paralyzed by dueling urges to open wider and draw herself in.

"I know what you were trying to prove, and you might have convinced the others, but not me. I saw the moment you realized he doesn't affect you like I do. I saw you realize no one does."

Her eyes closed so she wouldn't have to see him staring up at her, his head bobbing just above the water in between her legs. She could still hear the trickle of it parting as he moved in closer. She could still feel the heat radiating off his face, warming her inner thighs.

Who makes you feel good, Ben?

She inhaled again, the air heavier, even more intoxicating, saturated with the dark truth in his words.

"You didn't get half as wet sucking his tongue into your lush little mouth as you are right now just breathing me in." His grip moved higher on her leg. Teeth sank into the tender underside of her thigh just above her knee. "You like it when I'm jealous. It makes you feel powerful."

Her head shook as she corrected him. "I like that you can't hide it."

"I don't want to hide anything from you. But you keep shutting me down. Don't hide from me either. If you want me to lick up the mess you're making for me between those legs, open up—show me you know the difference between who you came with and who you come for."

Benj blinked her eyes open to find him lurking in the long shadow she cast over the pool. "There. Now I can apologize. Properly. For all the times I got us off track. When we're so good together just like this."

He waited, leaving it up to her whether or not to act

on the filthy oath he was swearing at her feet, hidden from view, his movements secret—unless someone came out and—

"There's no one here to see, Ben," he said as if reading her mind.

She'd been wrong about him—Milo Fox was constant, steadfast, reliably hell on her intentions. And if this week had proved anything, it was that she wanted him even when they weren't good together, she wanted him when they were bad.

Holding his gaze, she flattened her feet on the pool's tiled wall and slowly lifted herself up. Milo's hands skimmed over her exposed thighs and under the bit of skirt still covering her hips. He snagged both sides of her panties and slid them down her legs, letting the scrap of satin float away from them. She watched, growing breathless, as the fabric sank into the violet depth below, out of sight, unreachable.

"Ben," Milo whispered. "I'm sorry."

She inched forward, drawing to the precarious edge.

"So fucking sorry I ever hurt you."

She let one knee fall wide and Milo pressed an open-mouth kiss to the joint of her pelvis.

"I'll tell you however you want to hear it." He held himself to her, his hands wrapping around the outside of her legs, hauling himself up, the muscles of his shoulders tensing. She could feel his words, hot puffs warming her waiting pussy. "I'll say it whenever you want me to."

"Now would be nice," she replied on a shaky exhale.

"Now, then," he agreed with a slow smile. And then his mouth moved against her, saying everything she wanted to hear without any words. His tongue swirled around her clit, his fingers pressing into the tops of her thighs to leverage himself closer. Her hips rocked, bringing her perilously nearer to the water. His grip threatened to pull her under and she clung to the edge, ripping a fingernail against the stone.

Milo brushed his tongue flat and wide over her satin cunt. He dipped its tip into her heat once, twice, before diving deeper with all the devotion of a sacred prayer. A sharp gasp burst from her throat. How had she ever thought his mouth was problematic? Because she'd never felt the force of it on her clit in the light of a waning moon.

Her back arched as Milo sucked, bringing her closer still to the precipice. The pressure of his mouth carbonated her blood. The bittersweet agony of need bubbled to life inside of her. That certainty she craved crept up on her and she knew without a doubt she was going to come on his tongue and never be the same.

The orgasm to end all orgasms erupted from her core, an explosion of color sparking behind her eyes as her toes curled and her body throbbed with relief. A maniacal laugh clapped out of her mouth and she did nothing to stop it, letting it loose on the hillside. He'd cast another spell with his magic mouth, granting her another moment released from the turmoil of her thoughts, of second-guessing them both. Her legs clamped around his face. She wanted to keep him where he was until the feeling fizzled—

"What's so funny?"

New shadows disrupted the wide swath of light pouring out of the house. Benj pushed back, away from the edge, away from Milo, her feet slipping against the wet tiles, her knees trembling with aftershocks of pleasure.

Her pussy was still contracting when she looked back to find Jem and Jackson in the doorway.

"I got Benj wet."

Embarrassment flushed her cheeks in the dark. "Splashed——he splashed me." She glared at Milo whose eyes glimmered now with obvious delinquency while his glistening chin rested on hands innocently folded over the pool deck.

"Your car'll be here in ten, I'm gonna walk Jem out."

Benj hummed her assent and waved them off before climbing to her feet.

Milo swam after her. "Stay tonight."

"I'm working tomorrow. My kit is at home."

"Stay an hour. I'll drive you later."

"Jackson already got me a car."

Milo lunged up on the stone, grabbed her hand, and tugged her into the pool. Benj plummeted downwards, falling sideways into the deep end, into him.

Still so foolishly into him.

She broke the surface gasping and splashing, laughing and cursing. Furious and relieved. Furious to be relieved. He ran her so hot and cold she didn't know what she was feeling. The layers of her long skirt clung to her legs as she kicked to keep up with Milo swirling around her, a predatory thrill on his face. He pinned her in, the tiled wall at her back, and kissed the plea into her mouth, forcing her wayward intentions further afield. "Just stay."

Her mouth plundered his in return, her hands combing through the wet spikes of his hair as she held him to her. Their touching lips made her forget her reasons, her doubts. When they were like this, the possibilities for their future were endless.

"Stay," he insisted.

Maybe it would be different this time. He was different—he made her feel different. He made her feel so exceptionally good.

Milo sucked the hinge of her jaw, leaving her mouth free for the final say.

"Okay."

Chapter Twenty-Eight

Their mouths sliding together and apart in the lapping hush of the pool wall, Milo kissed Benj the same way he always did: like his life depended on it. He told her with his lips and his tongue that she was the only thing he'd ever wanted this much. There wasn't a desire or a dream or a destiny he could imagine that compared to the magic pull of Benjamina Wasik. Every time he set his sights on her felt like waking up all over again. Starting new, his focus clear. Even having her now, the wanting only compounded, increasing in urgency with every movement, every taste he coaxed from her body—some latent fear that each could be the last.

Not this time. This time Milo wanted more of Benj—more without limit. All of her, his selfish heart decided, he wouldn't settle for anything less.

One arm around her waist, holding her to him, Milo used his free hand to drag them through the water. Grasp to grasp, they moved along the wall toward his bedroom. Floundering up the pool steps, gravity replaced the weightless thrill of caressing Benj under the surface with a heavier need to remove the waterlogged clothes clinging to her body. Until Jackson's reappearance dampened the mood.

"Nice to see you guys waited for the all clear that everyone is gone. Really top-notch front you're running here."

Milo stepped protectively in front of Benj, the thin cotton of her white shirt melting into her skin. She laced her fingers with his and gave an appreciative squeeze.

Jackson stood with a glass in each hand and used one to motion to the pergola. "Are we gonna do this thing or what?"

Benj pressed a kiss to the back of Milo's shoulder. The fingers she'd coiled around his forearm uncurled. She began moving away and his hand tightened around hers.

"You two need to talk alone—" She took another step back. "I'm gonna dry off."

Their fingers slipped slowly apart, their arms stretched wide across the growing distance between them.

There would be more, Milo reassured himself. Benj was staying. He had to talk to Jackson and then there'd be no more obstacles. Nothing else keeping them apart.

The coin flipped in his mind. Nothing else keeping them together either. There'd be no external forces, no more excuses to see each other. They'd have to rely on a joint willingness to keep it up, to make it work.

His skin prickled, drenched and growing cold. Milo let his hand drop away first, refusing to let the past spook him. Benj's willingness was apparent in her continued presence. She had agreed to stay. No rules, no act. She'd agreed when it meant they'd only be themselves. Benj had said okay and he believed her.

Milo watched her plod into his bedroom, taking a few extra beats to see her safely inside and calm the pounding arousal in his body before following Jackson to the patio's lounge seating. He pulled a towel from the basket next to the table and unrolled it with a shake. Scruffing it over his head, he sank into the empty cushion at the end of the couch opposite his brother.

A tumbler from a set of thick, blue-rimmed Mexican glassware sat in front of him, the liquid inside clear. "Reposado?" he guessed, knowing Jackson wasn't a fan of the unaged blanco.

Milo brought the drink to his nose as Jackson shook his head.

"Guess again."

He didn't need to. The smell had already hit him, the potency of unrestrained alcohol urging him back, the taste of home drawing him in. Milo blinked against the tingle in his nostrils, wide eyes asking Jackson *how?*

"Soph shipped me a bottle."

"That's risky."

"High risk, high reward."

"What's the reward?"

Jackson clinked his glass against Milo's. Sophie, the family cultivator, certainly would have been pleased to see them sitting together, preparing to work out their differences.

The cheers ringing in his ears, Milo gave in to impulse and sipped, holding the clean flavor on his tongue for as long as he could before swallowing it back and savoring the nutty warmth of the sunflower's aftertaste.

Jackson's eyes squeezed shut, his mouth pulling in an uncharacteristic grimace. "Woo!" His head gave a sharp shake. "Fuck that's good."

"The best." Milo watched the lights in the valley through the blur of his glass. "I tried calling you—"

"Did you?" Jackson put his drink on the low table. "What were you going to say? I'm fascinated by your version of events here. What earthly reason could you have to explain this week?"

"Jack—"

"No, I'm really curious, how long exactly were you planning to be me? What was the end game here?"

"I wasn't—"

"If I hadn't come home early, would you have filmed? Would you have—"

"No." Milo shouldered his way into the conversation, refusing to let Jackson hijack it again. This was the talk he'd been waiting to have. For a week. For six months. For ten years, if he was honest. It was long overdue, and it was his to run. "No. I wouldn't have filmed because—what you know, what you refuse to accept—is that I'm quitting."

When Jackson didn't respond, Milo said it again. "I'm quitting."

"I heard you."

"Good."

"But—"

"No. I'm quitting. It's not a discussion."

"So you came here to—"

Milo's palm opened like it was obvious. "To tell you."

"You wanted to tell me, 'I'm quitting.'" Jackson's top lip protruded doubtfully. "Long flight for a little line."

"Yeah well. You tried calling me too. The voice mail you left me on Saturday night contributed pretty heavily to my decision to do this in person."

Jackson reacted to the mention of the drunken voice

mail with the same grimace that had accompanied his sip of sunshine. "That voice mail was—"

"Concerning. You sounded really worked up, Jack."

"I'm a passionate guy."

"Felt like maybe you shouldn't be alone hearing tough news. Like maybe you wouldn't be able to handle it very well."

Jackson laughed, reaching for his drink again. "I appreciate the concern. But according to Max, you're the one currently filling our grandfather's shoes."

"I'm not taking that part. It isn't true. Why would you believe that? When we both know you're Max's favorite. He's never put my interests first." Milo closed his fist. "Did you know he got Benj fired from *Twin Pistols 2?*"

"You can't hold that against him."

"That sounds like a yes." Sunshine burned in his gut, billowing anger rising into his throat. Milo swallowed it back.

"He's always had our backs. With that photographer who tried to hustle me—"

"And what was it you were doing the night that pap caught you up to your nostrils in cocaine, if not following in Grant Fox's footsteps?"

"My point," Jackson said with a glare, "is that Max made that go away."

Max had, hadn't he? He'd done the same thing earlier in the week, when that same pap had turned up outside Benj's house. Same guy, same Max. Same call.

"I don't trust him." Milo looked his brother in the eye. "I fired him last night."

Jackson responded with a faux salute, his glass up and his head bowing. "Good for you."

Irrepressible anger sparked the tractor fuel of low-grade emotion and high-proof liquor swirling in Milo's blood. "It is good for me! I don't want this. I've never wanted it. And you know I've never wanted it." Milo shot back the rest of his sunshine, swearing at the harsh burn that coursed through him. "Fuck, why did you even ask me to come out here with you?"

"Why did you say yes?"

"I shouldn't have. I should have left after *Hey Batter!* tanked—"

"It didn't *tank*. It's found a cult following!"

"—I should never have stayed. But I was worried what would happen if I left you here."

"And now you're not? Now you're more worried about yourself? Because you busted up your head?"

"Yeah, Jack." Milo echoed his brother's derision. "It's because I busted up my head."

"They aren't going to let that happen again. That was a total fluke—"

"I know it's not going to happen again. Because I'm done."

"You think it should have been me?"

"No. I'd never think that. It's not about you. I'm just done."

They stared at each other, would-be mirror images. Twin frowns on their faces, chests in sync with heavy breaths. But they weren't the same. They'd never been the same.

Jackson set his glass down again without taking a sip. "So that's it."

"That's it."

"And the ficus?"

"Sophie didn't tell you anything, huh?" Milo lurched

forward for Jackson's drink, gulping it down with a jerk of his head and feeling the angry hum in his veins strengthen to a violent roar. "How is it fair that she's been keeping you in the loop on my life, while I've been in the dark about what's going on with you? Why would you call her first, Jack? After everything I've done—I took that fall for you."

"You think I don't know that? I think about that every day. And I knew you had to be holding it against me—"

"I'm not—"

"But that was an accident—now you're sabotaging my life on purpose to get back at me. How is it fair you've convinced the world I'm involved with some woman I barely know? Did you even care what you could have messed up for me? What connections I've made out here without you? No. You just wanted your happy ending. Since when are you so selfish, Milo?"

"Selfish? I did that for you. Maybe I shouldn't have. Maybe Benj was right and you were angling for some free publicity at Nelle's expense."

"You wanna know what I was doing over there?" Jackson leaned his elbows on his knees. "Nelle and I met this woman Lo at a party like a year ago. I needed her contact info, so I stopped by to get it—"

"And then what?"

"And then nothing. It was a long night, Nelle said I could stay. I woke up to Max calling, suggesting I get my head on straight before filming."

"Max sent you out of town *before* you'd left Nelle's?" Before the photo was taken. Milo tongued the roof of his mouth. "And he picked you up? He knew when you were leaving?" He knuckled a knot forming above his eyebrow. How had he not considered this before? There were four people who knew Jackson was at Nelle's, not three. Factor in Max's history of interfering, and the case closed itself with a snap.

"What? Now you think Max set this up? Why would he? We're both his clients."

"Nelle's not. She's Mina's. And Mina's leaving the firm." Benj stood just outside the house in dry clothes, her wet hair combed back. She tossed a phone at Jackson. "This was ringing."

Jackson looked at the screen. "Speak of the devil. I tried him before coming out here."

"And he's already calling you back?" Milo slapped his knees and stood. "Must be nice being you, Jack."

"You would know."

Milo's head spun only slightly when he swung it back to his brother. Jackson's eyes had a liquid shine, his voice a jagged edge. That heartbreak Milo had heard on the phone was visible even without his face blown up on a big screen. It was the *Twin Pistols 2* standoff, playing out right in front of him. But Jackson wasn't going to shoot him over this betrayal. Jackson was going to be fine. He'd get over it. He'd move on, just like Milo. His gaze shifted back to Benj in those pink yoga pants and her tie-dye hoodie, the skin of her waist glowing pale in the moonlight.

Jackson would understand when he had everything he wanted too.

"I hope it works out with you and Lo." Milo gathered the glasses to head inside.

"I got her number for you, dickface."

"If I'm a dickface, what does that make you?"

Benj interrupted, setting her hands on her hips and

widening the gap between her shirt and pants. "Lo from Salty Tequila?"

"I don't want her number," Milo assured her, shooting a glare at Jackson.

"You sure about that?" Jackson asked. "She knows what she's doing—production, marketing, all of it."

The phone stopped ringing, the silence sudden and lasting. Tangled roots held Milo in place and his progress toward Benj stalled.

"Are you..." Milo trailed off, trying to form the question that would give him the right answer. Because there was a definite wrong answer, according to the apprehensive clench of the organs behind his ribs. "Are you getting into the tequila business?"

Jackson smoothed his mustache, looking to Milo like a black-and-white villain when he said, "I'm getting in on the family business. You and Soph were really partnering on Sunshine without me?"

"I'm not partnering with Soph, she's just providing the seeds." Milo's thumb found an air bubble trapped in one of the glasses. He scratched at it with his nail while Jackson explained.

"Lo said that's admirable but impractical. You can't make a real profit if you're only using that limited crop source. She suggested a line of—"

"No."

"Milo—"

"No, Jack, no. This isn't—" Milo felt his breath coming fast and heavy. Heat bloomed under his skin, a feverish, frenetic energy underlining his response. He wished this were a phone call, like the ones he'd made earlier in the week. Then all he'd have to do was hang up. He'd only wondered if those other potential partners would force him out. He knew Jackson could do it, if Milo didn't stop him. "This is mine. You can't just swoop in and take the lead in this production too."

"Too? We had equal billing on *Twin Pistols*."

"*Twin Pistols* isn't real, Jackson. Nothing here is real! Nothing here matters. Not to me. That's what I've been trying to tell you."

"You told me. You delivered your big line—so you can go now, right?"

"I will. I'm gone."

Jackson smirked. "And I'll call you about next steps for the company."

"No. I'm saying no." The power of the word kicked up Milo's conviction, his thoughtless rant picking up steam. Benj had silenced him, Max had ignored his calls, and Jackson didn't want to hear it, but he had something to say. Something that was ugly and wrong but held a seed of truth anyway. Something that wanted out, like him. "I'm not gonna be sidelined this time." This time he was going to be selfish. The only way he'd free that air bubble from the glass was to smash it on the patio stones. "I'm not living in anyone's shadow. I'm doing it my way and I don't want you to be a part of it. That goes for everything. I'm not touching *anything* involving you."

"That's good to know. Seeing as *I'm* involved with Jackson." The dark look on Benj's face contrasted with her outfit's cheerful color story. "You got more, Milo? More you've been holding back? Keeping to yourself?"

"Ben, I didn't mean—"

"No, you never do. You guys are best friends, huh? Is this what loyalty looks like to you? I would *never* talk to Nelle like that."

Her out-of-character judgment had Milo lashing back. "You'd just skip her calls."

Jackson's phone had started ringing again and he answered it. "Hold on, Max, my brother started imploding and I want to see how it ends."

"Give me that—" Milo grabbed for the phone. He had to stop Benj looking at him like this was all his fault. "Why'd you do it, Max? Why'd you set Nelle up?"

Max's laugh was loose with Saturday night revelry. "I didn't set up Nelle—"

Jackson shook a triumphant fist at the phone.

"—I was setting up her team so she'd see what I can do for her, that they can't."

That was all Benj needed to hear. She turned on her heel and went back inside. Milo should have followed her, made sure she was okay, but he had one more point to prove. Jackson was his best friend, and his career meant everything to him. Milo couldn't let his brother leave it in hands as dirty as Max's.

"So you make the threat, and then you make the threat disappear to endear the client to you?" Milo locked eyes with Jackson. "That's kind of an unsettling thought, considering the time you helped Jackson out of a jam."

"Milo? Don't read into it, kid." Max's voice scraped through the phone. "This is between me and Hassan. She owes me her career. And she wants to thank me by taking one of my highest profile clients? That's not respect—I'm old-school. I don't play like that. You tell anybody and I'll make sure you never get another fucking job again."

"Guess I can tell anyone I want then." Milo dropped

the phone in Jackson's lap and hustled after Benj. He was alive with feeling and accomplishment. That's what he'd wanted, for each aspect of his life to matter, to mean something. There was air in his lungs and blood in his veins and soon Benj would be in his arms. "Max confessed—Ben, and I told him I quit—"

Milo's vision blurred in the large living space, his glasses still on the side table next to his bed. It took several squinting passes of the room for him to declare it empty.

Jackson followed him into the house, arguing into the phone. "But what you're calling 'old-school' actually sounds really fucked up and not how I want my business conducted."

"Ben?"

Milo's strained gaze narrowed in on the black hole at the end of the room. The front door Benj had left open to the night. Milo ran, his wet feet slapping the slate tiles. Benj was loading her bag into the back seat of a black sedan at the bottom of the drive. Her shoulders jumped when he called her name, but she climbed in without looking back, talking into her phone.

The car began pulling away and Milo swore, racing after it in nothing but his swim shorts. The slope of the drive lent him momentum and for a few seconds he tricked himself into thinking he could catch her.

He couldn't. After two bends in the road, the car was gone. And Benj with it.

Milo's pace cut out, and he stared down the empty road, his breath coming in erratic bursts. This wasn't happening. Not again. He wouldn't let it.

He limped back home, his progress aggravatingly slow. The chase had taken a toll on his knee. But he forced himself through the pain, forced himself to keep going, making it back to the rise of the drive.

Jackson waited on the stoop, holding the high ground that Milo had clearly lost. "Tough Saturday night all around."

Milo hobbled past him.

"Max just lost his third client this week."

Without breaking his already fragmented stride, Milo focused on the garage doors.

"I was afraid to do it alone," Jackson called after him, true emotion spiking his voice. "I didn't want to end up like him."

That, Milo couldn't ignore. He didn't want to be responsible for any more heartache. "Grant Fox lived a lonely, miserable life until he was out of money and time because he didn't care about the people who loved him."

"Exactly."

"That's not you, Jackson. That's not going to be either of us." Milo started for the garage doors again, but, Jackson, spry on his feet, beat him there.

"I can't let you go after her."

"Respectfully, Jack, fuck off."

"She left of her own volition. Respectfully, Milo, she called it a night."

"So what am I supposed to do?"

"What can you do? This was going to end, Milo. I was always coming back. It was never real."

"It was real for me."

"And her? What happens if you go after her right now? What does that look like for her in the press? *Half-naked Milo Fox gets DUI chasing down brother's girlfriend?*"

He hated that Jackson was right. He bent at the waist, his side stitched together with pain.

That cliff Milo'd been trying to forget about? It wasn't looming ahead of him and Benj. It was already above them—they had started at the bottom of it. Started in a circumstance they had to climb their way out of.

His head lifted as he rubbed at the tender spot behind his ribs. "I want to tell her how I feel."

"So call her—once. Text her, if you think you can put it all in writing. Don't bombard her. You have to give it a day. At least. You're gonna have to wait, until this all settles down."

"I don't want to wait. I've waited three years. I want her now."

A smile lit Jackson's face. "Yeah. I can see that. But you gotta get your tractor back in line first. Maybe put on some pants."

A rush of affection for his brother sent Milo staggering into him. "I didn't mean it, Jack."

Jackson hugged him back, his voice choppy when he said, "You think I don't know that?" He held Milo closer. An explanation stuttered out of him, a rough draft of emotions he'd been keeping to himself. "Milo, I wasn't trying to take anything from you. I wanted to help. I wanted to fix it. I just didn't know how to talk to you. I'm still—And I do trust you. But how can you trust me? Of course you were done. Of course you got as far away from me as you could. If I hadn't been hungover that day of filming, if I hadn't asked you to— It was *my* fault you got hurt."

"No. It wasn't."

"And it tore us apart—"

"No. It didn't." They might have different paths but they'd always be brothers. Their lives weren't duplicates, but they would always be entwined. Milo had never wanted that to change. "It didn't, Jack. It couldn't."

Milo let Jackson help him back inside. His anger had finally burned out, released from where he'd kept it inside him but leaving an ashy taste in his mouth. He tried Benj's phone, which rang once before she sent it to voice mail.

Jackson brought him an ice pack to ease the pain in his knee, and another shot of sunshine to ease everything else. Milo stared at his phone until the screen went blurry, trying to think of something he could say to Benj to make it better. Some grand pronouncement worthy of the best screenwriter. Something that didn't sound completely insane and over the top when he read it back to himself.

Give it a day, Jackson had said. But there wasn't a day to give it. Benj could be in New York or London or Sydney by the time she was ready to talk to him.

It took the better part of an hour for him to figure it out. She'd already told him the simplest fucking thing to say. He typed the two words and hit send, waiting another hour for a response that never came.

I'm sorry wasn't enough.

Daily Star–t
Sunday, April 24

Have you considered the possibility that you're playing it too safe?

Chapter Twenty-Nine

"And I haven't even told you the worst part." Skylar Davies paused to sip from the straw sticking out of a red can of sparkling wine and Benj blinked, coming back to the present in the sudden silence.

"The worst part of what?"

"Of last night? The shit show that was my rehearsal dinner?"

"Sorry, of course. I got lost for a second." Benj shoved a few more bobby pins into her mouth to prevent herself from saying more and giving away how little attention she'd been paying while autopiloting through the repetitive action of curling strands of Skylar's hair around a wide wand. She gave an encouraging hum and Skylar picked up where she'd left off.

This was the job. The one she'd been protecting all week. That's where her mind should be.

Clamp, twist, release. Clamp, twist, release.

Just like her heart on the Milo Fox program.

A jolt tightened Benj's hamstrings. Fuck. *Stop!* She scolded herself. But not even Skylar's steady stream of family drama could distract her from thinking about Milo Fox today.

Benj had her own Worst Part from last night.

Her prediction had been realized. What she'd thought was going to happen had solidified into what actually had.

She had proof that someone had set Nelle up. She had proof that the heartlessness she suspected of Milo was still there, buried under the layers of his stage-craft. Sure, he'd been the one who'd gotten to the bottom of Max's deception, but first he'd taken shots at his brother and her.

She'd decided then and there it was time to disengage from the roller coaster of Milo's mouth before it swept her up again. She'd decided to separate herself from the anxiety of possibility, walking easy-breezy out of that house. Her bag had been by the door, the car had already been called. Each piece of her exit was simple and solid as a stepping-stone, set and waiting.

That had been her stop, and she'd had to get off before she'd missed it. She'd had to ignore Milo calling her name, calling her back, and focus ahead instead.

Mina had picked up on the second ring. "This can't wait until Monday?"

"It was Max Field. Trying to screw you over for defecting to Aya's office. He's behind the photo. He started all of this."

Mina's silence was heavy as steel. "Thanks. I'll handle it. And we can talk about Basic Witch with Nelle on the flight to New York."

The Worst Part of last night had been trying to convince herself she'd gotten what she wanted.

That calm that had carried her out of Milo's house didn't last. The steps weren't so clear after that. The separation not so easy. Agitation had mounted from deep in her bones as she'd fixated on what Milo had said, the hurt in his voice as he'd called her name into the night. In the stale stillness of her abandoned apartment, Benj felt…shitty.

It didn't help that she'd left it a mess, rushing around to pack the bag she'd taken to Milo's. She'd ransacked her drawers, a pant leg overflowing from one while a sleeve hung out the side of another. Apparently, in her haste, she'd knocked over the cup of water by her bed. She'd found it on its side, the magazines on the chair nearby warped, the pages crinkled like crimped hair.

This was what she'd done to her life to catch a little dick. A voice in her head had tried to call her out on that lie, but Benj flung herself into action, fixing what she could, distracting herself from thinking too hard about what the truth would be. She'd clicked on the TV, filling her little world with other women's stories, ones that were over-the-top on purpose. The ensuing, impromptu midnight cleaning-organizing-packing frenzy had left her one-room studio in worse shape than she'd found it. She'd ended up on the floor, the TV muted, the *WoCA* drama unable to compete with her own, wringing the grey beanie she'd uncovered in her hands like she could rip it in half. The knit was too thick, too sturdy, and her rough grip only released Milo's scent into the room, grassy and consuming.

She usually loved the way smells intertwined themselves with memory, how they triggered feeling. Now she had too many wrapped up in Milo. She'd have to navigate the world like a minefield. She wouldn't be able to pretend to forget him this time.

Benj had tossed the hat down and climbed on top of the clothes and products piled in her bed, dozing in and out until it was time to get up and go to work.

She'd kept her spiking emotion at bay rolling an icy
jade stone over her puffy face.

Clamp, twist, release.

Benj pinned another coil to Skylar's head, heat rising through her skin as she tried to fight it back. She
regretted that she was also a guest at the wedding.
That she couldn't leave after doing Skylar's postcer-
emony touch-up, go home and take a nice cold shower
and shock her system back into shape. The Worst Part
was that she wasn't okay.

Sudden emotion broke free inside her, rushing unrestrained into her eyes. Benj brought her elbow to her
face, wiping the moisture on her sleeve and making as
though dust had gotten in her eye.

A minor irritation. One week of smoke and mirrors.
Not enough to tear herself up about.

Another game: two truths and a lie.

But she wasn't going to go to pieces over Milo Fox.

"So," said Skylar, as they waited for the curls to cool
and set. "You want me to angle the bouquet your way?"

"No point in wasting it on me—" Benj searched her
canisters for a texture spray to ensure the curls held
their bounce, ignoring the fire that burned her cheeks.
"Jackson and I have already decided to be friends.
We're both busy. The timing isn't right. The chemistry isn't where it needs to be."

"Coulda fooled me."

Another burst of chaotic feeling erupted inside her,
startling a laugh from her throat. "Yeah. Same."

While Skylar posed for photos, Benj broke into her
client stash of under-eye patches and changed slowly
into her outfit for the reception, an aqua minidress
made from velour that ruched across her middle and

rose into a high cuff at her neck—tight and bright, hugging her in all the right places, though she'd picked it for its square-shouldered boss energy. For the way it made her feel like herself.

But when she looked in the mirror, she didn't recognize the glossy-eyed, vacant version of Benjamina Wasik that stared back at her. A full face of makeup didn't help. And even when she tried fluffing her aura, the attempt was halfhearted. Her curved hands cupped and lifted the air, coming closer to her face, making it impossible to ignore the wear and tear this week had had on her manicure, if nothing else.

With the ceremony over and Skylar's makeup refreshed, Benj entered the reception, letting out a little gasp. Wisteria hung from the ceiling in long tendrils. Peonies cascaded from the head table to a scallop-patterned dance floor. Flickering candles nestled among the bouquets infused the room with a golden glow. It was all the opulence Skylar had described, and still no match for the starry sparkle of her eyes when her father had walked her down the aisle, holding her close before letting her go.

Benj had never seen so many flowers in one place, so much golden light—except in the photograph that hung over Milo's dresser.

Pushing her square shoulders back, she marched forward to table thirteen. She only had to get through the next few hours without falling apart and making a scene. Then she'd finish what she'd started. She'd clean. She'd organize. She'd pack. One step at a time until she took off with Nelle, leaving Milo and his stupid hat where they belonged: behind her.

It was time for a change.

The familiar ensemble of Lewis, Jackson, Jem, and

the Vus greeted her approach. Jackson's back was to her. A prickle of apprehension shortened her steps as she neared him. Something was off in his posture, a tension across the dark shoulders of his suit that she normally associated with—

Benj stopped before her steps became noticeably unsure. Heat rushed up her neck when Milo turned, catching her in the trap of his gaze.

No. She shook her head, now appallingly light and easily dizzied. No. She'd gotten off this ride. There was no reason for them to have switched back.

With or without reason, the man before her was unmistakably the one she'd run from last night. His tangerine shirt collar was unbuttoned and his throat bobbed with a thick swallow. His clean-shaven cheeks were raised up and he looked at her from behind his glasses with bald-faced longing and hope, right there at the table for everyone to see.

"We saved you a seat." Jem gestured to the empty chair next to Vanessa, setting her outdated CHA and NEL earrings swinging. "Over there."

"Hey hon." Benj tore her gaze from the exposed scar at Milo's hairline as Jackson leaned around the table's large centerpiece. "You're with me."

A wave of vertigo nearly knocked her over and she stumbled gratefully into the waiting spot next to him. The sturdy cushion caught her. She'd misunderstood. Milo was here with Jem. The perpendicular oval back forced her upright. Skylar had chosen form over function but what did it matter when nothing about this situation was going to be comfortable.

Jackson palmed the rounded rail behind Benj's head. "You look gorgeous, how was work?"

Benj could feel eyes on her. She willed the attention away, taking the cue from Jackson and trying to prove there was nothing to see here.

"Kinda draining, honestly." Benj straightened the forks next to her plate. "I'm beat. I didn't sleep well and I've got to pack for New York, so I'm gonna dip out of here after we eat."

"Okay, great." Jackson glanced down the curve of the table to where Jem and his brother sat.

Benj refused to follow his gaze. There'd be nothing gained in that direction. She did, however, lower her voice to make a request. "Can you wait until we're officially over to hook up with her?"

"Like you waited to hook up with my brother?" Jackson matched her low tone. "Sorry, look—it's better for you if I do you dirty. When you and Milo make it to press, people'll be more sympathetic."

"We're not going to make it to press."

"Yeah, you're right. Has-been celebs and their low-profile girlfriends don't get many headlines."

Vanessa leaned in on her other side before Benj could set Jackson straight. "What are we whispering about? Jem and Milo? I don't buy it. Looks more like she's trying to make Jackson jealous. Are we concerned that it's working? I think it might be working."

Jackson winked in Jem's direction and Benj sat back against the World's Least Comfortable Chair. "We're not concerned. I could have told her Jackson and I already decided to be just friends."

"No!" Shock tugged Vanessa's brows up. "But—"

"It's fine." Benj waved away the concern. Fine and done and nothing. It wasn't a lie when she said it about Jackson. She dabbed her knuckle on the underside of one eye to lift a heavy lash, and then let her voice carry as she added, "So all that is completely unnecessary."

With a sharp tilt of her head, she met Milo's eye. Purpose gleamed in his dark irises.

What did he think he was doing as Jem's plus-one? Making her jealous? A decisive nuh-uh. He was way out of line if that's what he thought was happening.

And yet he was doing the absolute most to get under her skin. He was Milo with the volume pumped up. Was she concerned that it was working? She thought it might be working. The slow burn of his steadfast attention had begun to thaw the frozen pit in her stomach. Emotion she'd been trying to choke back all day rose in her throat. When he rested both elbows on the table and held her gaze, the look he gave her landed on the feral side of hungry.

If Benj hadn't already been sitting, another spinning wave of vertigo would have taken her down. As the particulars dropped into place, a brand-new realization winded her. What he'd been trying to tell her, what she'd been refusing to believe. A one-two punch of what she hadn't seen coming, of why Milo was here: He'd come as himself. And he'd come for her.

Oh.

Oh no.

Chapter Thirty

Milo couldn't take his eyes off Benj. He wouldn't. He was scared if he did, she'd disappear again, spirited away, a wisp of dream escaping into the dark of night.

A server paused at Benj's shoulder, a bottle of wine nestled in his palm, his other hand tucked neatly behind his back. "Rosé?"

"As much as you can." Benj eagerly lifted her glass, urging the server to fill it well past the bowl's apex.

Next to Milo, Jem exaggerated a yawn.

"Let us live!" Vanessa snapped, holding her own glass out to the server.

Milo ignored the salad placed in front of him. Nothing appealed to him like the woman in the bright blue dress, wine cooling her temple. He'd seen the moment she realized why he was here. Her lips had parted, the bottom one weighed down by that pouty disbelief of hers. Her leg would have started bouncing by now, hidden by the white linen but causing a small earthquake for anyone lucky enough to be near her. As she ate mechanical bites of asparagus and tiny, just-sprung lettuce leaves, he could tell her heart wasn't in it. She'd be plotting her next move, trying to outmaneuver him.

He had to do this carefully. She was leaving tomorrow and he didn't know when—if—he'd get another shot.

The wedding band's lead singer prompted them all to cheer, introducing Skylar and Ivo and their first dance. Every head in the room turned to see. Every head but Milo's.

His focus remained aimed at Benj and he had no intention of missing her. Not when he was so wrapped up, so infinitely invested in the continuation of their story. His hands ached where he clasped them together above the table. He wanted desperately to be closer to her. He envied the flush that caressed her cheeks. He envied the air she pulled shakily into her lungs. He envied the moisture that glistened in her eyes, never to fall, not if she could help it. Anything that worked its way through her, into her depths, that she kept to herself. Anything that wasn't him.

By the time Ivo and Skylar left the dance floor and relocated to the head table, the waiters were clearing their plates and the band had pivoted into a classic, the familiar strands of Sam Cooke engulfing the room. In Milo's periphery, the table began to empty, couples flocking to the dance floor, starting with the Vus.

Jem tapped her lip with a finger and swung it between Milo and Jackson, chanting, "Eeny-meeny-miny-moe," landing on Jackson with a flirtatious grin. "Dance with me?"

Jackson rose, loose-limbed and up for anything.

Jem took his offered hand, adding rather boldly as they strode away, "Don't worry, B, I brought you a consolation prize."

Around the room, forks scraped plates, glasses clinked, conversation ebbed and flowed in a steady murmur. But at table thirteen, an impactful silence deadened the air.

Benj shoved to her feet. Jackson's chair angled out from the table, blocking her path, and as she fumbled around it, she plowed into a waiting Milo. Right where he wanted her.

"I want to dance too." He snaked a hand around her waist, keeping her on her feet.

Benj eyed the door off his shoulder, weighing her chance of escape. She had to know there was none. If she made a break for it, he'd follow. Milo had a singular goal and he was dead set on achieving it.

Working his hand into the stubborn clench of her palm, he tried again. "I know dancing's not enough. But give me a chance to do it right."

When he tugged her gently toward the dance floor, she lagged after him, her course involuntary as driftwood's. She was trying to remain unaffected, detaching like she had last night. If she fought him every step of the way, he'd be right there with her, fighting at her side. Fighting for her.

His own gait assured, Milo pulled Benj in close, swaying slowly though the beat had a little more give to it.

"You're only getting one song." Benj adjusted her hand on the stiff shoulder of his jacket, as though readying to push him back. He wasn't surprised when she tried to take the lead. "Why don't I give you a boost—you want to start over."

"That's not—"

"You can't, Milo. You can't start over every time you get something wrong. Life begins once. There is no cut. The camera rolls until you die."

"Wow. Hot take." He eased her closer and for some reason she let him. "I don't want to start over. I'm sorry about—"

A humorless laugh snagged in her throat. "Right, I got your text."

"Was there another format you prefer?"

At the mention of his apology, she stepped back. Milo only moved after her, like it was part of the dance.

"Ben." He shifted them together again, taking control of their movement. "Stop hiding from this. You did the same thing last night."

"Yeah, well, when you said nothing here is real to you, that put a nice pin in things for me." Her voice had thinned to vapor, but her arm slipped over his, her hand curling back on his shoulder, the heat of her palm seeping into him.

He couldn't help thinking that was a good sign and he pressed forward. "If you can quit looking for the hidden 'truths' in what I'm saying—"

"What was hidden in that exactly? Which part wasn't true?"

"Which part?" His gaze searched around the room, looking for help before landing on her. Why had he ever looked anywhere else? "That I could possibly have been talking about you. It's this place—what I was doing with my life—that was killing me, Ben. And it was only after I literally almost died pretending to be my brother that I could admit that to myself. I've only ever told you the truth. That I want you. I've always wanted you. I'm saying it to you as clearly as I can."

She closed her eyes, leaning into him, still refusing to let any tears fall. Whichever direction he went, her body followed. He wanted her to question what she was fighting so hard against. Why couldn't she see what he did? The two of them were inevitable.

Another attempted argument left her mouth. "You said you were leaving."

He lifted his shoulder, her chin bobbing with it. "I am leaving. So are you—there's nothing to read into about that." He struggled to choose his words, picking each slowly, stitching his thoughts together, one by one. "Geography isn't the obstacle. We can be together anywhere. If you let us exist outside of the construct you've built. You—" Hurt lowered his voice as he skirted the truth of the problem. "You said you would stay."

Benj missed a step but it didn't matter. He was there, ready to catch her. Why couldn't she see it? Why wouldn't she?

"I'm never gonna get it right every time." It pained him to admit it. He wanted to meet her standards, however high she set them. That was what Benjamina Wasik deserved: whatever she wanted. He wanted it to be him. "What I said about Jackson—he and I worked it out. And even if we didn't, if I wanted nothing to do with him—you're separate from that. You've never been his to me. You've always been mine. And if you want me as me, I'm all yours."

"Milo—"

He rushed to finish, cutting her off before she could protest. "I can prove it to you. I couldn't be Jackson. But give me a chance to be me. It'll be the last one I need. I won't fuck that up." Now he waited for her answer. His cheek pressed against hers, his jaw stretching with frustration at her silence. "You don't believe me. You don't trust me not to hurt you."

"I…" Benj leaned back to look at him.

"What else do you need from me, Ben?" He'd done everything he could think to show her he'd changed. Now all he could do was guess. "You want me to do *Twin Pistols 3*, I'll do it if I get to wake up with you each day."

"Why would I fucking want that, Milo?"

Sweat dampened his shirt under the heat of her touch. He was going too fast, off the rhythm now but he couldn't seem to slow down. "What can I do?"

"I don't know—I need—" She cast a wild look at the door and his heart beat faster. Her lips were tacky when she peeled them apart. "You want me? Take me. Steal me. Make a scene. Right here for everyone to see—prove it. Kiss me."

Milo's palm spread wider on her back, pushing at the thick fabric of her dress, looking for the usual gap in her clothes. Tonight Benj was completely impenetrable. She lifted her chin, knowing she'd given him no way in, and only one way out.

He considered it. He could shrug, *fair enough*, kiss her and have her. Then everyone would know—everyone would know. If he kissed her in this room full of gossips and cameras, it'd be news before the song ended. He'd be breaking his promise, he'd be the source of an article making Benj look *terrible*.

But if he didn't—

If he didn't kiss her, she'd think he wasn't willing to do anything, absolutely anything, to prove that being part of her life was the only way he wanted to live. Why would she ask for this? She couldn't want the bad press of being seen with both brothers in one week. Mina had told her to keep the optics clean. No more turbulence. Milo would decimate himself for her solace, but he wouldn't light any fuse if she wasn't clear of the blast area.

The possibilities tormented him. Hurt her or kiss her or both. Break one promise, or another. She hadn't given him an out at all.

He searched her face for any sign of a feint. She had to be testing him. But Benjamina Wasik didn't bluff. He realized then that it wasn't what she wanted, as much as what she didn't. And she didn't want to choose him. She wanted her hand forced.

Milo's eyes squeezed shut and when he opened them a tear had splashed a clear line down her face. It probably meant nothing that she'd used waterproof mascara, but he couldn't help thinking she'd known, all along, that he was going to make her cry. That she'd anticipated it.

His voice came out hoarse. "Not like this."

It wasn't fair. It wasn't enough. He wanted something more. He couldn't pull her into this pool, she had to dive in on her own. She had to make her decision for herself. She had to choose him too. Those were his terms. He had to let her go until she met them. He had to believe she'd decide to meet them.

Milo crushed his mouth hard into Benj's scalp, spinning them in a tight circle, spiraling too fast and stopping short. "I don't have to steal you. You're mine."

People were clapping over a drawn-out drum crash, signaling the end of the dance and Milo's chance with Benj. His head should have been throbbing from the excess noise, but it was his chest that threatened to collapse. The lambent reflections in Benj's glassy eyes held the truth, whether he knew what it was or not.

But before he let go, before he bowed out, Milo went

all in, hoping eventually Benj would call. "I'll wait. And when you're ready—when you make the decision and make me yours, I'll be there." A closing dare dropped his voice to a whisper. "Don't let me have the last word, Ben. Don't even let there be one."

Daily Star–t
Monday, April 25

It isn't like you to lack compassion. But you already knew that.

Chapter Thirty-One

In the jet's airy white noise, Benj couldn't stop hearing the raspy ring of a crash cymbal. The sound of a song concluding endlessly dragged her back to those final moments with Milo, when she'd been completely aware of him, roused by the tone of his honesty. Before he'd twisted out of her hot grasp and left her dazed and alone.

Benj's hand flexed as if to release the memory. Why hold on to it? Their charade was a wrap. The applause still echoed in her ears.

Mina lifted her gaze over the top of a slim computer open on the jet's veneer tabletop. "She's crying again."

With her flannel shirtsleeves over her knuckles, Benj pressed them to her lower lids, letting the fabric absorb the liquid from her overflowing eyes. "I am not."

But Mina's cabin announcement had already summoned Nelle from the lounge area. As Nelle settled into the seat next to Benj, she offered her own mock assessment. "You wouldn't want to be crying, would you? Not when you're always so concerned about dehydrating on a plane. But, since you aren't crying and

we aren't talking about it, I can go off about this outfit, right? Plaid and floral is a lot, Benj."

Frowning, Benj adjusted the oversized shirt she'd
thrown over her jersey jumpsuit. "It's comfortable."

"And the hat? The hat is for comfort?"

Benj's fingertips brushed the grey wool cuffed over
her forehead. "I went to bed with my hair wet. Then I
overslept. I was running behind and it was by the door.
I didn't want to miss the flight."

"You wanna try that again without the excuses?"
Nelle's nails tapped the table. "What happened at the
wedding? How did it all end up?"

Did it matter how? It was finished. Again. The first
time because Milo kissed her, the second time because
he didn't. A sob Benj couldn't hold back folded her
over the table.

Nelle's arms wrapped around her. Her voice washed
over Benj's head, soothing words meant to make her
feel better. "I'm sorry. I'm so sorry. I shouldn't have
let you do this—you said he'd hurt you and I shouldn't
have let him do it again."

"It wasn't him."

That's what Benj had realized last night, when Milo
had called her out for leaving his house on Saturday
night. Electric understanding had shot through her,
making her miss a step. She'd said she'd stay. And then
she hadn't. She'd gone back on her word. She'd done
it without thinking. Without considering Milo's feelings. She hadn't played fair.

And Milo had kept trying, as if the game hadn't
been rigged against him. She'd watched his mouth
twisting, turning over every word before he spoke.
Working so hard to make sure he didn't say the wrong

thing. Didn't make a single mistake. He couldn't even have a fight with his brother without her upgrading it to original sin, sure he was showing his true colors. But he'd been clear about what he was feeling for days now. And she'd done a bang-up job of convincing them both that hers were the only feelings allowed to matter between them.

Nelle pulled back to meet Benj's eye. She was right, tangentially. What Benj had going on wasn't a good look. Milo had only held up the mirror.

Benj swiped her sleeve at her wet cheek, the *M*s wrinkled in her knuckles hidden under the damp cloth. Those initials that proved she should have known better. That she'd done this to herself. "It was me." She tasted salt on her upper lip. "I'm not myself when I'm with him. I'm judgy and I'm mean and I'm—"

"Uncompromising?"

"That too. He asked me what I needed, to move forward."

"And?"

Benj had demanded certainty. She'd demanded a kiss. Her lashes had been wet and heavy, but Milo had been the one to shut his eyes. Her stomach dropped again at the thought, plummeting lower, having further to fall.

She'd known then he was going to refuse, but she'd entertained other possibilities: *Maybe being right was overrated. Maybe she could change her mind, still take it back—*

Then Milo had opened his eyes and she'd seen the torment, and the resolve.

Maybe there were worse things to lose than control.

Benj's lungs stuttered. "And I made it impossible for him. So now it's done and it's all my fault."

"It's Max's fault," Mina corrected. "And you got Nelle out of this unscathed. I'm not going to forget that. So, what do we want to talk about first: Nelle's collaboration with you, or her secret project with Bran?"

Benj whipped her head to the side. "Are you fucking pregnant?"

"What? No! You and my mother. No." Nelle swept her hands in an X across her body, but she smiled as she continued. "Bran and I have been writing. We're thinking of producing an album and touring together." She dipped her chin and added pointedly, "There are always ways to make relationships work. You could call him."

"My phone died last night."

"You know a good trick for that is plugging it in." Nelle's eyes glowed like good bourbon in soft candlelight.

Benj swallowed.

She could call Milo. She still wanted another day, she could take it. She could fix everything before they touched down in New York. She could call Milo and try again—they'd both be on the East coast—

"No." Mina shut her laptop with a smack and Nelle sat back. But the manager pinned Benj with a stare. "Not yet. What you're feeling right now is for you, don't be so ready to rush through it."

She was ready. She was always ready to step in, to help out, to show she cared. Always—it's who she was. Except with Milo.

When you're ready, he had said on the dance floor, knowing she wasn't. Her mind had reeled away from the word, thinking it part of his larger taunt. But Mina had repeated it. Mina who was on the same team as her. Mina whose job it was to make the right things happen. Mina who had just given Benj the best advice she'd ever gotten.

Compounding realizations kept Benj from responding. Maybe the internet psychic was tangentially right too. Maybe those *M*s also represented people looking out for her.

Benj had told herself all the wrong true things.

Milo was selfish. It didn't stop him from proving he cared deeply for her.

Milo was to blame. But so was she. *So was she.*

It can hurt. It would, no matter what Milo said, or what he did. Because she wasn't over what had happened. She hadn't had time to let it go. She couldn't convince herself that he didn't deserve her worst. She couldn't trust herself to stop demanding more of him. This time she was breaking her own heart, fracturing herself to hold on to the hurt. What good was his apology if she wasn't ready to forgive him? What good was being together when she wasn't being herself?

She had to be done with that before they spoke again. She'd already accepted he was a better man. On the other side of the glass, she wanted to be a better Benj.

Benj hiked her feet into her seat. Easier said than done. Milo was proof that real growth didn't happen overnight. True character developed slowly like flavor. It would take time to sort through her own mistakes, to view them as part of a broader plan. Her knees flapped impatiently. She couldn't seek him out yet. Not ever, not if she wasn't ready for long distance and unwithheld trust and showing Milo the best of herself instead of hiding it. She had to mind her business, not interrupt the process. If she cheated, if she didn't get right with herself first, she'd lose him—she'd never really have had him.

If only it had started some other way, if it hadn't begun as a problem and continued as a hoax—

Benj peeled the hat off her head, not caring about the mess revealed underneath. The truth was in her hands. At the end of the day, nothing would have made a difference, she and Milo had started something they couldn't finish.

Daily Star–t
Wednesday, June 1

Trust yourself, you're the only one who can.

Chapter Thirty-Two

Benj didn't call.

She didn't call from New York, where she was for a week with Nelle kicking off the new album. Or from the promo stops in London or Tokyo. He didn't hear from her in Dublin or Manchester for the first two stops on the tour. And she didn't call during the week they were back in London again for a weekend at the O2.

A month. Milo had gone an entire month without Benjamina Wasik and he wasn't sure how much more he could take. His punk mouth had got him into this situation. Telling her he'd wait—now he had to do it.

If he had kissed her—

No. He rubbed both sides of the short, even beard covering his cheeks and templed his hands over his lips. No. Kissing her at the wedding hadn't been an option. Not without hurting her. And he wasn't going to fucking do that. So he'd wait. Wait for her to be ready.

Patience was the name of the new game, one Milo fully intended to play until he had her. And he'd given it a real gentleman's effort. But every moment they were apart felt wasted. The mere thought of her brought all his impulses bubbling to the surface. And when the tour moved to Paris for another double-header at the

Stade de France, he shot off a late-night email, for-
warding Benj a proof of the *Independent Spirits Magazine* article about his new partnership with Lo from
Salty Tequila. Proof of his continued progress, his ability to follow through.

Maybe she'd read it and see. Lo was interested in
things moving quickly. She'd come up with a business
plan that worked for all of them: a ridiculously small re-
serve label, sixty-some bottles of pure Sunshine made
from Sophie's seeds to appease Milo's vision, with a
separate line of liqueurs that would be more wide-
spread, more accessible. Even if Benj only looked at
the headline—*Twin Distills*—that might be enough to
warrant an email back, or a text or—

Milo's phone buzzed on the side table, rattling
against the white porcelain saucer under his coffee cup.
His pulse raced seeing her name on the caller ID. Scared
to believe his luck, he swiped urgently across the screen.

"Ben?"

"Where should I send your hat?"

Milo sat up at the sound of her voice, the overstuffed
white duvet rustling loudly, drowning out some of what
she'd said. He climbed out of the bed, standing in the
middle of the room where there'd be no interference.
"My hat?"

"I still—I was planning to mail it back to you but I
haven't had the chance."

"Keep it. It might rain next week in Amsterdam."
He pressed a knuckle to his top lip, worried he'd over-
stepped, said too much.

"How do you know I'll be in Amsterdam?" The accusation in her tone sent him pacing to the window.
She worked it out before he got there. "You googled

Nelle's tour? Jem wasn't lying when she said it was a fine line between stalker and admirer."

"Which side am I on?"

Benj skipped over his question. "If you don't need it…"

Milo closed his eyes and waited to hear what she wanted, though whatever it was his answer would be the same: *Yes. Take it. Have it. Keep it.* Whatever she wanted, he'd do. And not because he wanted the motherfucking hat.

"Maybe I could give it back to you the next time I see you."

"That." He pulled his fist away from his mouth. "Let's do that."

"Okay, well. I guess you know I'm not back in the States until July. Maybe you could drive up to the Philadelphia show?"

Another month. He wouldn't make it. "You don't want me to fly out to see you?"

A pause preceded her soft declaration. "I don't want to make you. I know how you feel. Too far to fall and all that."

She clearly didn't know how he felt. He'd have to tell her again and hope it stuck. "Ben. I want to see you now."

"Milo, I'm in Paris."

Milo gestured unhelpfully to the view she couldn't see. "So am I."

"No, you aren't."

The Eiffel Tower narrowed to a point off the hotel room's balcony, proving her wrong.

"I told you I'd be there, when you were ready. I didn't want to wait a minute more than I had to. I didn't like the ocean between us. Meet me today. Meet me now." He stared across the rooftops, trying to evaluate the stillness from the other end of the line. Should he tell her more? How he'd gone back to Maryland, to the earth that made up his bones, and hadn't felt completely at home because his soul was restless, seeking her out?

Probably not, considering she hadn't ruled out calling him a stalker. And he doubted his ability to get that many words to come out right. Arguably, his simple declarations, the *I want you*s and the *You're mine*s, didn't do much to refute the stalker label either.

A police car blared a warning outside and a minute later Milo heard it in his ear, the siren taunting him, proving just how close they were—how far—and jarring an answer out of her.

"Where are you?"

"The Four Seasons. You?"

"The Ritz." She stretched another seemingly endless silence between them, loading it with the importance of her decision. "Meet me outside Café Verlet."

"When?" The question burst from him with desperation he couldn't conceal.

"Now."

Milo had never gotten dressed faster in his life. Impatience rattled inside him during the ten-minute ride, a pinball he'd swallowed, ricocheting off his nerves. He bounced in the back seat of the taxi, handed over a wad of euros without looking at it, shoved out onto the sidewalk, and scanned for Benj in the rounded entrance.

The driver called him back, waving a few bills out the window. "*C'est l'amour, non?*"

"What?"

"You keep your change," he said with a heavy French accent and a light wink.

"Oh, thanks." Milo shoved the euros into his pocket. He turned back to the café.

And there she was.

Benj stood in the recessed glass door, lush greenery hanging over her. Her hair was pulled up in a casual ponytail leaving her collar bare in an off-shoulder shirt that almost reached the top of a flared knee-length skirt. Framed by the café's windows, a disposable coffee cup in each hand, she looked like she always did—perfect. Like she belonged just where she was.

After a month without eyes on her, Milo couldn't help but stare. "Hi."

Her lips parted and she took a half step back at his greeting. Then she blinked, inching forward. "That's some bedhead this late in the day."

"My sleeping schedule's all off. Conference calls on LA time."

She offered him one of the coffees.

He didn't need it. Not when she was so near. "We're not going to share?"

"We want different things."

Milo's breath came out all wrong, her words puncturing the hope he'd harbored since deciding to follow the tour. "What are you saying?"

The teeniest gold triangles glinted in her earlobes as her head tilted. "You like yours black. I don't. Keep up." She extended the coffee again and he took it.

Benj led Milo up the narrow street. They turned right and followed the sidewalk through an arcade. Something about her was different. As they made their way into a manicured park, Milo tried to place it.

A small, square bag bobbed on her hip. That was new. He was used to seeing her with baggage, prepared for anything. Sipping from one hand, she swung the other tantalizingly close to his like it wouldn't be a big deal to her if they touched. He was used to her rebelling against his presence, not welcoming the possibility that her skin might graze his at any moment. Her strides over the cobbled, scallop-patterned streets were light and purposeful, the opposite of her leaden, reluctant steps on the similarly embellished dance floor where he'd last seen her. Was her hair a shade blonder too, or was the halo effect around her the dreamy way afternoon sun filtered through Paris?

It didn't matter. Her composure was more than skindeep. It was her aura, Milo determined, fluffed like sugar into cotton candy. That was what time away from him had done. She was different, she was better. Now all she had to do was say it.

In the middle of a pedestrian crossing over the river, Benj slowed and Milo readied himself for what he knew was coming. He followed as she approached a railing covered in locks, pulling on a U-shaped shackle, testing its strength, delaying the inevitable.

"This is that bridge?"

"You're thinking of the Ponts de Arts, down that way. Same thing happens here, but this one's not famous." Benj rested her elbows on the flat top rail, watching him, a familiar challenge in her sharp gaze. "You said you'd wait."

There it was. He should have done it right.

"I did." Milo set his still-full coffee on the ledge, brimming with fresh regret. "I tried."

"You tried. And that article? It said you're doing a

line of flavored Sunshine. Starting with fig, and coffee, and coconut, and almond—am I not supposed to read into that?"

"You are." He sank a hand into his messy hair. "You know I couldn't kiss you because—"

"I know." Her eyes closed. "You have to stop."

"Stop what?" Milo knotted his hands at the back of his head, bracing for the answer.

"Stop trying to prove yourself to me." The end of her ponytail swung as she stepped closer to him, hypnotizing him for half a moment. Making him want to comply. But her scent on the air—crisp and soft, spring leading into summer, good growing conditions—alerted him to his own needs. The promise he'd made her was to be himself, and Milo Fox Miller wasn't ever going to stop wanting to belong next to her.

"I can't."

While she waited for him to elaborate, he took off his glasses, cleaned the lenses methodically with his shirt. As they'd walked, he'd put artless words to their synced steps: *Forgive me. Trust me. Love me.* At the core of each wish: *me, me, me.*

His glasses back in place, Milo told her the truth as he saw it. "I know I'm selfish and I'm exasperating and you deserve more—"

A single navy-tipped nail jabbed into his chest, backing him into the railing. "Why? Why would I deserve more?"

"Because you're... Ben." He held his palms open, frustrated by the seeming simplicity of his own explanation. "You're you."

"And that's enough? That's all I have to be?"

He tucked a strand of pale hair behind her ear,

searching her almond eyes. Did she really have to ask? "Yes."

She knocked his hand away, somehow tangling their fingers together. "Stop."

"No."

"That's so not right, Milo." There was certainty in her tone, a ring of finality that made him want to crush something—his mouth to hers, preferably, but he couldn't let the thrill of a single kiss cost him another three years without her.

Then her hand squeezed their palms together and her body was pressing into his.

Milo's brow creased with confusion. If the position hadn't been achingly familiar—her hair tickling his jaw, the water, the breeze, the planks, the buzz of people around them—her words would have given life to the memory.

"Just pretend."

He hesitated to ask, but she'd told him to keep up. "Pretend what?"

"Pretend you don't have to prove yourself to me."

The feel of her, the smell of her, the reality of her—that was all Milo could think about. If this was the end, he wanted it to last. He didn't want to pretend it away. He wouldn't.

"You're not pretending," she accused him.

"I am," he lied.

"No. You're not." Then she turned her face, resting the opposite cheek on his shoulder. The imprint of her mouth warmed his neck, and his breath shook on a deep inhale. He wasn't pretending, and neither was she.

"You're already enough. I don't get to deserve you. You don't have to earn me." Pushing up on her tiptoes, she wrapped her arms around his neck. His folded behind her automatically, locking them together. "You're not a consolation prize and I should have been looking out for you—and not because an internet psychic told me to, but because you deserve that too—" Milo opened his mouth and she covered it with her hand. "Let me finish. You need to know that I'm sorry too. That this goes both ways. I didn't treat you the way I want to treat people. I wanted to get you back and then I wanted to get you *back* but first I needed to be okay with feeling like I'd made a mistake, that I may make another one. That was super hard for me and I didn't want to rush it, not when it was you I'd lose if I didn't do it right. That's why I didn't call. I've been trying to make sure that when I saw you again, I could see you again."

Milo tightened his hold on her, asking through her fingers, "And?"

Ben's smile started slow. "Hi, Milo."

His name. Her lips. Their chance.

Milo's heart expanded painfully in his chest and Benj moved her hand to the spot like she could feel it. He swallowed. He'd been listening, but he had to be sure he'd heard her. Maybe this was just Paris, the place where she made exceptions. He needed to know that the rules were off. That they were on, completely. "Let me just make sure I've got this. You want me to be me, and you'll be you, and we'll continue what we started?"

"Looks like I was pretty clear." Benj bit her bottom lip and released it. "If I fuck it up first, I'll buy dinner."

He laughed, feeling a grin flash across his face, fast and loose. "Fair enough."

Running a hand down her spine, he found the warm skin above her skirt. This was Benj: open and honest. Real. Admitting to her own perfection like it was some kind of flaw.

"We're going to love each other," she assured him, trying to cover the sentiment with a cheeky head tilt, but he saw through it. Her clear eyes stared up into his. "If you're alright with that."

Everything he ever wanted was in front of him, the answer the easiest thing he'd ever agree to. "I'm down." He was going to kiss her, have her, be hers. But just before he did, Milo told Benj what he should've said to begin with. "I'm yours."

* * * * *

Acknowledgments

This book wouldn't be a book without Elaine Spencer, Kerri Buckley, and everyone at Carina Press—and I'm so very excited to get to thank Deborah Nemeth again for her impeccable insight and guidance.

Thank you to the friends and family who have been understanding of my poor correspondence etiquette while drafting. I appreciate you not judging when I send a meme on Instagram while leaving your texts unread. I appreciate you being family and friends, friends and family.

Thank you to the writers I admire and who inspire me. Those that I don't know: I love your books and your songs and your podcasts, it's a thrill to spot you crossing the street, and thank you for joining in on my spirit guide meditations. And the writers I do know: Indie City, Sisterhood of the Horizontal Writers, "Michelles," to name a few, I'm here for all your texts about process and progress and questionable practices (despite what I said above about my lapses in message etiquette—I am here for it, even when I'm not there for it). And new to this book is Pub Club! Lynnette, I can't say enough how good our meetups have been for my writing, my parenting, and my soul.

Kate! It's me! Your steadfast encouragement helped write this book—you are wildly good at friendship and I'm wildly happy Co–Star endorses ours.

Sarah, you literal daydream, it's hard to find a category to put you in because you are friend, family, and writer. I'm beyond lucky that in addition to all the wonderful things you are, I get to call you my first and favorite reader.

And Mom, thanks for letting me borrow your memories.

I've plugged lots of my favorite things in this book, and that list wouldn't be complete without Georgia and Alex. Thank you both for being mine; I'm so grateful to be yours.

About the Author

A fan of topknots, fried Brussels sprouts, and other peo-ple doing the dishes, Hanna Earnest lives, laughs, and writes in Chicago, contributing to the world's supply of book boyfriends and girl crushes.

She wants to be friends on Twitter and Instagram @hannaearnest. Find out more at www.hannaearnest.com.

Chapter One

The drumming was louder now. Three even beats tapped out by two candy-shell nails on the bar, punctuated by a one-count pause held just long enough to infuse the silence with her displeasure before the rhythm repeated.

Meeting Nelle tonight had been a mistake. A year had passed since the magic moment she'd slipped her number into Bran's pocket at the Cleffy after-party, her breath raising the hairs on his neck as she whispered into his ear, "You're it." That last image of her stood out in his memory like the bas-relief of her raised and defined shoulder blades in the open-back dress she'd worn as she walked away from him. He'd been dazzled—there was no other way to describe it—dazed by her radiance. Charmed by her audacity to go after what she wanted, her confidence to approach him even as the requisite supermodel held tight to his arm.

And he'd been an idiot to assume he could recapture that spark. He wasn't the same person he'd been a year ago. He'd cracked and broken since then. And Nelle had changed too. That night she had been green, nominated for best new artist, and now, based on the super-charged buzz surrounding her second album, her star had risen. Nothing could touch her. Whatever might have fizzed between them that night had gone flat now. Maybe it had never really been there. Maybe he'd just been surprised, lured in by all that gold-tinged skin, by a bold display he hadn't expected from a media darling with a good-girl image like Nelle's.

Tonight he could barely focus on her. The sun had been in his eyes the whole drive into the city, glinting off the skyline as it set at his back, angry and red. He'd spent the day squinting against excess light. Everything had been too bright—the glare off the topcoat of snow covering a field of graves blinding him worse than any stage lights he'd encountered. He'd had no relief from it, his sunglasses broken and twisted in his jacket pocket. A jacket that was woefully thin against Chicago's December chill.

All that sun and no warmth.

It was a good thing he was so numb.

One, two, three, Nelle drummed again.

Bran filled the gap, setting his empty pint glass on the polished wood, the dull thud familiar, a bass note of a chord he'd heard before. They were sat on either side of a rounded corner, an arrangement that afforded room for intimacy had they been angled towards each other, but instead seemed to accentuate their opposition in the moment. They sat as disinterested strangers, each facing the man in rolled shirtsleeves busy behind the bar.

Bran leaned his elbows on the curved countertop and motioned for the bartender, not missing the man's sharp glance at the untouched cocktail in front of the woman next to him. Their server had definitely recognized her, based on the reverence with which he had placed her drink down, a two-handed approach complete with a respectfully low head bow. Nelle's face and voice had been everywhere for the last two years and even in the bar's dim light she was recognizable: amber eyes like scotch on ice under thick dark lashes and thick dark brows set in a heart-shaped face. And that hair—trademark black waves fell over her shoulders as she sat straight in the low-backed bar stool.

"Another Two Hearted," Bran said. The barkeep stalled, waiting for Nelle's reaction. Bran's own fame was apparently of little consequence to the waiter. Sure, his band, Judith From Work, had broken up. But Bran had been on the scene for years before Nelle. And he'd just come off his first solo tour, which had been deemed a critical and commercial success—if not as lucrative as his label had wanted because he'd played smaller venues. And what about hometown advantage? Shouldn't that tip the scales in his favor?

But the barkeep only had eyes for Nelle. She noticed the delay and set the man into motion with a smile. "And can we have some French fries, please, when you have a second?" she added with an aggressive pleasantry that made Bran's molars ache.

"French fries?"

"Did you want a burger?" Nelle's voice, while high in tone, had a steely weight, like it was anchored deep inside of her. Tonight it held an unmistakable edge. The clear metallic scrape of a knife against the sharpening stone.

Bran shifted in his chair. "This is a Michelin-starred restaurant. We don't need to eat at the bar—I can get us a table."

"So can I." Her cheerful yellow fingertips took up

their rhythm on the counter again. "I don't think we'll be here long enough."

He didn't doubt that assertion. There wasn't anything here for either of them, it seemed. And the longer they stayed, the more likely it was someone would notice and think the encounter more than it was.

Across the restaurant a light flashed and Bran and Nelle both swung instinctively towards it to determine the source. But the flare was just a candle flame momentarily enhanced by the curved water jug of a passing waiter.

Bran exhaled slowly. "Because we won't be able to get through a meal before the paps catch us?"

Nelle curved her hand protectively around the stem of her coupe glass, a lemon peel on a metal spear resting across the rim. "Because this isn't going how I thought it would."

Honesty saturated her voice. Genuine emotion that carried through her music, unfiltered even in recordings. And in person it just about devastated him. He'd wanted something else from this too, but he wasn't going to say it. And it wasn't her fault: he shouldn't have agreed to see her. Not today.

Bran rubbed his eyes and looked down, landing on the brimming drink in front of Nelle. She lifted the shallow bowl and Bran followed it up to her mouth as she sipped the cloudy liquid and back down, replaced soundlessly on the bar. His gaze idled on the red smudge of her lips imprinted on the glass.

Okay, so that was one reason he'd gone against his better judgment and come tonight. He hadn't been able to stop thinking about that mouth for months. Every time he heard her voice on the radio or caught a glimpse of her on some magazine cover, he'd obsess about the full-lipped curve of that smile she'd given him when the heat of her skin radiated through the lining of his pocket.

She wasn't smiling now, pulling her hands into her lap and twisting one of a half dozen rings she wore staggered above and below her knuckles like notes on sheet music. The obsidian stone disappeared once, twice, before she released it, squared her shoulders, and tried valiantly to engage him in conversation again. "Don't worry about photos."

"You don't mind?" His head tilted to the side as he considered the statement. Maybe she liked it—the attention. She was good at getting it.

"Of course I mind. But they don't know we're here. They won't bother us."

"They won't?"

"It isn't like that here. It's the Midwest. It's home. It's safe."

Home? Not really. Not anymore.

"It's like that everywhere for us. Don't tell me you're that naïve."

Nelle lifted her glass again. "I'm not. Andre and I have an arrangement."

"Who's Andre?"

Nelle motioned to the barkeep and the garnish slid into her drink with a soft clink.

"You paid him?"

"We took a photo together."

Bran laughed, the sound as hollowed out as he felt. "Oh, that'll stop him. I thought you said you weren't naïve."

A glare narrowed her eyes. "I'm not. There's nothing wrong with trusting people to help you."

She waited a beat for him to respond, giving him the chance to show some willingness, some effort on his part to salvage the conversation. But he was done here. It wasn't enough to risk the blog fodder that would be twisted out of pictures of them having dinner together.

When he didn't say anything, her lips pressed together. She'd reached her limit too. He was surprised she'd let it get this far. Nelle didn't need to sit here. She was like him. She had options, anywhere she went. Better for her to use them. And he'd have the next drink alone. Take a nap in the car. Forget the company he'd hired to ship it back to California, he'd drive it himself. The album he'd promised his label by the New Year hadn't materialized. New music just wasn't coming to him. A spontaneous road trip wouldn't put the album any further off course. Maybe he'd even be inspired. Maybe he'd find what he was looking for rolling across the great American plains. Or maybe the blazing desert sun would leave him as dry and shriveled as his current creative vision.

Nelle uncrossed her legs and inched to the front of her seat. "I really thought you'd be different."

"Yeah?" He spun his own stool to get his knees out of her way, make it easier for her to go.

"But you're just a talented dickhead."

A lot of things had been said about Bran Kelly. He'd worked his way into the spotlight by nineteen, becoming the lead singer of a world-renowned band, so people who'd been inclined to comment had had seven years to come up with some shit. But no one had ever called him a talented dickhead.

And Nelle wasn't stopping there. "If you just wanted to have a drink, flirt a little, go back to my hotel, no pressure—we could have done that. Instead you show up late in that ridiculous car, slam a beer, and call me naïve? At the very least I expected some originality from Bran Kelly—but I've heard this one. A couple versions, actually. And I don't care for a repeat."

She stretched one black ankle boot to the ground while reaching for the big leather bag hanging from a hook under the bar. Behind her, large windows framed the dark city street, his car parked across it next to an empty lot. It unnerved him that she'd seen him arrive, like a perspective in the wrong direction, a Nighthawk looking out, studying him. Headlights from a passing car cut across the room, outlining her edges in a burst of backlighting. Bran's eyes widened, taking in her flared leather miniskirt and tight black turtleneck sweater. A silhouette of black on black. Even her thick hair, loose and cascading down her back, shone with the ebony gloss of night.

Bran had wanted the day to be over and suddenly it was—of course partial credit could be given to how quickly the sun set in December, how early, but for a moment it seemed like Nelle conjured the darkness that appealed to his tired eyes. And she alone was defined in it, by it, fierce and powerful—a goddess whose blessing he craved.

And he felt it—saw again that brazen determination that had mesmerized him a year ago. A shiver rocked his shoulders as the door at his back opened, letting in a gust of winter air. He was awake. He was wired—charged by her tractor-beam stare. The words pulled up from deep inside him, the rush of creation pricking across his skin.

She turned midnight.

A lyric flashed in his mind.

He needed her to stay. He needed her to do that again. Another flash, another spark leaping from her to him, like static electricity jumpstarting his process.

Bran blinked. Then he was on his feet, filling the cramped space between their stools before she could.

"Wait—wait—" Bran shook his hair and settled it back into place in one involuntary movement. He scrambled to remember the reasons she was going. "I've had a long day. I'm sorry. I'll nurse the next beer."

For the first time since landing in the seat next to her he locked his eyes on hers for more than a fleeting glance. They glowed like sun caught in honey and he felt just as stuck.

"I didn't mean to be late. I was speeding. You gotta know I was—who goes the speed limit in a Ferrari, right?"

Her eyes sizzled with annoyance and he remembered her calling the car ridiculous.

Bran was so used to being the force in a room, the sun around which everyone seemed to gravitate. Normally it was his electric-blue eyes that shocked people into stunned silence. He was off balance when he was with Nelle, when it was his body that spun towards hers, his lungs that struggled under her gaze. Whatever he had that drew people in, she had it too. Only hers was fresher. Not yet faded. And it pulled something to the surface in him—something he recognized, something he'd lost.

Queen of light.

Another lyric. Another ray of hope breaking through his blocked mind. The hazy shape of a song formed in his periphery.

He had to make her stay.

Skewered by her gaze, Bran prepared another admission, willing to humble himself to any level, if she'd just sit back down. "Admittedly, yes, the car is a little over the top. It's the first big thing I bought." She had to understand. "You must have done something with your signing bonus?"

"I paid my parents' mortgage."

Maybe not.

He couldn't keep the desperation out of his final plea. "Please stay."

Half standing, she deliberated silently for a long, torturous minute while Bran held his breath. Finally, when his lungs had begun to ache, she settled herself back in her seat. And as relieved as he was, he had no idea why. Maybe she was curious about what had changed his attitude? Maybe she just wanted to finish her drink. It didn't matter. He had a second chance to focus on her. To catch any flashes of her brashness and hope for another burst of inspiration.

She crossed her legs and leaned as far back from him as she could. "I'm not sleeping with you now."

Bran let out a shaky laugh. "I wouldn't expect you to."

As Nelle gulped the last of her cocktail, lips puckering, it dawned on him that was all she'd been interested in. This could have been easy. Both of them intent on quick access to passion—if only he hadn't been so distracted, so stupid. That ship had sailed. But she was still here, the sour twist easing from her mouth. He could settle for a little conversation and a little hope.

He picked up the beer Andre had delivered to take a restorative gulp and caught Nelle's watchful glance. He sipped instead, to prove he could behave. The beer was cold and bitter and he held it in his mouth as she leaned forward. She took the pint from his hand, her eyes locking on his as she swigged it back, leaving him his own print of her lips on the rim as she set it down. Bran swallowed. A hidden sweetness coated his tongue. How had he not been paying his full attention to this girl?

"I'm not sleeping with you either," he told her when he recovered himself.

Unmistakable interest lit her face. "Because you've rekindled things with Francesca."

He raised his eyebrows. "Have I?"

"You haven't heard? They're saying it was backstage at the Victoria's Secret show."

"That's news to me. I haven't been in New York since October."

"*News* is a strong word for it. Same source reported my butt implants." She angled her hips to give him a glance at her backside. "Nice, right?"

And he'd been fixated on her mouth. The things he could do to an ass like that. He swallowed again. "Very natural."

"Well. It is. So." Her gilded lids glittered as she shifted her attention to the barkeep, thanking him with a smile for removing her empty glass. She stretched, the sweater pulling tight over her breasts, her sleek hair dancing over the crescent arch of her spine. Curves and shadows. This was the performer in her, aware of his attentiveness, feeding off her audience.

"I'm not with Francesca anymore. I'm not with anyone." He put his arm on the low back of her chair, thumbing the nailhead trim that lined the edge.

"But you're not sleeping with me?"

"I'm considering celibacy."

She bent towards him. "Bran Kelly. Celibate. This is a line, right? You tell a girl you're withholding your dick from the world to make her want you more? The rock-star thing not working for you anymore?"

It wasn't a line. But a solution he'd entertained earlier—when he wasn't close enough to smell the Chanel at her neck. When it felt like his only option was something drastic he'd never have considered before.

His aforementioned dick twitched at her casual shout-out and Bran tried to quiet that urge. She inspired something more valuable in him, but maybe he could turn this around and satisfy them both. He was aware of the night stretching before them, long and cold.

He had to grip the back of her seat to stop himself from sifting his fingers through the bottom inch of her hair. When Nelle coasted a hand through the waves, Bran swayed forward to inhale. Her hair swung over her shoulders, falling over the back of Bran's hand, and he had the sudden sensation that he had slipped, the stomach lurch of losing your footing.

Black like ice, queen of light, she turned midnight.

The line flickered through Bran's mind and he resisted the impulse to pull out his phone and type it into his notes. That would look like texting—and definitely not help his case. His fingers tensed at his side. He repeated the words in his head, trying to combat the anxiety of losing them, unaware of how the desire tethered itself to the woman sitting next to him.

Nelle pressed forward, still hunting down answers. "What is it then? A New Year's resolution—a quarter-life crisis?"

"More of a clarity thing."

"Pussy clouds the mind?"

A smile tugged at Bran's mouth. "They're wrong about you. You've got an edge."

"Because I said *pussy*?"

"Because you pursued me while I was with someone else."

Now he wished for blaring sunlight, to see for sure that her face had gone pink with a blush of his making.

Andre arrived with a second cocktail, and Nelle swiveled towards him with another practiced smile. "And we're gonna split a burger." She glanced down before meeting Bran's eyes again. "I should apologize for that."

"But?"

"I wouldn't mean it."

A soft silence settled between them, the thick snow outside muffling the sounds of the city. Her mouth curved, finally for him, and an uptick of tempo thumped in his heart.

The candle across the room winked again. Bran touched her elbow, the fabric of her sweater soft, thinner than he'd expected. "You're sure Andre has your back with the paps? I can't help thinking they'd kill for this."

She recrossed her legs, her feet tangling momentarily with his. He widened his thighs, making room for her to fit the V of her stacked knees between them. "*If* this were happening—they'd be all over us in a minute. Reporting our breakup while speculating that we're engaged—contrasting headlines over a photo of us buying groceries and holding hands—"

"That's why I have a no-hand-holding policy. Makes it too easy for them."

"And if I eat one gyro too many: bump watch."

She was right. That's exactly what they always did. Take any scrap of his life they could find to churn out stories he barely recognized as his life. Soon they'd have more than fragments to work with, soon they'd have every detail that made Bran Kelly who he was. The private stuff that made him feel like a real person.

And he didn't know how to stop it.

"Everything they can find, sold to the highest bidder." He moved his hand from her sleeve before his grip tightened. He shouldn't be talking about this. Not when he was trying to focus on Nelle, let her be the distraction from his other problems.

But she was nodding, rebalancing the metal toothpick across her glass. "Better than making things up."

His response arose from the ease of talking to someone who really understood. "Does it bother you more when they're wrong or when they're right?"

"It bothers me that I can't have any secrets." She gave up on balance and let the lemon peel splash back into her drink. "It bothers me that I don't think I can keep any."

"Then you need a tighter circle. Or a smaller one."

"Is that what you do? Keep a circle so small and tight you suffocate inside it, your secrets preserved as your body rots?"

"You're pretty dark for a pop princess."

"You're pretty chaste for a rock god."

A second line flared in his mind, warm with the

possibility of what it could become, and he tried to burn it to his memory.

The French fries arrived in a paper cone with a little dish of pale aioli. The smell filled Bran's nose and his mouth watered. That numbness had kept him from registering how hungry he'd gotten.

Nelle had a crispy golden strand in her hand before Andre had managed to set the plate down. "And you know how they call you Bran and Fran? If we got married they'd call me Nelly Kelly."

Bran froze, hot fries searing his fingertips. "Would they?"

This time it wasn't a lyric rising in his mind. But an idea that only a man as blindly desperate as he currently was would consider.

She nodded with confidence. "Of course they would."

Even if he was in straits dire enough to come up with a scheme like that, Nelle certainly wouldn't accept. She was a catalyst, and he was reacting too quickly. Besides, she didn't need a last name. Why would she take his?

So Bran filled his mouth with fries and swallowed the idea with them.

Don't miss All the Best Nights *by Hanna Earnest, available now.*

www.CarinaPress.com